DEVIL
BONES

KATHY REICHS

SCRIBNER

NEW YORK   LONDON   TORONTO   SYDNEY

SCRIBNER
A Division of Simon & Schuster, Inc.
1230 Avenue of the Americas
New York, NY 10020

First Scribner hardcover edition August 2008

SCRIBNER and design are registered trademarks of The Gale Group, Inc.,
used under license by Simon & Schuster, Inc., the publisher of this work.

For information about special discounts for bulk purchases,
please contact Simon & Schuster Special Sales at 1-800-456-6798
or business@simonandschuster.com.

DESIGNED BY ERICH HOBBING

Manufactured in the United States of America

1   3   5   7   9   10   8   6   4   2

Library of Congress Control Number: 2008013676

ISBN-13: 978-0-7432-9438-6
ISBN-10: 0-7432-9438-6

Dedicated to

Police Officer Sean Clark
November 22, 1972–April 1, 2007

and

Police Officer Jeff Shelton
September 9, 1971–April 1, 2007

And to all who have died protecting the citizens of
Charlotte-Mecklenburg, North Carolina

Sergeant Anthony Scott Futrell	*July 17, 2002*
Police Officer John Thomas Burnette	*October 5, 1993*
Police Officer Anthony A. Nobles	*October 5, 1993*
Patrol Officer Eugene A. Griffin	*November 22, 1991*
Police Officer Milus Terry Lyles	*August 6, 1990*
Police Officer Robert Louis Smith	*January 15, 1987*
Patrol Officer Timothy Wayne Whittington	*July 16, 1985*
Patrol Officer Ernest Coleman	*July 1, 1982*
Patrol Officer Edmond N. Cannon	*November 23, 1981*
Officer Ronnie E. McGraw	*October 18, 1970*
Sergeant Lewis Edward Robinson, Sr.	*May 4, 1970*
Police Officer Johnny Reed Annas	*May 21, 1960*
Detective Charlie Herbert Baker	*April 12, 1941*
Officer Rufus L. Biggers	*February 12, 1937*
Officer Charles P. Nichols	*April 17, 1936*
Patrol Officer Benjamin H. Frye	*June 9, 1930*
Detective Thomas H. Jenkins	*October 21, 1929*
Officer William Rogers	*August 30, 1929*
Detective Harvey Edgar Correll	*January 22, 1929*
Patrol Officer Robert M. Reid	*January 1, 1927*
Rural Police Officer John Franklin Fesperman	*February 16, 1924*
Officer John Robert Estridge	*March 29, 1913*
Rural Police Officer Sampson E. Cole	*January 1, 1905*
Officer James H. Brown	*August 2, 1904*
Patrol Officer James Moran	*April 4, 1892*

ACKNOWLEDGMENTS

Thanks go to Dr. Richard L. Jantz, statistical guru behind Fordisc 3.0; to Dr. M. Lee Goff, a most excellent bug guy (his real name is Madison); to Dr. Peter Dean, coroner extraordinaire; and to Dr. William C. Rodriguez, one of the wisest forensic anthropologists in the kingdom. Dr. Leslie Eisenberg, Dr. Norm Sauer, and Dr. Elizabeth Murray also gave input on bone minutiae.

Sergeant Darrell Price, Sergeant Harold (Chuck) Henson, and Detective Christopher Dozier, Charlotte-Mecklenburg Police Department, answered cop questions. Mike Warns shared knowledge and opinions on many things. What he didn't know, he found out.

Dr. Wayne A. Walcott, Senior Associate Provost, UNC-Charlotte, provided information on the availability of scanning electron microscopes on campus. UNCC has five. Who knew?

I appreciate the continued support of Chancellor Philip L. Dubois of the University of North Carolina–Charlotte.

I am grateful to my family for their patience and understanding, especially when I am grumpy. Or away. Special thanks must go to my daughter, Kerry, who took time to discuss my book while writing her own. (Yay! First novel: *The Best Day of Someone Else's Life*, available the spring of 2008!) Extra credit to Paul Reichs for reading and commenting on the manuscript.

Deepest thanks to my awesome agent, Jennifer Rudolph Walsh; to my brilliant editors, Nan Graham and Susan Sandon; and to my magnificent publisher, Susan Moldow. Thanks to Kevin Hanson and Amy Cormier in Canada. I also want to acknowledge all those who work so very hard on my behalf, especially: Katherine Monaghan, Lauretta Charlton, Anna deVries, Anna Simpson, Claudia Ballard, Jessica Almon, Tracy Fisher, and Michelle Feehan.

If there are errors in this book, they are my fault. If I have forgotten to thank someone, I apologize.

DEVIL
BONES

*M*Y NAME IS TEMPERANCE DEASSEE BRENNAN. *I'M FIVE-FIVE, feisty, and forty-plus. Multidegreed. Overworked. Underpaid.*

Dying.

Slashing lines through that bit of literary inspiration, I penned another opening.

I'm a forensic anthropologist. I know death. Now it stalks me. This is my story.

Merciful God. Jack Webb and *Dragnet* reincarnate.

More slashes.

I glanced at the clock. Two thirty-five.

Abandoning the incipient autobiography, I began to doodle. Circles inside circles. The clock face. The conference room. The UNCC campus. Charlotte. North Carolina. North America. Earth. The Milky Way.

Around me, my colleagues argued minutiae with all the passion of religious zealots. The current debate concerned wording within a sub-section of the departmental self-study. The room was stifling, the topic poke-me-in-the-eye dull. We'd been in session for over two hours, and time was not flying.

I added spiral arms to the outermost of my concentric circles. Began filling spaces with dots. Four hundred billion stars in the galaxy. I wished I could put my chair into hyperdrive to any one of them.

Anthropology is a broad discipline, comprised of linked subspecialties. Physical. Cultural. Archaeological. Linguistic. Our department has the full quartet. Members of each group were feeling a need to have their say.

George Petrella is a linguist who researches myth as a narrative of individual and collective identity. Occasionally he says something I understand.

At the moment, Petrella was objecting to the wording "reducible to" four distinct fields. He was proposing substitution of the phrase "divisible into."

Cheresa Bickham, a Southwestern archaeologist, and Jennifer Roberts, a specialist in cross-cultural belief systems, were holding firm for "reducible to."

Tiring of my galactic pointillism, and not able to reduce or divide my ennui into any matters of interest, I switched to calligraphy.

Temperance. The trait of avoiding excess.

Double order, please. Side of restraint. Hold the ego.

Time check.

Two fifty-eight.

The verbiage flowed on.

At 3:10 a vote was taken. "Divisible into" carried the day.

Evander Doe, department chair for over a decade, was presiding. Though roughly my age, Doe looks like someone out of a Grant Wood painting. Bald. Owlish wire-rims. Pachyderm ears.

Most who know Doe consider him dour. Not me. I've seen the man smile at least two or three times.

Having put "divisible into" behind him, Doe proceeded to the next burning issue. I halted my swirly lettering to listen.

Should the department's mission statement stress historical ties to the humanities and critical theory, or should it emphasize the emerging role of the natural sciences and empirical observation?

My aborted autobiography had been smack on. I *would* die of boredom before this meeting adjourned.

Sudden mental image. The infamous sensory deprivation experiments of the 1950s. I pictured volunteers wearing opaque goggles and padded hand muffs, lying on cots in white-noise chambers.

I listed their symptoms and compared them to my present state.

Anxiety. Depression. Antisocial behavior. Hallucination.

I crossed out the fourth item. Though stressed and irritable, I wasn't hallucinating. Yet. Not that I'd mind. A vivid vision would have provided diversion.

Don't get me wrong. I've not grown cynical about teaching. I love being a professor. I regret that my interaction with students seems more limited each year.

Why so little classroom time? Back to the subdiscipline thing.

Ever try to see just a doctor? Forget it. Cardiologist. Dermatologist. Endocrinologist. Gastroenterologist. It's a specialized world. My field is no different.

Anthropology: the study of the human organism. Physical anthropology: the study of the biology, variability, and evolution of the human organism. Osteology: the study of the bones of the human organism. Forensic anthropology: the study of the bones of the human organism for legal purposes.

Follow the diverging branches, and there I am. Though my training was in bioarchaeology, and I started my career excavating and analyzing ancient remains, I shifted into forensics years ago. Crossed to the dark side, my grad school buddies still tease. Drawn by fame and fortune. Yeah, right. Well, maybe some notoriety, but certainly no fortune.

Forensic anthropologists work with the recently dead. We're employed by law enforcement agencies, coroners, medical examiners, prosecutors, defense attorneys, the military, human rights groups, and mass-disaster recovery teams. Drawing on our knowledge of biomechanics, genetics, and skeletal anatomy, we address questions of identification, cause of death, postmortem interval, and postmortem alteration of the corpse. We examine the burned, decomposed, mummified, mutilated, dismembered, and skeletal. Often, by the time we see remains, they're too compromised for an autopsy to yield data of value.

As an employee of the state of North Carolina, I'm under contract to both UNC-Charlotte, and to the Office of the Chief Medical Examiner, which has facilities in Charlotte and Chapel Hill. In addition, I consult for the Laboratoire de sciences judiciaires et de médecine légale in Montreal.

North Carolina and Quebec? Extraordinaire. More on that later.

Because of my cross-border treks and my dual responsibilities within North Carolina, I teach only one course at UNCC, an upper-level seminar in forensic anthropology. This was my biannual semester in the classroom.

And the conference room.

I look forward to the teaching. It's the interminable meetings that I detest. And the faculty politics.

Someone moved that the mission statement be returned to committee for further study. Hands rose, mine among them. As far as I was concerned, the thing could be sent to Zimbabwe for permanent interment.

Doe introduced the next agenda item. Formation of a committee on professional ethics.

Inwardly groaning, I began a list of tasks requiring my attention.

1. Specimens to Alex.

Alex is my lab and teaching assistant. Using my selections, she would set up a bone quiz for the next seminar.

2. Report to LaManche.

Pierre LaManche is a pathologist, and chief of the medico-legal section at the LSJML. The last case I'd done before leaving Montreal the previous week was one of his, an auto-fire victim. According to my analysis, the charred corpse was that of a thirty-something white male.

Unfortunately for LaManche, the presumed driver should have been a fifty-nine-year-old Asian female. Unfortunately for the victim, someone had pumped two slugs into his left parietal. Unfortunately for me, the case was a homicide and would probably require my presence in court.

3. Report to Larabee.

Tim Larabee is the Mecklenburg County medical examiner, and director of the three-pathologist Charlotte facility. His had been the first case I'd done upon returning to North Carolina, a bloated and decomposed lower torso washed up on the shore of the Catawba River. Pelvic structure had indicated the individual was male. Skeletal development had bracketed the age between twelve and fourteen. Healed fractures of the right fourth and fifth metatarsals had suggested the possibility of an ID from antemortem hospital records and X-rays, if such could be found.

4. Phone Larabee.

Arriving on campus today, I'd found a two-word voice mail from the MCME: *Call me.* I'd been dialing when Petrella came to drag me into the meeting from hell.

When last we'd spoken, Larabee had located no missing person reports that matched the Catawba River vic's profile. Perhaps he'd now found one. I hoped so, for the sake of the family. And the child.

I thought of the conversation Larabee would have with the parents. I've had those talks, delivered those life-shattering pronouncements. It's the worst part of my job. There is no easy way to tell a mother and father that their child is dead. That his legs have been found, but his head remains missing.

5. Sorenstein recommendation.

Rudy Sorenstein was an undergraduate with hopes of continuing his studies at Harvard or Berkeley. No letter from me was going to make that happen. But Rudy tried hard. Worked well with others. I'd give his mediocre GPA the best spin possible.

6. Katy shopping.

Kathleen Brennan Petersons is my daughter, living in Charlotte as of this fall, employed as a researcher in the public defender's office. Having spent the previous six years as an undergraduate at the University of Virginia, Katy was desperately in need of clothes made of fabric other than denim. And of money to buy them. I'd offered to serve as fashion consultant. There's irony. Pete, my estranged husband, was functioning as ways and means.

7. Birdie litter.

Birdie is my cat. He is fussy concerning matters of feline toilette, and expresses his displeasure in ways I try to prevent. Inconveniently, Birdie's preferred litter brand is available only in veterinary offices.

8. Dental checkup.

The notification had been delivered with yesterday's mail.

Sure. I'd get right on that.

9. Dry cleaning.

10. Car inspection.

11. Shower door handle.

I sensed, more than heard, an odd sound in the room. Stillness.

Glancing up, I realized attention was focused on me.

"Sorry." I shifted a hand to cover my tablet. Casually.

"Your preference, Dr. Brennan?"

"Read them back."

Doe listed what I assumed were three hotly contested names.

"Committee on Professional Responsibility and Conduct. Committee on the Evaluation of Ethical Procedures. Committee on Ethical Standards and Practices."

"The latter implies the imposition of rules set by an external body or regulating board." Petrella was doing petulant.

Bickham threw her pen to the tabletop. "No. It does not. It is simp—"

"The department is creating an ethics committee, right?"

"It's critical that the body's title accurately reflect the philosophical underpinnings—"

"Yes." Doe's reply to my question cut Petrella off.

"Why not call it the Ethics Committee?"

Ten pairs of eyes froze on my face. Some looked confused. Some surprised. Some offended.

Petrella slumped back in his chair.

Bickham coughed.

Roberts dropped her gaze.

Doe cleared his throat. Before he could speak, a soft knock broke the silence.

"Yes?" Doe.

The door opened, and a face appeared in the crack. Round. Freckled. Worried. Twenty-two curious eyes swiveled to it.

"Sorry to interrupt." Naomi Gilder was the newest of the departmental secretaries. And the most timid. "I wouldn't, of course, except . . ."

Naomi's gaze slid to me.

"Dr. Larabee said it was urgent that he speak with Dr. Brennan."

My first impulse was to do an arm-pump *Yes!* Instead, I raised acquiescent brows and palms. *Duty calls. What can one do?*

Gathering my papers, I left the room and practically danced across the reception area and down a corridor lined with faculty offices. Every door was closed. Of course they were. The occupants were cloistered in a windowless conference room arguing administrative trivia.

I felt exhilarated. Free!

Entering my office, I punched Larabee's number. My eyes drifted to the window. Four floors down, rivers of students flowed to and from late-afternoon classes. Low, angled rays bronzed the trees and ferns in Van Landingham Glen. When I'd entered the meeting the sun had been straight overhead.

"Larabee." The voice was a little on the high side, with a soft Southern accent.

"It's Tempe."

"Did I drag you from something important?"

"Pretentious pomposity."

"Sorry?"

"Never mind. Is this regarding the Catawba River floater?"

"Twelve-year-old from Mount Holly name of Anson Tyler. Parents were on a gambling junket in Vegas. Returned day before yesterday, discovered the kid hadn't been home for a week."

"How did they calculate that?"

"Counted the remaining Pop-Tarts."

"You obtained medical records?"

"I want your take, of course, but I'd bet the farm the broken toes on Tyler's X-rays match those on our vic."

I thought of little Anson alone in his house. Watching TV. Making peanut butter sandwiches and toasting Pop-Tarts. Sleeping with the lights on.

The feeling of exhilaration began to fade.

"What morons go off and leave a twelve-year-old child?"

"The Tylers won't be getting nominations for parents of the year."

"They'll be charged with child neglect?"

"Minimally."

"Is Anson Tyler the reason you called?" According to Naomi, Larabee had said urgent. Positive ID's didn't usually fall into that category.

"Earlier. But not now. Just got off the horn with the homicide boys. They may have a nasty situation."

I listened.

Trepidation quashed the last lingering traces of exhilaration.

"No doubt it's human?" I asked.

"At least one skull."

"There's more than one?"

"The reporting unit suggested the possibility, but didn't want to touch anything until you arrived."

"Good thinking."

Scenario: Citizen stumbles onto bones, calls 911. Cops arrive, figure the stuff's old, start bagging and tagging. Bottom line: Context is lost, scene is screwed. I end up working in a vacuum.

Scenario: Dogs unearth a clandestine grave. Local coroner goes at it with shovels and a body bag. Bottom line: Bits are missed. I get remains with a lot of gaps.

When faced with these situations, I'm not always kind in my remarks. Over the years, my message has gotten across.

That, plus the fact that I teach body recovery workshops for the ME in Chapel Hill, and for the Charlotte-Mecklenburg PD.

"Cop said the place stinks," Larabee added.

That didn't sound good.

I grabbed a pen. "Where?"

"Greenleaf Avenue, over in First Ward. House is being renovated. Plumber knocked through a wall, found some sort of underground chamber. Hang on."

Paper rustled, then Larabee read the address. I wrote it down.

"Apparently this plumber was totally freaked."

"I can head over there now."

"That would be good."

"See you in thirty."

I heard a hitch in Larabee's breathing.

"Problem?" I asked.

"I've got a kid open on the table."

"What happened?"

"Five-year-old came home from kindergarten, ate a doughnut, complained of a bellyache, hit the floor. She was pronounced dead two hours later at CMC. Story to tear your heart out. An only child, no prior medicals, completely asymptomatic until the incident."

"Jesus. What killed her?"

"Cardiac rhabdomyoma."

"Which is?"

"Big honking tumor in the interventricular septum. Pretty rare at her age. These kids usually die in infancy."

Poor Larabee was facing more than one heartbreaking conversation.

"Finish your autopsy," I said. "I'll handle the chamber of horrors."

Charlotte began with a river and a road.

The river came first. Not the Mississippi or Orinoco, but a sturdy enough stream, its shores rich with deer, bear, bison, and turkey. Great flocks of pigeons flew overhead.

Those living among the wild pea vines on the river's eastern bank called their waterway Eswa Taroa, "the great river." They, in turn, were called the Catawba, "people of the river."

The principal Catawba village, Nawvasa, was situated at the headwater of Sugar Creek, Soogaw, or Sugau, meaning "group of huts," a development not based solely on proximity to the water. Nawvasa also snugged up to a busy route of aboriginal commerce, the Great Trading Path. Goods and foodstuffs flowed along this path from the Great Lakes to the Carolinas, then on down to the Savannah River.

Nawvasa drew its lifeblood from both the river and the road.

The arrival of strange men on great ships ended all that.

For helping in his restoration to power, England's King Charles II awarded eight men the land south of Virginia and westward to the "South Seas." Charlie's new "lord proprietors" promptly sent people to map and explore their holdings.

Over the next century, settlers came in wagons, on horseback, and wearing out shoe leather. Germans, French Huguenots, Swiss, Irish, and Scots. Slowly, inexorably, the river and the road passed from Catawban to European hands.

Log homes and farms replaced native bark houses. Taverns, inns, and shops sprang up. Churches. A courthouse. At an intersection with a lesser trail, a new village straddled the Great Trading Path.

In 1761, George III married Duchess Sophia Charlotte of Mecklenburg-Strelitz, Germany. His seventeen-year-old bride must have caught the imagination of those living between the river and the road. Or perhaps the populace wished to curry favor with the mad British king. Whatever the motive, they named their little village Charlotte Town, their county Mecklenburg.

But distance and politics doomed the friendship to failure. The American colonies were growing angry and ripe for revolt. Mecklenburg County was no exception.

In May 1775, peeved at his majesty's refusal to grant a charter for their beloved Queens College, and incensed that redcoats had fired on Americans in Lexington, Massachusetts, Charlotte Town's leaders assembled. Dispensing with diplomacy and tactful phrasing, they drafted the Mecklenburg Declaration of Independence in which they declared themselves "a free and independent people."

Yessiree. The folks who wrote the Mec Dec didn't mess around. A year before the Continental Congress put pen to paper, they told old George to take a hike.

You know the rest of the story. Revolution. Emancipation and civil war. Reconstruction and Jim Crow. Industrialization, meaning textiles and railroads in North Carolina. World wars and depression. Segregation and civil rights. Rust Belt decline, Sun Belt renaissance.

By 1970, the Charlotte metro population had grown to roughly 400,000. By 2005, that number had doubled. Why? Something new was traveling the path. Money. And places to stash it. While many states had laws limiting the number of branches a bank could have, the North Carolina legislature said "be fruitful and multiply."

And multiply they did. The many branches led to many deposits, and the many deposits led to very much fruit. Long story short, the Queen City is home to two banking-industry heavies, Bank of America and Wachovia. As Charlotte's citizenry never tires of chortling, their burg ranks second only to New York City as a U.S. financial center.

Trade and Tryon streets now overlie the old trading path and its intersecting trail. Dominating this crossroads is the Bank of America Corporate Center, a fitting totem in sleek glass, stone, and steel.

From Trade and Tryon, old Charlotte's core spreads outward as a block of quadrants called, uncreatively, First, Second, Third, and Fourth Wards. Blinded by a vision of their town as a child of the New South, Charlotteans have historically cared little about preserving these inner-city zones. The single, and relatively recent, exception has been numero quatro.

The northwestern quadrant, Fourth Ward, was built by the town's nineteenth-century elite, then slipped into genteel decay. In the mid-seventies, spurred by the steel-magnolia force of the Junior League ladies, and some friendly financing by the banks, Fourth Ward became the focus of intense restoration effort. Today, its grand old homes share narrow streets with old-timey pubs and quaint modern townhouses. Gas lamps. Brick pavers. Park in the middle. You get the picture.

Back in the day, Second Ward was the flip side of lily-white Fourth. Lying southeast of the city center, Log Town, later known as Brooklyn, occupied much of the ward's acreage. Home to black preachers, doctors, dentists, and teachers, the Brooklyn neighborhood is now largely extinct, cleared for the construction of Marshall Park, the Education Center, a government plaza, and a freeway connector to I-77.

First and Third Wards lie to the northeast and southwest, respectively. Once crowded with depots, factories, rail yards, and mills, these quartiers are now crammed with apartments, townhouses, and condos. Courtside. Quarterside. The Renwick. Oak Park. Despite the city's policy of raze and replace, here and there a few old residential pockets remain. Larabee's directions were sending me to one in Third Ward.

Exiting I-77 onto Morehead, my gaze took in the monoliths forming the city skyline. One Wachovia Center. The Westin Hotel. The seventy-four-thousand-seat Panthers stadium. What, I wondered, would the residents of Nawvasa think of the metropolis superimposed on their village?

I made a left at the bottom of the ramp, another onto Cedar, and rolled past a cluster of recently converted warehouses. A truncated rail line. The Light Factory photo studios and gallery. A homeless shelter.

On my right stretched the Panthers training complex, practice fields muted green in the predusk light. Turning left onto Greenleaf, I entered a tunnel of willow oaks. Straight ahead lay an expanse of openness I knew to be Frazier Park.

A bimodal assortment of homes lined both sides of the street. Many had been purchased by yuppies desiring proximity to uptown, modernized, painted colors like Queen Anne Lilac or Smythe Tavern Blue. Others remained with their original African-American owners, some looking weathered and worn among their gentrified neighbors, the deed holders awaiting the next tax reevaluation with trepidation.

Despite the contrast between the born-agains and the yet-to-be-re-created, the work of caring hands was evident up and down the block. Walks were swept. Lawns were mowed. Window boxes overflowed with marigolds or mums.

Larabee's address belonged to one of the few exceptions, a seedy little number with patched siding, sagging trim, and peeling paint. The yard was mostly dirt, and the front porch featured a truckload of non-degradable trash. Pulling to the curb behind a Charlotte-Mecklenburg PD cruiser, I wondered how many wannabe purchasers had knocked on the bungalow's faded green door.

Alighting, I locked the Mazda and took my field kit from the trunk. Two houses down, a boy of about twelve shot a basketball into a garage-mounted hoop. His radio pounded out rap as his ball *thupped* softly on the gravel drive.

The walkway was humped where bulging tree roots snaked beneath. I kept my eyes down as I mounted warped wooden steps to the porch.

"You the one I gotta talk to so's I can go home?"

My gaze moved up.

A man occupied a rusted and precariously angled swing. He was tall and thin, with hair the color of apricot jam. Embroidered above his shirt pocket were the name *Arlo* and a stylized wrench.

Arlo had been seated with knees wide, elbows on thighs, face planted on upturned palms. Hearing footsteps, he'd raised his head to speak.

Before I could respond, Arlo posed a second question.

"How long I gotta stay here?"

"You're the gentleman who called in the nine-one-one?"

Arlo grimaced, revealing a rotten tooth among the lower rights.

I stepped onto the porch. "Can you describe what you saw?"

"I done that." Arlo clasped dirty hands. His gray pants were ripped at the left knee.

"You've given a statement?" Gently. The man's body language suggested genuine distress.

Arlo nodded, head moving crosswise to a torso canted at the same slope as the swing.

"Can you summarize what you saw?"

Now the head wagged from side to side. "The devil's work."

OK.

"You are Arlo . . . ?"

"Welton."

"The plumber."

Arlo gave another bobble-head nod. "Been banging pipes for thirty years. Never come across nothing like this."

"Tell me what happened."

Arlo swallowed. Swallowed again.

"I'm changing out fittings. The new owner's missus is planning to put in some newfangled washer setup, some kinda green thing saves the environment. It'll need different pipe fittings. Lord knows why she wants to start with that, place needing all it does. But that's not my business. Anyways, I start in on the wall and drop a piece of brick that takes a bite outa the flooring. I think to myself, Arlo, you cut that flooring, they're gonna take the cost of repairs outa your wages. So I roll back the flooring, and what do I find but a big ole wood plank."

Arlo stopped.

I waited.

"Don't know why, but I give the thing a nudge with my toe, and the end raised up in the air."

Again Arlo paused, recalling, I suspected, a bit more than a nudge.

"This plank was part of a hatch that opened?"

"Thing was covering some kinda hidey-hole. I'll admit, curiosity got the better of me. I took my flashlight and shined it on down."

"Into a subcellar."

Arlo shrugged. I allowed him time to continue. He didn't.

"And?" I prompted again.

"I'm a churchgoing man. Every Sunday and Wednesday. Never seen the devil, but I believe in him. Believe he's in the world, working his evil amongst us."

Arlo ran the back of a hand across his mouth.

"What I seen was Satan himself."

Though the day was still warm, I felt a chill ripple through me.

"You reported that you saw a human skull." All business.

"Yes'm."

"What else?"

"Don't want to put words to wickedness. It's best you see with your own eyes."

"Did you go down into the subcellar?"

"No way."

"What did you do?"

"I hauled my butt upstairs fast as I could. Called the police." Arlo emphasized the first syllable and gave it a very long *o*. "Can I go now?"

"The officer is downstairs?"

"Yes'm. Follow the hall, then through the kitchen."

Arlo was right. It was best I saw with my own eyes.

"Thank you, Mr. Welton. It shouldn't be long."

I crossed the porch and entered the house. Behind me, the swing rattled as Arlo's face dropped back to his hands.

The front door opened directly onto a narrow corridor. To the right was a bile green living room. A broken window had been sealed with cardboard duct-taped into place. The furnishings were sparse. A moth-eaten armchair. A sofa badly clawed by a cat.

To the left was a dining room, bare except for a knotty-pine sideboard, a mattress, and a stack of tires.

Continuing down the central hall, I turned left into a kitchen that would already have been retro in '56. Round-top Philco fridge. Kelvinator stove. Red Formica and chrome dinette set. Speckled gray Formica countertops.

A door stood open to the left of the Kelvinator. Through it I could see wooden stairs and hear radio static drifting up from below.

Shifting my kit to my right hand, I gripped the banister and started to descend. Two treads down, small hairs began rising on the back of my neck.

Unconsciously, I switched to breathing through my mouth.

3

THOUGH FAINT, THE ODOR WAS UNMISTAKABLE. SWEET AND FETID, it heralded the presence of rotting flesh.

But this wasn't the cloying, gut-churning smell with which I am so familiar. The reek of active putrefaction. Of innards ravaged by maggots and scavengers. Of flesh greened and bloated by water. No other stench can compete with that. It seeps into your pores, your nostrils, your lungs, your clothing, rides you home like smoke from a bar. Long after showering, it lingers in your hair, your mouth, your mind.

This was gentler. But still undeniable.

I hoped for a squirrel. Or a raccoon that had gnawed through a wall and become trapped in the basement. Recalling Larabee's words, and Arlo's agitation, I doubted either scenario was likely.

The temperature dropped with each downward tread. The dampness increased. By the time I reached bottom, the banister felt cool and slick to my palm.

Amber light seeped from a bulb dangling from a fuzzy overhead cord. Stepping onto hard-packed earth, I looked around.

Barely six feet high, the cellar had been divided into a number of small rooms arranged around a central open space. Plywood walls and prefab doors suggested partitioning had taken place long after the home's construction.

Every door in my sight line was open. Through one I could see shallow shelving, the kind used to store home-canned jam and tomatoes. Washtubs were visible through another. Stacked boxes through another.

A Charlotte-Mecklenburg uniform waited at the far end of the cellar, past a furnace that looked like a Jules Verne contraption. Unlike the other three, the door at his back looked old. The oak was solid, the varnish thick and yellowed with age.

The cop stood with feet spread, thumbs hooking his belt. He was a compact man with Beau Bridges brows and Sean Penn features, not a good combination. Drawing close, I could read the plaque on his shirt. *D. Gleason.*

"What have we got?" I asked, after introducing myself.

"You met the plumber?" Gleason lowered the volume on a speaker mike clipped to his left shoulder.

I nodded.

"Around sixteen hundred hours, Welton phoned in a nine-one-one. Said he'd found dead people in a crawl space. I caught the call, spotted remains which I believed to be human. Reported in. Desk told me to stay put. I told Welton to do the same."

I liked Gleason. He was concise.

"You go belowdecks?"

"No, ma'am." A second bulb hung in the room at Gleason's back. The angled light falling through the door threw shadows from his brows and carved his already too chiseled features deep into his flesh.

"The ME said you suspected more than one body."

Gleason waggled a hand. Maybe yes, maybe no.

"Anything down here I should know about?"

I was remembering a pizza parlor basement in Montreal. Detective Luc Claudel had pegged rats while I'd dug bones. I pictured him underground in his cashmere coat and Gucci gloves, almost smiled. Almost. The bones had turned out to be those of adolescent girls.

Gleason misinterpreted my question. "Appears to be some sort of voodoo thing. But that's your call, doc."

Right answer. Skeletons often appear sinister to the uninitiated. Even gleaming white anatomical specimens. The thought lifted my spirits. Maybe that's what this would turn out to be. A fake skull long forgotten in a cellar.

I flashed again on the pizza parlor case. The initial concern there had been PMI. Postmortem interval. How long since death? Ten years? Fifty? A hundred and fifty?

Another hopeful scenario. Perhaps the skull would turn out to be an ancient head pilfered from an archaeological site.

Lab models and relics don't smell of rot.

"Fair enough," I said to Gleason. "But I was wondering about rats, snakes?"

"So far, no company. I'll watch for party crashers."

"Much appreciated."

I followed Gleason through the doorway into a windowless room measuring about ten by twelve. Two brick walls appeared to be exterior, part of the original foundation. Two were interior. Workbenches pressed against those walls.

I did a quick scan of the jumbled contents atop the tables. Rusty tools. Boxes of nails, screws, washers. Coiled wire. Chain linking. A vise.

Large rolls of textured gray plastic lay below the workbenches. Dirt coated the underside of each.

"What's with the plastic?"

"G-floor."

I cocked a questioning brow.

"Rollout vinyl floor covering. I installed it in my garage last year. Normally, the stuff's secured with adhesive and seaming strips. Here it was just spread over the dirt and a hatchway."

"Welton rolled it and set it aside."

"That's his story."

Save for the workbenches and the vinyl flooring, the room was empty.

"Opening is over here." Gleason led me to the corner at which the exterior walls met.

A one-by-two-foot breach was evident at roughly shoulder level in the easternmost wall. Jagged edges and a marked color difference attested to the brevity of the opening's existence. Shattered brick and plaster littered the floor below. Welton had broken through to the plumbing at that location.

Through the gap I could see labyrinthine piping. On the ground, just out from the rubble, gaped a black rectangle, partially covered by a battered hatch of wood planks.

Setting my kit to one side, I peered down into the blackness. It yielded no clue of what lay below.

"How far to the bottom?"

"Twelve, fifteen feet. Probably an old root cellar. Some of these houses still have them."

I felt the familiar crawly sensation. The tightness in my chest.

Easy, Brennan.

"Why so deep?" I asked, forcing my voice calm.

Gleason shrugged. "Warm climate, no refrigeration."

Opening my kit, I unfolded and stepped into coveralls. Then I settled on my stomach, face over the hole.

Gleason handed me his flash. The shaft danced down makeshift wooden steps whose angle of descent was precariously steep, more a ladder than a stairway.

"Stuff's over by the east wall."

I shot the beam in that direction. It picked out rusted metal, flecks of red, yellow. Something ghostly pale, like cadaver flesh. Then I saw it.

The skull rested on some sort of short, round pedestal, lower jaw missing, forehead strangely mottled in the small oval of light. An object was centered on top of the cranial vault.

I stared. The empty orbits stared back. The teeth grinned, as though daring me to approach.

Pushing to all fours, I sat back and brushed dirt from my chest and arms. "I'll take a few shots, then we'll remove the plank and I'll go down."

"Those treads appear to have some years on them. How about I test to see if they're safe?"

"I'd prefer you stay topside, lower equipment as I need it."

"You got it."

The click of my shutter. The skitter of dirt cascading from the undersurface of the hatch cover. Each sound seemed magnified in the absolute stillness of the cellar. Irrationally, I couldn't shake the feeling that the hush was ominous.

After gloving, I shoved my Maglite into my waistband. Then I tested the first riser. Solid enough. Turning my face toward the steps, I gripped the banister with one hand and clutched the risers with the other as I descended.

The air grew dank. The odor of death strengthened. And my nose began picking up ribbons of other things, olfactory hints more than solid smells. Impressions of urine, sour milk, decaying fabric.

Six rungs down, almost no light penetrated from above. I paused, allowing my pupils to adjust. Allowing my nerves to come to grips with their environment. The tunnel I was descending through was two feet square, damp, and smelly.

My heart was banging now. My throat felt constricted.

There you have it. Brennan, the legendary tunnel rat, was claustrophobic.

Breathe.

Death-gripping the side rails, I descended four more steps. My head cleared the tunnel into a larger space. As I moved to the fifth, a sliver pierced the latex sheathing my left palm. My hand jerked reflexively.

More self-coaching.

Calm.

Breathe.

Two more rungs.

Breathe.

My toe touched solid ground with an odd little click. Gingerly, I explored behind me with my foot. Found nothing.

I stepped from the stairs. Closed my eyes, a reflex to stem the pounding adrenaline. Pointless. It was pitch black.

Releasing the banister, I flicked on my flash, turned, and swept the beam above and around me.

I was standing in an eight-foot cube whose walls and ceiling were reinforced by rough wooden beams. The dirt floor was covered with the same rollout vinyl that had been used overhead.

The action was off to my right. Cautiously, I edged in that direction, beam probing the shadows.

Cauldrons, one large, one small. Rusty saucepan. Plywood. Tools. Statues. Candles. Beads and antlers suspended overhead.

Gleason had called it correctly. The chamber housed some sort of ritualistic display.

The large cauldron appeared to be the focal point, with the rest of the paraphernalia fanning out from it. Stepping over a semicircle of candles, I pointed my light toward center stage.

The cauldron was iron and filled with dirt. A macabre pyramid rose from its center.

An animal cranium formed the base. Judging by shape, and by what I could see of the teeth, I guessed it came from a small ruminant, maybe a goat or sheep. Remnants of desiccated tissue lined the orbits and orifices.

Centered on the ruminant was the human skull that had so frightened the plumber. The bone was smooth and fleshless. The vault and forehead were oddly luminescent, and darkened by an irregular stain. A stain the exact red-brown of dried blood.

A small avian skull topped the human *cabeza*. It, too, retained scraps of dried skin and muscle.

I angled my beam to the floor.

Positioned at the cauldron's base was what looked like a section of railroad track. On the track lay a decapitated and partially decomposed chicken.

The source of the odor.

I inched my light left to the saucepan. Three hemispheric objects took shape. I bent for a closer look.

One turtle carapace. Two halves of a coconut shell.

Straightening, I sidestepped right past the large cauldron to the smaller. It, too, was soil packed. On the soil surface lay three railroad spikes, an antler, and two strands of yellow beads. A knife had been thrust into the fill to the depth of its handle.

A chain wrapped the cauldron's exterior, just below the rim. A machete leaned against its left side. A sheet of plywood was propped against its right.

I moved to the plywood and squatted. Symbols covered the surface, executed, I suspected, with black Magic Marker.

Next in the row was a cheap plaster statue. The woman wore a long white gown, red cape, and crown. One hand held a chalice, the other a sword. Beside her was a miniature castle or tower.

I tried to recall the Catholic icons of my youth. Some manifestation of the Virgin Mary? A saint? Though the visage was vaguely familiar, I couldn't ID the lady.

Shoulder to shoulder with the statue stood a carved wooden effigy with two faces pointing in opposite directions. Roughly twelve inches tall, the humanoid figure had long, slender limbs, a potbelly, and a penis upright and locked.

Definitely not the Virgin, I thought.

Last in line were two dolls in layer-cake ruffled gingham dresses, one yellow, one blue. Both dolls were female and black. Both wore bracelets, hoop earrings, and medallions on neck chains. Blue sported a crown. Yellow had a kerchief covering her hair.

And a miniature sword piercing her chest.

I'd seen enough.

The skull was not plastic. Human remains were present. The chicken hadn't been dead long.

Perhaps the rituals performed at the altar were harmless. Perhaps not. To be certain, proper recovery protocol had to be followed. Lights. Cameras. Chain-of-custody documentation to ensure possession could be proved every step of the way.

I headed to the stairs. Two treads up I heard a noise and raised my eyes. A face was peering down through the opening.

It was not a face I wanted to see.

ERSKINE "SKINNY" SLIDELL IS A DETECTIVE WITH THE CHARLOTTE- Mecklenburg PD Felony Investigative Bureau/Homicide Unit. The murder table.

I've worked with Slidell over the years. My opinion? The guy's got the personality of a blocked nostril. But good instincts.

Slidell's Brylcreemed head was turtling over the tunnel's opening.

"Doc." Slidell greeted me in his usual indolent way.

"Detective."

"Tell me I can go home, knock back a Pabst, and root for my boys on SmackDown."

"Not tonight."

Slidell sighed in annoyance, then withdrew from sight.

Climbing upward, I recalled the last time our paths had crossed.

August. The detective was entering the Mecklenburg County Court-house. I'd just testified and was heading out.

Slidell isn't what you'd call a fast thinker on his feet. Or on the stand. Actually, that's an understatement. Sharp defense attorneys make hamburger of Skinny. His nervousness had been apparent that morning, his eyes circled with dark rings suggesting a lot of tossing and turning.

Emerging from the ladder well, I noted that Slidell looked marginally better today. The same could not be said of his jacket. Green polyester with orange top stitching, the thing was garish, even in the subterranean gloom.

"Officer here says we got us a witch doctor." Slidell lifted his chin in Gleason's direction.

I described what I'd seen in the subcellar.

Slidell checked his watch. "How 'bout we toss this thing in the morning?"

"Got a date tonight, Skinny?"

Behind me, Gleason made a muffled sound in his throat.

"Like I said. Six-pack and Superstars."

"Should have set your TiVo."

Slidell looked at me as though I'd suggested he program the next shuttle mission.

"It's like a VCR," I explained, yanking off a glove.

"I'm surprised this hasn't drawn attention." Slidell was looking at the opening by my feet. He was referring to the media.

"Let's keep it that way," I said. "Use your cell phone to call CSS."

I pulled off the torn glove. The heel of my thumb was red, swollen, and itchy as hell.

"Tell them we'll need a generator and portable lights." Both gloves went into my kit. "And something that can lift a cauldron of dirt."

Head wagging, Slidell began punching his mobile.

Four hours later, I was pouring myself into my Mazda. Greenleaf was bathed in moonlight. I was bathed in sweat.

Emerging from the house, Slidell had spotted a woman shooting with a small digital camera through a kitchen window. After dispatching her, he'd chain-smoked two Camels, mumbled something about deeds and tax records, and gunned off in his Taurus.

The CSS techs had left in their truck. They'd deliver the dolls, statues, beads, tools, and other artifacts to the crime lab.

The morgue van had also come and gone. Joe Hawkins, the MCME death investigator on call that night, was transporting the skulls and chicken to the ME facility. Ditto the cauldrons. Though Larabee would be less than enthused about the mess, I preferred sifting the fill under controlled conditions.

As anticipated, the large cauldron had posed the greatest difficulty. Weighing approximately the same as the Statue of Liberty, its removal had required winching, a lot of muscle, and a lexicon of colorful words.

I pulled out and drove up Greenleaf. Ahead, Frazier Park was a black cutout in the urban landscape. A jungle gym rose from the shadows, a silvery cubist sculpture poised over the dark, serpentine smile of the Irwin Creek gulley.

Doubling back down Westbrook to Cedar, I skirted the edge of uptown and drove southeast toward my home turf, Myers Park. Built in the 1930s as Charlotte's first streetcar burb, today the sector is overpriced, oversmug, and over-Republican. Though not particularly old, the hood is elegant and well-landscaped, Charlotte's answer to Cleveland's Shaker Heights and Miami's Coral Gables. What the hell, we're not Charleston.

Ten minutes after leaving Third Ward I was parked beside my patio. Locking the car, I headed into my townhouse.

Which requires some explanation.

I live on the grounds of Sharon Hall, a nineteenth-century manor-turned-condo-complex lying just off the Queens University campus. My little outbuilding is called the "Annex." Annex to what? No one knows. The tiny two-story structure appears on none of the estate's original plans. The hall is there. The coach house. The herb and formal gardens. No annex. Clearly an afterthought.

Speculation by friends, family, and guests ranges from smokehouse to hothouse to kiln. I am not fixated on identifying the original builder's purpose. Barely twelve hundred square feet, the structure suits my needs. Bedroom and bath up. Kitchen, dining room, parlor, and study down. I took occupancy when my marriage to Pete imploded. A decade later, it still serves.

"Yo, Bird," I called out to the empty kitchen.

No cat.

"Birdie, I'm home."

The hum of the refrigerator. A series of soft bongs from Gran's mantel clock.

I counted. Eleven.

My eyes snuck to the message indicator on my phone. Not a flicker.

Depositing my purse, I went straight to the shower.

As I exorcised cellar grime and odor with green tea body gel, rosemary mint shampoo, and water as hot as my skin could stand, my thoughts drifted to the perversely dark voice mail light, to the voice I was hoping to hear.

Bonjour, Tempe. I miss you. We should talk.

Pop-up image. Lanky build, sandy hair, Carolina blue eyes. Andrew Ryan, *lieutenant-détective,* Section des crimes contre la personne, Sûreté du Québec.

So there's the Quebec thing. I work two jobs, one in Charlotte, North Carolina, USA, one in Montreal, Quebec, Canada, where I am forensic anthropologist for the Bureau du coroner. Ryan is a homicide detective with the provincial police. In other words, for murders in *La Belle Province,* I work the vics and Ryan detects.

Years back, when I began at the Montreal lab, Ryan had a reputation as the station-house stud. And I had a rule against office romance. Turned out the *lieutenant-détective* was lousy with rules. When hopes of salvaging my marriage finally hit the scrap heap, we began seeing each other socially. For a while, things went well. Very well.

My mind ran an X-rated slide show of memorable plays. Beaufort, South Carolina, the first deflected pass, me in cutoffs sans panties, aboard a forty-two-foot Chris-Craft at the Lady's Island Marina. Charlotte, North Carolina, the first touchdown, me in a man-eater black dress and one of Victoria's most secret thongs.

Recalling other sports moments, I felt a wee tummy flip. Yep, the guy was that good. And that good-looking.

Then Ryan blew a hole in my heart. The daughter he'd newly discovered but had never known, Lily, was rebellious, angry, addicted to heroin. Racked with guilt, Daddy had decided to reconnect with Mommy and launch a joint effort to save daughter.

And I was out like last year's shade of lipstick. That was four months ago.

"Screw it."

Face upturned to the spigot, I belted out a jumbled version of Gloria Gaynor.

"I will survive. I've got all my life to live—"

Suddenly, the water went cold. And I was starving. Totally engaged in processing the cellar, and nerve-fried by the underground context in which I was forced to work, I'd been oblivious to hunger. Until now.

Bird strolled in as I was toweling off.

"Sorry," I said. "Night op. No choice."

The cat looked skeptical. Or quizzical. Or bored.

"How about a hit of zoom-around-the-room?"

Bird sat and licked one forepaw, indicating forgiveness would not be hurried with a catnip bribe.

Pulling on a nightshirt and fuzzy pink socks, I returned to the kitchen.

Another character weakness. I hate errands. Dry cleaning. Car maintenance. Supermarket. I may construct lists, but follow-through is usually delayed until I'm back-against-the-wall. Consequently, my larder offered the following delicacies:

One frozen meat loaf entrée. One frozen chow mein entrée. Cans of tuna, peaches, tomato paste, and green beans. Mushroom, vegetable, and chicken noodle soup. Packages of dried macaroni and cheese and mushroom risotto.

Bird reappeared as the chow mein was leaving the microwave. Setting the tray on the counter, I got catnip from the pantry and placed it in his mouse.

The cat flopped to his side, clawed the toy with all fours, and sniffed. His character weakness? He likes to get high.

I ate standing at the sink while Bird jazzed his pheromonic receptors on the floor at my feet. Then Ozzy Osbourne and I hit the sack.

Though I was anxious to begin my analysis of the skull and cauldrons, Tuesdays I belonged to UNCC.

Much to Slidell's annoyance.

As appeasement, I agreed to drop by the MCME at the butt crack of dawn. Skinny's wording, not mine.

I spent an hour sampling from the chicken and the goat head, and double-checking the bugs I'd collected from the cellar. Fortunately, I'd taken time on-site to separate and label them.

Insects packaged and shipped to an entomologist in Hawaii, I rushed to campus to teach my morning seminar. In the afternoon I advised students. Legions of them, all concerned about upcoming midterms. Dusk was nothing but a memory when I finally slipped away.

Wednesday, I was again up with the sun. Rising at daybreak is not my style. I wasn't enjoying it.

The Mecklenburg County Medical Examiner is located at Tenth and College, on the cusp of uptown, in a building that started life as a Sears Garden Center. Which is exactly what it resembles, sans the pansies and philodendra. Squat and featureless, the one-story brick bunker is also home to several Charlotte-Mecklenburg PD satellite offices.

In tune with the original mall theme, landscaping consists of an acre of concrete. Bad news if you're hoping for a shot at *Southern Homes and Gardens.* Good news if you're trying to park your car.

Which I was, at 7:35 A.M.

Card-swiping myself through double glass doors, I entered an empty reception area. A purring silence told me I was first to arrive.

Weekdays, Eunice Flowers screens visitors through a plate-glass window above her desk, granting entrance to some, turning others away. She does scheduling, types and enters reports, and maintains hard-copy documents in gray metal cabinets lining the walls of her domain.

Regardless of the weather, Mrs. Flowers's clothes remain pressed, her hair fixed with balanced precision. Though kind and generous, the woman inevitably makes me feel messy.

And her work space totally confounds me. No matter the chaos throughout the rest of the lab, her desktop is perpetually clean and clutter-free. All papers stay militarily squared, all bulletin board Post-its aligned and equi-spaced. I am incapable of such tidiness, and suspicious of those who are.

I knew the gatekeeper would arrive in fifteen minutes. Precisely. Mrs. Flowers had clocked in at 7:50 for more than two decades, would continue to do so until she retired. Or her toes pointed north.

Turning right, I walked past a row of death investigator cubicles to a large whiteboard on the back wall. While penning that day's date in the square beside my name, I checked those beside the names of the three pathologists.

Dr. Germaine Hartigan was away for a week of vacation. Dr. Ken Siu had blocked off three days for court testimony.

Bummer for Larabee. He was on his own this week.

I looked at the intake log. Overnight, two cases had been entered in black Magic Marker.

A burned body had been found in a Dumpster behind a Winn-Dixie supermarket. MCME 522-08.

A jawless human skull had been found in a cellar. MCME 523-08.

My office is in back, near those of the pathologists. The square footage is such that the room probably qualifies by code as a closet.

Unlocking the door, I slid behind my desk and placed my purse in a drawer. Then I pulled a form from plastic mini-shelving topping a filing cabinet at my back, filled in the case number, and wrote a brief description of the remains and the circumstances surrounding their discovery. Worksheet ready, I hurried to the locker room.

The MCME facility has a pair of autopsy suites, each with a single table. The smaller of the two has special ventilation for combating odor.

The stinky room. For decomps and floaters. My kinds of cases.

After laying out cameras, calipers, a screen, picks, and a small trowel, I crossed to the morgue. The stainless steel door whooshed open, enveloping me in the smell of refrigerated flesh. I flicked on the light.

And said a prayer of thanks to Joe Hawkins. Metaphorically.

On Tuesday, I'd been too grumpy because of the butt-crack hour to notice. The dilemma struck me as I was changing into scrubs. If the cauldrons were on the floor, how would I move them?

No problem. Hawkins had left both on the gurney he'd employed to transport them from Greenleaf. Gathering the cardboard box containing the skulls and the chicken, I toed the brake release, turned, and rump-pushed the door. It flew open.

Hands caught me as I sailed into a full-out pratfall. Recovering, I turned.

Tim Larabee resembles a wrangler who's spent far too much time in the desert. A marathon junkie, daily training has grizzled his body, fried his skin, and hollowed his already lean cheeks.

Larabee's eyes were apologetic. Eyes set way too deep. "Sorry. I didn't know anyone else was here."

"My fault. I was leading with my ass."

"Let me help you."

As we maneuvered the gurney out of the cooler and into the autopsy room, I told him about the cellar.

"Voodoo?"

I shrugged. Who knows?

"Guess you won't be X-raying the fill." Larabee slapped one iron cauldron.

"Flying blind," I agreed, pulling on gloves. "But I'll have Joe shoot the skulls as soon as he gets here."

Larabee indicated the box. "Quick look-see?"

I opened the flaps. Each skull was as I'd left it, encased in a labeled ziplock. No need to check the bag. The stench told me it still contained the chicken.

While the ME gloved, I removed the human skull and centered it on a cork ring balancer on the autopsy table.

"Mandible?"

I shook my head no.

Larabee ran a fingertip over the forehead and crown. "Looks like wax," he said.

I nodded in agreement.

Larabee touched the stain haloing the borders of the overlying goo. "Blood?"

"That's my guess."

"Human?"

"I'll take a sample for testing."

Larabee gestured with an upturned palm. I knew what he wanted.

"This is only preliminary," I warned.

"Understood."

I took the cranium in my hands, palate and foramen magnum pointing up.

"I'll wait for the X-rays, of course, but it looks like the third molars were just erupting, and there's minimal wear on the others. The basilar suture has recently fused." I referred to the junction between the sphenoid and occipital bones at the skull base. "That configuration suggests an age in the mid to late teens."

I rotated the skull.

"The back of the head is smooth, with no bump for the attachment of neck muscles." I pointed to a triangular lump projecting downward below the right ear opening. "The mastoids are small. And see how this raised ridge dies out at the end of the cheekbone?"

"Doesn't continue backward above the auditory meatus."

I nodded. "Those features all suggest female."

"The brow ridges aren't much to write home about."

"No. But at this age that's not definitive."

"What about race?"

"Tough one. The nasal opening isn't all that wide, but the nasal bones meet low on the bridge, like a Quonset hut. The inferior nasal border and spine are damaged, so it's hard to evaluate shape in that region." I turned the skull sideways. "The lower face projects forward." I looked down onto the crown. "Cranial shape is long but not excessively narrow."

I replaced the skull on its ring.

"I'll run measurements through Fordisc 3.0, but my gut feeling is Negroid."

"African-American."

"Or African. Caribbean. South American. Central—"

"A black teenaged girl."

"That's only preliminary."

"Yeah, yeah. PMI?"

"That'll take some work."

"A hundred years? Fifty? Ten? One?"

"Yes," I said. "I FedEx'ed the bugs yesterday."

"I didn't know you were here."

"It was in and out early," I said.

"Now what?" Larabee asked.

"Now I sift through two cauldrons of dirt."

The door opened and Joe Hawkins stuck his head through the gap.

"You see what I left in the coffee room yesterday?"

Larabee and I shook our heads no.

"I was at the university all day," I said.

"I was in Chapel Hill," Larabee said.

"Just as well. You ain't gonna like it."

5

We followed Hawkins down a short corridor to a small staff lounge. The left side was a mini-kitchen, with cabinets, sink, stove, and refrigerator. A phone and a small TV sat at one end of the counter. A coffeemaker and a basket holding sugar and dried cream packets sat at the other. A round table and four chairs took up most of the right side of the room.

Joe Hawkins has been hauling stiffs since the Eisenhower years, and is living proof that we're molded by what we do. Cadaver thin, with dark-circled eyes, bushy brows, and dyed black hair slicked back from his face, he is the archetypical B-movie death investigator.

Unsmiling, Hawkins crossed to the table and jabbed a finger at an open copy of Tuesday's *Charlotte Observer.*

"Yesterday's paper."

Larabee and I leaned in to read.

Local section. Page five. Three column inches. One photo.

Demons or Dump?

Police were baffled Monday night when a 911 call sent them to a house on Greenleaf. While renovating, a plumber had stumbled onto more than rusty pipes. Within hours, skulls, cauldrons, and an assortment of strange items were removed from the home's basement and transported to the MCME morgue and the CMPD crime lab.

Directing the recovery operation were forensic anthropologist Dr. Temperance Brennan and homicide detective Erskine Slidell. Though queried, police refused to comment on whether any remains were human.

The plumber, Arlo Welton, recounted knocking through a wall into a mysterious subterranean cellar. Welton described an altar and satanic paraphernalia that, in his opinion, clearly indicated demonic ritual.

Devil worship? Or underground Dumpster? The investigation is ongoing.

The photo was grainy, taken from too great a distance with too little light. It showed Slidell and me standing beside the crooked porch swing. My hair was cascading from a topknot. I was wearing the jumpsuit. Skinny was picking something from his ear. Neither of us looked ready to appear on *The View.* Photo credit was given to Allison Stallings.

"Sugar," Larabee said.

"Shit," I said.

"Nice 'do."

My finger told Larabee what I thought of his humor.

As though on cue, the phone rang. While Hawkins picked up, I reread the article, feeling the usual irritation. While I'm an avid consumer of news, both print and electronic, I detest having journalists in my lab or at my field recoveries. In my view, cameras and mikes don't go with corpses. In their opinion, neither the lab nor the crime scene are mine and the public has a right to know. We coexist in a state of forced accommodation, yielding only as necessary.

Allison Stallings. The name wasn't familiar. Perhaps a new hire at the paper? I thought I knew everyone covering the police beat in town.

"Mrs. Flowers has been flooded with calls from the press." Hawkins was holding the receiver to his chest. "Been saying 'no comment.' Now that you're here, she wants direction."

"Tell them to drop dead," I said.

" 'No comment' is good," Larabee overruled.

Hawkins transmitted the message. Listened. Again, pressed the phone to his shirtfront.

"She says they're insistent."

"Mysterious? Satanic?" My voice oozed disdain. "They're probably hoping for a boiled baby for the five o'clock news."

"No comment," Larabee repeated.

I spent the rest of the day with the Greenleaf materials.

After photographing the human skull, I began a detailed analysis, starting with the teeth.

Unfortunately, only ten of the original sixteen uppers remained. Nothing sinister. Dentition fronting the arcade is single-rooted. When the gums adios, the incisors and canines aren't far behind.

Dental Aging 101. Choppers don't arrive fait accompli. No scoop there. Everyone knows mammal teeth come in two sets, baby and adult. And that each set makes its entrance as a specialty troupe. Incisors, premolars, canines, molars. But dental development is more complex than simply a play in two acts. And much of the action takes place offstage.

Here's the script. First, a crown bud appears deep in the jaw. Enamel is laid onto that bud as a root begins growing downward or upward into the socket. The crown emerges. The root elongates, eventually forming a tip. In other words, following eruption, formation continues until the root is complete. Simultaneously, other teeth play out their scenes according to their own entrance cues.

Cranial X-rays showed partial eruption of the third maxillary molars, and partial completion of the second molar roots. That combination, along with recent basilar suture closure, suggested an age of fourteen to seventeen. My gut instinct favored the upper end of that range.

A reassessment of cranial traits did not change my initial impressions of gender and ancestry. Nevertheless, as a cross-check, I took measurements and entered them into my laptop.

Fordisc 3.0 is an anthropometric program that employs a statistical procedure called discriminant function analysis, or DFA. DFA's rely on comparison to reference groups composed of known membership, in this case skulls of individuals whose race and sex have been documented, and whose measurements have been entered into the database. "Unknowns," such as the Greenleaf skull, are compared to the "knowns" in the reference groups, and evaluated as to similarity and difference.

For sex determination there are a number of reference groups, each composed of known males and known females of specific racial or ethnic backgrounds. Since tight-fitting cheekbones and a relatively long skull ruled out Asian and Native American ancestry in this case, I ran comparisons using Caucasoids and Negroids.

No surprise. No matter black or white, the Greenleaf skull classified with the girls.

Evaluation of race is a bit more complicated. Just as they are for sex determination, the potential reference groups are composed of both sexes of known blacks, whites, American Indians, and Japanese, as well as Guatemalan, Hispanic, Chinese, and Vietnamese males. That's what the Fordisc database holds.

I ran a two-way comparison between black and white females.

My unknown classified with the former. Barely.

I checked the interpretive stats.

A posterior probability, or PP, gives the probability of group membership for an unknown based on its relative proximity to all groups. Major assumptions are that variation is roughly the same *within* groups; that means and values differ *between* groups; and that the unknown actually belongs to one of the reference groups you're using. That last isn't necessarily true. A DFA will classify any set of measurements, even if your unknown is a chimp or hyena.

A typicality probability, or TP, is a better indicator of actual group membership. TP's suggest the likelihood of an unknown belonging to a particular group based on the average variability of all the groups in the analysis. TP's evaluate absolute distances, not relative distances, as with PP's.

Think of it this way. If you have to fit your unknown into one of the program's reference groups, a PP tells you which is the best choice. A TP tells you if that choice is realistic.

The PP on my screen said that for my unknown, black ancestry was a greater likelihood than white. The TP suggested her head wasn't put together like those of the black ladies in the data bank.

I remeasured and recalculated.

Same result.

Numbers go one way, overall deductive judgment goes another? Not uncommon. I stick with experience. And, since genes pay no heed to stats, I knew there was the possibility of mixed ancestry.

Flipping to the cover sheet, I filled in boxes on my case form.

Sex: Female.

Ancestry: Negroid. (Possible Caucasoid admixture.)

Age: Fourteen to seventeen years.

Sweet Jesus. Just a kid.

Staring into the empty orbits, I tried to visualize who this young woman had been. Felt sad at the loss. My mind could conjure up rough images of her appearance based on the black girls I saw around me. Katy's friends. My students. The kids who hung out in the park across College Street. I could envision dark hair and eyes, chocolate skin. But what had she felt? Thought? What expression had molded her features as she fell asleep each night, woke each morning?

Fourteen to seventeen. Half woman, half child. Had she liked to read? Ride a bike? A Harley? Hang out at the mall? Did she have a steady boyfriend? Who was missing her?

Had malls existed in her world? When did she die? Where?

Do what you do, Brennan. Learn who she was. What happened to her.

Setting sentimental musing aside, I refocused on the science.

The next boxes on the form asked for PMI and MOD. Postmortem interval. Manner of death.

With dry bone, leached of flesh and organic components, time since death can be even tougher to nail than race.

Gently, I hefted the skull in one palm, testing its weight. The bone looked and felt solid, not porous or degraded like old cemetery remains or archaeological materials. All visible surfaces were stained a uniform tea brown.

I looked for cultural alterations, such as tooth filing, cranial binding, occipital flattening, or surgical boring. Zip.

I checked for indications of coffin burial. The skull retained no funerary artifacts such as morticians' molding wax, trocars, or eye caps. No threads or fabric shreds. There was no embalmed tissue. No flaking of the cortical bone. No head or facial hair.

I shined a small flashlight through the foramen magnum, the large hole through which the spinal cord enters the brain. Except for adherent dirt, the vault interior was empty.

Using a dental pick, I scraped at the endocranial soil. A small cone formed on the gurney. Though slightly shinier, the soil looked similar to that in the cauldron. It yielded one pill bug, one puparial case, and no plant inclusions.

Still using the pick, I tipped the skull and probed the nasal and auditory openings. More dirt trickled onto the cone.

Scooping the cranial soil, the bug, and the casing into a ziplock, I wrote the MCME ID number, date, and my name on the outside of the plastic. The sample might never be processed, but better to err on the side of caution.

Using a scalpel, I chipped flakes from the candle wax coating the outer surface of the crown and sealed them into a second ziplock. Scrapings of the "blood" stain went into a third.

Then I turned back to the X-rays. Slowly, I worked through the frontal, lateral, posterior, superior, and basal views Hawkins had provided.

The skull showed no signs of trauma or disease. No metallic trace that would indicate gunshot wounding. No fractures, bullet entrance or exit holes, or sharp instrument gashes. No lesions, defects, or congenital anomalies. No restorations, implants, or indicators of cosmetic or corrective surgery. Not a clue as to the girl's dental or medical history. Not a hint concerning the reason for her death.

Frustrated, I reexamined both the skull and the X-rays under magnification.

Nope. The cranium was remarkably unremarkable.

Discouraged, I ran through a mental checklist of methods for PMI estimation with dry bone. Ultraviolet fluorescence, staining for indophenol and Nile blue, supersonic conductivity, histological or radiographic structure analysis, nitrogen or amino acid content evaluation, Bomb C14 testing, calculation of fat transgression, carbonate, or serological protein levels, benzidine or anti–human serum reaction.

Though I'd forward the pill bug and casing to the entomologist, I doubted either would be of much use. They could have come from the fill, drifting into the skull years after the girl had died.

The Bomb C14 was a possibility. Testing might show whether death occurred, roughly, before or after 1963, the end date for atmospheric testing of thermonuclear devices. But based on bone quality, I doubted PMI could be greater than fifty years. Besides, given budgetary restraints, Larabee would never cough up the funds for C14.

Revving up a Stryker saw, I removed a small square of bone from the right parietal and sealed it into a ziplock. Then I extracted and added a right second molar. Even if we couldn't afford C14 testing, we might need the specimens for DNA sequencing.

Samples bagged, I finished entering my observations onto my case form.

PMI: Five to fifty years.

MOD: Unknown.

I could picture Slidell's expression when I reported that. I wasn't looking forward to the conversation.

Discouraged, I turned to the nonhumans.

Yep. Goat and chicken.

Both skulls retained remnants of desiccated flesh. I found a few larvae and puparial cases inside the vault and auditory canals of the goat.

I'd already sampled from the chicken on Tuesday, and knew it had held the motherlode. Adult flies. Larvae. The body had even yielded a few beetles and a number of very large roaches. I'd await word from the entomologist, but I had no doubt Chicken Little had gone to her reward in the past few months.

I turned my attention to the large cauldron.

First I took photos. Then I placed a stainless steel tub in the sink, settled a screen over it, masked, and began troweling. The dirt *shished* softly as it fell through the mesh. An earthy smell rose around me.

One scoop. Three. Five. A few pebbles, snail shells, and bug parts collected in the screen.

Twelve scoops in, I sensed resistance. Abandoning the trowel, I dug by hand. In seconds, I'd freed a shriveled mass measuring approximately two inches in diameter.

Laying my find on the gurney, I gingerly explored with my fingers.

The mass was shrunken, yet spongy.

Apprehension began to tap at my brain. What I was handling was organic.

As I teased away dirt, detail emerged. Gyri. Sulci.

Recognition.

I was poking at a hunk of mummified gray matter.

My own neurons fired up a name.

Mark Kilroy.

I pushed it back down.

The human brain measures in at approximately 1,400 cubic centimeters. This thing could claim but a fraction of that.

Goat? Chicken?

A sudden grisly thought. One lobe of a human cerebrum?

That was a question for Larabee.

After bagging and tagging my find I continued with the fill.

And made my next chilling discovery.

6

At first I thought it was a holy card, a mass-produced devotional used by the Catholic faithful. My sister, Harry, and I used to collect them as kids. A bit smaller than a driver's license, each card depicts a saint or biblical scene and provides a suitable prayer. The good ones promise indulgence, time off the purgatory sentence you've got to serve for screwing up on Earth.

It wasn't. When removed from its plastic wrapping, the image that emerged was actually a portrait, the kind that shows up in school yearbooks.

The subject was shown from the waist up, tree-leaning, face turned toward the lens. She wore a brown long-sleeved sweater that allowed a peek of stomach. One hand pressed the tree, the other thumb-hooked a belt loop on a faded pair of jeans.

The girl's hair was center parted, swept back and flipped up behind her ears. It was black. Her eyes were dark chocolate, her skin nutmeg. She looked about seventeen.

I felt a constriction in my chest.

A black teenaged girl.

My eyes jumped to the gurney. Dear God, could this be her skull? If so, how had it ended up in that basement? Had this girl been murdered?

I looked back at the portrait.

The girl's head was subtly tipped, her shoulders lightly raised. Her lip corners rose in an impish grin. She looked happy, bursting with self-assurance and the promise of life. Why was her photo buried in a cauldron?

Could Arlo Welton be right? Had he uncovered an altar used for satanic ritual? For human sacrifice? I'd read news stories, knew that, though rare, such atrocities did take place.

The phone shrilled, sparing further contemplation of the dreadful possibilities.

"Weren't we the early bird today." As usual, Mrs. Flowers sounded a yard north of chirpy.

"I have a lot to go through."

"The media is in a dither over this basement thing."

"Yes."

"The phone's been ringing off the hook. Well, I guess they don't really have hooks anymore. Metaphorically speaking, of course."

I looked at the wall clock. Twelve forty.

"They'll move on once something new die-verts their attention. Thought I'd let you know. There's a detective steaming your way."

"Slidell?"

"Yes, ma'am. Partner's with him."

"Warning heeded."

I was hanging up when the autopsy room door swung in. Slidell entered, followed by a gangling skeleton toting an Italian leather briefcase.

Skinny Slidell and Eddie Rinaldi have been partners since the eighties, to the puzzlement of all, since the two appear to be polar opposites.

Rinaldi is six feet four and carries a little over 160. Slidell is five-ten and carries a whole lot more, most of it south of where his waist should be. Rinaldi's features are sharp. Slidell's are fleshy and loose, the bags under his eyes the size of empanadas.

Why the Skinny handle? It's a cop thing.

But the differences aren't limited to physique. Slidell is messy. Rinaldi is neat. Slidell inhales junk food. Rinaldi eats tofu. Slidell is Elvis, Sam Cooke, and the Coasters. Rinaldi is Mozart, Vivaldi, and Wagner. Slidell's clothes are blue-light special. Rinaldi's are designer or custom-made.

Somehow the two stick. Go figure.

Slidell removed knockoff Ray-Bans and hung them by one bow in his jacket pocket. Today it was polyester, a plaid probably named for some golf course in Scotland.

"How's it hangin', doc?" Slidell sees himself as Charlotte's very own Dirty Harry. Hollywood cop lingo is part of the schtick.

"Interesting morning." I nodded at Rinaldi. "Detective."

Rinaldi flicked a wave, attention fixed on the cauldrons and skulls.

That was Rinaldi. All focus. No jokes or banter. No complaining or bragging. No sharing of personal problems or victories. On duty, he was perennially polite, reserved, and unflappable.

Off duty? No one really knew much. Born in West Virginia, Rinaldi had attended college briefly, then come to Charlotte sometime in the seventies. He'd married, his wife had died shortly thereafter of cancer. I'd heard talk of a child, but had never witnessed the man mention a son or daughter. Rinaldi lived alone in a small brick house in a sedate, well-groomed neighborhood called Beverly Woods.

Other than his height, lofty taste in music, and penchant for expensive clothing, Rinaldi had no physical traits or personality quirks that other cops poked fun at. To my knowledge, he'd never been the butt of jokes concerning screwups or embarrassing incidents. Perhaps that's why he'd never been tagged with a nickname.

Bottom line: Rinaldi was not the guy I'd invite to my margarita party, but, if threatened, he was the one I'd want covering my back.

Slidell raised and waggled splayed fingers. "Some cretin's idea of a Halloween freak show, eh?"

"Maybe not."

The waggling stopped.

I summarized the biological profile that I'd constructed from the skull.

"But the stuff's older than dirt, right?"

"I estimate the girl's been dead no less than five, no more than fifty years. My gut goes with the front end of that range."

Slidell blew air through his lips. His breath smelled of tobacco.

"Cause of death?"

"The skull shows no signs of illness or injury."

"Meaning?"

"I don't know."

"Where's the jaw?"

"I don't know."

"Now we're getting somewhere."

Calm, Brennan.

"I found this in the large cauldron. About four inches down in the fill."

I placed the school picture on the gurney. The men stepped forward to view it.

"Anything else?" Slidell's eyes remained on the photo.

"Hunk of brain."

Rinaldi's brows floated up. "Human?"

"I hope not."

Rinaldi and Slidell looked from the photo to the skull to the photo and back.

Rinaldi spoke first. "Think it's the same young lady?"

"There's nothing in the cranial or facial architecture to exclude the possibility. Age, sex, and race fit."

"Can you do a photo superimposition?"

"Not much point without the lower jaw."

"I suppose that also holds true for a facial approximation."

I nodded. "The image would be too speculative, might distract rather than help with an ID."

"Sonovabitch." Slidell's head wagged from side to side.

"We'll start checking MP's." Rinaldi was referring to missing persons files.

"Go back ten years. If nothing pops, we can expand the time frame."

"Not much sense sending her through NCIC."

NCIC is the FBI's National Crime Information Center, a computerized index of criminal records, fugitives, stolen properties, and missing and unidentified persons. By comparing details entered by law enforcement, the system is able to match corpses found in one location with individuals reported missing in others.

But the database is huge. With only age, sex, and race as identifiers, and a time frame of up to fifty years, the list generated would look like a phone book.

"No," I agreed. "Not without more."

I told the detectives about the insects and the chicken.

Rinaldi grasped the implication. "The cellar is still being used."

"Based on the condition of the chicken, I'd say within the last few months. Perhaps more recently than that."

"You saying some witch doctor took a kid underground and cut off her head?"

"I am not." Cool. "Though I'd guess that's exactly what happened to the chicken."

"So this wing-nut plumber is right?"

"I'm suggesting there is a possibility—"

"Witch doctors? Human sacrifice?" Rolling his eyes, Slidell *do-do-do-do*'ed the *Twilight Zone* theme.

Though relatively few, there are people on this planet with a talent for irking me, for provoking me to blurt things I wouldn't otherwise say. Slidell is one of those special souls. I hate losing control, vow each time it won't happen again. Repeatedly, with Slidell, that vow is shattered.

It happened now.

"Tell that to Mark Kilroy." The comment flew out before I had time to consider.

There was a moment of silence. Then Rinaldi pointed one long, bony finger.

"Kid from Brownsville, Texas. Disappeared in Matamoros, Mexico, back in eighty-nine."

"Kilroy was sodomized, tortured, then killed by Adolfo de Jesus Constanzo and his followers. Investigators found his brain floating in a cauldron."

Slidell's eyes snapped down. "What the hell?"

"Kilroy's organs were harvested for ritual use."

"You saying that's what we got here?"

Already, I regretted seeding Slidell's imagination with mention of the Kilroy case.

"I have to finish with the cauldrons. And hear what the crime lab comes up with."

Slidell scooped up and passed the class photo to his partner.

"Based on clothing and hair, the image doesn't look that old," Rinaldi said. "We could broadcast it, see if someone recognizes her."

"Let's wait on that," Slidell said. "We start flashing the mug of every kid we can't find, eventually Mr. and Mrs. Public tune out."

"I agree. We don't even know that she's missing."

"Can't be too many studios shooting bubble gummers in this burg." Slidell pocketed the photo. "We'll start by working those."

I nodded. "Might not be from this burg. What did you learn about the Greenleaf property?"

Rinaldi pulled a small leather-bound notepad from the inside breast pocket of a jacket jarringly different from that of his partner. Navy, double-breasted, very high-end.

A manicured finger flipped a few pages.

"The property changed hands rarely after purchase by a family named Horne in the postwar years, and only among relatives. We're talking World War Two, here." Rinaldi looked up from his notes. "We can check older records should circumstances warrant."

I nodded.

"Roscoe Washington Horne owned the house from 1947 until 1972; Lydia Louise Tillman Horne until 1994; Wanda Belle Sarasota Horne until her death eighteen months ago."

"Ye old family plantation," Slidell snorted.

Rinaldi continued from his notes.

"Upon Wanda's death, the property went to a grandnephew, Kenneth Alois Roseboro."

"Did Roseboro live in the house?"

"I'm looking into that. Roseboro sold to Polly and Ross Whitner. Both are transplanted New Yorkers. She's a teacher. He's an account manager with Bank of America. Transfer of title took place on September twentieth of this year. The Whitners are currently living in a rental apartment on Scaleybark. It appears that major renovations to the Greenleaf house are planned." Rinaldi closed and tucked away the tablet.

There was a moment of silence. Slidell broke it.

"We made the papers."

"I saw the article. Is Stallings a regular at the *Observer*?"

"Not one we know of," Rinaldi said.

Slidell's faux Ray-Bans slid into place.

"Shoulda shot that little gal on sight."

Lunch consisted of a granola bar bolted down with a Diet Coke. After eating, I found Larabee in the main autopsy room cutting on the Dumpster corpse.

I filled him in on my progress and on my conversation with Slidell and Rinaldi. He listened, elbows flexed, bloody hands held away from his body.

I described the brain. He promised to take a look later that day. I was back with the cauldrons by two.

I'd been sifting for twenty minutes when my cell phone sounded. The caller ID showed Katy's work number.

Degloving one hand, I clicked on.

"Hi, sweetie."

"Where are you?"

"The ME office."

"What?"

Lowering my mask, I repeated what I'd said.

"Is it really Satanists?"

"You saw the paper."

"Nice pic."

"So I've been told."

"My guess is fraternity prank. This town's *waaay* too proper for devil worship. Satanism means eccentricity. Exotica. Nonconformity. That sound like stodgy old Charlotte to you?"

"What's up?" I asked, recognizing the sound of discontent.

Katy had, this year, completed a bachelor of arts degree in psychology, an accomplishment six long years in the making. In the end, graduation hadn't been spurred by academic passion, but by threats of parental termination of funding. It was one of the rare issues on which Pete and I had agreed. Six is a wrap, kiddo.

The reason Katy lingered so long an undergrad? Not lack of intelligence. Through five majors, she maintained a grade point average of 3.8.

Nope. It wasn't due to a shortage of brainpower. My daughter is bright and imaginative. The problem is she's restless as hell.

"I'm thinking of quitting," Katy said.

"Uh-huh."

"This job is dull."

"You chose to work for the public defender's office."

"I thought I'd get to do—" Expelled air. "I don't know. Interesting stuff. Like you do."

"I'm sifting dirt."

"You know what I mean."

"Sifting dirt is tedious."

"What dirt?"

"From the cauldrons."

"Beats sifting papers."

"Depends on the papers."

"Finding much?"

"A few things." No way I'd mention the photo or the brain.

"How many cauldrons?"

"Two."

"How far along are you?"

"I'm still on the first."

"If you're striking out, switch cauldrons."

Typical Katy. If bored, move on.

"That doesn't make sense."

"Jesus, you're rigid. Why the hell not?"

"Protocol."

"Switching back and forth won't change what's inside."

I couldn't disagree with that.

"How's Billy?" I asked.

"A peckerhead."

OK.

"Buy you dinner?" I asked.

"Where?"

"Volare at seven."

"Can I order the sole?"

"Yes."

"I'll be there. Assuming I haven't died of boredom."

I resumed screening.

Snails. Rocks. Puparial cases. Roaches. A dermestid beetle or two. A millipede. That was exciting.

By three I was yawning and my thoughts were wandering.

My eye fell on the other cauldron.

I'd already shot stills and labeled evidence bags. New ground would perk me up, I told myself. Sharpen my observational skills.

Lame.

Why the hell not?

Better.

After cleaning both the trowel and the screen, I inserted my blade.

And immediately hit pay dirt.

7

NINETY MINUTES LATER THE SMALL CAULDRON SAT EMPTY. A macabre assortment of objects lined the counter behind me.

Twenty-one sticks.

Four strings of beads, one white, two alternating red and black, one alternating black and white.

Seven railroad spikes, four painted black, three painted red.

Avian bones, some chicken, others probably pigeon or dove.

Blood-stained feathers.

Two sawn bones, both from nonhuman limbs. By consulting Gilbert's *Mammalian Osteology*, I identified one as goat, the other as domestic dog.

Two quarters, four nickels, and one dime. The most recent was stamped 1987.

I felt mild satisfaction. The placement of the coin deep within the fill suggested 1987 as a baseline date for the packing of the cauldron. That date fell within my estimated PMI range for the skull.

Get real, Brennan. The skull could have joined the display long after the cauldron was filled, or have become a skull long before.

Nevertheless, energized, I returned to the large cauldron.

Ever been on a road trip and decided you needed KFC? Passed a million, but now not a single exit's offering chicken. You pull off, eat a burger. Within a mile there's the Colonel smiling from a billboard.

That's what I'd done. I'd given up too soon.

On the second trowel dive the large cauldron began to produce. Sticks. Beads. Necklaces. Feathers. Iron objects, including railroad spikes, horseshoes, and the head of a hoe. Pennies, the legible dates ranging from the sixties to the eighties.

I checked the clock. Five fifty-five. Choice. Drive home to shower and blow-dry? Sift on, toilette here, and meet Katy wet-headed?

I resumed digging and screening.

Six ten. My trowel struck something hard. As with the brain matter, I shifted to quarrying with my fingers.

A brown button appeared. I burrowed around it. The button became a mushroom, cap on top, thick-stemmed below. The cap was dimpled by one small pit.

Uh-oh.

I followed the stem.

Larabee opened the door, spoke. I answered, not really listening. He moved in beside me.

The stem angled from a tubular base shooting horizontally across the cauldron. I dug, estimating length and, as contour emerged, diameter.

Within minutes, I could see that the tube ended in two round prominences, condyles for articulation in a bipedal knee.

"That's a femur," Larabee said.

"Yes." I felt a neural hum of excitement.

"Human?"

"Yes." I was flipping dirt like a ratter scratching at a burrow.

A second button appeared.

"There's another underneath." Larabee continued his play-by-play. "Also lying sideways, head up, but oriented in the opposite direction."

I glanced at the clock.

Six forty-two.

"Crap."

"What?"

"I have to meet my daughter in twenty minutes."

Grabbing my cell, I dialed Katy.

No answer. I tried her mobile. Got voice mail.

"Let this go until morning," Larabee said. "I'll secure everything."

"You're sure?"

"Scram."

I raced to the locker room.

❊   ❊   ❊

Fortunately, I didn't have far to go.

Since high school, Volare has been Katy's favorite eatery. In those days the restaurant was housed in a Providence Road strip mall, in space that allowed but a dozen tables. Several years back, the owners relocated to a larger, freestanding building in Elizabeth, the Queen City's only neighborhood named for a woman. Irony there?

Here's the scoop. In 1897 Charles B. King picked Charlotte as the site for a small Lutheran college, and named the school in honor of his mother-in-law, Anne Elizabeth Watts. Smooth move, Charlie.

In 1915, Elizabeth College moved to Virginia. In 1917, a fledgling hospital purchased the property. Almost a century later, the original building is gone, but the Presbyterian Hospital complex occupying the site is massive.

Bottom line. The college split, but the name stuck. Today, in addition to Presby, Independence Park, and Central Piedmont Community College, Elizabeth is home to a hodgepodge of medical offices, cafés, galleries, resale shops, and, of course, churches and tree-shaded old homes.

At 7:10, I pulled to the curb on Elizabeth Avenue. Yep. The old gal also scored a street name.

Hurrying to the door, I felt a twinge of regret. Sure, it's now easier to reserve a table at Volare, but the intimacy of the smaller venue is gone. Nevertheless, the food still rocks.

Katy was at a back table, sipping red wine and talking to a waiter. The guy looked captivated. Nothing new. My daughter has that effect on those who pee standing.

I thought of Pete as I often did when I saw her. With wheat blond hair and jade green eyes, Katy is a genetic ricochet of her father. I am reminded of the resemblance when I see either one.

Katy waved. The waiter yammered on.

"Sorry I'm late." Sliding into a chair. "No excuse."

Katy arched one carefully groomed brow. "Nice 'do."

I was hearing that a lot lately.

"Who knew the wet look was coming back?"

The waiter asked if I'd like a beverage.

"Perrier with lime. Lots of ice."

He looked at Katy.

"She's an alkie." My daughter has many endearing qualities. Tact is not among them. "But I'll have another Pinot."

The waiter set off, charged with a papal command.

Katy and I ignored the menus. We already knew everything on them.

"Split a Caesar salad?" I asked.

"Sure."

"Sole meunière?"

Katy nodded.

"I think I'll go for the veal piccata."

"You always go for the veal piccata."

"That's not true." It was close.

Katy leaned forward, eyes wide. "So. Voodoo, vampires, or vegan devil worshippers?"

"Nice alliteration. When are we going shopping?"

"Saturday. Don't ignore my question. The cellar?"

"It was used for something"—what?—"ceremonial."

Two jade eyes rolled skyward.

"You know I can't talk about an ongoing investigation."

"What? I'm going to call in a scoop to WSOC?"

"You know why."

"Jesus, Mom. This dungeon is practically in Coop's backyard."

Katy was living two blocks from Greenleaf, in the townhouse of a mysteriously absent gentleman named Coop.

"It's hardly a dungeon. Tell me again. Who is Coop?"

"A guy I dated in college."

"And where is Coop?"

"In Haiti. With the Peace Corps. It's a win-win. I get a break on rent. He gets someone looking after his place."

The waiter delivered drinks, then stood smiling at Katy, pen and hopes poised.

I recited our order. The waiter left.

"What's up with Billy?"

Billy Eugene Ringer. The current boyfriend. One in a trail leading back to Katy's middle school years.

"He's a dickhead."

A promotion or demotion from peckerhead? I wasn't sure.

"Care to be more specific?"

Theatrical sigh. "We're incompatible."

"Really."

"Rather, he's *too* compatible." Katy took a hit of Pinot. "With Sam Adams and Bud. Billy likes to drink beer and watch sports. That's it. It's like dating a gourd. You know?"

I made a noncommittal noise.

"We have nothing in common."

"It took you a year to figure that out?"

"I can't imagine what we talked about in the beginning." More Pinot. "I think he's too old for me."

Billy was twenty-eight.

Katy's palm smacked the tabletop. "Which brings us to Dad. Can you believe this shit with Summer? I don't understand why you're being so cooperative."

My estranged husband was almost fifty. We'd lived apart for years, but never divorced. Recently Pete had requested that we file. He wanted to remarry. Summer, his beloved, was twenty-nine.

"The woman squeezes puppy glands for a living." Katy's tone redefined the term scornful.

Summer was a veterinary assistant.

"Our marital status is strictly between your father and me."

"She's probably sucked his brain right out through his—"

"New topic."

Katy drew back in her chair. "OK. What's up with Ryan?"

Mercifully, our salad arrived. As the waiter ground pepper from a mill the size of my vacuum, I thought about my own on-again off-again, what, boyfriend?

What was Ryan doing now? Was he happily reunited with his long-ago lover? Did they cook together? Window-shop while strolling hand in hand along rue Ste-Catherine? Listen to music at Hurley's Irish Pub?

I felt a heaviness in my chest. Ryan was gone from my life. For now. For good? Who knew?

"Hell-o?" Katy's voice brought me back. "Ryan?"

"He and Lutetia are trying to make it as a couple. To provide stability for Lily."

"Lutetia is his old girlfriend. Lily is his kid."

"Yes."

"The druggie."

"She's doing well in rehab."

"So you're just out on your ass."

"Lily's going through a rough patch. She needs her father."

Katy chose not to reply.

The waiter arrived with our food. When he'd gone, I changed direction.

"Tell me about work."

"Shoot-me-in-the-head dull."

"So you've said."

"I'm a glorified secretary. Scratch that. There's nothing glorified in what I do."

"Which is?"

"Maintain folders. Feed info into a computer. Assemble criminal histories. My most exciting task to date was a credit check. Heart-pounding."

"Did you think you'd be arguing before the Supreme Court?"

"No." Defensive. "But I didn't expect mind-numbing drudgery."

I let her vent on.

"I make next to nothing. And the people I work with are slammed by their caseloads and just want to negotiate pleas and move on to the next file. They don't have time for a lot of interaction with staff. Talk about boring. There's only one guy with spunk, and he's got to be fifty." Katy's tone changed ever so slightly. "Actually, he's bodaciously hot. If he weren't so old I wouldn't mind slipping off *his* tighty whities."

"Too much information."

Katy rolled on.

"You'd like this guy. And he's single. It's really sad. His wife was killed on nine-eleven. I think she was an investment banker or something."

"I'll find my own men, thanks."

"All right, all right. Anyway, half the staff are fossils, the other half are too harried to notice there's a world outside the PD's office."

I was beginning to grasp the problem. Billy was no longer making grade, and no twenty-something cute-boy lawyer was waiting in the wings.

We ate in silence for a few moments. When Katy spoke again I could tell her thoughts had circled.

"So what are we going to do about Summer?"

"For my part, nothing."

"Jesus, Mom. The woman hasn't finished forming a full set of molars."

"Your father's life is his own."

Katy said something that sounded like "cha," then fork-jabbed her fish. I took another mouthful of veal.

Seconds later I heard a whispered "Ohmygod."

I looked up.

Katy was gazing at something over my shoulder.

"Ohmygod."

8

"W<small>HAT?</small>"

"I don't believe it."

"*What?*"

Bunching her napkin, Katy pushed away from the table and strode across the restaurant.

I turned, confused and anxious.

Katy was talking to a very tall man in a very long trench coat. She was animated, smiling.

I relaxed.

Katy pointed at me and waved. The man waved. He looked familiar.

I waggled my fingers.

The two started toward me.

The NBA build. The loose gait. The black hair parted by Hugh Grant himself.

Ping.

Charles Anthony Hunt. Father, a guard first for the Celtics, later for the Bulls. Mother, an Italian downhill skier.

Charlie Hunt had been a classmate at Myers Park High. Lettered in three sports, served as president of the Young Democrats. The yearbook predicted him the grad most likely to be famous by thirty. I was voted most likely to do stand-up.

Following graduation, I'd left Charlotte for the University of Illinois, gone on to grad school at Northwestern, then married Pete.

Charlie had attended Duke on a hoops scholarship, then UNC–Chapel Hill law. Over the years I'd heard that he'd married and was practicing up North.

Charlie and I both played varsity tennis. He was all-state. I won most of my matches. I found him attractive. Everyone did. Change was sweeping the South in the seventies, but old mores die slowly. We didn't date.

The Labor Day weekend before our collegiate departures, Charlie and I swung a bit more than our rackets. The match involved tequila and the backseat of a Skylark.

Cringing inwardly, I refocused on my veal.

"Mom."

I looked up.

Charlie and Katy were at my side, both flashing copious dentition.

"Mom, this is Charles Hunt."

"Charlie." Smiling, I extended a hand.

Charlie took it in fingers long enough to wrap the Toronto Sky-Dome. "Nice to see you, Tempe."

"You two know each other?"

"Your mama and I went to high school together." Charlie's accent was flatter and more clipped than I remembered, perhaps the result of years spent up North, perhaps the product of intentional modification.

"You never let on." Katy punched Charlie's bicep. "Objection, counselor. Withholding evidence."

"Katy's brought me up to date on all your achievements." Charlie was still enveloping my fingers, giving me his "no one in the universe exists but you" stare.

"Has she." Reclaiming my hand, I glanced narrow-eyed at my daughter.

"She is one proud young lady."

The proud young lady gave an unbelievably staged laugh. "Mom and I were just talking about you, Charlie, and in you waltz. What a coincidence."

Like garlic and bad breath are coincidental, I thought.

"Should my ears be burning?" Boyish grin. He did it well.

"It was all good," Katy said.

Charlie looked appropriately surprised and modest.

"I should be moving on," he said. "I was passing, saw Katy through the window, thought I'd pop in to tell you what a terrific job she's doing for us."

"She's certainly enjoying the challenge," I said. "Especially the data entry. Katy loves logging info into computers. Always has."

This time it was Katy squinting at me.

"Well, we are certainly enjoying having her in the office."

I had to admit, with the emerald eyes and lashes to die for, Charlie Hunt was still leading-man handsome. His hair was black, his skin a pleasant compromise between Africa and Italy. Though the coat masked his midsection, he appeared to carry little more poundage than he had in the Skylark.

Charlie made a move to leave. Katy scrunched a "say something" face at me and upcurled her fingers.

Tipping my head, I grinned at her. Mutely.

"Mom's working on that basement cauldron thing," Katy said, way too brightly. "That's why her hair is"—she flapped a hand in my direction—"wet."

"She's just fine." Charlie beamed at me.

"She looks better with mascara and blusher."

My blushless cheeks burned.

"Painting that face would be a sin. Like colorizing a Renoir. Y'all take care now."

Charlie turned, hesitated, turned back, Columbo-style.

Here it comes, I thought.

"I suppose we play on opposite teams."

My look must have revealed confusion.

"You jail 'em, I bail 'em."

I floated a brow.

"Might make for some interesting coffee conversation."

"You know I can't discuss—"

"'Course you can't. No law against reminiscing."

The man actually winked.

By the time I got home it was almost ten. Katy had already left a message on my voice mail, a reiteration of the conversation we'd had post-Charlie. Don't be mad. Give him a chance. He's cool.

Charlie Hunt might be a prince, but I wasn't going to date him. A fix-up by my offspring was humiliation I didn't need.

There were two other messages. Pete. Phone me. A landscaping company. Buy our yard service.

Disappointment. Then the usual mental sparring.

You really thought Ryan would call?

No.

Right.

Whatever.

He's living with another woman.

They're not married.

He could have rung from his cell.

Cell.

Grabbing my purse, I pulled out my mobile and checked for messages.

Let him go.

I miss talking with him.

Talk to the cat.

We're still friends.

Move on.

Settling in bed, I clicked on the news.

A fifty-seven-year-old teacher was suing the school district, alleging age discrimination as the reason for her firing. An unemployed trucker had won fifteen million dollars in the Powerball lottery.

Bird hopped up and curled at my knee.

"Good for the trucker," I said, stroking his head.

The cat looked at me.

"The man has five kids and no job."

Still no feline opinion.

A couple had been arrested for stealing copper wiring from a Tuckaseegee Road business. In addition to larceny, the resourceful pair were being charged with contributing to the delinquency of minors. Mom and Dad had brought the kids along on the break-ins.

Authorities were investigating the shooting death of a sixty-four-year-old man in his Pineville home. Though police had found no evidence of foul play, the death had been ruled suspicious. The medical examiner would be performing an autopsy.

I drifted off.

"—worship of Satan right here in the cellars and back rooms of our city. Pagan idolatry. Sacrifice. Bloodletting."

The voice was baritone, the vowels thicker than sap.

My eyes flew open.

The clip was just ending. Overweight and red-faced, Boyce Lingo was delivering one of his media-grab rants.

"Those who follow Lucifer must be dealt with swiftly and harshly. Their evil must be stopped before it seeps into our playgrounds and schools. Before it threatens the very fabric of our society."

Preacher turned county commissioner, Lingo was a case study of extremist ideology, pseudo-Christianity, pseudo-patriotism, and thinly veiled white-male supremacy. His was a constituency that wanted the economy unregulated, the welfare state small, the military strong, and the citizenry white, native born, and strictly New Testament.

"You moron!" Had I been holding the remote, it would have gone sailing.

Birdie shot from the bed.

"You boneheaded twit!" My palms smacked the mattress.

I heard soft padding, assumed Birdie was increasing his distance. I didn't care. Tonight's grandstanding was typical Lingo. The man had a pattern of attaching himself to anything of media interest for a minute of air time or a half inch of print.

Killing the TV and lamp, I lay in the dark, tense and angry. I tossed, kicked the covers, punched the pillow, thoughts and images kaleido-scoping in my brain. The cauldrons. The putrefied chicken. The human cranium and femora.

The school portrait.

Who was she? Had Skinny's decision been wise? Or should we be broadcasting the girl's image?

Had the photo already flashed on TV screens somewhere far away, in a market disconnected from the coverage that entered Charlotte homes? Had some anchor reported a missing teen, vanished while on her way home from a ball game, from having pizza with friends? When? Had it been before the advent of centers for missing children and Amber alerts?

Had her parents made pleas to the camera, Mom crying, Dad steely-voiced? Had neighbors and townsfolk offered solace, inwardly thankful that their own children were safe? That, this time, tragedy had not selected them?

How had the picture ended up in that cauldron? The skull? *Was* it her skull?

And what about the leg bones? Did both come from a single individual?

Did the skull, the femora, and the photo represent one person? Two? Three? More?

My clock radio said 11:40. Twelve twenty. One ten. Out in the garden, a million tree frogs croaked. Erratic gusts scratched leaves across my bedroom window screen.

Why so warm this deep into the fall? It would be cold in Quebec by now. Montreal might even be sporting a dusting of snow.

I thought about Andrew Ryan. I did miss him. But the pragmatist brain cells were definitely right. I had to move on.

I smiled recalling Katy's postprandial "coincidence." Her matchmaking had started several years back, intensified with the arrival of Summer. Judd the pharmacist. Donald the veterinarian. Barry the entrepreneur. Sam the what? I never was sure. I refused all offers.

My daughter, the yenta of Dixie.

Now it was Charlie, the public defender.

Katy did have a point. Charlie Hunt was smart, good-looking, available, and interested. Why not give it a try?

Charlie was a 9/11 widower. That meant he carried baggage. Was he ready for a relationship? Was I? I also toted a satchel or two.

Puh-leeze. The man offered coffee.

Lyrics popped into my head. England Dan and John Ford Coley.

I'm not talking 'bout moving in,
And I don't want to change your life . . .

There you go.

Moving in. Moving on.

Good old Pete was moving on.

Pete and Summer.

What was Summer's last name? Glotsky? Grumsky? I made a note to ask.

Again and again, my thoughts veered back to the cellar.

I remembered the doll with the miniature sword piercing her chest. The knife.

The chicken had been decapitated. Had the goat been slaughtered in a similar fashion?

Had there really been a human sacrifice? Like Mark Kilroy, the college student killed in Matamoros. Lingo insinuated as much, but he was just yapping. He had no information. But then, neither did I.

I resolved to find some.

9

Though I'd slept little, I again rose at dawn. Coffee and a muffin, and I was on my way to the MCME.

By eight thirty both femora lay on the counter. So did three other sections of long bone. The latter were sawn, and came from a small mammal. Or mammals. Since no anatomical landmarks remained, the osteology text was of no use. I'd need histology to determine species and numbers.

By ten I'd emptied the large cauldron. The remaining soil produced three more red beads, a segment of antler, probably deer, and a small plastic skeleton.

After photographing the collection, I turned to the human femora.

The two leg bones were similar in size and robusticity. Both were slender and lacked prominent muscle attachment sites. One was a left, the other a right. Both were straight, with little shaft concavity, an African-American more than European trait.

As with the skull, I took measurements. Maximum length. Bicondylar breadth. Midshaft circumference. When I'd completed two sets of nine, I ran the numbers through Fordisc 3.0.

Both bones classified as female. Both classified as black.

I turned my attention to age.

As with the cranium, long bones come with some assembly required. Here's how it works.

As the tubular part, or shaft, elongates throughout childhood, caps, condyles, crests, and tuberosities form around it. It is the joining together of these fiddly bits to the straight bit, sometime in mid to late adolescence, that gives each bone its characteristic shape.

Union occurs in set sequence, at roughly predictable ages. Elbow. Hip. Ankle. Knee. Wrist. Shoulder.

Both femora exhibited identical patterns. The hip ends were fully adult, meaning full fusion of the heads to the necks, and of the lesser and greater trochanters to the shafts. At the other end, squiggly lines above the joint surface indicated the articular condyles were still wrapping things up at the knee. The picture suggested death sometime in the late teens.

The leg bones came from a young black female. So did the skull.

I felt, what? Relieved? Resigned? I wasn't sure.

I flashed on the girl in the photo. The very modern photo.

I surveyed the cauldrons and the artifacts they had held. Thought of the chicken, the goat, the statue, the dolls, the carved wooden effigy.

The human remains.

Deep down, I had a strong hunch what it all meant.

Time for research.

Ninety minutes later I'd learned the following:

A belief system that combines two or more cultural and spiritual ideologies into a single new faith is called a syncretic religion.

In the Americas, most syncretic religions are of Afro-Caribbean origin, having developed during the eighteenth and nineteenth centuries as a result of the slave trade. Forbidden the right to follow their traditional beliefs, African slaves disguised their practices by assigning images of Catholic saints to their gods.

In the United States, the best-known syncretic religions are Santería, voodoo, and brujería. Most followers live in Florida, New Jersey, New York, and California.

Santería, originally called Lucumi, emerged in Cuba and evolved from the southwestern Nigerian Yoruba culture. In Brazil it's known as Candomble; in Trinidad, as Shango.

Santería recognizes multiple gods, called *orishas*. The seven big dogs are Eleggua, Obatalla, Chango, Oshun, Yemaya, Babalu Aye, and

Oggun. Each has his or her own function or power, weapon or symbol, color, number, feast day, and favorite form of offering.

Each deity has a corresponding Catholic syncretism. Eleggua: Saint Anthony of Padua, the Holy Guardian Angel, or the Christ Child; Obatalla: Our Lady of Las Mercedes, the Holy Eucharist, Christ Resurrected; Chango: Saint Barbara; Oshun: Our Lady of Charity; Yemaya: Our Lady of Regla; Babalu Aye: Saint Lazarus; Oggun: Saint Peter.

The deceased rank with the *orishas* in Santería, thus ancestor worship is a central tenet. Both the gods and the dead must be honored and appeased. The concepts of *ashe* and *ebbo* are fundamental.

Ashe is the energy that permeates the universe. It's in everything—people, animals, plants, rocks. The *orishas* are mega-repositories. Spells, ceremonies, and invocations are all conducted to acquire *ashe*. *Ashe* gives the power to change things—to solve problems, subdue enemies, win love, acquire money.

Ebbo is the concept of sacrifice. It's what you do to get *ashe*. *Ebbo* can be an offering of fruit, flowers, candles, or food, or it can involve animal sacrifice.

Priests and priestesses are known as *santeros* and *santeras*. The priestly hierarchy is complex, the highest rank being *babalawo*. As with the papacy, girls need not apply. They can be powerful priestesses, but the top job is closed to them.

Except for the extra gods, and the barnyard animals, the setup sounded pretty Catholic to me.

Voodoo originated in Dahomey, now the Republic of Benin, among the Nagos, Ibos, Aradas, Dahomean, and other cultural groups, and evolved in Haiti during the time of slavery.

Voodoo has many deities, known collectively as *loa*, each corresponding to a Catholic saint. Dambala is Patrick, Legba is Peter or Anthony, Azaka is Isidor, and so on. Like the *orishas*, each has his or her own icon, realm of responsibility, and preferred offering.

Voodoo altars are kept in small rooms known as *badji*. Rituals are similar to those performed in Santería. The priesthood is loosely organized, with men called *houngan*, women *mambo*. As with Santería, the focus is on white, or positive, magic.

But voodoo has its dark side, the *bokors*. Hollywood's portrayal of these specialists in left-handed, or black, magic has given rise to the image of the evil sorcerer casting spells to cause calamity, or to raise zombie slaves from the grave. It is this stereotype that taints the public perception of voodoo.

Brujería, which combines Aztec myth, European witchcraft, and Cuban Santería, has Mexican cultural and religious roots. In the sixteenth century, when Spanish priests declared the pagan goddess Toantzin to be a Roman Catholic, Toantzin's priestesses went underground and became *brujas.* Theology evolved to center on Our Lady of Guadalupe, an omniscient and all-powerful goddess who grants human wishes when appropriately propitiated.

Each *bruja* keeps her spells in a *libreta,* similar to a Book of Shadows in traditional witchcraft. Most practice solo, but occasionally several organize into groups similar to covens.

I was taking notes from an article in the *Journal of Forensic Sciences* when Mrs. Flowers rang. Slidell and Rinaldi were in the house.

The wind had been frisky when I'd left home, tickling leaves from trees and swirling them across lawns and walks. Slidell looked like he'd traveled through a wind tunnel. His tie was shoulder-tossed and his hair was doing Grace Jones on one side.

"What's breaking, doc?" Slidell righted his neckwear and ran a palm across his crown. It helped some.

"Two human leg bones, both from a teenaged black female."

"The same person as the skull?" Rinaldi was impeccable, with each thin gray strand aligned on his skull.

"Probably. Any luck with the photography studios?"

Rinaldi shook his head.

"I took samples for DNA testing." I gave him my artifact sheet. "That lists the contents of both cauldrons."

Opening his briefcase, Rinaldi handed me a brown envelope marked *CMPD Crime Lab.* While he and Slidell scanned my inventory, I flipped through the photos.

Save for better lighting and more detail, the objects were as I recalled from the cellar. Based on my research, I now recognized the statue as Saint Barbara.

"You catch Lingo last night?" Slidell's question was directed at me.

"Oh, yeah," I said.

"Any truth there?"

"Look at this."

I singled out a close-up of the plywood with the Magic Marker glyphs. Slidell picked it up. Rinaldi moved to his side.

"See any pentagrams or inverted crosses?"

"No."

"I doubt this is Satanism."

"Great. We know what it ain't." Slidell raised theatrical palms. "What the hell is it, voodoo?"

"More like Santería."

"That some occult herb-doctor thing?"

"Yes and no."

I explained the basics. Syncretism. *Orishas. Ashe* and *ebbo.*

Rinaldi took notes with a Mont Blanc pen.

When I'd finished, I pulled a second photo from the stack and indicated the statue. "Saint Barbara is the cover image for Chango." I chose another shot and, one by one, tapped the necklaces. "Alternating red and black beads, Eleggua. Alternating red and white, Chango. Yellow and white, Oshun. All white, Obatalla."

I selected a photo showing the two-faced effigy. "Eleggua, the trickster god."

"Describe these deities." Rinaldi poised pen over paper.

I took a minute to compose my thoughts.

"They're not unlike Catholic saints. Or Greek gods. Each has a function or power. Chango controls thunder, lightning, and fire. Babalu Aye is the patron of the sick, especially skin diseases. Each can help with certain things and inflict certain punishments. For example, Obatalla can cause blindness, paralysis, and birth deformities."

"Piss off Babalu and you break out in boils?"

"Leprosy or gangrene." Curt. I was not appreciating Slidell's sarcasm.

"*Ashe* is parallel to the Christian concept of grace," Rinaldi said.

"In a way," I agreed. "Or mana. Believers strive to acquire *ashe* because it provides the power to change things. *Ebbo* is like penance, or kneeling on ashes."

"Give-ups during Lent."

I smiled at Rinaldi's comparison. "Catholic?"

"With a name like Rinaldi?"

"Every year, mine was chocolate."

"Comics."

"These synthetic religions, they roll with offing animals?" Slidell asked.

"Syncretic. Yes. Since different types of sacrifice suit different problems, a serious difficulty or a tough request may require a blood offering."

Slidell threw up his hands. "Santería, voodoo, who gives a shit? They're all crazoids."

"The doc's saying there are important differences." Rinaldi, the voice of reason. "Santería evolved in Cuba, that's Spanish. Voodoo evolved in Haiti, that's French."

"*Ex-cuse-ay-moi.* How many of these wing nuts we got floating around? A handful?"

"Santería, probably several million. Voodoo, maybe as many as sixty million worldwide."

"Yeah?" Slidell considered, then, "But we're talking win me the lottery, cure my kid's bellyache, help get my pecker up, right?"

"Most followers of voodoo and Santería cause no harm, but there is a dark side. Ever hear of Palo Mayombe?"

Two negative head wags.

"Palo Mayombe combines the belief systems of the Congo with those of the Yoruba and Catholicism. Practitioners are known as *paleros* or *mayomberos*. Rituals center not on *orishas*, but on the dead. *Paleros* use magic to manipulate, captivate, and control, often for their own malevolent purposes."

"Go on." Slidell's voice was now devoid of humor.

"The *paleros*'s source of power is his cauldron, or *nganga*. It's there that the spirits of the dead reside. Human skulls or long bones are often placed in the *nganga*."

"Obtained how?" Rinaldi asked.

"Most are purchased from biological supply houses. Occasionally, remains are stolen from cemeteries."

"So how's this kid fit in?" Slidell was looking at the skull.

"I don't know."

"How's the animal snuffing fit in?"

"A *palero* makes a request. Cause sickness, an accident, death. When the spirit of the *nganga* delivers, blood is offered as an expression of gratitude."

"Human blood?" Rinaldi asked.

"Usually goat or bird."

"But human sacrifice is not unheard of."

"No."

Slidell jabbed a finger. "The kid in Matamoros."

I nodded. "Mark Kilroy."

Rinaldi underlined something in his notebook. Underlined it again.

Slidell opened his mouth to speak. His phone rang. Clamping his jaw, he clicked on.

"Talk."

Slidell was moving through the door when Larabee appeared in it, face so tense it looked molded to the bone.

"What's happened?" I asked Larabee.

"When?" Slidell's voice floated in from the hall.

"Just got a call about a body at Lake Wylie," Larabee said to me. "I may need your help."

"Sonovabitch." Slidell sounded agitated.

"Why?" I asked.

"We're on it." Slidell's phone snapped shut.

"Vic's missing his head," Larabee said.

10

Larabee rode in the van with Hawkins. Though Slidell offered a lift, I was familiar with his auto hygiene. Less tolerant than Rinaldi, I took my own car.

Twenty minutes after departing the MCME, I was exiting I-485 onto Steele Creek Road. Following Hawkins's directions, I forked southwest onto Shopton Road, crossed Amohr Creek, then made a series of turns through a pocket of forest that had temporarily escaped the developer's ax. Though vague on my exact position, I had a sense the McDowell Nature Preserve lay roughly to the south, the Gaston County line somewhere to the west.

One more left and I spotted a CMPD patrol unit backlit by an expanse of choppy blue water. A uniformed cop was half sitting, half leaning against a rear quarter panel. Pulling to the shoulder, I got out and walked toward him.

Stretching from Mountain Island Dam in the north to Wylie Dam in the south, Wylie is one of eleven lakes in Duke Power's Catawba River chain. On maps, the thing resembles a furry vein snaking from the Tar Heel into the Palmetto State.

Despite the nuclear power plant humming on its southwestern shore, Lake Wylie is ringed by a number of upmarket developments— River Hills, the Palisades, the Sanctuary.

Palisaded against whom? I often wondered. Sanctuary from what? Day-Glo bass and eight-legged toads?

Whatever the threat, there were no fortified mansions on this piece of the lakeshore. The few homes I'd passed were strictly vinyl siding, aluminum awnings, and rusting carports. Some were little more than shacks, remnants of a time when Charlotteans went to "the river" to escape the press of urban living. Little did they know.

On spotting me, the cop pushed upright and assumed a wary stance. His face and body were lean, his shades straight out of *The Matrix.* At five yards out I could read the name *Radke* on a small brass plaque on his right breast.

I flicked a wave. It was not returned.

Behind Radke, a plastic-tangled lump lay on the shore.

I gave my name and explained who I was. Relaxing a hair, Radke chin-cocked the lump.

"Body's over there. This cove's a magnet for crap."

My face must have registered something. Surprise? Reproach?

Reddening, Radke chest-folded his arms. "I'm not referencing the vic. I mean, it appears a lot of stuff washes up here. It's a crazy strong wake zone."

My eyes drifted past Radke. On sunny weekends, Wylie is a gnat swarm of boats. Today a half dozen putted and skimmed nearby.

"You search the area?"

"I walked the shore maybe twenty yards in either direction. Poked around in the trees. Nothing systematic."

I was forming a follow-up question, when I heard an engine, then the sound of crunching gravel. Turning, I saw a Ford Taurus nose up to the bumper of my Mazda.

Two doors opened. Rinaldi unfolded from one and stick-walked toward us. Slidell heaved from the other and lumbered after, Ray-Bans flashing as his head swiveled left then right.

"Officer." Slidell nodded in Radke's direction.

Radke returned the nod.

Nods. Rinaldi-Brennan. Brennan-Rinaldi.

"Whadda we got?" Slidell was surveying the lake, the shoreline, the woods, assessing.

"Headless body."

"So I've heard."

"Guy found it while walking his dog."

"Must live under a lucky star."

"My money's on the pooch."

"You put that in your report, Radke?"

"Dog didn't seem too concerned about credit."

Slidell ignored the attempt at levity. "What's his story?"

"Just taking a dump."

The Ray-Bans crawled to *The Matrix.*

"That was funny, Radke. That line about the dog. What I got a problem with is your timing. You gotta practice that. Plan your jokes so's they don't take up no part of my day."

Shrugging, Radke pulled out a notepad.

"Guy's name is Funderburke. Lives up the road, walks the dog at seven, at midday, and again around six. Says the body showed up sometime between their morning and noon outings on Tuesday."

"He check it out?"

"Not until today. Says he figured it was trash. And the dog wanted his nap." Pause. "Name's Digger."

"I'll make a note."

"With two g's." Deadpan.

I liked Radke.

"He open the package?"

Radke shook his head. "Saw one foot. Called nine-one-one."

Leaving the men, I moved off toward the body, mind logging impressions.

Ground hard-packed. Pines and hardwoods thick to within five feet of the shore. Embankment muddy, sloping, and strewn with debris.

I made a mental inventory. Beer and soda cans, food wrappers, plastic six-pack loops, a waterlogged sneaker, a chunk of Styrofoam, a tangle of fishing line.

The body lay on, not under, the trash, looking pitifully small against the backdrop of lake and horizon. Flies danced the blue plastic in a continuous action-reaction ballet.

Snapping on gloves, I moved close and dropped to a squat. The humming swelled to a frenzied buzzing as flies darted, bodies iridescent green in the sunlight.

Most people are disgusted by flies. And rightly so. Like those bouncing off my face and hair, many species breed and feed on decaying organic matter. And they're not picky about the menu. Feces or Whoppers, it's all just chow. So is flesh, human or otherwise.

Though repulsive, necrophagous insects are useful citizens. With their single-minded focus on eating and reproducing, they speed decomp along its inevitable path. Key players in nature's recycling plan, they work hard at returning the dead to the earth. From a forensic perspective, bugs kick ass.

But, for now, I ignored them.

I also ignored the object of their interest, save to note that it was loosely wrapped in blue plastic sheeting. I couldn't tell if the wrapping had been intentionally placed, or if the body had become entangled accidentally while free-floating in the lake.

But I did note the absence of smell. Odd, given recent warm temperatures. If the body had been here since Tuesday morning, things should have been cooking inside that plastic.

Rising, I checked the immediate surroundings. No boot prints. No tire treads. No drag marks.

No cast-off shoes or articles of clothing. No recently overturned rocks.

No head.

In less than a minute, motor and tire sounds overrode the drone of the *Caliphoridae.*

I glanced toward the road.

Larabee was striding in my direction, camera in one hand, field kit in the other. Hawkins was opening the rear doors of the van. Both wore Tyvek coveralls.

The flies went bananas when Larabee joined me.

"Blowflies. I hate blowflies."

"Why blowflies?"

"The noise. Buzzing creeps me out."

I told Larabee what Radke had said.

The ME looked at his watch. "If Funderburke's right, we've got a time frame of roughly forty-eight hours."

"Forty-eight hours here," I said, pointing at the ground.

People have a habit of moving corpses. So does water. PMI could have been forty-eight hours or forty-eight days.

Either way, there should have been odor.

"Good point." Larabee batted a fly from his forehead.

While Hawkins shot video and stills, Larabee and I walked the shoreline. Beside us, waves lapped the mud, indifferent.

When we'd finished, we executed a grid in the woods, moving side by side, searching with our eyes and our feet. We spotted nothing suspicious. No head.

When we returned to the body, Hawkins was still shooting. Slidell and Rinaldi were with him. Pointlessly, each detective held a handkerchief to his nose. One was monogrammed, made of linen. The other was red polyester. Funny the things you notice.

"That should do her." Hawkins let the camera drop to his chest. "Pop the cork?"

"Mark the plastic where you make your cuts." Larabee's voice sounded flat. I suspected he was feeling as unenthused as I.

When Hawkins stepped to the body, flies rose in a crazed nimbus of protest.

Using a Scripto, the death investigator drew a line on the plastic then slashed along its length. Should matching this segment of plastic to a source roll become necessary, tool mark analysts could easily separate Hawkins's blade mark from those made by the perpetrator when cutting the sheet.

The corpse lay with rump up, legs tucked, chest and face to the ground. Had there been a face. The torso ended at a midshoulder stump that was dotted with fly eggs. The anus also showed moderate insect activity.

"Naked as a jaybird." Spoken through red polyester.

Hawkins resumed shooting. Larabee and I masked and stepped in.

"Looks young," Rinaldi said.

I agreed. The limbs were slender, body hair was scarce, and the feet were free of bunions, calluses, thickened nails, or other indicators of advanced age.

Slidell bent sideways and squinted under the upraised buttocks. "Got a full load."

Though inelegantly stated, Slidell's observation was correct. The genitalia were male and fully adult.

"No doubt he's a white boy," Rinaldi said. The skin was ghostly, the fine covering of hair a light, golden blond.

I dropped to my knees. The flies went mad. Waving them aside, Larabee joined me.

Up close I could see pale yellow bone glistening in the flesh of the truncated neck. The bright pink flesh. Something odd there.

"Wound looks red as a porterhouse." Larabee spoke my thought.

"Yes," I agreed. "The head hasn't fallen off, it was severed. Given a PMI of two days, the whole body's surprisingly well-preserved."

Larabee palpated a defect at the level of the tenth rib, in the right muscle mass paralleling the spinal column.

"Any guess on that?"

The indentation looked like a series of six short parallel lines, with a seventh crossing at a ninety-degree angle.

"Contact with some sort of debris?" I didn't really think so.

"Maybe." Larabee examined one upturned palm then the other. "No defense wounds. Looks like we may get usable prints." To Hawkins. "Make sure to bag the hands."

"This guy come out of the water?" Slidell asked.

"Doesn't look like most floaters I've seen," I said.

"No signs of aquatic scavenging," Larabee said.

"Immersion time could have been brief."

Larabee shrugged agreement. "In any case, there's no need to check for water in the lungs. If he did wash out of the lake, he definitely wasn't breathing when he went in."

"So, how much time we looking at?" Slidell asked.

"The body's been *here* long enough for blowflies to arrive and oviposit, and for a few eggs to hatch." I'd noticed that the few larvae present were young, and that there were no pupae or empty casings.

"You gonna translate that for us average mopes?"

"Flies would have found the body in minutes, especially with such a massive open wound. Eggs would have been laid in a matter of hours. Hatching would have occurred anywhere from twelve to forty-eight hours later, depending on temperatures."

"It's been warm," Rinaldi said.

"That would speed things up."

"So whaddya think?" Slidell repeated his question, this time with a note of annoyance.

Given Funderburke's story, I thought something was off. I kept it to myself.

"I'm not an entomologist," I said. "I'll collect samples for analysis."

In addition to the lack of smell and paucity of insect activity, another thing bothered me. If the body had been dumped where it lay, or if its time in the lake had been brief, that might explain the absence of aquatic scavenging. But Funderburke's story placed it on the shore last Tuesday morning. The local wildlife should have opened a soup kitchen. Why no signs of animal damage?

Slidell was about to comment when two CSS techs emerged from the trees. The woman was tall, with puffy cheeks and braids pinned to her head. The man was sunburned and wore Maui Jims.

Larabee filled them in. Neither seemed interested in lengthy explanations. Fair enough. They were facing a long afternoon of documenting and collecting evidence and remains.

We waited while markers were placed, photos were taken, and measurements were made. Prelims finished, both techs looked to the ME.

Turning to me, Larabee arm-gestured an invitation.

We stepped to the corpse, me at the hips, Larabee at the shoulders.

Behind us a boat whined approach, then retreat. A series of waves slapped the shore.

"Ready?" Above his mask, the ME's brows were grimly knitted. The moment of truth. The turning of the body.

I nodded.

Together, we rolled the corpse onto its back.

Everyone there was a veteran, used to murder, mutilation, and all the horror one human can inflict on another. I doubt anyone present had seen this before.

Rinaldi spoke for us all.

"Holy hell."

11

Though contact with the ground had discouraged most flies, a few hardy ladies had managed to maneuver beneath the body. A white circle seethed in the pale, hairless chest. A smaller oval churned on the belly.

"What the hell?" Muffled through red polyester.

Leaning close, I could see that the egg masses weren't evenly distributed, but appeared to cluster into patterns. With one gloved finger, I nudged outlier eggs back toward thicker bands that seemed to rim and crisscross the circle.

And felt coldness congeal in my chest.

The eggs formed an inverted five-point star.

"It's a pentagram," I said.

The others remained silent.

Using the same finger, I proceeded to "clean up" the oval until that pattern was clear: 666.

"That don't say *Old Time Gospel Hour* to me." Slidell's voice was thick with revulsion.

"How . . . ?" Rinaldi's question trailed off.

"Flies are like the rest of us," I said. "Given a choice, they take the easy route. Orifices. Open wounds."

Slidell knew what I was saying. "The kid was carved up."

"Yes."

"Before or after his head was whacked off?" Angry.

"I don't know."

"So Lingo's right."

"We shouldn't jump to—"

"You got another theory?"

I didn't.

"Let's go." Stone-jawed, Slidell strode off.

"He means no disrespect." Rinaldi's tone was apologetic. "His niece had some problems in high school." He stopped, considered whether to elaborate. Decided against it. "Anyway, he's anxious to wrap up the Greenleaf business. We've got a line on Kenneth Roseboro, the kid that inherited the house."

"Wanda Horne's nephew," I said.

"Yes." Again, Rinaldi offered nothing further. "You want a cadaver dog to come sweep the area, maybe try to sniff out the head?"

I nodded.

"I'll call in a request."

When I returned from the car with my field kit, Hawkins was shooting video and the CSS team was walking the area. Already the shoreline was dotted with orange markers indicating the presence of potential trace evidence. Cigarette butts. Candy wrappers. Tissues. Most of it would turn out to be useless, but at this stage no one knew what was relevant and what was present due to accidental association.

Opening my kit, I spread out supplies. Beside me, the ME unsheathed a thermometer for insertion into the anus. Or the egg mass. I couldn't be sure. For two hours we gathered and labeled evidence, Larabee on the corpse, Brennan on the bugs.

First I took close-ups, in case something matured into something else in transit to the entomologist. I'd made that mistake once.

Using a dampened child's paintbrush, I then scraped up eggs. Half I preserved in diluted alcohol. RIP. The rest I wanted alive for the entomologist to raise to maturity for species identification. That lucky half I placed in vials with beef liver and damp tissue.

Then, I went for maggots. Since the few larvae present appeared to be of the same species and newly hatched, I didn't worry about separation according to size, merely area of collection: neck, anus, surrounding soil. As with the eggs, one half went into vials with air, food, and perching material. The other half went into hot water, then an alcohol solution.

After netting and packaging adult flies, I gathered representatives of every species present within a yard of the body. My inventory included two black beetles, a long brown crawly thing, and a handful of ants. The yellow jacket got a pass.

Bugs sealed and labeled, I collected soil samples, then made notes about the habitat: freshwater lake, hardwoods and pines, semiacid soil, elevation five hundred to six hundred feet, temperature ranging from midsixties to mideighties Fahrenheit, low humidity, full sunlight.

Finally, I jotted comments concerning the body. Naked. Prone, buttocks raised, arms straight at the sides. Decapitation, no blood or bodily fluids at the scene. Head missing. Incised wounds on chest and belly. Minimal decomp. No aquatic or animal scavenging. Egg masses at neck and anus with internal temperatures of 97 and 98 degrees Fahrenheit, respectively. Unknown cause of death.

It was half past four when I finished. Larabee and Hawkins were leaning on the back of the van, drinking bottled water.

"Thirsty?" Hawkins asked.

I nodded.

Hawkins pulled a six-ouncer from a cooler and tossed it to me.

"Thanks."

We all drank and stared at the lake. Larabee spoke first.

"Slidell's convinced we got devil worshippers in our midst."

"Commissioner Lingo will have a field day." I couldn't keep the disdain from my voice.

Hawkins shook his head. "Old Boyce was sounding off less than twenty-four hours after you and Skinny wrapped up in that cellar."

"Don't you know? Lingo has a hotline to God."

Larabee snorted.

"Remember that stabbing off Archdale?" Hawkins tipped his bottle in Larabee's direction. "Lesbian lady took issue with her partner coyoting around? Body bag's barely zipped and Lingo's pontificating on the evils of homosexuality."

"Not a peep last week when that trucker blew his ex-wife's boyfriend away. That was a righteous heterosexual murder," Larabee said. "Biblical motive. If I can't have her, nobody can."

"If Lingo gets wind of this one, he'll roll it into his current soap opera." Hawkins tossed his empty bottle onto a Winn-Dixie bag beside the cooler. *The Devil Goes Down to Georgia.*

"He'll be dead-ass wrong," I said.

"You don't get satanic vibes from this?" Larabee asked.

"From this one, yes. From that cellar, no."

I described what I'd found.

"Don't sound like Baptists to me," Hawkins said.

I outlined what I'd told Slidell and Rinaldi about syncretic religions. Santería. Voodoo. Palo Mayombe.

"Who's into animal sacrifice?"

"All of them."

"Satanists?"

"Yes."

"Where's your money?" Larabee's bottle joined Hawkins's.

"The colored beads, the coins, and the Catholic saint point to Santería. The wooden sticks and the padlocked *nganga* suggest Palo Mayombe."

"The human remains?"

I raised my hands, frustrated. "Take your pick. Voodoo. Santería. Palo Mayombe. Satanism. But the cellar had no inverted pentagrams or crosses, no six-six-six symbols, no black candles or incense. Nothing typical of devil worship."

"Nothing like this kid here." Larabee tipped his head toward the lake.

"No."

"You think there's a link?"

I pictured the mutilated body lying on the shore.

The cauldron skull and leg bones.

I had no answer.

Wending toward the highway, I passed two cars. One pleased me. The other did not.

The SUV held the search dog promised by Rinaldi. I wished the canine better luck than I'd had in locating the missing head.

The Honda Accord was driven by the same woman I'd seen outside the Greenleaf house Tuesday night. What had the *Observer* photo credit been? Allison Stallings.

"Just friggin' great." I palm-smacked the wheel. "Who the hell are you, Allison Stallings?"

Noting her plate number, I wished Radke luck in keeping Stallings far from the body.

My mobile rang as I was merging from the entrance ramp onto I-77. Traffic was heavy, but not yet the bumper-to-bumper crush it would be.

The caller ID showed an unfamiliar number with a 704 area code.

Curious, I clicked on.

"Go Mustangs," a male voice said.

I was tired, preoccupied, and, to be honest, disappointed the call was local and therefore not from Ryan. My reply wasn't overly courteous.

"Who is this?"

The response was the first line of the Myers Park High School fight song.

"Hi, Charlie."

"Up for that coffee?"

"It's not a good time."

"Six o'clock? Seven? Eight? You name it."

"I've been in the field all day. I'm tired and grubby."

"As I recall, you clean up real good." An old Southern expression.

I am competitive. Play hard. Work hard. Some people manage to do those things and remain well-groomed. I'm not among them. Following our tennis tournaments, Charlie usually looked like a *GQ* model. I usually looked like a badly permed shih tzu.

"Thanks. I think."

"Katy tells me you like lamb chops."

The veering segue caught me off guard.

"I—"

"My specialty. How about this? You shower while I hit the Fresh Market. We meet at my place at seven. You relax while I toss a salad and throw chops on the grill."

Whoa, big fella!

"Katy's invited, of course. I'll catch her before she leaves here."

I suspected his co-conspirator was right at his side.

"It's been a long day," I said.

"A shower will make a new woman of you."

"But the old one will still have to work in the morning." That sounded lame even to me.

"Look. You like lamb chops, I like lamb chops. You don't feel like cooking. I do."

He had me there.

"I have to go to the ME office to FedEx some bugs."

"Dead ant, dead ant." Sung to the opening bars of *The Pink Panther* theme.

"Mostly flies." I couldn't help grinning.

Curtis Mayfield. No lyrics.

"*Superfly*," I guessed.

"Very good," Charlie said.

"I can't stay late."

"I won't let you."

A car cut into my lane, forcing me to brake hard. The phone dropped to my lap. Steering one-handed, I groped it back to my ear.

"You still there?"

"Thought you'd hung up on me," Charlie said.

Looking back, I probably should have.

My clothes went directly into the laundry. My body went directly into the shower.

Emerging, I found Birdie batting a blowfly around the bathroom floor. Before I could act, he ate it.

"Gross, Bird."

The cat looked proud. Or smug. Or introspective, pondering the nuances of fly.

Smiling, I spread orange blossom body cream onto my skin.

Charlie was right. I felt rejuvenated. Cheery, even. Going out was a good idea. Making new friends was a healthy move.

A group of memory cells offered a collage of images, fuzzy, like snapshots left out in the rain.

The Skylark.

Charlie in cutoffs. Just cutoffs.

Me in shorts and a tank with bling on the front. A sparkly butterfly. Or was it a bird? Hair doing that layered, flippy seventies thing.

Upholstery stinging my sunburned back.

Maybe this wasn't such a peachy idea.

Reacquainting with *old* friends, I amended my thinking. Friends. Just friends.

Uh-huh, the memory cells said.

Moving to the bedroom, I clicked on the news and crossed to the dresser.

"—sorcerers and fornicators and murderers and idolaters, and everyone who loves and practices falsehood. Those words of Revelation never sounded more true. Lucifer is right here, at our own city gates."

I froze, panties half out of the drawer.

12

B OYCE LINGO WAS ON THE STEPS OF THE NEW COURTHOUSE, cameras and mikes aimed at his face. Behind him stood a middle-aged man with buzz-cut hair, Brad Pitt cheeks, and a prominent chin. From the conservative dress, I guessed he was an aide. Navy jacket, white shirt, blue tie, gray pants. He and Lingo looked like fashion clones.

The commissioner was staring straight into the lens.

"Another body was discovered today. Another innocent slaughtered, his head cut off, his flesh desecrated. Why such brutality? To serve Satan. And what do the authorities say? 'No comment.'"

My fingers curled around the panties.

"They will not comment on a headless body identified three days ago, a twelve-year-old child dragged from the Catawba River. They will not comment on a human skull found last Monday in a Third Ward basement."

I stood rigid.

"No comments, indeed." Lingo shook his head in theatric dismay. "Why alert the public to the godless depravity invading our city?"

Lingo paused for effect.

"Citizens of Charlotte-Mecklenburg, we must not accept 'no comment.' We must demand answers. Swift and forceful action. We must insist that these murderous devil worshippers *not* be allowed to go unpunished.

"Let me share a story. A sad story. A horrifying story. In London, in

2001, a tiny, headless body was found in a river. The child is called Adam because, to this day, his name is unknown. What *is* known is that little Adam was smuggled to England by human traffickers to serve as a human sacrifice."

Lingo wagged a finger at the camera.

"We must protect our children. These evildoers must be rooted out. The guilty must be arrested and prosecuted to the full extent of the law. Satan's minions must be driven from amongst us. Our city has no room for a Night Stalker. An Andrea Yates. A Columbine. A poor little Adam."

Birdie was licking orange blossom from my leg. I couldn't take my eyes from Lingo. Richard Ramirez? Andrea Yates? Eric Harris and Dylan Klebold?

"It's up to each and every one of us to insist that these killings receive top priority. We must be adamant. We must urge our brothers and sisters in government and law enforcement to don the armor of God and fight the Prince of Darkness. We must join hands and hearts to cleanse our great city and county of this cancer."

The broadcast cut back to the anchor. He talked of Anton LaVey, founder and high priest of the Church of Satan until his death in 1997, and author of the *Satanic Bible.* A list of Web sites scrolled behind him.

> Kids and Teens for Satan
> Synagogue of Satan
> Church of Satan
> Superhighway to Hell
> Satanic Network
> Letters to the Devil

Birdie nudged my leg.

Dropping the undies, I scooped and hugged my cat to my chest, a sense of foreboding rippling through me.

The coverage wrapped up with footage from LaVey's 1993 documentary, *Speak of the Devil.*

The clip had barely ended when my landline rang.

"You talk to Lingo?"

"Of course I didn't talk to Lingo." I matched Slidell's outrage with outrage.

"The pompous old lizard just held a press conference."

"I caught most of it."

"Accused the cops of a cover-up. Told Joe Citizen to ready up his noose for lynchings in the name of the Lord. Won't that just stir up a freakin' hornets' nest."

Though Slidell was exaggerating, in large part, I agreed.

"How's this asshole get his information?"

"As I was leaving the scene today I saw Allison Stallings driving toward it."

"The dame what was creeping around on Greenleaf Avenue?"

No one but Slidell had said "dame" since the fifties. On the upside, at least he knew one other French expression besides *ex-cuse-ay-moi*.

"Yes," I said.

"I made a call. Stallings don't work for the *Observer.*"

"So why's she showing up at my scenes?"

"I damn well intend to find out."

For a moment, no one spoke. In the background I could hear Slidell's TV mimicking mine.

"You think Stallings is tipping Lingo?"

"It's possible."

"What's in it for her?"

"The guy's a grandstander. Maybe she's a wannabe, or a freelancer selling pics here and there to the press. Maybe she thinks Lingo will blow the situation into a bigger story than it might otherwise be, score her some fame and fortune."

I waited while Slidell chewed that over.

"So where's Stallings get her info?"

"She could have a police scanner."

"Where's a little girl like that gonna come up with a police scanner?" Slidell said *police* with a very long *o* and a whole lot of scorn.

"RadioShack."

"Get out. How's she gonna know to operate a gizmo like that?"

Slidell's ignorance of technology always astounded me. I'd heard rumors that Skinny had yet to make the move to touch-tone dialing at home.

"It's not rocket science. The thing sweeps through a group of frequencies searching for one in use, then stops so you can listen. Like the SCAN button on your car radio." I couldn't believe Slidell was hearing this for the first time. "Stallings could have picked up on Rinaldi's request for a cadaver dog. Or maybe Lingo has a scanner of his own."

I waited out more mental mastication. Then, "Who's this Antoine LeVay?" Slidell's tone had edged down a notch.

"Anton. He founded the Church of Satan."

"That's real?"

"Yes."

"How many members?"

"No one really knows."

"Who's this other kid Lingo's talking about?"

"Anson Tyler. Lingo's way off base there. Tyler's whole upper body was missing, not just his head."

"Missing where?"

"When a corpse floats, the heavy parts hang down. A human head weighs about four to five kilos." I stopped. Could Slidell convert metric? "About the same as a roaster chicken. So the head detaches early."

"That don't answer my question."

"The missing parts are wherever the current took them."

"So you're saying there's no link between this Catawba River kid and the kid we found today?"

"I'm saying Anson Tyler lost his head due to natural processes, not intentional decapitation. There wasn't a single cut mark anywhere on his skeleton."

"What about the skull in the cauldron?"

"That's a tougher call."

"You find tool marks on that?"

"No."

"On the leg bones?"

"No."

"That bit about the kid in London, that true?"

"Yes."

"Tell me 'bout that."

"In 2001, the headless, limbless body of a four-to-six-year-old boy was pulled from the Thames below the Tower Bridge. The cops named him Adam. The postmortem showed he'd only been in that part of the world a short time."

"Based on what?"

"The food in his stomach and the pollen in his lungs. It also showed that he'd ingested a potion containing poisonous Calabar beans in the forty-eight hours prior to his death."

"And?"

"Calabar causes paralysis while keeping the victim conscious. It's used commonly in witchcraft rituals in West Africa."

"Go on." Slidell's voice was pure steel.

"Adam's bones were also analyzed to determine geographical origin."

"How's that play?"

"Foodstuffs bear traces of the soil in which they were grown or reared." I kept it simple. "Samples taken from Adam and compared to places around the world suggested he came from the vicinity of Benin City, in Nigeria. Investigators went to Africa, but discovered little."

"Any arrests?"

"No. But there are persons of interest. Mostly Nigerians, some of whom have been linked to human trafficking."

"But there's insufficient evidence to bring charges." Skinny has never been a champion of individual civil liberties. His disgust was evident.

"You've got it."

As dual voices reported sports scores in my bedroom and across town in a condo I didn't want to picture, I debated in my mind. Tell Slidell the most worrying element and risk sending him off in the wrong direction? Keep it to myself and risk impeding the investigation?

"There's more," I said. "Authorities in London claim that in recent years some three hundred black boys have gone missing from the system and not returned to school or reappeared. Only two have ever been traced."

"Where the hell are the families?"

"When questioned, caregivers and relatives say the boys have left the UK to return to Africa."

"And no one can confirm."

"Exactly."

"Cops think these kids have been murdered?"

"Some do."

My eyes drifted to the clock radio. Six thirty. I was naked, sans makeup, with tangled wet hair that looked like seaweed.

And due at Charlie's in thirty minutes.

I needed to hurry. But I wanted to know what Slidell and Rinaldi had learned about the property on Greenleaf.

"What did you find out about Kenneth Roseboro?"

"Kenny-boy's some kinda musician living in Wilmington. Claims the minute Aunt Wanda went belly-up and the place was his, he ran an ad and rented the dump out."

As Slidell talked I tried donning the panties one-handed.

"Roseboro never lived in the house?"

"No."

"How many tenants occupied the premises?"

"One. Upstanding citizen name of Thomas Cuervo. T-Bird to his friends and business associates."

"What business?"

"Pissant little shop out South Boulevard." Slidell snorted. "La Botánica Buena Salud. Natural cures, vitamins, herbal remedies. I can't believe people blow money on that horseshit."

While I didn't totally disagree with Slidell, I wasn't in the mood for his thoughts on holistic healing.

"Does Cuervo have a record?"

"In addition to brain tonics and flatulence powders, T-Bird has periodically dealt in stronger pharmaceuticals."

"He's a drug dealer?"

"Penny-ante stuff. Nickel bags. Racked up some drunk and disorderlies."

As I did my Karate Kid crane kick maneuver, the panties caught on my upraised foot. I toppled and my elbow slammed the wall.

"Shit!"

Birdie shot under the bed.

"What the hell are you doing?"

"Why did Roseboro decide to sell?" I chucked the skivvies to rub my elbow.

"T-Bird skipped, owing a lot of back rent."

"Skipped where?"

"Roseboro claims he'd really like to know."

"Did you ask about the cellar?"

"I'm saving that for our early morning chat."

"Mind if I observe?"

Pause.

"What the hell."

I PARKED ON THE BORDER BETWEEN FOURTH AND FIRST WARDS. Walking along Church Street, I couldn't help thinking the quarter was a poster for Charlotte's uptown revival.

Charlie's unit was midpoint in a row of nine spanking-new townhouses. Kitty-corner from it was the McColl Center for Visual Art, a studio and gallery complex recently created within a renovated church.

One empty lot down from the former house of worship, mounded rubble attested to a recent implosion. Way past its shelf life, the old Renaissance Place Apartment building had been toppled to make way for a spiffy new tower.

Two blocks southeast, I knew other buildings had also been earmarked for demolition, including the Mecklenburg County Government Services Center, our very own reborn Sears Garden Shop. Everyone at the MCME was dreading the move.

C'est la vie, Charlotte-style. A new landscape rising from the old.

I rang Charlie's bell at 7:23, damp hair yanked into a high ponytail. Fetching. But I had managed mascara and blusher.

My summons was answered by a host who looked exceedingly good. Wash-faded jeans. Slip-on loafers, no socks. Zip-front sweater showing just a hint of chest.

"Sorry I'm late."

"No problemo." Charlie buzzed my cheek. He smelled good, too. Burberry?

Flashbulb image of the Skylark.

Taking in my leggings and new Max Mara tunic, Charlie nodded approval. "Yessiree. She cleans up real good." He gave the modifier at least five *e*'s.

"You used that same line earlier today."

"Experience has taught me the value of moderation."

"Moderation."

"If I let loose unbridled wit, women show up from all over town. I once crafted three smooth lines in a single evening. Cops had to set up barricades."

"How annoying for the neighbors."

"I got a letter of complaint from the homeowners association."

I rolled my eyes.

"Walk or ride?" Charlie asked.

I tipped my head in question.

"The place has four levels."

"There's an elevator," I guessed.

Charlie gave a humble what's-one-to-do? smile.

"Are we going to the top?"

"Kitchen's on two."

"I'll rough it," I said.

Leading the way, Charlie explained the layout. Office and garage down, living-dining room, kitchen, and den on two, bedrooms on three, party room and terrace on four.

The decor was Pottery Barn modern, done using a palette of browns and cream. Probably umber and ecru in designer-speak.

But the furnishings showed a personal touch. Paintings, most modern, a few traditional and obviously old. Sculptures in wood and metal. An African carving. A mask I guessed was Indonesian.

As we climbed, I couldn't help noticing photos. Family gatherings, some with faces colored like choices in coffee, others with skin in the mocha-olive range.

Posed shots of a tall black man in a Celtics jersey. Charles "CC" Hunt in his NBA days.

Framed snapshots. A ski trip. A beach outing. A sailing excursion. In most, Charlie stood or sat beside a willowy woman with long black hair and cinnamon skin. The wife who died on 9/11? I spotted my answer in a wedding portrait on the living room mantel.

I looked away, saddened. Embarrassed? Charlie was watching. His eyes clouded but he made no comment.

The kitchen was all stainless steel and natural wood. Charlie's culinary efforts covered one granite countertop.

He waved a hand over the platters. "Rosemary-rubbed lamb chops. Marinated zucchini. Mixed salad à la Hunt."

"Impressive." My eyes drifted to the table. It was set for two.

Charlie noticed my noticing.

"Unfortunately, Katy had a prior engagement."

"Uh-huh." Washing her hair, no doubt.

"Wine? Martini?"

Apparently my daughter hadn't mentioned my colorful past.

"Perrier, please."

"Lemon?"

"Perfect."

"Nondrinker?" Spoken from behind the opened refrigerator door.

"Mm."

Though Charlie knew I'd knocked back my share of beers in high school, he didn't ask about my changed relationship with booze. I liked that.

"Join me on the terrace? The view's not bad."

I've never been an autumn person. I find the season bittersweet, nature's last gasp before the clocks are turned back and life hunkers down for the long, dark winter.

Forget Johnny Mercer's "Autumn Leaves." In my view the original French title had it right. *"Les feuilles mortes."* The dead leaves.

Maybe it's because of my work, my daily intimacy with death. Who knows? Give me crocuses and daffodils and little baby chicks.

Nevertheless, Charlie's "not bad" was an understatement. The evening was so sparkling it seemed almost alive, the kind you get when the summer pollen has settled and the fall foliage has yet to gear up for action. A zillion stars dotted the sky. The illuminated towers and skyscrapers made uptown resemble a Disney creation. Mr. Money's Wild Ride.

As Charlie grilled, we talked, testing pathways. Naturally, the first led down memory lane.

Parties at "the rock." Spring break at Myrtle Beach. We laughed hardest at memories of our junior float, a tissue-paper and chicken-wire whale with booted legs kicking from its open mouth. *Whale Not Swallow De-Feet.* At the time we'd thought the pun Groucho Marx clever.

We cringed at recollections of ourselves during the all-time nadir in fashion history. Crushed-velvet jackets. Crocheted beer label hats. Macramé purses. Candies pumps.

No reference was made to the Skylark.

Chops and veggies grilled, we descended to the dining room. As our comfort level grew, conversation turned to more serious issues.

Charlie talked of a teen whose defense he was handling. Mildly retarded, the boy had been charged with murdering two of his grandparents.

I discussed the cauldron bones, Anson Tyler, and Boyce Lingo's latest showboating. Why not? Between them, Lingo and Stallings had put practically all of it out there.

"Lingo's suggesting the cases are linked?" Charlie asked.

"He's implying it. He's wrong. First of all, Anson Tylor wasn't decapitated. And, while I'll admit that the Lake Wylie mutilation suggests Satanism, there's no hint of devil worship in the Greenleaf cellar. The barnyard animals, the statue of Saint Barbara, the carving of Eleggua, the cauldrons. It all smacks of some form of Santería."

"Ignore him. Lingo's positioning for a run at a state senate seat and needs publicity."

"Who votes for that jackass?"

Charlie took my question as rhetorical. "Dessert?"

"Sure."

He disappeared, returned with pie slices the size of warships.

"Please tell me you didn't make this."

"Banana cream purchased at Edible Art. Though galactic, sadly, my powers have boundaries." Charlie sat.

"Thank God."

Two bites and I winged back to Lingo. This round, I really cranked up.

"Lingo's hysterics about Satanists and child murder are going to scare the hell out of people. Worse. He could inspire the right-wing loony fringe to start burning crosses on the lawns of Ashkenazim and Athabascans. I've seen it happen. Some holier-than-thou nitwit hits the airwaves, next thing you know folks are organizing down at the minimart to go out and kick ass." I air-jabbed my fork for emphasis. "Statues? Beads? Coconut shells? Forget it. Satan wasn't on the A list down in that cellar."

Charlie raised his palms in my direction. "Put down your weapon and we all walk away."

I lay my fork on my plate. Changed my mind, picked it up, and dived back into the pie. I'd hate myself later. Tough.

"Lingo really pissed you off," Charlie said.

"It's one of his specialties." Garbled through crumbs and banana.

"You done venting?"

I started to protest. Stopped, embarrassed.

"Sorry. You're right."

We both ate in silence. Then, "Athabascans?"

I looked up. Charlie was smiling.

"Ashkenazim?"

"You know what I mean. Minority groups that are not understood."

"Aleuts?" he suggested.

"Good one."

We both laughed. Charlie reached out, stopped, as though surprised by the action of his hand. Awkwardly, he pointed one finger.

"You have whipped cream on your lip."

I made a swipe with my napkin.

"So," I said.

"So," he said.

"This was nice."

"It was." Charlie's face was fixed in an expression I couldn't interpret. Awkward beat.

I rose and began gathering dishes.

"Not a chance." Shooting to his feet, Charlie took the plates from my hands. "My house. My rules."

"Dictatorial," I said.

"Yes," he agreed.

An hour later I lay curled in my bed. Alone. Perhaps it was the pantytumble incident. Whatever. Birdie was keeping his distance.

The room was silent. Slivers of moonlight slashed the armoire.

Given the calm of the room and the demands of the day, I should have fallen asleep quickly. Instead, my thoughts spun like whirligig blades.

I'd enjoyed Charlie's company. Conversation had been easy, not strained as I'd anticipated.

Sudden realization. I'd done most of the talking. Was that good? Was Charlie Hunt the silent, pensive type? Still waters running deep? Shallow waters barely running at all?

Charlie had appeared to understand my frustration with Lingo. Though I had, indeed, been venting, he hadn't treated me like a sleep-deprived toddler.

Our dialogue had been strictly present tense. No mention of past marriages, lost loves, murdered spouses. No discussion of the years between the Skylark and now.

I remembered the wedding picture. Charlie's expression. What was it I'd seen in his eyes? Resentment? Guilt? Grief for a woman blown up by fanatics?

Not that I wanted to share secrets with Charlie Hunt. I hadn't mentioned Pete and his twenty-something fiancée, Summer. Or Ryan and his long-ago lover and damaged daughter. Ours had been a mutual, unspoken complicity, both dancing around the edges of our respective pasts. It was better that way.

Ryan.

I hadn't expected Ryan to call. Yet, arriving home, I'd felt hope on seeing the pulsing red beacon.

Three voice-mail messages. Katy. Pete. Hang-up.

My daughter wanted to discuss Saturday's shopping excursion. Sure she did.

My estranged husband hoped to arrange a dinner for me to meet Summer. That was as likely as pork chops on Shabbat.

The blades twirled crazily.

Ryan.

Was he happy reunited with Lutetia? Was it really over between us? Did I care?

Easy one.

Should I care?

Pete.

Don't go there.

Charlie.

Enough.

The Lake Wylie corpse.

What had bothered me about the body? The paucity of maggots, given Funderburke's statement? The absence of smell or signs of scavenging? The missing head? The symbols carved into the flesh?

Duh, yeah.

Was the Lake Wylie case somehow tied to the Greenleaf cellar? If so, how? The former suggested Satanism. The latter looked like Santería or a variant such as Palo Mayombe.

What had happened to the Lake Wylie kid's head?

Sudden image. The hunk of brain buried in the cellar cauldron.

Was it human? Note: Ask Larabee.

My pessimist brain cells threw out a thought.

Mark Kilroy's brain was found floating in a cauldron.

Adolfo de Jesus Constanzo and his followers were an aberration of Palo Mayombe. They were not Satanists.

Kenneth Roseboro.

Was Roseboro being truthful about the house on Greenleaf? His tenant? Where was T-Bird Cuervo?

Cuervo. Wasn't that Spanish for "crow"? Thomas Crow. T-Bird. Cute.

What story would Roseboro tell in the morning?

The mutilated kid at Lake Wylie.

The cauldron bones.

The school portrait.

Boyce Lingo.

Charlie Hunt.

Pete's nuptials.

Ryan's détente with Lutetia.

And on.

And on.

Jumbled images. Confused musings.

But not as confused as they were about to become.

14

THE CMPD IS HEADQUARTERED IN THE LAW ENFORCEMENT Center, a geometric hunk of concrete looming over the corner of Fourth and McDowell. Across the intersection is the new Mecklenburg County Courthouse, site of Boyce Lingo's most recent performance.

All detective units are on the second floor at Law Enforcement. At 8:00 A.M. I presented ID, passed security, and rode the elevator ass to elbow with cops and civilians gripping cups from Starbucks and Caribou Coffee. Conversations centered on the upcoming long weekend.

Columbus Day. I'd totally forgotten that Monday was a holiday.

No picnic or barbecue for you. Loser.

Kenneth Roseboro presented himself ninety minutes later than Slidell had ordered. His tardiness did not put Skinny in the best of moods.

Nor did the sludge that passed as coffee in the homicide squad room. While waiting, Slidell and I knocked back a full pot. Rinaldi was out showing the cauldron portrait to school photographers, so I was on my own with his partner's bad humor.

This did not put *me* in the best of moods.

Slidell's desk phone finally rang at 9:37. Roseboro was in interrogation room three. The sound and video systems were up and running.

Before entering, Slidell and I paused to view Wanda Horne's nephew through a one-way mirror.

Roseboro was seated, sandaled feet jiggling, spidery fingers interlaced on the tabletop. He was maybe five-two, a hundred and twenty pounds, with an oddly elongated head that balanced on his neck like a budgie on a perch.

"Nice hair," Slidell snorted.

Roseboro's scalp was looped by concentric circles of ridges and furrows.

"He's got a three-sixty wave," I said. "Like Nelly."

Slidell looked at me blankly.

"The rapper."

The look did not change.

"Jaunty shirt," I segued. It was lime and large enough to shelter a racehorse.

"Aloha." Slidell hiked his pants. The belt settled above a roll that masqueraded as his waist. "Let's sweat this prick."

Roseboro started to rise when we entered the room.

"Sit," Slidell barked.

Roseboro folded.

"Glad you could make it, Kenny."

"Traffic was heavy."

"Shoulda set out earlier." Slidell regarded Roseboro as he though he were scum in a drain.

"I didn't have to come here at all." Roseboro's tone fell somewhere between sulky and bored.

"You've got a point there." Slapping a folder onto the table, Slidell dropped into a chair opposite his interviewee. "But an upstanding citizen like you, what's a little personal inconvenience, right?"

Roseboro shrugged one bony shoulder.

I seated myself next to Slidell.

Roseboro's eyes slid to me. "Who's the chick?"

"The *doctor* helped me clean out your cellar, Kenny. You got something to say about that?"

"How much I owe you?" Smirking.

"You think this is funny?"

Again, the shoulder hitch.

Slidell turned to me. "You hear something funny?"

"Not yet," I said.

"I didn't hear nothing funny." Slidell refocused on Roseboro. "You've got problems, Kenny."

"Everyone's got problems." Nonchalant.

"Everyone don't have a little palace on Greenleaf."

"I told you. I haven't been in that house since I was nine years old. Blew my mind when the old lady left it to me."

"Auntie's favorite nephew."

"Auntie's only nephew." Still unconcerned.

"No kids of her own?"

"One. Archie."

"And Archie would be where these days?" Slidell kept his voice set on scornful.

"Cemetery."

"That's amazing. I ask where's Archie, you come back with cemetery. A sidesplitter, right off your head." Again, Slidell turned to me. "Isn't he something? Firing off one-liners, just like that?"

"Hilarious," I agreed.

"Archie died in a wreck when he was sixteen."

"Condolences for your loss. Let's talk about the cellar."

"Best I can remember, there were spiders, rats, rusty old tools, and a shitload of mold." Roseboro snapped a finger, as though in sudden understanding. "That's it. You're busting me for failure to maintain safe housing for my pets. Animal endangerment, right?"

"You really are a scream, Kenny-boy. Bet you're hoping to make the comedy channel." Another Slidell lob to me. "What do you think? We'll be surfing one night, there'll be Kenny with a mike in one hand?"

"Seinfeld got his start doing stand-up."

"Only one problem." Slidell drilled Roseboro with a look that said he was far from amused. "You ain't going to be standing up, or walking out, or going nowhere, you don't start making a little effort here, asshole."

Roseboro's face showed only indifference.

"Chateau Greenleaf?" Slidell clicked a ballpoint to readiness over a yellow legal pad.

"As far as I know the cellar was used as a laundry and pantry. And I think there was a workshop down there."

"Wrong answer."

"I have no idea what you're talking about, man."

"I'm talking about murder, you dumb fuck."

Roseboro's apathy showed its first fault line.

"What?"

"Give it up, Kenny. Maybe you skate on freedom of religion."

"Give what up?"

"John Gacy. Jeffrey Dahmer. Rule number one, dumb ass. Never stash body parts in your own crib."

"Body parts?" Roseboro was definitely interested now.

Slidell only glared.

Saucer-eyed, Roseboro directed a question to me. "What is he talking about?"

Slidell opened the folder and, one by one, slapped scene photos onto the tabletop. The cauldron. The statues of Saint Barbara and Eleggua. The dead chicken. The goat skull. The human remains.

Roseboro viewed but didn't touch the prints. After a full ten seconds, he wiped a hand across his mouth.

"This is bullshit. I've got no way of knowing what a tenant drags into my basement. I told you. I never set foot in the place."

Slidell gave him silence. As is common, Roseboro felt compelled to fill it.

"Look. I got a letter from some pinstripe saying the house was mine. I signed the papers, ran an ad. Guy named Cuervo called, agreed to a one-year lease."

"You background him?"

"I wasn't offering space in Trump Tower. We agreed on a price. Cuervo ponied up the cash."

"When was this?"

Roseboro searched the ceiling, the fingers of one hand worrying a scab on the back of the other. Finally, "A year ago March."

"You got a copy of the lease?"

"I never got around to writing one up. Cuervo forked over every month, never asked for anything. After a while, I forgot about paperwork. Stupid, as things turned out."

"How'd Cuervo pay?"

"I already said. Cash."

Slidell wiggled his fingers in a give-me-more gesture.

"He mailed it. I couldn't have cared less if the guy had a bank account, and I wasn't about to drive to Charlotte each month."

"Your little arrangement didn't have nothing to do with the IRS, now did it?"

Roseboro's fingers went into overdrive. "I pay my taxes."

"Uh-huh."

Flecks of crusty endothelium were building on the tabletop.

"You want to give that a rest," Slidell said. "You're turning my stomach."

Roseboro dropped both hands to his lap.

"Tell me about Cuervo."

"Latino. Seemed like a nice enough dude."

"Wife? Family?"

Another shoulder hitch. "We weren't exactly pen pals."

"He legal?"

"What am I, border patrol?"

Slidell dug a printout from his folder. The photo looked dark and blurry from where I sat.

"That him?"

Roseboro glanced at the face, nodded.

"Go on." Slidell took up his pen. I suspected the note-taking was mostly for show.

Again, Roseboro shrugged. He really had the move down.

"After June, the guy stopped paying, stopped answering his cell phone. By September I was so pissed I drove up here to toss his ass out." Roseboro shook his head in disillusionment over his fallen fellow man. "Shithead was gone. Really screwed me."

"You're bringing tears to my eyes, Kenny, you being such an honorable guy and all. Cuervo clear out his stuff?"

Roseboro shook his head. "Left everything. It was crap."

"You got his number?"

Roseboro unhooked his mobile, powered on, and scrolled the address book.

Slidell jotted down the digits. "Go on."

"Nothing else to tell. I hired a Realtor and sold the place. End of story."

"Not quite." After gophering the stack, Slidell slid free a shot of the human skull. "Who's this?"

Roseboro's eyes dropped to the print, snapped back up. "Jesus Christ. How would I know?"

Slidell removed a copy of the school portrait from his folder and held it up. "And this?"

Roseboro looked like a man whose mind was racing. For composure? Comprehension? Explanation? A way out?

"I've never seen that kid in my life. Look. I may have tried to scam on a few taxes, but, honest to God, I know nothing about any of this. I swear." Roseboro's gaze jumped from Slidell to me and back. "I live in Wilmington. Been there for five years. Check it out."

"Count on it," Slidell said.

"You want, I'll take a lie detector. Now. I'll do it now."

Wordlessly, Slidell gathered the prints, placed the folder on the tablet, and pushed to his feet.

I stood.

Together, we started for the door.

"What about me?" Roseboro whined at our backs. "What's going to happen to me?"

Slidell spoke without turning.

"Don't schedule no auditions."

"Impressions?" I asked when we were back in Slidell's office.

"He's a sniveling little weenie. But my gut says he's telling the truth."

"You're thinking Cuervo?"

"Or Auntie."

I shook my head. "Wanda died a year and a half ago. I'm almost certain the chicken was killed within the last few months. I'll phone my entomologist, see if he'll hazard a preliminary opinion."

"If Wanda's clear, then I gotta like Cuervo. Assuming Roseboro's not taking us for a ride."

"May I see the mug shot?"

Slidell dug the printout from the folder.

The quality was, indeed, lousy. The man was all teeth and wrinkles, with thick gray hair swept back from his face.

"If Cuervo is Latino, Santería makes sense," Slidell said. "Or that other one."

"Palo Mayombe." I hoped that wasn't it. If so, I hoped it was not of the Adolfo de Jesus Constanzo variety. "What about Roseboro?"

"I'll let him cool his heels, then go in for some more face time. Fear has a way of jogging the gray cells."

"Then?"

"I'll cut him loose and start looking for Cuervo. Start with his cell phone."

"And the INS. Cuervo could be undocumented."

Slidell rolled his eyes at my use of the term. "Him being illegal could explain Roseboro's desire for cash and carry only."

"Rinaldi call in?"

Slidell checked his voice mail and mobile, then shook his head.

"I'm going to the ME office," I said. "Let me know if Rinaldi learns anything. If not, maybe it's time to put the girl's face out there. I'll phone when Larabee and I finish with the Lake Wylie torso."

"Sounds like a plan," Slidell said.

We didn't know that another plan was already unfolding. A plan traveling a deadly collision course with our own.

15

Weekends mean paychecks and opportunities for knocking back booze. Consequently, the number of brawls, batteries, mishaps, and misfortunes swells from quittin' time on Friday till church on Sunday. Week's opening can be bedlam at a morgue. Week's close, on the other hand, is often tranquil.

Such was not the case this Friday morning.

Two blocks out I knew something was wrong. Vehicles filled the few slots fronting the MCME and lined the curbs on College and Phifer.

Drawing close, I could read logos. *WBTV. WSOC. WCCB. News 14 Carolina.*

Gunning into the lot, I threw the car into park, flew out the door, and raced toward the building. TV crews, print reporters, and photographers blocked the front entrance. Head lowered, elbows winging, I charged into the pack.

"Dr. Brennan," a voice said.

Ignoring it, I plowed forward, anger tensing every muscle in my body. After much shoving by me and name-calling by others, I finally broke through.

Boyce Lingo was holding court at the top of the steps. As before, Crew-Cut-Squirrel-Cheeks was covering his flank.

"We are a tolerant society." Lingo's kindly smile faded to stern. "But now is not a time for indulgence. An attitude that permits devil worship permits every other brand of evil. Drunkenness, adultery, idolatry, homosexuality. All manner of antifamily moral perversion."

I stepped forward, arms raised like a school crossing guard. "This press conference is over."

Lenses swiveled in my direction. Microphones shot toward my face.

I heard murmuring. My name. *Anthropologist. UNCC.*

"Your presence here is hampering our ability to do our jobs."

Lingo froze, arms V-ed downward, fingers intertwined in front of his genitals.

"You must all leave."

"Is it true Anson Tyler's head was cut off?" a reporter called out.

"It is not," I snapped, immediately regretted being sucked into an answer.

"What can you tell us about the Tyler case?" a woman's voice asked.

"No comment." Glacial.

"What about the body found at Lake Wylie?" Yelled from the back of the mob.

"No comment."

"The commissioner says satanic symbols were carved into the flesh."

"No. Comment."

I glared at Lingo, fury firing from nerve ending to nerve ending.

"Why not admit the truth, Dr. Brennan?" Lingo, the concerned activist.

"You wouldn't know the truth if it bit you on the ass."

A small, collective gasp. A few nervous giggles.

"The people of Charlotte deserve answers."

"The people of Charlotte do *not* deserve you generating baseless fears." Compared to Lingo's syrupy baritone, my voice sounded shrill.

Lingo smiled benignly, a loving parent observing an ill-tempered child. I wanted to kick the sanctimonious bastard right down the steps.

"Is it LeVay? Church of Satan?" Shouted.

"Is it true these people are torturing and killing animals?"

"How big is the Charlotte coven?"

"Disperse now or the police will be called to clear the premises."

My threat was ignored.

"Do the cops have a suspect?"

"Why the cover-up?"

A mike veered close. I slapped it aside. The boom winged back, scraping my cheek.

I lost it.

"There! Is! No! Cover-up! There is no goddamn conspiracy!"

Lenses clicked furiously.

"You are being manipulated!" Stepping forward, I grabbed a television camera and turned it onto the crowd. "Look at yourselves. This is a scalp hunt!"

Behind me I heard the glass door swing open.

"Hit the road!"

Fingers wrapped my wrist.

Yanking free, I made underhanded sweeping gestures with my fingers.

"Quick! Maybe you can find a nun who's been raped. Or a bludgeoned granny eaten by her poodle."

"Easy." Whispered. Turning my shoulders, Larabee nudged me toward the entrance.

Before the door closed, I managed to toss off one last suggestion.

Ten minutes later I'd regained my composure.

"How bad was it?"

Larabee recapped the highlights.

"*Clusterfuck?*"

Larabee nodded.

"The mikes caught it?" A headache knocked at the back of each eyeball.

"Oh, yeah."

"Oh, God."

"Him, too. Let's hope word doesn't reach the chief."

North Carolina has a statewide medical examiner system, with the chief ME's office in Chapel Hill.

"He'll be pissed."

"He will," Larabee agreed.

"What now?"

"You and I autopsy the Lake Wylie kid."

And that's what we did.

By three, X-rays glowed from light boxes, fingerprint forms covered one countertop, organ slivers floated in jars, and bone specimens lay in stainless steel bowls. Liver, pancreas, lung, stomach, kidney, and brain for the ME. Clavicular extremities, pubic symphyses, cervical vertebrae, and a two-inch plug of femoral shaft for me.

The pentagram and 666 signs hung ghostly pale in their formalin bath. Gray-pink craters marked the excision sites in the chest and belly.

Normally, when all cutting and weighing and observing is completed, an assistant closes the body, organizes the specimens, and cleans up so the pathologist can proceed to other aspects of the postmortem.

Today, Larabee and I lingered, baffled and frustrated.

"It's ass backwards." As Larabee spoke, Hawkins returned organs to the open chest cavity. "There's more aerobic decomposition than anaerobic putrefaction."

"As though the body had decomposed from the outside in, rather than the inside out," I said.

"Exactly. And there's too little of either, given a minimum PMI of forty-eight hours."

"Temperatures have been in the eighties all week," I said. "That stretch of shoreline gets full sun for more than ten hours a day. The corpse was loosely wrapped. Given that combination, things should have headed south fast."

"Very fast," Larabee agreed.

"And there should be signs of animal scavenging."

"Yes."

Hawkins transferred the liver. It made a soft, wet plop.

"And there's nothing to indicate this body spent time in the lake."

"Zip."

"So what's going on?"

"Got me."

Hawkins hooked a short curved needle into the boy's chest. The skin tugged up as he drew together the edges of the Y incision.

"Stomach contents suggest the kid ate several hours before death. Beans. Peppers. Some kind of citrus, lemon, maybe lime."

"Hopefully we'll get a hit off the prints," I said.

"You're putting his age at sixteen to eighteen?"

I nodded. My preliminary was based on the clavicle, the pubic symphyses, and the X-rays.

"Could be a pisser. Teenagers vanish every day." Larabee tipped his head in the general direction of uptown. "Most are right out there, living on the streets. Parents start looking, a kid goes to ground. Someone stops showing up, the gang figures the kid's moved on."

Hawkins turned to Larabee. The ME nodded.

Hawkins shifted the body from the table to a waiting gurney, covered it with plastic, released the foot brake, and rolled it into the corridor. The door clicked into place behind him.

"I'll check the vertebrae," I said. "If there's an arrest, cut marks could prove useful."

"Assuming the perp kept his tool and the cops find it. You thinking saw?"

"Striations suggest a toothed or serrated blade. I'll examine everything under magnification."

Larabee stripped off his gloves. "I'll contact Slidell, get the prints into the system."

I remembered. "Have you looked at the brain?"

Larabee nodded. "I'm no neuroanatomist, but the organization looks human to me."

"Could try a precipitin test."

I referred to a procedure in which anti–human antibodies, produced by injecting a rabbit with human blood, are placed on a gel diffusion plate with an unknown sample. If a precipitin line forms where the two samples meet, then the unknown sample is not from a human being. The test can be performed using antidog, antideer, or anti–whatever species is in question. Though usually done with blood, I suspected it might work with brain matter.

"Worth a try," Larabee said.

"I'll get on it."

Circling the empty table, I picked up my bowls and headed for the stinky room.

I was right about the cut marks.

Though neck bones are not ideal for preserving blade characteristics, the fourth cervical vertebra had been sliced transversely, preserving a series of striae exhibiting concave bending with fixed-radius curvature sweeping away from, not around, the breakaway point. The fifth vertebra had a single false start measuring .09 of an inch in width. Every cut surface had a uniform, almost polished appearance. I found little entrance or exit chipping.

Everything suggested a power circular saw.

After photographing the sawn vertebrae, I called the entomologist to whom I'd sent the Greenleaf cellar specimens on Tuesday morning. He had them. He'd looked at them.

He talked about coffin flies from the chicken and empty puparial cases from the goat head. He went on about *Collembola, Dermestidae,* and cockroaches in the dirt. He gave me numbers and statistical probabilities.

I asked for a bottom line.

Pending final observations, in his opinion, the chicken had been dead roughly six weeks.

I outlined the facts of the Lake Wylie case, and told him another set of samples was en route to his lab.

He said hot damn.

I told him we suspected a body dump, but wanted to rule out that the victim had come from the lake. He said send the plastic wrapping. I agreed.

I bolted a quick sandwich, then began making thin sections from the bone plug removed from the Lake Wylie corpse. If Slidell bombed with the prints, I hoped histology would help me refine my age estimate.

Normally the procedure is grindingly tedious. Using a very sharp diamond blade, you cut cross-sectional slices of bone measuring one hundred microns in thickness. Or, at least they used to. The micron was officially abolished in 1967 by the CGPM, the intergalactic council on weights and measures. The micron is now the micrometer. No matter. The little bugger is still .00004 of an inch. That's why the slices are called thin sections.

Once placed on slides, the thin sections are eyeballed with a light microscope at a magnification of 100X. Then you count stuff.

Here's the premise. Bone is a dynamic tissue, constantly repairing and replacing itself. Throughout life, the microscopic bits increase in number. Therefore, a tally of osteons, osteon fragments, lamellae, and canal systems provides a means of evaluating adult age.

My scores supported my initial estimate of sixteen to eighteen years. No surprise.

But something else was.

While counting, I noticed odd discolorations in several of the Haversian canals, the tiny tunnels that allow nerves and vessels to traverse a bone's interior.

Some sort of invasive microorganism? Soil staining? Mineral deposition? Microfracturing?

Though I doubled the magnification, the irregularities still weren't clear. The defects could be meaningful or nothing at all. To be certain I'd need mongo magnification. That meant scanning electron microscopy.

Grabbing my cell, I dialed a colleague in the optoelectronics center at UNCC. A cheery voice told me its owner would return on Tuesday and wished me an enjoyable holiday weekend.

In addition to tired and frustrated, I once again felt like the world's biggest loser.

I was leaving a decidedly less chirpy message, when a call beeped in. I finished and switched over.

Slidell was at the front door. Waiting. Impatiently.

I looked at the clock. Mrs. Flowers had been gone for hours.

Walking to the lobby, I admitted Slidell.

"Thought I'd maybe die of old age out there."

"I'm working two cases at once." I ignored Slidell's dig.

"Got an age on the Lake Wylie kid?"

"Sixteen to eighteen."

"Cuttin' tool?"

"Power saw, circular blade."

"Yeah?"

"Yeah."

Slidell pooched out his lips, nodded, then slipped a paper from his pocket.

"Got something you're gonna like."

I held out a hand.

He was right.

I liked it.

16

SLIDELL HAD OBTAINED A WARRANT FOR CUERVO'S SHOP.

"I'm impressed." I was.

"Erskine B. Slidell don't let no grass grow. And, by the by, Thomas Cuervo's a card-carrying citizen of these United States."

"Really?"

"Looks like Mama managed to slip ashore, give birth, collect little Tommy's papers, then hightail it back to Ecuador. In the eighties, Cuervo started traveling in and out of the country regularly. Been here steady since ninety-seven. INS has no permanent address for him, either here or south of the border."

"That's not surprising."

"After a second, decidedly shitcan session with Roseboro, I cruised by Cuervo's little pharmacy. Place was closed, but I shopped his picture around. Thought I was in Tijuana, for Christ sake."

Slidell made a gesture whose meaning was lost on me.

"Finally smoked out a pair of hombres"—pronounced *home-brays*—"admitted to a passing acquaintance. Boys had some trouble speaking English, but whaddya know, flashed a couple twenties, their communication skills took a sharp upward turn. Seems hawking tonic and weed are but two of Señor Cuervo's talents. The guy's some kinda hotshot faith healer."

"A *santero*?"

"Or maybe that other thing."

"*Palero?*"

Slidell nodded.

Palo Mayombe.

Mark Kilroy.

I pushed the thought to deep background.

"Where's Cuervo now?"

"Cisco and Pancho were a bit vague on that. Said the shop's been closed for a couple of months. Suggested Cuervo may have gone back to Ecuador."

"Does he have family here in Charlotte?"

"Not according to the two amigos."

"How did you get a judge to cut paper?"

"Seems old T-Bird had other reasons for making himself scarce. Little matter of an outstanding warrant."

"Cuervo failed to show for a court hearing?" I guessed.

"Drug charge. August twenty-ninth."

"Any luck with his cell phone?"

"Records show no incoming or outgoing calls since August twenty-fifth. Tracking individual numbers will take some time."

"You going to toss the shop now?"

Slidell shook his head. "Tomorrow. Tonight I gotta run Larabee's prints."

That made sense. The Lake Wylie case was definitely murder. We weren't even certain the Greenleaf cellar involved criminal activity.

I retrieved the print forms from the main autopsy room and gave them to Slidell.

"I want to be there," I said.

"Eh," he said.

I took that as assent.

When Slidell had gone, I looked at my watch. Eight forty. Apparently Skinny's social life was as pathetic as mine.

I was rebagging the skull when a ping sounded in my brain. You know. You've had them. In comics they appear as overhead bulbs with radiating lines.

Prints.

Wax.

What are the chances?

It happens.

Using a scalpel, I cut intersecting lines in the wax coating the top of the skull, outlining a roughly two-inch square. With some teasing, a flake lifted free.

I repeated the process until the entire wax cap lay in pieces on a stainless steel tray. One by one I viewed each under the scope.

I was three-quarters through when I saw it on the concave side of a segment that had adhered to the right parietal. One perfect thumbprint.

Why the undersurface? Had the wax lifted the print from the underlying skull? Had the perp's finger contacted the hot wax as it was poured or as it dripped from a candle?

It didn't matter. The print was there and it could lead to a suspect.

Feeling pumped, I dialed Slidell. His voice mail answered. I left a message.

After photographing the print with direct then angled light, I examined every flake twice, upside and downside. I found nothing.

The clock said 10:22.

Time to go.

I was pulling into my drive when Slidell called.

His news trumped mine.

"James Edward Klapec. Went by Jimmy. Seventeen. Looks better with his head. But not much."

Slidell's comment irked me even more than usual. We were talking about a dead child. I said nothing.

"Parents live down east, near Jacksonville," Slidell continued. "Father's a retired marine, pumps gas, mother works in the commissary at Camp Lejeune. Dropped a dime, found out little Jimmy split last February."

"Did the parents know he was living in Charlotte?"

"Yeah. The kid phoned every couple months. Last call came sometime in early September. They weren't sure the exact date. Keep in mind, these folks ain't checking the mail for an invite from MENSA."

I wondered how Slidell knew about MENSA, but let it go.

"The Klapecs didn't come to Charlotte to take their son home?"

"According to Dad, the kid was sixteen and could do as he pleased." Slidell paused. "That's what he said, but this shitbird read like an open book. The kid was queer and Klapec wanted nothing to do with him."

"Why do you say that?"

"Called him a faggot."

Clear enough.

"Why was Klapec in the system?"

"Kid was a chicken hawk."

That made no sense. In the parlance of my gay friends, chicken hawks were older gay men looking for young blood.

"I know you're going to explain that," I said.

"Punks that hang around gay bars waiting for prey. You know, circling, like chicken hawks. Great lifestyle. Do a john, score some dough, get wasted."

Deciding the term in this context was a cop thing, I let it go.

So the Lake Wylie boy had followed a common path for runaways. Kid leaves home expecting a Ken Kesey Merry Pranksters bus ride, ends up eating garbage from Dumpsters and turning tricks. It's a heartrending but predictable course.

"Did you speak with the mother?"

"No."

"Did you mention the condition of the body?"

There was a brief silence. Then, "Maybe we'll find the head and they don't have to know."

So Badass Slidell had a heart after all.

I described the wax print.

"Worth running," Slidell said. "Klapec worked a patch in NoDa, around Thirty-sixth and North Davidson." NoDa. North Davidson. Charlotte's version of SoHo. "Rinaldi's gonna float his picture, see what the homeys are willing to share. Before he heads up there I'll have him collect your wax and run it by the lab."

"What time are you tossing Cuervo's shop?"

"Eight. Sharp. And, doc?"

I waited.

"You oughta stay out of the spotlight."

Overnight, a front swaggered down from the mountains and kicked aside the warm comforter swaddling the Piedmont. I awoke to the smell of wet leaves and the sound of rain drumming my window. Beyond the screen, magnolia branches worked hard in the wind.

Cuervo's shop was located just south of uptown, in a neighborhood that wasn't a Queen City showplace. Many enterprises were fifties and sixties Dixie, chicken and burger franchises, body shops, barbecue joints. Others catered to more recent arrivals. Tienda Los Amigos. Panadería y Pastelería Miguel. Supermercado Mexicano. All were housed in strip malls well past their prime.

La Botánica Buena Salud was no exception. Brick, with a dark, brown-tinted window, the operation was flanked by a tattoo parlor and a bronzing salon. An ice cream shop, an insurance agency, a plumbing supply outfit, and a pizzeria completed the assemblage.

A beat-to-crap Mustang and an ancient Corolla occupied a narrow band of asphalt fronting the shops. Each gleamed as though buffed by a proud new owner. A good drenching will do that for old junkers.

I parked and tuned into WFAE. Sipping coffee from a travel mug, I listened to *Weekend Edition.*

Ten minutes passed with no sign of CSS or Slidell. So much for eight sharp.

Rain turned the neon lights on the tattoo parlor to orange and blue streaks. Through the wash on my windshield I watched a homeless man pick through trash, waterlogged sweatshirt hanging to his knees.

Scott Simon was reporting on mutated frogs when my eyes drifted to the driver's-side rearview. Slidell was framed in the glass. Below it letters announced: *Objects in mirror are closer than they appear.*

A sobering thought.

Killing the engine, I got out.

Slidell was also breakfasting on the run, a Bojangles sausage biscuit and a Nehi orange.

"Hell of a downpour, eh?" Garbled.

"Mm." Water was soaking my hair and running down my face. I raised the hood of my sweatshirt. "Is CSS coming?"

"Thought we'd poke around first, see if they're needed."

Preferring to examine his scenes pristine, undisturbed, Slidell's normal MO was to allow himself time alone before calling in the techs.

Downing the last of his biscuit and soda, Slidell bunched and stuffed the wrapper into the can, then unpocketed and flourished a set of keys. "Asshole at the management office has punctuality issues."

Up the strip, a storm drain had clogged, turning the asphalt into a shallow pond. Together, Slidell and I slogged to the shop.

I waited while he tried key after key. A bus whooshed past, water spraying from all of its tires.

"Want me to try?" I offered.

"I got it."

Keys continued jangling.

Rain pelted Slidell's windbreaker and dripped from the bill of his cap. My sweatshirt grew heavy, began to lengthen like that of the bum.

Far off a car alarm whooped.

Finally, something clicked. Slidell pushed. The door opened with a soft tinkling of bells.

The shop was murky and jammed with so many smells it was hard to ID any single contributor. Tea. Mint. Dust. Sweat. Other odors only teased. Fungus? Cloves? Gingerroot?

My eyes were still adjusting when Slidell found the lights.

The square footage was approximately twenty by twenty. Aluminum shelves lined the walls and formed rows down the center. Slidell headed down one.

I headed down another, reading random labels on my right. Energy enhancers. Brain rejuvenators. Tooth and gum restorers.

Pivoting, I scanned the products at my back. Skin poultices. Fertility oils. Aloe balms. Tinctures of slippery elm, barberry, fennel, juniper.

"Here's a good one." Slidell's voice sounded loud in the musty stillness. "Parkinson's kit. No more tremors, my ass." I heard the tick of glass hitting metal, then footsteps. "Here we go. Passion oil. An ancient Hindu recipe. Right. That'll make your johnson sit up and smile."

Though I didn't disagree, I offered no comment.

Beyond the shelving, a wooden counter paralleled the shop's rear wall. On it sat an old but ordinary-looking cash register. Centered behind it was a curtained doorway.

Slidell joined me, features crimped with disdain.

"Looks like pretty standard fare," I said.

"Uh-huh." Slidell lifted a hinged wooden flap connecting the far end of the counter to the wall. "Let's see what the Prince of Passion keeps stashed in back."

Crossing the threshold was like entering a different time and place. Even the smells underwent a metamorphosis. Beyond the curtained doorway, the overall impression was of flora and fauna and things long dead.

The space was windowless, and little illumination seeped in from out front. Again, Slidell located a switch.

In light cast by a single overhead bulb I could see that the room was roughly ten by fifteen. As in front, shelves lined both sides. Wood, not aluminum. Those on the right were divided into compartments measuring eight inches square. A small bundle lay centered in each cubby.

The shelves on the left had been converted into pull-out bins, the kind from which seeds or flour might be sold in bulk.

A table ran the length of the back wall. Spread along it were an old-fashioned two-plate scale and approximately twenty glass jars. Some housed recognizable things. Gingerroot. Tree bark. Thistle. Others contained dark, gnarled objects whose provenance I could only guess.

In front of the table sat two folding chairs. Equidistant between them was a large iron cauldron.

"Well, hell-o," Slidell said.

To the right of the table was a half-open door.

Striding forward, Slidell reached in and felt the wall with his fingers. In seconds, amber light revealed a rust-stained toilet and sink.

I was moving toward the cubbyhole cabinet when a bell tinkled.

I froze. Brushed eyes with Slidell. He flicked a low backward wave with one hand.

Silently, we eased to the left of the door. Slidell's hand rose to his hip. Backs pressed to the wall, we waited.

Footsteps crossed the shop.

The curtain flicked sideways.

Had Hatshepsut's mummy appeared in that doorway I couldn't have been more surprised.

The girl was young, maybe sixteen or seventeen, with nutmeg skin and center-parted hair tucked behind her ears. Only her waistline differed from the school portrait. Based on belly size, I guessed she was almost full term.

The girl scanned the room, expression watchful and alert.

"Está aquí, señor?" Whispered.

I held my breath.

Still clutching the curtain, the girl stepped forward. Backlight from the shop sparkled moisture in her hair.

"Señor?"

Slidell's hand dropped. Nylon swished.

The girl's face whipped our way, eyes wide. Flinging aside the curtain, she bolted.

Without thinking, I blew past Slidell and raced across the shop. By the time I cleared the shelving, the girl was out the door.

Rain still poured from the sky and sluiced along the pavement. Head lowered, I pounded after my quarry, water pluming up from my sneakers.

I had the advantage. I wasn't pregnant. By the pizzeria, I'd closed the gap enough to lunge and catch hold of the girl's sweater. Reaching back, she knuckle-drilled my hand again and again.

It hurt like hell. I held on.

"We just want to talk," I shouted through the downpour.

The girl gave up pummeling my carpals to claw at her zipper.

"Please."

"Leave me alone!" Struggling to shrug free of the sweater.

I heard splashing behind me.

"Hold it right there, little lady." Slidell sounded like a whale spouting air.

The girl's thrashing grew desperate. Rain flicked from her hair, sending spray across my face.

"Let me be. You got no—"

Slidell pinwheeled the girl and clamped her arms to her sides.

She kicked back with one foot. A heel connected.

"Sonova—"

"She's pregnant," I yelled.

"Tell that to my goddamn shinbone."

"It's OK," I said in what I hoped was a reassuring voice. "You're not in trouble."

The girl glared at me, fury in her eyes.

I smiled and held her gaze.

The girl squirmed and kicked.

"Your choice." Slidell panted. "We do this civilized, or I cuff you and we do it downtown."

The girl stilled, perhaps laboring through her alternatives. Then her shoulders slumped and her hands balled into fists.

"Good. Now I'm going to let you go and you're not gonna do nothing stupid."

We all stood there, breath coming in gasps. After a moment, Slidell released his grip and stepped back.

"Now. We walk to my car, all calm and collected."

The girl straightened and her chin tipped up in defiance. I could see a small gold cross lying in the hollow of her throat. Below it, a pulse beat hard.

"We all on the same page?" Slidell asked.

"Whatever gets you off," the girl said.

Regripping the girl's arm, Slidell motioned for me to follow. I did, watching drops dimple the lake at my feet.

Slidell eased the girl into the passenger seat. As he circled the hood

I displaced a mashed pizza box, a Chinese takeout bag, and a pair of old sneakers, and climbed in back. The Taurus's interior smelled like week-old underwear.

"Jesus." The girl's left hand rose to cover her nose. The fourth finger wore no ring. "Something die in here?"

Sliding behind the wheel, Slidell slammed and leaned against the door, then pointed a key in her direction.

"What's your name?"

"What's yours?"

Slidell badged her.

The girl blew air through her lips.

"What's your name?" Slidell repeated his question.

"Why you want to know?"

"In case we lose touch."

The girl rolled her eyes.

"Name?"

"Patti LaBelle."

"Buckle up." Slidell yanked and clicked his seat belt, then jammed the key into the ignition.

The girl raised a hold-it palm, then lay both hands on her belly. "All right."

Slidell relaxed into the seatback. "Name?"

"Takeela."

"That's a good start."

Eye roll. "Freeman. Takeela Freeman. You want I should spell that?"

Slidell produced a notebook and pen. "Phone number, address, name of parent or guardian."

Takeela scribbled, then tossed the tablet onto the dash. Slidell picked it up and read.

"Isabella Cortez?"

"My grandmother."

"Hispanic." More statement than question. "You live with her?"

Tight nod.

"How old are you, Takeela?"

"Seventeen." Defensive.

"You in school?"

Takeela shook her head. "It's all bullshit."

"Uh-huh. You married?"

"More bullshit."

Slidell gestured at Takeela's belly. "We got a daddy?"

"Nooo. I'm the sweet Virgin Mary."

"What?" Sharp.

"Why you want to fry my ass?"

"The father's name?"

Heavy sigh. "Clifton Lowder. He lives in Atlanta. We're not mad at each other or split up or nothing. Cliff's got kids there."

"And how old is Cliff Lowder?"

"Twenty-six."

Slidell made a sound like a terrier choking on liver.

"Is there a Mrs. Lowder in Atlanta?" I asked.

Takeela jabbed a thumb in my direction. "Who's she?"

"Answer the question. Mr. Wonderful got a wife?"

Takeela shrugged one shoulder. *So what?*

I felt a wave of emotions. Anger. Sadness. Revulsion. Mostly revulsion. Slidell nailed it.

"What kind of yank-off works the school yard for nooky?"

"I told you. I ain't in school."

"Good career planning. Big Cliff weigh in on that decision?"

"He treats me good."

"Yeah. And I'll bet he's a swell dancer. The asshole knocked you up, kitten. Then he dumped you."

"I already tole you. I ain't been dumped."

"Will Mr. Lowder be helping with the baby?" I tried to sound sympathetic.

Another shrug.

"When's your birthday?" Slidell's tone was as far from sympathetic as a tone can be.

"What? You gonna put me in your address book? Send me a e-card every year?"

"Just wondering your age when you and loverboy tripped the light fantastic. If you weren't sixteen, he could be looking at statutory rape."

Takeela's mouth clamped into a hard line.

I changed gears. "Tell us about Thomas Cuervo."

"Don't know no Thomas Cuervo."

"You just left his shop," Slidell snapped.

"You talking 'bout T-Bird?"

"I am."

Another shrug. "I was out walking, saw T-Bird's door open."

"Walking. In a typhoon."

"I wanted primrose oil to rub on my belly."

"Can't have stretch marks ruining our runway dreams."

"Why you so mean?"

"Must be a gift. Where is T-Bird?"

"How the hell would I know?"

For a full minute no one spoke. Rain drummed the roof and ran in rivulets down the windows.

After watching a plastic bag skitter across the street and paste itself to the windshield, I broke the silence.

"Do you live with your grandmother, Takeela?"

"So?"

"I've heard that T-Bird is a wonderful healer."

"Last I looked, that ain't illegal."

"No," I said. "It's not illegal."

"Why'd T-Bird have your picture?" Slidell cut in.

"What picture?"

"The picture laying on my desk. The picture we can go downtown and peruse together."

Takeela splayed her fingers and widened her eyes. "Ooh! That's me looking real scared."

Slidell's jaw muscles bulged. His gaze slid to me. I squinted "Cool it."

"T-Bird has been missing for several months," I said. "The police are concerned he may have come to harm."

For the first time she turned to face me. I saw turmoil in her eyes.

"Who'd want to hurt T-Bird? He just help people."

"Helps them how?"

"If someone need something special."

I pointed to the cross on her neck. "You're Christian?"

"That's a dumb question. Why you ask that?"

"T-Bird is a *santero*?"

"The one ain't got nothing to do with the other. You want to pray, you go to church. You want action, you go to T-Bird."

"What kind of action?"

"You got a cough. You need a job. Whatever."

Suddenly it clicked.

"You went to T-Bird because you're pregnant."

Takeela gave a quick, noncommittal shrug.

Abortion? Healthy baby? Girl versus boy child? What had this girl sought from a *santero*?

Leaning forward between the seats, I placed a hand on her arm.

"You gave T-Bird your class photo to use in a ritual."

Suddenly, the defiance was gone. Now she just looked tired and wet. And pregnant. And very, very young.

"I wanted Cliff to take care of me and the baby."

"But he won't leave his wife," I guessed.

"He gonna change his mind." Unconsciously, one hand stroked her belly.

"Do you know where T-Bird might have gone?" Softly.

"No."

"Does he have family?"

"I don't know nothing 'bout no family."

"When did you last see him?"

"Maybe in the summer."

"Is there anything you *can* tell us?"

"All I know is, my grandma say you need something, T-Bird make it happen."

Takeela laced her fingers over her unborn child and looked at Slidell.

"You gonna charge me with a crime?"

"Don't leave town," Slidell said. "We may get to do this again real soon."

"Next time get party hats." Takeela hit the handle, pulled herself out, and started up the sidewalk.

Sudden thought. Would she be insulted? What the hell. I knew her future should she follow her current course. Single motherhood. Minimum-wage jobs. A life of long hopes and empty wallets.

I got out.

"Takeela."

She half turned, hands resting lightly on her swollen middle.

"If you like, I can make some calls, see what sort of aid might be available."

Her eyes drifted to my face.

"I can't promise anything," I added.

She hesitated a beat. Then, "Me neither, lady."

Jotting a number, I handed her my card.

"That's my private line, Takeela. Call anytime."

As I watched her walk away, Slidell got out of the Taurus. Together, we started back toward the *botánica*.

"So the kid in the cauldron ain't the kid in the photo."

"No," I agreed.

"So who the hell is she?"

Taking the question as rhetorical, I didn't answer.

"Don't matter. This creep still had some kid's skull and leg bones in his cellar. Cuervo's into more than just curing the clap."

I started to respond. Slidell cut me off.

"And what about Jimmy Klapec? No question 'bout that being murder. But you say that's Satanists and Cuervo ain't, right?"

I raised both hands in frustration.

"And where the hell's Rinaldi?" Slidell dug for his mobile.

Hurrying through the rain, I kept churning thoughts in my mind.

Takeela Freeman.

Jimmy Klapec.

T-Bird Cuervo.

Santería.

Palo Mayombe.

Satanism.

I had no idea that by day's end we'd score two more ID's, close a cold case, and come face-to-face with yet another perplexing religion.

18

An hour of searching turned up nothing sinister in Cuervo's shop. The *botánica* housed no skulls, slaughtered animals, or impaled dolls.

"So T-Bird limited his bone-collector act to the Greenleaf crib."

I set down the jar I was examining and glanced at Slidell. With his rain-pasted hair and clothing he looked like the couch potato from the Black Lagoon. But I wasn't exactly at my best either.

"Makes sense," I said. "The cellar was secret, more secure."

"Cauldrons are typical of that palo stuff." I wasn't sure if Slidell was asking a question or thinking out loud.

"Palo Mayombe. But Takeela's description of Cuervo makes him sound more like a garden-variety *santero*."

"If he's harmless, how come he's got cauldrons?"

"Santería has no hard-and-fast rules."

"Meaning?"

"Maybe T-Bird simply likes pots."

"And animal corpses." Slidell whacked the cauldron with the tip of a loafer. It made a hollow ringing sound. "Why's this one empty?"

"I don't know."

"And where the hell is this guy?"

"Ecuador?" I suggested.

"All I care, his ass can stay there. I should be working Klapec."

With that, Slidell disappeared through the curtain.

I followed.

Outside, the rain had diminished to a slow, steady drizzle. Slidell's cell rang as he was locking the shop.

"Yo."

I could hear a voice buzzing on the other end.

"The kid believable?"

The buzz resumed.

"Worth some shoe leather."

Shoe leather? I curbed an eye roll.

Slidell described our session with Takeela Freeman and our search of the *botánica*. There was more buzzing, longer this time.

"No shit." Slidell's eyes slid to me. "Yeah. She has her moments."

Slidell waited out a very long sequence of buzzes.

"That address current?"

Again, Slidell glanced at me. I couldn't imagine what was being said on the other end.

"You stick with Rick. I'll swing by Pineville. We'll hook up later this afternoon."

Buzz.

"Roger."

Slidell clicked off.

"Rinaldi?" I asked.

Slidell nodded. "Some homey saw Klapec with a john the night he dropped off the scanner. Older guy, wearing a baseball cap. Not a regular. Kid told Rinaldi the dude creeped him out."

"Meaning?"

"Who the fuck knows? Remember Rick Nelson? Rock and roller got killed in a plane crash back in the eighties?"

"Ozzie and Harriet."

"Yeah. Remember 'Travelin' Man'? Guy had chicks all over the world. Fraulein in Berlin, señorita in Mexico. Great song."

"What's Rick Nelson got to do with Rinaldi's witness?" I asked, heading off the possibility that Slidell might sing.

"Genius said Klapec's john looked like Rick Nelson in a baseball cap. Real brain trust, eh?"

"What's in Pineville?" I asked.

Slidell grinned and cocked his head.

Not in the mood for guessing games, I cocked mine back.

"Rinaldi says you're good."

"I am," I said. "What's in Pineville?"

"Asa Finney." Slidell's grin broadened, revealing something green between his right lower premolars. "Popped right out when Rinaldi ran your print."

"The one in the wax?"

"That very one."

"Why's Finney in the system?" I felt totally jazzed.

"D-and-D six years ago." Slidell referred to a drunk and disorderly charge. "Moron thought peeing on a gravestone was performance art."

"Who is he?"

"Computer geek. Twenty-four years old. Lives down in Pineville, works from home. You ready for this?"

I waggled impatient fingers.

"Finney's got a Web site."

"Millions of people have Web sites."

"Millions of people don't claim to be witches."

"You mean *santero*? Like Cuervo?"

"Rinaldi said 'witch.'"

That made no sense. Santería had nothing to do with witchcraft.

"We going down there now?"

Slidell was silent so long I was certain he was about to blow me off. His answer surprised me.

"We take one car," he said. "Mine."

Pineville is a sleepy little community curled up between Charlotte and the South Carolina state line. Like the Queen City, the burg owes its existence to trails and streams. Pre–Chris Columbus, one route ran westward to the Catawba Nation, the other was the good old Trading Path. The streams were Sugar Creek and Little Sugar Creek.

Farms. Churches. The railroad came and went. Mills opened and closed. The town's one claim to fame is being the birthplace of James K. Polk, eleventh president of the US of A. That was 1795. Not much has happened there since. In the nineties, the construction of an outer belt-way morphed Pineville into a bedroom burb.

Finney's house was a post-beltway newcomer with yellow siding and fake black shutters. A nice, neat, forgettable ranch.

« 139 »

A dark blue Ford Focus was parked in the driveway. Slidell and I got out and moved up the walk.

The stoop was concrete, the door metal and painted black like the shutters. A sculpture was centered on the door, a butterfly with lace enveloping the wings.

Slidell pressed the bell. Muted harp sounds trilled somewhere inside.

Seconds passed.

Slidell rang again, held the button.

Lots of harp.

We heard rattling, then the door swung in.

Hair swelled from Finney's forehead like a wave rolling from a beach. Comb tracks ran straight backward above each temple. His lashes were long, his smile bad-boy crooked. Had it not been for severely acne-scarred skin, the man would have been rock-star good-looking.

"You Asa Finney?" Slidell asked.

"Whatever you're selling I will not buy it."

Unsmiling, Slidell showed his badge. Finney studied it.

"What do you want?"

"Talk."

"This isn't—"

"Now."

Wary, Finney stepped back.

Slidell and I entered a tiny foyer with a gleaming tile floor.

"Come with me."

We followed Finney past a cheaply furnished living–dining room combo to a small kitchen at the back of the house. A faux pine table and chairs occupied the center of the room. A half-eaten carton of yogurt and a bowl of granola sat on a place mat, spoons jutting from each.

"I was eating lunch."

"Don't let us stop you," Slidell said.

Finney resumed his chair. I sat across from him. Slidell remained standing. Interrogation tactic: height advantage.

Finney finger-drummed the table. Nervous? Annoyed that Slidell had outwitted him by staying on his feet?

Slidell folded his arms and said nothing. Interrogation tactic: silence.

Finney draped his napkin over one knee. Picked up his spoon. Set it down.

I looked around. The kitchen was spotless. A carved stone mortar and pestle sat on one counter beside an herb garden nourished by long fluorescent bulbs.

Above the sink hung an intricately carved rendering of a naked, antlered figure with a stag to its left and a bull to its right. A ram-headed serpent coiled one arm.

Finney followed my line of vision.

"That's Cernunnos, the Celtic father of animals."

"Tell us 'bout that." Slidell's tone was glacial.

"Cernunnos is husbandman to Mother Earth."

"Uh-huh."

"He is the essence of the masculine aspect of the balance of nature. In that depiction the god is surrounded by a stag, a bull, and a snake, symbols of fertility, power, and masculinity."

"You get off on those things?"

Finney's gaze swung back to Slidell. "I beg your pardon?"

"Sex. Power."

Finney began picking at one of his cheeks. "What are you implying?"

"You live by yourself, Asa?" Interrogation tactic: subject switch.

"Yes."

"Nice house."

Finney said nothing.

"Must cost some bucks, a crib like this."

"I have my own business." Finney's scratching had created a flaming red patch among the pits. "I design video games. Manage some Web sites."

"Word is you got a dandy of your own."

"Is that why you're here?"

"You tell me."

Finney's nostrils narrowed, expanded. "The same old ignorant bigotry."

Slidell tipped his head.

"Look, it's no secret. I'm Wiccan."

"Wiccan?" Heavy with disdain. "Like witches and devil worshippers?"

"We consider ourselves witches, yes. But we are not Satanists."

"Ain't that a relief."

"Wicca is a neopagan religion whose roots predate Christianity by centuries. We worship a god and a goddess. We observe the eight sabbats of the year and the full-moon esbats. We live by a strict code of ethics."

"Those ethics include murder?"

Finney's brows dipped. "Wicca incorporates specific ritual forms, the casting of spells, herbalism, divination. Wiccans employ witchcraft exclusively for the accomplishment of good."

Slidell made one of his uninterpretable noises.

"Like many followers of minority belief systems, we Wiccans are continually harassed. Verbal and physical abuse, shootings, even lynchings. Is that what this is, Detective? More persecution?"

"I'm asking the questions." Slidell's drawl was pure ice. "What do you know about a cellar on Greenleaf Avenue?"

"Absolutely nothing."

I watched Finney for signs of evasiveness. Saw only resentment.

"Got cauldrons and dead chickens."

"Wiccans do not practice animal sacrifice."

"And human skulls."

"Never."

"How 'bout a guy named T-Bird Cuervo?"

There was a subtle tensing around Finney's eyes.

"He is not one of us."

"Ain't what I asked."

"I may have heard the name."

"In what context?"

"Cuervo is a *santero.* A healer."

"You two dance in the moonlight together?"

Finney's chin hiked up a notch. "Santería and Wicca are really quite different."

"Answer the question."

"I don't know the man."

Again, a crimping of the lower lids?

"You wouldn't be lying to me, now would you, Asa?"

"I don't have to sit still for your bullying. I know my rights. *Dettmer versus Landon.* 1985. A district court in Virginia ruled that Wicca is a legally recognized religion to be afforded all benefits accorded by law. Affirmed in 1986 by the Federal Appeals Court for the Fourth Circuit. Get used to it, Detective. We're legal and we're here to stay."

At that moment my cell chirped. The caller ID showed Katy's number. I rose and walked to the living room, closing the door behind me.

"Hey, Katy."

"Mom. I know what you're going to say. I'm always dumping you. And, yes, I've probably bailed way too many times. But I've been invited to this awesome picnic, and if you don't mind, I'd really, really like to go."

I was lost. Then I remembered. Saturday. Shopping.

"It's not a problem." I was speaking softly, trying not to be overheard.

"Where are you?"

"You go, enjoy."

Through the door I heard the cadence of voices, Slidell's harsh, Finney's affronted.

"You're sure?"

Oh, yeah.

"Absolutely."

As we spoke, I perused book titles on a set of wooden shelves pushed up against one wall. *Coming to the Edge of the Circle: A Wiccan Initiation Ritual; Living Wicca; The Virtual Pagan; Pagan Paths; Earthly Bodies Magical Selves: Contemporary Pagans and the Search for Community; Living Witchcraft: A Contemporary American Coven; Book of Magical Talismans; An Alphabet of Spells.*

On a lower shelf, two books caught my attention. *Satanic Bible* and *Satanic Witch*, both by Anton LaVey. How did those fit in?

"Charlie said you rocked the other night."

"Mm."

My eyes roved to a statue of a goddess with upraised arms, a stone bowl of crystals, a cornhusk doll. Hearing soft clacking, I looked up.

A miniature wind chime swayed from a hook screwed into the top outer frame of the bookcase. The shells hung on strings attached to a pink ceramic bird.

Katy said something that my brain failed to take in. My gaze was locked on an object barely visible behind the dangling cowries.

"Bye, sweetie. Have fun."

Pocket-jamming the phone, I dragged a chair to the bookcase, climbed up, and reached for the top shelf.

19

Barely breathing, I ran a mental checklist.

The mandible retained no incisors or canines. The wisdom teeth were partially erupted. All dentition showed minimal wear. The bone was solid and stained tea brown.

Every detail was consistent with the jawless Greenleaf skull.

Back in the kitchen, Finney was explaining the creation of script for video gaming. Slidell looked as though he'd swallowed raw sewage.

Both turned at the sound of the door.

Wordlessly, I placed the jaw on the table, slapped the LaVey books beside it.

Finney regarded me, a flush creeping up from his collar.

"You have a warrant to search my belongings?"

"It was in plain view on the bookshelf," I said.

"You invited us in," Slidell snapped. "We don't need no warrant."

"Those your books?" Slidell demanded.

"I strive to understand different perspectives."

"I'll bet you do."

"I'll do a full exam," I said. "But I'm certain this jaw belongs to the skull found in T-Bird Cuervo's cellar."

Finney's eyes dropped from my face. But not before I noted the lower lid tremble.

"So, asshole, you want to explain why this jawbone's in your crib, given you don't know Cuervo or his little shop of horrors on Green-leaf?"

Finney looked up and met Slidell's glare coming his way.

"Know what I'm thinking?" Slidell didn't wait for an answer to his question. "I'm thinking you and your pals killed some kid at one of your freakfests, then stashed her skull and leg bones to play your sick little games."

"What? No."

Striding to the table, Slidell leaned close to Finney's ear, as though preparing to share a private moment. "You're going down, asshole," he hissed.

"No!" High and whiny, more the wail of a teenaged girl than a grown man. "I want a lawyer."

Jerking Finney to his feet, Slidell spun and cuffed him. "Don't you worry. This town's got more lawyers than a bayou's got gators."

"This is harassment."

Slidell read Finney his rights.

Driving into the city, Finney sat with head down, shoulders slumped, cuffed hands clasped behind his back.

Slidell called Rinaldi, told him about the jaw and about Finney's arrest, and pushed back their rendezvous time. Rinaldi reported that his canvass was yielding good follow-up.

I asked Slidell to drop me at my car on his way to headquarters. An unpleasant sight greeted us at Cuervo's shop. Allison Stallings stood with face pressed to the glass, digital Nikon clasped in one hand.

"Well, isn't that just finger-lickin' brilliant."

Shoulder-ramming the door, Slidell heaved from behind the wheel and lumbered across the asphalt. I lowered my window. Finney raised his head and watched with interest.

"What the hell do you think you're doing?"

"Research." Grinning, Stallings framed Slidell in her LCD screen and clicked the shutter.

Slidell made a grab for the camera. Stallings raised it, snapped the Taurus, then dropped the Nikon into her backpack.

"Stay the hell away from my car and my prisoner," Slidell blustered.

"Let's go," I shouted, knowing it was too late.

Stallings beelined to the Taurus, bent, and peered into the backseat. Slidell stormed behind, face cherry pie red.

Before I could react, Finney leaned toward my open window and shouted, "I'm Asa Finney. I've done nothing wrong. Let the public know. This is religious persecution."

I hit the button. Finney kept shouting as my window slid up.

"I'm a victim of police brutality!"

Breathing hard, Slidell threw his girth into the driver's seat and slammed the door. "Shut the fuck up!"

Finney went mute.

Slidell jammed the gearshift. We shot backward. He jammed again and we flew from the lot, tires spitting up rainwater.

While Slidell booked Finney, I went to the MCME to determine if the jaw was, in fact, consistent with the cauldron skull. X-rays. Biological profile. State of preservation. Articulation. Measurements. Fordisc 3.0 assessment. Everything fit.

When finished, I extracted and bagged the mandible's left second molar. If needed, DNA comparison could be done between the jaw and the skull. Other than satisfying lawyers in court, the procedure was unnecessary. I had no doubt the mandible and cranium came from the same young black female.

Two questions remained. Who was she? How did part of her end up in that cauldron and part of her at Asa Finney's house?

When I got to police headquarters, Finney was in the interrogation room so enjoyed by Kenneth Roseboro the day before. The accused had made his one phone call. Slidell and I ate Subway sandwiches while awaiting the arrival of counsel.

That counsel appeared as I was downing my last mouthful of turkey and Cheddar.

Nearly causing me to choke.

Charlie Hunt looked even better than he had Thursday night. Double-breasted merino wool and shiny wingtips now replaced the jeans and loafers. Today, he carried a briefcase. And wore socks.

Charlie introduced himself to Slidell, then to me.

We shook hands crisply.

Slidell read the charge, illegal possession of human remains. He then described the evidence and explained the link between Finney and Cuervo's cellar. For good measure, he threw in the possibility of a tie-in to Jimmy Klapec.

"Based on what?" Charlie asked.

"A fondness for the writings of Anton LaVey."

"I'd like ten minutes alone with my client."

"Guy's a weirdo," Slidell offered.

"So's Emo," Charlie answered. "That doesn't make him a killer."

Together, we walked to interrogation room three.

"I don't mind you observing." One by one, Charlie looked us each in the eye. "But no mikes."

Slidell shrugged.

Charlie entered the room. Slidell and I positioned ourselves by the one-way glass.

Finney was on his feet. The men shook hands then sat. Finney talked, did a lot of gesturing. Charlie did a lot of nodding and scribbling.

Eight minutes after entering the cubicle, Charlie rejoined us.

"My client has information he is willing to share." As before, Charlie addressed both of us. I liked that.

"Coming to his senses," Slidell said.

"In exchange for full immunity covering any and all statements."

"This douche bag may have killed a kid."

"He swears he's harmed no one."

"Don't they all."

"Do you believe him?" I asked.

Charlie regarded me for a very long time. "Yes," he said. "I do."

"How'd he get this kid's jaw?" Slidell asked.

"He's willing to explain that."

"What's his relationship to Cuervo?"

"He claims they've never met."

"Uh. Huh. And I'm gonna be voted the king of good taste."

"That would be hereditary," I said.

Slidell shot me a questioning look.

"No voting in a monarchy."

Charlie ran a hand over his mouth.

"Hardy-friggin'-har-har." Slidell turned back to Charlie. "Your boy flips, he gets a pass on the jaw, and only the jaw. He testifies truthfully and we give him immunity on the possession of human remains charge.

I suspect he's lying, I find out he's plucked one feather off one lame-butt chicken, the deal's out the window."

"Fair enough," Charlie said.

"We do it with audio and video."

"Good," Charlie said.

The three of us trooped into the interrogation room. Charlie took a chair beside Finney. Slidell and I sat facing them.

Slidell told Finney the interview was being recorded.

Finney looked at his lawyer. Charlie nodded, told him to begin.

"High school was pure hell for me. My one friend was a girl named Donna Scott. A loner, like me. A reject. Donna and I connected by default, both having been exiled to the fringe, and because of our common interest in gaming. We both spent a great deal of time online."

"This Donna Scott live in Charlotte?"

"Her family moved to L.A. the summer before our senior year. That's when she came up with the plan." Finney looked down at his hands. They were trembling. "Donna got the idea from GraveGrab. It's a pretty cheesy game but she liked it, so we played. Basically, you run around a cemetery digging up graves and trying to avoid being killed by zombies."

"What was Donna's plan?" I asked.

"That we steal something from a grave. I didn't think we'd pull it off, but I figured going to a cemetery would be a trip." Finney drew a deep breath, exhaled through his nose. It sounded like air being forced through steel wool. "Donna was into the Goth scene. I wasn't, but I liked spending time with her."

"Did you carry through with the plan?" I asked.

Finney nodded. "Donna was excited about moving, but knew I was bummed. Her idea was that we'd split whatever we stole; she'd keep one half, and I'd keep the other. You know, the old trick where people write a note, or draw a map, then tear it in two. When you meet years later you match the halves. Donna said that way we'd stay spiritually connected."

"What graveyard?" Slidell.

"Elmwood Cemetery."

"When?"

"Seven years ago. August."

"Talk about it."

"Donna picked Elmwood because some old cowboy movie star is supposed to be buried there."

"Randolph Scott?" I guessed.

"Yeah. Since her name was Scott she thought it would be cool to get something from him."

Randolph Scott was male, white, and eighty-nine at the time of his death. That didn't track with my profile of a young black female.

"Did you succeed?" I asked.

"No. We met for a midnight showing of *Rocky Horror Picture Show*, then went over to Elmwood. The gate was open. Donna brought flashlights. I brought a crowbar."

Finney's eyes slid to his lawyer. Charlie nodded.

"We looked around for Scott's grave, but couldn't find it. Eventually, we stumbled onto an aboveground crypt, back in a different section, where there weren't so many big, fancy tombstones. Seemed like a place we wouldn't be spotted. The hinges were rusty. It took only a couple of shoves with the crowbar."

"Was a name engraved on a marker?" I asked.

"I don't remember. It was dark. Anyway, we went in, pried open a casket, grabbed a skull and a jaw and a couple of other bones, and ran. To be honest, I was pretty freaked by then, just wanted to be gone. Donna said I was being a candyass. She was psyched."

"Let me be sure I got this straight. You're saying you kept the jaw and Donna kept the rest?"

Finney nodded in answer to Slidell's question.

"How'd Cuervo get the bones?"

"I don't know."

"You got contact information for Donna?"

"No. Her family moved right after that. She said she'd write or call, but she never did."

"You never saw or talked to her again?"

Finney shook his head glumly.

"Who's her old man?"

"Birch. Birch Alexander Scott."

Slidell scribbled the name. Underlined it twice.

"Anything else?"

"No."

Silence crammed the small space. Finney broke it.

"Look. I was a messed-up kid. Four years ago, I discovered Wicca. For the first time, I'm accepted. People like me for who I am. I'm different now."

"Sure," Slidell said. "You're Billy Friggin' Graham."

"Wicca is an Earth-oriented religion dedicated to a goddess and god."

"Lucifer part of the lineup?"

"Because we embrace a belief system different from traditional Judeo-Christian theology, the ignorant believe we must also worship Satan. That if God is the sum of all good, there must be an equally negative being who is the embodiment of evil. Satan. Wiccans don't buy into that."

"You saying there's no devil?"

Finney hesitated, choosing his words.

"Wiccans acknowledge that all nature is composed of opposites, and that this polarity is a part of everyone. Good and evil are locked within the unconsciousness of every person. We believe it's the ability to rise above destructive urges, to channel negative energies into positive thoughts and actions, that separates normal people from rapists and mass murderers and other sociopaths."

"You use magic to do all this rising above?" There was menace in Slidell's voice.

"In Wicca, magic is viewed as a religious practice."

"This religious practice involve carving up corpses?"

"I've already told you. Wiccans perform no destructive or exploitive magic. We hurt no one. Why would you ask such a question?"

Slidell described Jimmy Klapec's corpse.

"You think *I* killed this boy?"

Slidell impaled Finney with a glare.

"I robbed a grave when I was seventeen. Got picked up once for relieving myself in public. Two stupid pranks. That's it."

The glare held.

Finney's eyes sliced from Slidell to Charlie to me. "You've got to believe me."

"Frankly, kid, I don't believe a thing you're telling me."

"Check it out." Finney was almost in tears. "Find Donna. Talk with her."

"You can bank on it."

20

WE CAUGHT A BREAK. OR FINNEY DID. SINCE THE ALLEGED grave grab had taken place after 1999, the incident was on the CMPD computer. Using the year of occurrence and Elmwood as identifiers, we pulled the report in minutes.

On the night of 3 August, an unknown suspect/suspects unlawfully entered crypt 109 located at Elmwood Cemetery. The reporting officer spoke with Mr. Allen Burkhead, cemetery administrator. Mr. Burkhead stated that upon arriving at the cemetery at 0720 hours on 4 August he discovered crypt 109 had been pried open. Mr. Burkhead did not believe the crypt was damaged when he left work at 1800 hours on 3 August. Once inside the crypt the suspect/suspects opened a coffin and violated the remains of Susan Clover Redmon by removing the skull. The Medical Examiner was notified, but declined to visit the site or to examine the body to determine if other bones were removed from the coffin. At the time of the incident the cemetery was closed and there are no witnesses. A record search revealed that Marshall J. Redmon (deceased) holds deed to the tomb. A Redmon family member, Thomas Lawrence Redmon, was located in Springfield, Ohio. Thomas Redmon has been notified and will be kept abreast of developments. I request this case remain open for further investigation.

I skimmed the rest of the information: *Reporting officer: Wade J. Hewlett. Incident address: 600 E. 4th St. Victims: Elmwood Cemetery; Marshall J. Redmon. Stolen property: human skull and jaw.*

Slidell determined that Hewlett was now assigned to the Eastway Division. He phoned and was placed on hold. Seconds later Hewlett picked up. Slidell switched to speakerphone.

"Yeah, I remember the B-and-E at Elmwood. Kinda sticks in my head, being the only grave robbery I've ever caught. Case went nowhere."

"You have a gut on it?"

"Probably kids. I caught a double homicide that week, so vandalism didn't top my dance card. We had no leads, nothing to work. Local Redmons were all dead or moved away. The one out-of-state relative we managed to locate didn't give a rat's ass. Eventually, I decided to just wait and see if the skull surfaced."

"Did it?"

"No."

I jumped in. "Why was the ME a no-show?"

"He asked my opinion. I told him nothing else in the tomb or in the coffin looked disturbed. He said he'd contact the family member living in Ohio."

"And?"

"Thomas Redmon said seal her up, call if you find the head."

"Real humanitarian," Slidell said.

"Redmon had never been to Charlotte, didn't know that branch of the family, hadn't a clue who was stored in that tomb."

"Did you check cemetery records on Susan Redmon?" I asked.

"Yeah. There wasn't much. Just the name, burial location, and date of interment. Apparently hers was the last coffin in."

"When was that?"

"Nineteen sixty-seven."

"How many others are in there?"

"Four in all."

"None of the others was vandalized?"

"Didn't appear to be. But nothing was in good shape."

Slidell thanked Hewlett and disconnected. For several seconds his hand lingered on the receiver. Then he turned to me.

"What do you think?"

"I think Finney's lying about Cuervo. Maybe Klapec."

"How 'bout we have us a crypt crawl?"

Elmwood isn't the oldest burial ground in Charlotte. That would be Settlers. Located on Fifth between Poplar and Church, Settlers Graveyard is lousy with Revolutionary War heroes, the Mecklenburg Declaration of Independence signers, and well-heeled antebellum movers and shakers.

Elmwood is a relative newcomer on the local cemetery scene. Opened in 1853, the first interment took place two years later, purportedly the child of one William Beatty. Record keeping was less than detailed back then.

Business at Elmwood was slow for a while. Sales picked up in the latter half of the century due to population increases associated with the arrival of textile mills. The last plot sold in 1947.

Designed from its inception to serve both the quick and the dead, Elmwood remains a popular venue for joggers, strollers, and Sunday picnickers. But its hundred acres offer more than azaleas and shade. The cemetery's design immortalizes in hardscape and landscape the changing attitudes of America's New South.

Like Gaul, the original graveyard was *omnis divisa in partes tres,* Elmwood for whites, Pinewood for blacks, Potters Field for those lacking bucks for a plot. Whites only, of course.

No roads connected Elmwood to Pinewood, and the latter could not be accessed via the main entrance to the former. Sixth Street for whites, Ninth Street for blacks. Sometime in the thirties, a fence was erected to ensure that racially distinct corpses and their visitors never commingled.

Yessiree. Not only did African-Americans have to work, eat, shop, and ride buses in their own special places, their dead had to lie in barricaded dirt.

Years after Charlotte outlawed discrimination in the sale of cemetery plots, the fence lingered. Finally, in 1969, after a public campaign led by Fred Alexander, Charlotte's first black city councilman, the old chain-linking came down.

Today everyone gets planted together.

Before leaving headquarters, Slidell dialed the number Hewlett had provided for Thomas Redmon. Amazingly, the man picked up.

Have a go, Redmon said. But, if possible, do everything on-site. Redmon was not a fan of rousing dead spirits.

Slidell also phoned the number listed for Allen Burkhead. Burkhead was still in charge of Elmwood and agreed to meet us.

Hewlett. Redmon. Burkhead. Three for three. We were clicking!

Burkhead was a tall, white-haired man who carried himself like a five-star general. He was waiting, crowbar in one hand, umbrella in the other, when we pulled up at the Sixth Street gate. It was raining again, a slow, steady drizzle. Heavy gray-black clouds looked ready to unload at the least encouragement.

Slidell briefed Burkhead, then we passed through the gates. The rain beat a soft metronome on the bill of my cap, and on the pack I carried slung over one shoulder.

Some people view silence as a void needing fill. Burkhead was one of them. Or maybe he was just proud of his little kingdom. As we walked, he provided unbroken commentary.

"Elmwood is a cultural encyclopedia. Charlotte's poorest and wealthiest lie here, Confederate veterans side by side with African slaves."

Not in this section, I thought, taking in the Neoclassical-inspired obelisks, the massive aboveground box tombs, the temple-like family crypts, the granite and marble carved in intricate detail.

Burkhead gestured with the crowbar as we walked, a guide identifying pharaohs in the necropolis at Thebes. "Edward Dilworth Latta, developer. S. S. McNinch, former mayor."

Massive hardwoods arced overhead, leaves shiny, trunks dark with moisture. Cypresses, boxwoods, and flowering shrubs formed a wet understory. Headstones curved to the horizon, gray and mournful in the persistent rain. We passed a monument to firemen, a tiny stone log cabin, a Confederate memorial. I recognized common funerary symbols: lambs and cherubs for children, blooming roses for young adults, the Orthodox cross for Greeks, the compass and square for Masons.

At one point Burkhead paused by a headstone engraved with an elephant image. Solemnly, he read the inscription aloud.

" 'Erected by the members of John Robinson's Circus in memory of John King, killed at Charlotte, North Carolina, September twenty-second, eighteen-eighty, by the elephant, Chief. May his soul rest in peace.' "

"Yeah?" Slidell grunted.

"Oh, yes. The beast crushed the poor man against the side of a rail-road car. The accident caused quite a sensation."

My eyes drifted to a marble statue of a female figure several graves over. Struck by the poignancy of her pose, I wove my way to it.

The woman was kneeling with one hand cradling her face, the other hanging limply, clutching a bouquet of roses. The detail in her clothing and hair was exquisite.

I read the inscription. Mary Norcott London had died in 1919. She was twenty-four. The monument had been erected by her husband, Edwin Thomas Cansler.

My mind floated a picture of the skull in my lab. Did it belong to Susan Clover Redmon?

Mary had been Edwin's wife. She'd died so young. Who had Susan been? What calamity had cut her life short? Ended her happiness, her suffering, her hopes, her fears?

Had grieving parents placed Susan's coffin lovingly in its tomb? Remembered her as a little girl coloring inside the lines, boarding the school bus with her brand-new lunch box? Had they cried, heartbroken at the promise of achievement never to be fulfilled?

Or had it been a husband who most mourned her passing? A sibling?

Slidell's voice cut into my musing. "Yo, doc. You coming?"

I caught up with the others.

Further east, the cemetery's subtly curvilinear design gave way to a gridlike arrangement of graves. The rain was falling harder now. I'd abandoned my soggy sweatshirt for an MCME windbreaker. Bad move. The thin nylon was keeping me neither warm nor dry.

Eventually we entered an area with few elaborate markers. The trees were still old and stately, but the layout appeared somehow more organic, less rigid. I assumed we'd crossed the boundary once secured by chain-linking.

Burkhead continued his guided tour.

"Thomas H. Lomax, A.M.E. Zion Bishop; Caesar Blake, Imperial Potentate of the Ancient Egyptian Arabic Order and leader of Negro Shriners throughout the nineteen-twenties."

The section's most prominent feature was a small, front-gabled structure of yellow and red brick. Raised bricks formed diamond-shaped decorative motifs on the side and rear elevations and spelled SMITH above the plain wooden door.

"W. W. Smith, Charlotte's first black architect," Burkhead said. "I find it fitting that Mr. Smith's tomb reflects his distinctive style of brickwork."

"How many stiffs you got in this place?" Slidell asked.

"Approximately fifty thousand." Burkhead's tone gave new meaning to the term "disapproving."

"Make a great setting for one of them zombie movies."

Squaring his already square shoulders, Burkhead pointed the crowbar. "The vandalism occurred over here."

Burkhead led us to a tiny concrete cube centered among a half dozen graves, each with a headstone bearing the middle or last name Redmon. The name also crowned the tomb's front entrance.

Handing me the crowbar, Burkhead collapsed his umbrella and leaned it against the crypt. Then he produced a key and began working a padlock affixed at shoulder height to the right side of the door.

I noticed that the lock appeared shinier and less rusted than the nails and hinges embedded in the wood. Adjacent to it, deep gouges scarred the jamb.

After freeing the prongs, Burkhead pocketed both lock and key, and gave the door a one-handed push. It swung in with a trickle of rust and a Hollywood creak.

As one, we pulled out and flicked on our flashlights.

Burkhead entered first. I followed. Slidell brought up the rear.

The odor was dense and organic, the smell of earth, old brick, decayed wood, and rotten fabric. Of moths and rat piss and dampness and mold.

Of Slidell's pastrami breath. The space was so small we were forced to stand elbow to elbow.

Our flashlights showed built-in ledges straight ahead and to the left of the door. Each held a simple wood coffin. Bad idea for riding out history. Good idea for a quick dust-to-dust sprint. Each box looked like it had gone through a crusher.

Wordlessly, Burkhead unfolded a photocopied document and stepped to the shelves opposite the door. Shadows jumped the walls as his gaze shifted back and forth from the paper in his hand to first the upper, then the lower coffin.

I knew what he was doing.

The dead do not always stay put. I once did an exhumation in which Grandpa was three plots over from the one in which he was supposed to have been buried. Another in which the deceased lay in a plot containing two stacks of three. Instead of bottom left, as shown in the records, our subject was second casket from the top right.

First rule in a disinterment: Make sure you've got the right guy.

Knowing the vague nature of old cemetery records, I assumed Burkhead was checking photos or brief verbal descriptions against observable details. Casket style, decorative hardware, handle design. Given the obvious age of the coffins, I doubted he'd be lucky enough to have manufacturers' tags or serial numbers.

Finally satisfied, Burkhead spoke.

"These decedents are Mary Eleanor Pierce Redmon and Jonathan Revelation Redmon. Jonathan died in 1937, Mary in 1948."

Moving to the side wall, Burkhead repeated his procedure. As before, it took him several minutes.

"The decedent on top is William Boston Redmon, interred February 19, 1959."

Burkhead's free hand floated to the lower coffin.

"This is the burial that was violated seven years ago. Susan Clover Redmon was interred on April 24, 1967."

Like her relatives, Susan met eternity in a wooden box. Its sides and top had collapsed, and much of its hardware lay on a piece of plywood slid between the casket and the shelf.

A crack ran a good eighteen inches along the left side of the cover. Over it, someone had nailed small wooden strips.

"Mr. Redmon declined to purchase a new casket. We did our best to repair and reseal the lid."

Burkhead turned to me.

"You will examine the decedent here?"

"As per Mr. Redmon's request. But I may take samples to the ME facility for final verification."

"As you wish. Unfortunately, the coffin key has gone missing over the years."

Stepping to one end of the shelf, Burkhead gestured Slidell to the other.

"Gently, Detective. The remains are no longer of any great weight."

Together, the men scooted the plywood forward and lowered it to the floor. The displaced casket filled the tiny chamber, forcing our little trio back against the walls.

With scarcely enough room to maneuver, I opened my pack and removed a battery-operated spot, a magnifying lens, a case form, a pen, and a screwdriver.

Burkhead observed hunched in the shadows of the easternmost corner. Slidell watched from the doorway, hanky to mouth.

Masking, I squatted sideways and began to lever.

The nails lifted easily.

SOUTHERNERS DON'T ATTEND WAKES. WE ATTEND VIEWINGS.
Makes sense to me. Drained of blood, perfumed, and injected with wax,
a corpse is never going to sit up and stretch. But it is laid out for one
final inspection.

To facilitate that last, pre-eternity peek, casket lids are designed like
double Dutch doors. Finney and his gal pal had taken advantage of that
feature, prying open only the hinged upper half.

OK for a snatch and run in the night. I needed full-body access.

Thanks to the vandalism and to natural deterioration, the top of
Susan's coffin had collapsed into a concavity running the length of the
box. Experience told me the cover would have to be lifted in segments.

After prying loose Burkhead's makeshift repair strips, I hacked
through corrosion sealing the edges of the lid. Then, like Finney, I laid
to with the crowbar.

Burkhead and Slidell helped, displacing decayed wood and metal to
unoccupied inches of floor space. Odor oozed up around us, a blend of
mildew and rot. I felt my skin prickle, the hairs rise along my neck and
arms.

An hour later the casket was open.

The remains were concealed by a jumble of velvet padding and drap-
ing, all stained and coated with a white, lichenlike substance.

After shooting photos, I gloved, uneasy about Hewlett's assessment
that nothing in the coffin had been violated but the head. If that was

true, what of the femora I'd found in Cuervo's cauldron? I kept my concerns to myself.

It took only minutes to disentangle and remove the funerary bedding covering the upper half of the body. Slidell and Burkhead observed, offering comments now and then.

Susan Redmon had been buried in what was probably a blue silk gown. The faded cloth now wrapped her rib cage and arm bones like dried paper toweling. Hair clung to the cushion that had cradled her head, an embalmer's eye cap and three incisors visible among the long, black strands.

That was it for the pillow. No head. No jaw.

My eyes slid to Slidell. He gave a thumbs-up.

I collected a sample of hair, then the incisors.

"Those teeth?" Slidell asked.

I nodded.

"Do you have dental records?" Burkhead asked.

"No. But I can try fitting these three into the sockets, and comparing them to the molars and premolars still in place in the jaw and skull."

Teeth and hair bagged, I continued my visual examination.

Susan's gown was ripped down the bodice. Through the tear I could see a collapsed rib cage overlying thoracic vertebrae. Three cervical vertebrae lay scattered above the gown's yellowed lace collar. Four others nestled between the soiled padding and the edge of the pillow.

Gingerly, I peeled away coffin lining until the lower body was also exposed.

The wrist ends of the radii and ulnae poked from both sleeve cuffs. Hand bones lay tangled among the folds of the skirt and along the right side of the rib cage.

The gown was ankle-length, and tightly adhered to the leg bones. The ankle ends of the tibiae and fibulae protruded from the hemline, the foot bones below, in rough anatomical alignment.

"Everything's brown like the Greenleaf skull," Slidell said.

"Yes," I agreed. The skeleton had darkened to the color of strong tea.

"What are those?" Slidell jabbed a finger at the scattered hand bones.

"Displaced carpals, metacarpals, and phalanges. She was probably buried with her hands positioned on her chest or abdomen."

As I snipped and tugged rotting fabric, I imagined Donna thrusting a hand into the covered lower half of the coffin, fingers groping blindly, grabbing, tearing, amped on adrenaline.

"Overlapping hands is a standard pose. Either on the belly or the chest. Often the departed are interred holding something dear."

Burkhead was talking to be talking. Neither Slidell nor I was listening. We were focused on the fragile silk covering Susan's legs.

Two last snips with the scissors, then I tugged free the remnants of the skirt.

One lonely kneecap lay between Susan's pelvis and her knees.

"So Hewlett screwed up," Slidell said.

"Both femora are gone." Relief was evident in my voice.

"I'm going to fry that pissant Finney. And his sicko girlfriend. We done here?"

"No, we are not done here," I snapped.

"What now?" Slidell's thoughts had already turned to tracking Donna Scott.

"Now I check for consistency between this skeleton and the skull and leg bones found in Cuervo's cauldron."

"I gotta make a call." Pivoting, Slidell strode from the tomb. In seconds, his voice floated in from outside.

Folding back the torn edges of the bodice, I lifted the right clavicle, brushed and inspected its medial end. The growth cap was partially fused, suggesting a young adult with a minimum age at death of sixteen.

I lifted and inspected the left clavicle. Same condition.

I was scribbling notes on my case form when Slidell reappeared.

"Asked Rinaldi about a query I popped through to LAPD before heading over here. About Donna Scott and her daddy, Birch."

"I thought Rinaldi was canvassing in NoDa."

"Chicken hawks went to ground. He's at headquarters, plans to head back out when they resurface after dark."

I resumed my analysis by removing and inspecting the right pelvic half. The shape was typically female. The pubic symphysis had deep horizontal ridges and furrows, and a slender crest of bone was in the process of fusing to the upper edge of the hip blade.

I made notes on my form, then picked up the left pelvic half. Adipocere, a crumbly, soaplike substance, clung to its borders and symphyseal face. Ten minutes of cleaning revealed characteristics identical to those on the right.

More notes.

I was examining the rib ends when Slidell's phone shattered the silence. Yanking the device from his hip, he shot outside. As before, his words were lost, but his tone carried in through the open door.

Slidell's second conversation was longer than his first. I was repositioning a vertebra when he reentered the tomb.

"LAPD got back to Rinaldi."

"That was quick," I said.

"Ain't computers grand?"

Burkhead had gone motionless. I could tell he was listening.

"Birch Alexander Scott purchased a home in Long Beach in February of 2001, moved in that summer with his wife, Annabelle, and two daughters, Donna and Tracy."

"That squares with Finney's story," I said.

"Things didn't go exactly as the old man intended. Two years after relocating, the guy was taken out by a massive coronary. Wife's still enjoying the house."

"What about Donna?"

"Sounds flaky as ever. Enrolled in the School of Cinematic Arts at the University of Southern California in 2002." Slidell put a sneer into the program title. "Dropped out in 2004 to marry Herb Rosenberg, age forty-seven. Ever hear of him?"

I shook my head.

"Guy's some bigwig freelance producer. Marriage lasted two years. Donna Scott-Rosenberg now lives in Santa Monica. Since July she's been working as a researcher for a TV series."

"Did Rinaldi get a phone number?"

"Oh, yeah." Slidell waggled his cell and disappeared again.

"Who is Donna Scott?" Burkhead asked.

"She may have been involved in the vandalism."

One by one, I assessed the maturity of the long bones.

Neck and shoulders screaming, I finally sat back on my heels.

Clavicles. Pelves. Ribs. Long bones. Every indicator suggested death between the ages of fifteen and eighteen.

Age. Gender. Height. Robusticity. Preservation. Staining.

Cuervo's cauldron contained the partial remains of a black female who'd died in her mid to late teens. A black female now missing her head, jaw, and thigh bones.

Susan Redmon was a perfect match for the girl in the cauldron.

It was full night when Slidell and I left Elmwood. Thick clouds blanketed the moon and stars, turning trees and tombstones into dense cutouts against a background only slightly less dense. A cold rain was still falling, and legions of tree frogs matched vocal offerings with armies of locusts. Or maybe they were crickets. Whatever. The sound was impressive.

Burkhead assumed responsibility for securing the remains and locking the crypt. I promised to return Finney's jaw and the cauldron skull and femora as soon as I'd satisfied my boss that they were, indeed, Susan Redmon's missing parts. He promised to do his best to persuade cousin Thomas to cough up for a new casket.

Slidell was restless and grumpy. Though he'd left messages, Donna Scott-Rosenberg had not phoned him back

Slidell called Rinaldi again as I was buckling my seat belt.

I looked at my watch. Nine fifteen. It had been a very long day. I'd eaten nothing since the turkey and Cheddar sub at headquarters.

Leaning back, I closed my eyes and began rubbing circles on my temples.

"Broad isn't burning up the line getting back to me. I'll give her till morning, then bring down some heat. Let's focus on Klapec. Anything new up there?"

Rinaldi said something. From Slidell's end of the conversation I gathered he'd returned to NoDa.

"Oh, yeah? This guy's really credible?"

Rinaldi spoke again.

"And he's willing to share?"

More listening on Slidell's end.

"See you at ten."

Slidell's mobile snapped shut.

We rode in silence. Then, "Ready to call it a day, doc?"

"What's Rinaldi got?" I mumbled.

"His hawk is willing to dish on this Rick Nelson john." Slidell stopped. "Know what I liked about Nelson? His hair. Guy had hair like a Shetland pony."

"What's the kid's story?" I brought Slidell back on track.

"Describes the guy as average height and build, white, a conservative dresser, not a talker. Says he used to do Ricky-boy until he got the crap beat out of him."

I opened my eyes. "The man was violent?"

"Kid claims the asshole tuned him up good."

"When was this?"

"June. When he refused to do him anymore, Klapec took over."

"Anything else?"

"Says he's got info, but it won't be free. There's a novel approach. Rinaldi's meeting him at ten."

"Where?"

"Some Mexican joint on North Davidson. I'm gonna stop by, provide a little sales incentive of my own. You want I should run you back to your wheels?"

My stomach chose that moment to growl.

"No," I said. "I want you should buy me an enchilada."

Located at Thirty-fifth and North Davidson, Cabo Fish Taco is a bit upmarket to qualify as a joint. The place is more Baja surfer meets Albuquerque artiste.

Slidell parked outside the old Landmark Building, now home to the Center of the Earth Gallery. Hanging in the window was a still life of a glass tumbler containing an egg yolk and two halves of a plastic Easter egg balanced on the rim.

Seeing the painting as we exited the Taurus, Slidell snorted and shook his head. He was about to comment when he spotted Rinaldi walking toward us, from the point where Thirty-fifth dead-ends at the tracks.

Slidell gave a sharp whistle.

Rinaldi's head came up. He smiled. I think. I'm not sure. At that moment, reality went sideways.

Rinaldi's hand started to rise.

A gunshot rang out.

Rinaldi's arm froze, half crooked. His body straightened. Too much. A second shot exploded.

Rinaldi spun sideways, as though yanked by a chain.

"Down!" Slidell shoved me hard toward the pavement.
My knees cracked cement. My belly. My chest.
Another shot rang out.
A vehicle screamed south on Davidson.
Heart hammering, I looked up, barely raising my head.
Gun drawn, Slidell was thundering up the block.
Rinaldi lay still, long spider limbs arrayed terribly wrong.

22

Scrabbling to my feet, I ran up Thirty-fifth.

Sirens wailed in the distance. The previously deserted sidewalks were filling with the curious. Ahead, a circle was forming around Rinaldi. Between pairs of legs I could see his motionless form, a dark tendril oozing toward the curb from below his chest.

Shoving aside gawkers, I made my way up the street. Slidell was kneeling, face splotchy, both hands pressed to his partner's chest.

My heart leaped into my throat.

Rinaldi's eyelids were blue, his face morgue white. Rain soaked his hair and shirt. Blood crawled the pavement and oozed over the lip of the curb. Too much blood.

"Get back!" Slidell screamed, voice tremulous with rage. "Give the man some goddamn air!"

The circle expanded, immediately began to contract. Cell phones clicked, capturing images of the gore.

The distant wails grew louder. Increased in number. I knew Slidell had called in the code for officer down. Units were responding from all over the city.

"Let me do that," I said, dropping beside Slidell. "You deal with the crowd."

Slidell's eyes whipped to mine. He was breathing hard. "Yeah."

I slid my hands onto Rinaldi's chest below Slidell's palms. I could feel trembling in his arm.

"Hard! You gotta press hard!" A vein pounded up the center of Slidell's forehead. Wetness haloed his hair.

I nodded, unable to speak.

Shooting upright, Slidell lurched toward the gawkers, feet slipping in the rain and the slick of Rinaldi's blood.

"Get the hell back!" Slidell's upraised palms were a horrifying crimson.

I dropped my gaze, thoughts pointed at only one goal.

Stop the blood!

"Give me some fucking room! Now!" Slidell bellowed.

Stop the blood!

Too much! Dear God, no one could survive such a loss.

Stop the blood!

Seconds passed. The rain fell in a slow, steady drizzle.

A siren screamed to a stop close by. A second. A third. Lights pulsated, turning the street into a flashing whirlpool of red and blue.

Stop the blood!

Doors opened. Slammed. Footsteps pounded. Voices shouted.

Stop the blood!

Sensing movement and space, I glanced up, palms still pressed to Rinaldi's chest.

Uniformed cops were now muscling the onlookers back.

My eyes returned to my hands, now glossy and dark.

Stop the blood!

Feet appeared at my side, one pair in boots, one in New Balance running shoes. Muddy. Wet.

Boots squatted and spoke to me. I barely heard through the mantra controlling my mind.

Stop the blood!

Boots placed his hands over mine on the blood-soaked shirt. I looked into his eyes. The irises were blue, the whites latticed by a network of tiny red veins.

Boots nodded.

I rose and stepped back on rubber legs.

I knew the drill. ABC. Airway. Breathing. Circulation. I watched numbly as the paramedics went through it, checking Rinaldi's trachea, bagging him with oxygen, evaluating his carotid pulse.

Then they strapped Rinaldi to a gurney, lifted him, and slammed the doors. I watched the ambulance race into the Charlotte night.

Leaving the scene to others, Slidell and I drove straight to CMC. On the way we passed dozens of squad cars speeding toward NoDa. Dozens more clogged the streets. The city throbbed with sirens and pulsating lights.

The ER waiting room already held a half dozen cops. Barely acknowledging their presence, Slidell barked his name and demanded Rinaldi's doctor.

A receptionist ushered us to restrooms so we could wash the blood from our hands and arms. Or maybe it was a nurse. Or an orderly. Who knew? Upon our return, she asked us to take seats and wait.

Slidell started to bluster. I led him by one arm to a row of interlocking metal seats. His muscles felt tense as tree roots.

Sensitive to Slidell's mood, everyone left us alone. Those in law enforcement understood. Their presence was enough.

Slidell and I dropped into chairs and began our vigil, each lost in thoughts of our own.

I kept hearing the shots, picturing Rinaldi's ghostly face. The blood. Too much blood.

Every few minutes Slidell would lurch to his feet and disappear outside. Each time he returned, cigarette smoke rode him like rain on a dog. I almost envied him the diversion.

Slowly, the number of cops increased. Plainclothes detectives stood in groups with uniformed patrolmen, faces tense, voices hushed.

Finally, a grim-faced doctor approached wearing blood-spattered scrubs. A stain on one sleeve mimicked the shape of New Zealand. Why would I think of that?

Slidell and I rose, terrified, hopeful. The doctor's badge said *Meloy*.

Meloy told us that Rinaldi had taken two rounds to the chest and one to the abdomen. One wound was through and through. Two bullets remained in his body.

"He conscious?" Slidell asked, face fixed in grim resolution.

"He's still in surgery," Meloy said.

"He gonna make it?"

"Mr. Rinaldi has lost a lot of blood. Tissue damage is extensive."

Slidell forced his voice even. "That ain't an answer."

"The prognosis is not good."

Meloy led us to a staff lounge and told us to stay as long as we wanted.

"When's he come off the table?" Slidell asked.

"That's impossible to say."

Promising to find us if there were developments, Meloy left.

Rinaldi died at 11:42 P.M.

Slidell listened stone-faced as Meloy delivered the news. Then he turned and strode from the room.

A cop drove me home. I should have said thanks, but didn't. Like Slidell, I was too battered for niceties. Later I learned her name and sent a note. I think she understood.

Once in bed, I cried until I could cry no more. Then I fell into a dreamless sleep.

I awoke Sunday morning feeling something was wrong, but unsure what. When I remembered, I cried all over again.

The *Observer*'s headlines were huge, the kind reserved for the outbreak of war or peace. Bold, two-inch letters screamed POLICE DETECTIVE SLAIN!

TV and radio coverage was equally frenzied, the rhetoric wildly speculative. *Gang murder. Assassination. Drive-by shooting. Execution-style killing.*

Asa Finney did not escape notice. Finney was described as a self-proclaimed witch arrested for possession of the Greenleaf cauldron skull, and as a person of interest in the Satanic killing of Jimmy Klapec.

Allison Stallings's photo of Finney appeared on the front page of the *Observer,* on the Internet, and behind somber reporters at TV anchor desks. Everywhere, reports emphasized the fact that Rinaldi had been investigating both the Greenleaf and the Klapec cases.

My early morning sampling of media coverage left me despondent. And the day went downhill from there.

Katy called around ten to say she was sorry about Rinaldi. I thanked her, and asked about the picnic. She said it was about as much fun as a boil on the butt. And now they were sending her to some backass place in Buncombe County to help sort and tag documents. I said that her recent negativity was a real downer. Or something equally imprudent. She said I was the negative one, that I criticized everything about her. Like what? Her taste in music. I denied it. She challenged me to name a single group she liked. I couldn't. And so on. We hung up, hostile and angry.

Boyce Lingo was on the air by noon, railing against decadence and corruption and insisting the world remake itself in his narrow image. As before, he encouraged his constituents to take a proactive stance against evil and to insist that their elected officials do likewise.

Boyce pointed to Asa Finney as an example of all that was wrong in today's society. To my dismay, he referred to Finney as a minion of Satan, and implied a link to Rinaldi's murder.

A Google of Allison Stallings eventually revealed that she was a writer of true crime with one publication under her belt, a low-budget mass market exposé of a domestic homicide in Columbus, Georgia. The book wasn't even listed on Amazon.

Stallings had also earned photography credits in the *Columbus Ledger-Inquirer*, and one big score with the Associated Press.

Dear God. The woman was snooping for book ideas.

Around three, I checked my e-mail. There was a message from the OCME in Chapel Hill. It made three points. The chief was deeply troubled by my rant Friday morning. I was to abstain from all contact with the press. I'd be hearing from him first thing on Tuesday.

Ryan didn't call.

Charlie didn't call.

Birdie threw up on the bathroom rug.

In between e-mails and phone calls and vomit and tears, I cleaned. Not the run-the-vacuum-swipe-a-dust-cloth type slicking-up. I attacked the Annex with fury, toothbrush-scrubbing the bathroom grout, scouring the oven, changing the AC filters, defrosting the freezer, discarding just about everything in the medicine cabinet.

The intense physical activity worked. Until I stopped.

At six, I stood in my gleaming kitchen, grief once again threatening to overwhelm my composure. Birdie was in bunker mode atop the refrigerator.

"This won't do, Bird," I said.

The cat studied me, still wary of the vacuum.

"I should do something to lift my spirits."

No response from the lofty height of the Sub-Zero.

"Chinese," I said. "I'll order Chinese."

Bird repositioned his two front paws, centering them under his upraised chin.

"I know what you're thinking," I said. "You can't constantly sit home eating out of little white cartons."

Bird neither agreed nor disagreed.

"Good point. I'll go to Baoding and order all my favorites."

And that's what I did.

And the day really hit the mung heap.

Though restaurant dining is among my favorite activities, I've always felt the need of a social component. When alone, I eat with Birdie, in front of the TV.

But Baoding is a southeast Charlotte end-of-the-weekend tradition. On Sunday evenings I always see faces I know.

That night was no exception.

Unhappily, these were not faces I wanted to, well, face.

Martinis are a Baoding specialty, particularly for those awaiting take-out. Not very Chinese, but there it is.

When I entered, Pete was at the bar, talking to a woman seated on his right. Both were drinking what I guessed were apple martinis.

Quick reversal of course.

Too late.

"Tempe. Yo! Over here."

Springing from his stool, Pete caught me before I could escape out the door.

"You have to meet Summer."

"It's not a good—"

Beaming, Pete tugged me across the restaurant. Summer had turned and was now gazing in our direction.

It was worse than I'd imagined. Summer was overblond, with breasts the size of beach balls, and far too little blouse to accommodate them. During introductions, she wrapped a territorial hand around Pete's upper arm.

I offered congratulations on their engagement.

Summer thanked me. Coolly.

Pete beamed on, oblivious to the hypothermics.

I asked how wedding plans were progressing.

Summer shrugged, speared an apple slice with a red plastic swizzle stick.

Mercifully, at that moment their order arrived.

Summer popped from her stool like a spring-loaded doll. Snatching the bag, she mumbled, "Nice to meetcha," and made for the door, leaving a gale of fleur-de-something in her wake.

"She's nervous," Pete said.

"Undoubtedly," I said.

"You OK?" Pete studied my face. "You look tired."

"Rinaldi was killed yesterday."

Pete's brows did that confusion thing they do.

"Eddie Rinaldi. Slidell's partner."

"The cop shooting that's been all over the news?"

I nodded.

"You've known Rinaldi forever."

"Yes."

"You were there?"

"Yes."

"Shit, Tempe. I'm really sorry."

"Thanks."

"You holding up all right?"

"Yes." I could manage only monosyllabic replies.

Pete took my hand. "I'll call you."

I nodded, faked a smile, afraid speaking would unleash the pain that was a tangible presence in my chest.

"That's my Tempe. Tough as a lumberjack."

Pete kissed my cheek. Then he was gone.

Closing my eyes, I gripped the back of Summer's empty bar stool. Behind me, conversation burbled. Cheerful diners, enjoying the company of others.

My nose took in sesame oil, garlic, and soy, smells from the happy years, when Pete, Katy, and I made Sunday-evening outings to Baoding.

The past few days had been overwhelming. Rinaldi. Katy. The chief. Boyce Lingo. Takeela Freeman. Jimmy Klapec. Susan Redmon. Now Pete and Summer.

I felt a tremor low in my chest.

Took a deep breath.

"Waiting for take-out?" The voice was right at my ear.

I opened my eyes. Charlie Hunt was leaning down, face close to mine.

"Buy you a Perrier?" Charlie asked.

What I did next I will always regret.

"Buy me a martini," I said.

23

I DON'T REMEMBER THE REST OF THAT NIGHT OR MUCH OF MON-
day. Arguing with Charlie. Driving. Tossing items into a supermarket
cart. Fighting with a corkscrew. Otherwise, thirty-six hours of my life
disappeared.

Tuesday morning I awoke alone in my bed. Though the sun was just
cresting the horizon, I could tell the day would be clear. Wind teased
the magnolia leaves outside my window, flipping some to show their
undersides pale against the dark green of their unturned brethren.

The jeans I'd worn Sunday lay kicked to a baseboard. My shirt and
undies hung from a chair back. I was wearing sweats.

Birdie was watching me from under the dresser.

Downstairs, the TV was blaring.

I sat up and swung my feet to the floor, testing.

My mouth felt dry, my whole body dehydrated.

OK. Not too bad.

I stood.

Blood exploded into my dilated cranial vessels. My eyeballs pounded.

I lay back down. The pillow smelled of Burberry and sex.

Dear God. I couldn't face students in my condition.

Staggering to my laptop, I sent an e-mail to my lab and teaching
assistant, Alex, saying I was ill and asking if she could proctor the
bone quiz then dismiss class.

When I raised my lids again the cat was gone and the clock said eight.

Forcing myself vertical, I trudged to the shower. After, my hands trembled as I combed wet tangles from my hair and brushed my teeth.

Downstairs, the classic movie channel was pumping out *The Great Escape*. I found the remote and clicked off as Steve McQueen cycle-jumped a barbwire fence.

The kitchen told the story like a graphic novel. Heaped in the sink were remnants of a frozen pizza and Dove Bar wrappers and sticks. Two empty wine bottles sat on the counter. A third, half-empty, had been abandoned on the table beside a single glass.

I ate a bowl of cornflakes and knocked back two aspirins with coffee. Then I threw up.

Though I rebrushed my teeth, my mouth still tasted noxious. I chugged a full glass of water. Tried Advil.

As expected, nothing helped. I knew only time and metabolism would provide relief.

I was crushing the pizza box when my mind began to dial into focus.

It was Tuesday. I'd spoken to no one since Sunday.

Though Monday was a holiday, I'd surely been missed.

Smashing the crumpled cardboard into the trash, I hurried to the phone.

Dead air.

I followed the cord to the wall. The connector was snugly snapped into its jack. I began checking extensions.

The bedroom handheld was buried under the discarded jeans. It had been left in talk mode, blocking operation of the rest of the system.

Had I turned it off? Had Charlie?

How long had the line been out of service?

After disconnecting, I hit TALK. Dial tone. I disconnected again.

Where was my cell? Using the house phone, I dialed that number. Nothing.

After considerable searching, I found the mobile downstairs in the back of a drawer in the study. It had been shut off.

Doubtful Charlie did that, I thought, wondering at my alcohol-addled motivation.

I was hooking the mobile to its charger when the landline rang.

"Where the bloody hell have you been?"

Slidell's tone sent an ice pick straight through my brain.

"It was a holiday," I said defensively.

"Well, ex-c-u-u-se me if murder don't take time off."

I was too sick to come up with a clever rejoinder. "You've made progress finding Rinaldi's shooter?"

Slidell allowed me several heel-cooling moments of muteness. Background noises suggested he was at police headquarters.

"I'm barred from the investigation. Seems I'm too *invested* to be objective." Slidell snorted. "Invested. They talk about me like they're talking about a goddamn portfolio."

It was probably a good decision. I kept the thought to myself.

"But I got a gut feeling this is all connected. I work Klapec and the Greenleaf cellar, eventually I nail the slime that took Rinaldi out."

Slidell stopped. Cleared his throat.

"I talked to Isabella Cortez."

"Who?" The name meant nothing to me.

"Takeela Freeman? Grandma?"

"Right. What did you learn?"

"Nada. But I also talked to Donna Scott-Rosenberg. The lady tells a good story. Her version puts the cemetery caper square on Finney."

"Big surprise. What does she say about Susan Redmon's remains?"

"Says when her family left for California she decided packing body parts would be too risky. Didn't want her old man to find them. Didn't want to leave them behind in the house. So she gave them to one of her Goth buddies, a kid named Manuel Escriva."

I was sweating and nausea was threatening again.

"Escriva wasn't hard to find. He's doing a nickel-dime for possession with intent to distribute. Took a drive up to central prison yesterday."

In one way Slidell and I are much alike. Though devastated by Rinaldi's death, neither of us would permit others to see our pain. But, while Skinny had carried on, I'd come apart. I'd blown off the investigation, and for the first time in my life, was failing to carry out my academic duties. Shame burned my already flushed face.

"Guy's an arrogant little prick. Took some bartering, but Escriva finally admits to selling the bones for fifty bucks."

"To whom?"

"Neighborhood witch doctor."

"Cuervo," I guessed.

"None other."

"Except for unlawful possession of human remains, that puts T-Bird in the clear."

"I ain't so sure. Escriva said Cuervo was into bad shit."

"Meaning?" The phone felt clammy in my palm.

"I pose that very question, Escriva just gives me this cocky little smirk, makes me want to rip his face off. Then he demands something it ain't possible to arrange with the warden. Things get a little heated. As I'm leaving he calls out. I turn around. He's still grinning, making some kind of voodoo symbol with his hands. He says, 'Beware the demon, cop man.' "

"You're saying Escriva accused Cuervo of devil worship?"

"That's my take."

"Did you ask Escriva where Cuervo might be?"

"He claims they've had no contact in five years."

"Did you ask about Asa Finney?"

"Swears he don't know him."

"What are you doing now?"

I heard movement, then Slidell's voice grew muffled, as though he'd covered the receiver with one hand. "Going through Rinaldi's notes."

"You still have them?" I was surprised the case notes hadn't been confiscated by the team investigating the shooting.

"I made photocopies yesterday morning." Slidell's words sharpened as he withdrew his lips from contact with the mouthpiece. "Trip to Raleigh ate up the rest of the day."

Probably a cover. I couldn't have looked at those notes yesterday, either.

"I need you to make it solid that Susan Redmon is our Greenleaf vic. Be a real pisser if that skull don't go with the stuff in that coffin."

I fought down a bitter taste in my throat. I'd be no good in the classroom, but at least I could do that.

"I'm heading to the lab now. I'm sorry about yesterday. Please keep me in the loop."

Slidell either grunted or belched.

After disconnecting, I splashed cold water on my face, then checked the messages on my cell.

One from Katy. One from Charlie. Three from Slidell. One from

Jennifer Roberts, a colleague at UNCC. Everyone said pretty much the same thing. *Call me.*

I tried Katy, but got her voice mail. Too early? Or had she already gone to work? Or departed Charlotte to work on the project in Buncombe County? I left basically the same message she had left me.

Slidell I would see soon. Talking to Charlie would require some preplanning. Calling Jennifer Roberts would blow my cover at UNCC. She'd have to wait.

Before leaving home, I tried a bowl of Campbell's chicken noodle soup.

That came up, too.

After brushing my teeth a third time, I gathered my keys and purse and headed out the door.

And nearly fell over a large Dean & DeLuca bag sitting on the stoop. A note had been paper-clipped to one handle.

Tempe:
   I know this is a rough time. I'm sorry if I offended you, but I was concerned for your safety. Please take this as a token of my sincere apology. And please, please. Eat.
   Call when you feel up to turning on the phone.

Charlie

I was mortified. Sweet Jesus. What had Charlie tried to prevent?

Placing the food on the kitchen counter, I grabbed a Diet Coke from the fridge, and started for the lab.

The movement of the car. The fumes. The soda. I almost lost it again.

OK. I would suffer until my body returned to normalcy. I would pay the price.

The upside was that the bender had played out at home. I'd harmed no one. I'd engaged in nothing more foolish than a sweaty tryst with an old high school flame.

Sadly, that last assumption would prove to be false.

Remember my comment concerning Mondays at a morgue? Double that for Tuesdays coming off holiday weekends.

All three pathologists were present, and the board showed eight new corpses. Since Rinaldi's was not among them, I assumed Larabee, Siu, or Hartigan had come in the previous day to perform that autopsy. Given the circumstances, my money was on the boss.

Again, I was overcome with guilt. While I'd been destroying brain cells in a grand mal of self-pity, others had been carrying on doing their jobs.

I went straight to the cooler and pulled out Cuervo's cauldron skull and leg bones and Finney's mandible. Since both autopsy rooms were in use, I spread plastic on my office desk, lay the remains on it, and added the teeth that I'd taken from Susan Redmon's coffin.

In two hours, I was finished. Every tooth fit. Every detail of age, gender, ancestry, and state of preservation matched. The measurements I'd taken in the tomb were compatible with those I'd taken from the skull. Fordisc 3.0 agreed. If needed I could run DNA comparisons, but I was convinced the skull, mandible, and coffin remains belonged to the same individual.

Now and then I saw Hawkins or Mrs. Flowers or one of the pathologists hurry past my open door. Larabee stopped at one point, looked at me oddly, moved on. No one ventured into my office.

I was composing my report on Susan Redmon when Mrs. Flowers rang to announce the call I'd been dreading. Dr. Larke Tyrell, head of North Carolina's medical examiner system, was on the line from Chapel Hill.

"Could you possibly say that I'm not here?" I asked.

"I could." Prim.

"I'm a little under the weather today."

"You look a bit peaked."

"Perhaps you could suggest that I've left early?"

"I suppose you might."

Grateful, I didn't ask what she meant.

Returning to the Redmon report proved futile. I couldn't concentrate sufficiently to string words into meaningful sentences. I needed to stick to tasks that were more concrete. Visual.

For lack of a better idea, I returned to the cooler, withdrew Jimmy Klapec's vertebrae and the mutilated tissue that had been excised from his chest and belly and set them on the desk beside Susan Redmon's bones. Then I got out the school portrait of Takeela Freeman and the mug shots of Jimmy Klapec and T-Bird Cuervo and added them to the assemblage.

I was staring at the sad little collection, hoping for some sort of epiphany, when Larabee entered my office without knocking. Crossing to the desk, he loomed over me.

"You look awful."

"I think I've got the flu."

I could feel Larabee studying my face. "Maybe something you ate."

"Maybe," I said.

Larabee knew my history. Knew I was lying. Wanting to hide the guilt and self-loathing, I kept my eyes down.

Larabee continued looming. He was very good at it.

"What's all this?"

I told him about Susan Redmon.

Larabee picked up the jar and inspected the two hunks of Jimmy Klapec's carved flesh.

"Slidell's convinced this all ties together." I swept a hand over the desk. "Crack this, he says, we'll crack Rinaldi's murder."

"You're not convinced?"

"He was working the cases."

"Rinaldi was a cop."

We both knew what he meant. Disgruntled drug lords. Vengeful inmates. Dissatisfied victims. Most do little beyond fantasizing the settling of perceived scores. A dangerous few take action.

Larabee swapped the excised specimens for the mug shot of T-Bird Cuervo.

"Who's this guy?"

"Thomas Cuervo, an Ecuadoran *santero* who rented the Greenleaf property from Kenneth Roseboro. Went by T-Bird."

"The house with the cauldrons and skulls in the basement?"

I nodded. "Trouble is, Cuervo's vanished. Either no one knows or no one's willing to say where he is."

Larabee studied the mug shot a very long time. Then, "I know exactly where he is."

24

LARABEE LED ME THROUGH THE COOLER INTO THE FREEZER, TO A
gurney rolled to the far back wall. Unzipping the body bag, he revealed
a very icy corpse.

"Meet Unknown 358-08."

I studied the face. Though blanched, distorted, and badly abraded,
there was no question it belonged to T-Bird Cuervo.

"How long has he been in storage?"

Larabee consulted the tag. "August twenty-sixth."

That definitely put Cuervo in the clear on Klapec and Rinaldi.

"Why didn't I know this body was back here?"

"He arrived the day you left for Montreal. The case didn't call for an
anthro consult. By the time you returned, I'd put him on ice."

And I'd had no reason to venture into the freezer.

"He's your boy, right?"

I nodded, arms hugging my sides in the cold.

"Poor bastard took on a Lynx. Just south of the Bland Street Station."

Larabee was referring to the brand-new light-rail arm of CATS, the
Charlotte Area Transit System. A bit much with the Panthers and
Bobcats, I know. But then, mass transit planners aren't known for their
subtlety.

"Cuervo was hit by a train?"

"Crushed his legs and pelvis. He carried no ID, and no one ever
claimed him."

"Did you run prints?" My teeth weren't chattering, but they were thinking about it.

"Yeah, right. This guy was dragged almost fifty feet. Palms and fingers were raw meat."

"How did it happen?"

"The driver thought he saw something on the track, threw his emergency brake and blew his horn, but couldn't stop. Apparently a train going fifty-five miles per hour takes up to six hundred feet to come to a complete halt."

"Ouch." I was amazed Cuervo wasn't in worse shape.

"The cross arms were lowered and the bells and lights were activated before the train approached the station. The driver had also blown his horn."

"Was the driver tested?" I was amazed I hadn't heard about this incident.

"Drug and alcohol clean."

"Cuervo was alive when the train hit him?"

"Definitely."

"And you had no reason to doubt that his death was an accident?"

"No. And his blood alcohol level was .08. Is the guy legal?"

"Cuervo held both U.S. and Ecuadoran citizenship."

"Any family here?"

"Apparently not. He lived alone on Greenleaf, operated a shop called La Botánica Buena Salud off South Boulevard. The INS has no permanent address for him either here or in Ecuador."

"Makes it tough to track next of kin."

Larabee zipped the bag and we exited to the corridor.

Back in my office, I dialed Slidell.

"I'll be a sonovabitch."

"Yeah," I agreed.

For a full thirty seconds, the only sounds I heard were phones ringing on Slidell's end of the line.

"This morning I did some canvassing along that road leading to where Klapec was found. You'll never guess what's tucked away in those woods."

"Why don't you tell me." Though the freezer had calmed my tremors and settled my stomach, already I was perspiring and my head was starting to rumble. I was not in the mood for Twenty Questions.

"A camp. I'm not talking Camp Sun in the Pines, you know, canoe-ing and hiking and 'Kumbaya.' I'm talking Camp Full Moon. As in witches and warlocks baying at it."

"Wiccan?"

"Yep. And, according to the neighbors, who ain't exactly thrilled with all the jujuism in their backyards, things were cooking the night before Klapec turned up."

I started to ask what that meant, but Slidell kept on talking.

"Drumming, dancing, chanting."

"The activity could be completely unrelated to Klapec."

"Right. A friendly little wienie roast. I want to see Cuervo."

"Come on down."

Slidell hesitated a beat. Then, "And I want your take on something Eddie wrote."

I'd barely hung up when my cell phone sounded.

Nine-one-nine area code.

Larke Tyrell.

My fragile gut clenched in anticipation of the upcoming conversa-tion.

I'd just qualified for certification by the American Board of Forensic Anthropology when Tyrell was appointed the state's chief medical examiner. We met through work I was doing for the North Carolina State Bureau of Investigation, reassembling and identifying two drug dealers murdered and dismembered by outlaw bikers.

I was one of Tyrell's first hires as a consulting specialist, and though our relationship was generally congenial, over the years we'd had our differences. As a result, I'd learned that the chief could be cynical and exceedingly dictatorial.

I drank water from the glass at my elbow, then, carefully, clicked on.

"Dr. Brennan."

"Tempe. Sorry to hear you're not feeling shipshape." Born in the lowcountry to a Marine Corps family, then a two-hitch marine him-self before med school, Tyrell spoke like a military version of Andy Griffith.

"Thank you."

"I'm concerned, Tempe."

"It's just a flu."

"About your outburst with Boyce Lingo."

"I'd like to explain—"

"Mr. Lingo is irate."

"He's always irate."

"Do you have any idea the public image nightmare you've created?" Tyrell was fond of the rhetorical question. Assuming this was one, I said nothing.

"This office has an official spokesperson whose responsibility it is to interact with the media. I can't have my staff airing their personal views on medical examiner cases."

"Lingo foments fear so he can make himself look like a hero."

"He's a county commissioner."

"He's dangerous."

"And you think throwing a tantrum for the press is the way to neutralize him?"

I closed my lids. They felt like sandpaper sliding over my eyeballs.

"You're right. My behavior was inexcusable."

"Agreed. So explain why you ignored my direct order?" Tyrell sounded angrier than I'd ever heard him.

"I'm sorry," I said lamely. "You've lost me."

"Why would you brief a reporter when I requested you cease all contact with the press?"

"What reporter?"

I heard paper rustle.

"Allison Stallings. Woman had the brass ones to call my office for confirmation of information that should have been confidential. Tempe, you know that data pertaining to a child is particularly sensitive."

"What child?"

"Anson Tyler. It's beyond my comprehension how you could have shown so little respect for that dead little boy and his poor, grieving family."

The sweat felt cold on my face. I had no memory of talking to Allison Stallings.

But Monday was a blank. Was it possible I'd made contact, hoping, in some boozy delusion, to clear up the misconception that Anson Tyler's death was connected to that of Jimmy Klapec? To clarify that the Catawba River headless body was not linked to the Lake Wylie headless body? Or to the cauldron head we now knew to be Susan Redmon's?

Or had Stallings called me? Was that why I'd shut down and shoved my mobile into a drawer?

Tyrell was still talking, his voice somber.

"—this is a serious breach. Disregarding my order. Disclosing confidential information. This behavior can't be ignored. Action must be taken."

I felt too weak to argue. Or to point out that Stallings was not a reporter.

"I will think long and hard what that action should be. We'll talk soon."

I put the phone down with one trembling hand. Finished the water. Dragged myself to the lounge and refilled the glass from the tap. Downed two aspirins. Returned to my office. Took up the Klapec report. Set it down, unable to think through the pounding in my head.

I was sitting there, doing nothing, when Slidell appeared with a grease-soaked bag of Price's fried chicken. Normally, I'd have pounced. Not today.

"Well, don't you look like something the dog threw up."

"And you're a picture of manly vitality?"

Unkind, but true. Slidell's face was gray and a dark crescent underhung each eye.

Placing the chicken on the file cabinet, Skinny dropped into a chair opposite my desk. "Maybe you should go home and rack out."

"It's just a bug."

Slidell regarded me as a cat might a sparrow. I was sure he could smell the wine sweat coating my skin.

"Yeah," he said. "Those bugs can be a bitch. Where's Cuervo?"

I led him to the freezer. He asked the same questions I'd asked Larabee. I relayed the information the ME had provided.

Back in my office, the fried poultry smell was overwhelming. Slidell dug in the bag and began on a drumstick. Grease trickled down his chin. It was all I could do not to gag.

"Sure you don't want some?" Garbled.

I shook my head. Swallowed. "What is it you want me to read?"

Wiping his hands on a napkin, Slidell pulled papers from a pocket and tossed them on the blotter.

"Eddie's notes. That's your copy."

I unfolded and scanned the pages.

Like the man, the handwriting was neat and precise. So was the thinking.

Rinaldi had recorded the time, location, and content of every interview he'd conducted. It appeared that those he'd questioned either lacked or withheld contact information. Ditto for surnames.

"He got only first names or street names," I said. "Cyrus. Vince. Dagger. Cool Breeze. And no addresses or phone numbers."

"Probably didn't want to spook the little freaks by pushing too hard." Slidell's jaw muscles bunched. As though suddenly devoid of appetite, he shoved a half-eaten chicken breast into the bag and sailed it into my wastebasket. "Probably figured he could find them later if needed."

"He used some kind of shorthand system."

"Eddie liked to get his thoughts down quick, but he worried some scumbag defense attorney might latch on to his first impressions and make a big deal of them in court if they later turned out to be off. So's not to provide ammo, he kept his comments cryptic, that's what he called it. Cryptic. I thought maybe you could make something of it."

Rinaldi had questioned a chicken hawk named Vince on Saturday. I read the entry.

JK. 9/29. LSA with RN acc. to VG. RN - PIT. CTK. TV. 10/9-10/11? CFT. 10. 500.

"Vince must be the informant Rinaldi mentioned when you talked by phone as we were leaving Cuervo's shop. Maybe he's VG. JK could be Jimmy Klapec. RN could be the john Vince described as looking like Rick Nelson."

Slidell nodded.

"The numbers are probably dates," I went on. "LSA is standard code for 'last seen alive.' Maybe September twenty-ninth is the last day Vince remembered seeing Klapec with this Rick Nelson character."

"So far we're on the same page," Slidell said. "But Funderburke first spotted Klapec's body on October ninth, called it in on the eleventh. If that's what this Vince is saying, where's Klapec from late September until early October when he gets himself dead? Assuming Funderburke and his pooch ain't totally wacko."

I was too busy running possibilities to answer.

"CFT would be Cabo Fish Taco," I said. "He was meeting Vince there at ten. Maybe Vince wanted five hundred dollars for his information."

"TV?"

"Vince had seen Rick Nelson on television?"

"PIT? CTK?"

"PIT is the airport code for Pittsburgh. Maybe those are abbreviations for cities."

I logged onto the computer and opened Google.

"CTK is the code for Akron, Ohio," I said.

"What's the significance of that?"

"I don't know."

Slidell laced his fingers on his belly, dropped his chin, and thrust out his legs. His socks were Halloween orange.

"Eddie did some digging while waiting to go back out to NoDa," he said. "Read his last entry."

RN = BLA = GYE. Greensboro. 10/9. 555-7038. CTK-TV-9/27. VG, solicitation 9/28-9/29.

GYE 9/27?

I Googled the two three-letter combos.

"BLA is the airport in Barcelona, Venezuela," I said, somewhat deflated. "GYE is in Guayaquil, Ecuador."

"If he's referencing cities by code, why write out Greensboro?"

It was a good point.

"The seven-digit sequence looks like a phone number," I said lamely.

"It is."

"Whose?"

Slidell's answer was a shocker.

25

"I PUNCH IT UP, A VOICE TELLS ME I'VE REACHED COMMISSIONER Lingo's office."

"Why would Rinaldi have Lingo's number?"

"Good question."

I reread Rinaldi's last entry.

VG, solicitation 9/28-9/29.

"VG could be Vince. Maybe Rinaldi learned the kid's last name, and the fact that he was busted for solicitation."

"Right around the time we're guessing Klapec disappeared."

"Why did Rinaldi think that was worth noting?"

Slidell shrugged. "Can't hurt to pull arrest records for those dates. If nothing else, it might give us Vince's last name. Kid's in the wind, by the way. No one's seen him since Saturday."

"Where does he live?"

"His buddies ain't busting their balls to share, but they think he was mostly sleeping on the streets."

"Do you plan to pay Lingo a visit?"

"Later. Right now I'm retracing Eddie's steps, seeing what I can score on this dipshit Vince."

"Strictly regarding Klapec," I said.

"Strictly."

"Anything new on Asa Finney?"

"Unless I find a smoking howitzer in the guy's shorts, he sees a judge on the bones rap, posts bond, and they kick him tomorrow."

"What's your take on him?"

Slidell snorted. "Could have been a stud except for the head-on with zits."

I ignored the unkind remark. Finney couldn't help the condition of his skin. "But a killer?"

"Finney's a witch. Witch camp's a spit from the Klapec scene. Neighbors report a lot of drumming and rattling the night before the kid's body turns up. One says he saw a Ford Focus leaving the area long after the party was over."

I remembered the car in the Pineville driveway.

"Finney drives a Focus," I said.

"Don't take a genius to connect the dots." Again, the tensing of the jaw. "I'm thinking Finney's wizard pals maybe also capped Eddie."

"Why?"

"He was learning too much."

As I started to reply Slidell shot upright in his chair.

"Rick Nelson." A beefy finger jabbed the air in my direction. "Except for the zits, Finney's a dead ringer for Rick Nelson. Think about it. The hair. The come-fuck-me smile. Sonovabitch."

"You're suggesting Finney is the violent john described by Vince?"

Slidell stood and circled to my side of the desk. The finger flipped the pages of Rinaldi's notes.

RN-PIT. CTK. TV.

"Eddie was saying Rick Nelson with pits. Zit pits. That's just what he'd say. I'll be goddamned."

"Maybe." I was unconvinced.

"What? It describes Finney to a T. Maybe that'll give us enough to hold the little prick on Klapec."

"I'd still run the Akron angle." I truncated Slidell's objection. "See if Finney booked a flight or has ties there."

"Yeah. Yeah."

We fell silent, staring at Rinaldi's enigmatic code.

After several seconds, I sensed a shift in Slidell's attention, felt his eyes crawl my face. I didn't look up. Didn't want to pursue the conversation I suspected was coming.

Instead of commenting, Slidell yanked a spiral from his pocket, scribbled, then tore out and laid the page on my desk.

"My girlfriend used to catch a lot of these bugs. You feel like it, you call her."

I heard footsteps. Then my office was still.

Again, shame scorched my face. Larabee knew. Slidell knew. Who else had seen through my pathetic flu story?

I was reading Slidell's scrawl when the ME stuck his head in the door.

"Get in here quick—" Seeing my look, he stopped. "What?"

"Slidell has a girlfriend."

"No way."

"Verlene Something with a W." The name was spelled Wryznyk.

"I'll be damned." Larabee remembered his purpose in coming. "Lingo's foaming at the mouth again."

"God almighty!"

I followed Larabee into the lounge. Every station was carrying coverage of the Rinaldi shooting. The TV was tuned to one of them.

Lingo was holding forth outside a cemetery. Police barricades were going up on the street around him.

"—no longer sacred? When lawbreakers butcher those who risk their lives to keep our city safe? Those brave officers who protect our homes and keep our children from harm? I'll tell you what it is. It is the beginning of the end for decent society.

"I am standing at the entrance to Sharon Memorial Park. Detective Edward Rinaldi will be buried here tomorrow. He was fifty-six, a policeman for thirty-eight years, a beloved member of this community, a God-fearing man. Detective Rinaldi is not alone."

Lingo read from a list in his hand.

"Officer Sean Clark, thirty-four. Officer Jeffrey Shelton, thirty-five. Officer John Burnette, twenty-five. Officer Andy Nobles, twenty-six."

Lingo's eyes rolled up.

"I name but a few of the fallen." The porcine face creased in concern. "Does the fault lie solely with the evildoers?" Solemn head shake. "I think not. The fault lies with a system of laws designed to protect the guilty. With libertine scientists who undermine the efforts of our brothers and sisters in uniform."

I felt my innards curdle.

"Many of you witnessed the assault on my person last Friday. Dr. Temperance Brennan, employed by *your* university, by *your* medical examiner, institutions funded by *your* tax dollars. Dr. Brennan has seen the carnage. She knows of the battle raging on our streets. Does she work to convict those like Asa Finney? Those who have chosen the serpent's path? Quite the opposite. She makes excuses for these criminals. Defends their pagan practices."

Lingo drilled the camera with a look of heart-stopping sincerity.

"It is time for change. As your elected representative, I intend to see that change brought about."

There was an aerial shot of the scene, then the program cut to an anchorwoman. Above her left shoulder, a street map diagrammed the course of the next day's funeral procession.

"Services will begin with eleven o'clock mass at St. Ann's Catholic Church. The cavalcade will then proceed along Park, Woodlawn, Wendover, Providence, and Sharon Amity. Those streets will be closed to traffic until midafternoon.

"Since Sunday, members of law enforcement have been arriving from all over the country. Those unable to attend mass or to march in the procession will gather at the cemetery. Thousands are expected to turn out along the route to bid final farewell to Detective Rinaldi. Motorists are encouraged—"

Larabee snapped off the set.

"Who votes for freaking lunatics like Lingo?"

We both knew the answer.

"You did the autopsy?" I asked, steeling my voice, avoiding eye contact.

"Monday."

"Any surprises?"

"One through-and-through gunshot wound at the T-12 level. Two XTP's lodged in the thorax. I removed one from the right lung, the other from the heart."

Larabee didn't have to explain. I knew the bullet. Extreme Terminal Performance. A nasty little slug designed to expand for maximal organ damage.

Grabbing a Diet Coke, I returned to my office. The phone was blinking.

Both messages had been left by UNCC colleagues. Marion Ireland was returning my call concerning use of the scanning electron microscope. Jennifer Roberts simply asked again that I phone her.

I gulped more Coke. It was definitely helping to settle my stomach. But the headache was still off the Richter, and my enthusiasm for human interaction was low.

My booze-battered cortex offered a list of excuses. The conscience guys countered each one.

Scanning electron microscopy is now irrelevant.

Not your thinking on Friday.

Klapec's been ID'ed. Histological age estimation is now superfluous.

Why the shadowing in the Haversian systems?

The cortical guys had no hypothesis.

Do it, Brennan.

Could be pointless.

Can't know until you try.

Score a win in the conscience column.

After another Coke hit, I dialed. Ireland answered on the first ring. I asked about her weekend, sat out the answer, then explained my puzzlement concerning the irregularities in the thin sections I'd made from Jimmy Klapec's femur.

"At a magnification of one hundred, everything looks dandy. When I crank it to four hundred, I pick up odd discolorations in some of the Haversian canals. I don't know what they are."

"Fungal? Pathological? Taphonomic?"

"That's what I'd like to clarify."

"It will take a while to prepare your specimens. I'll have to etch them with nitric acid, place them in a vacuum dessicator, then dust them with gold palladium."

"I can drop them off anytime."

"If all goes well, they should be ready by late afternoon tomorrow."

That would work. Rinaldi's funeral was at eleven.

"I'll be there within the hour."

Allowing no time for a second cerebral spat, I dialed Roberts. She, too, was right by her phone.

"Dr. Roberts."

"It's Tempe."

"Thanks so much for calling me back. I'm sorry I bothered you on a holiday weekend. I should have known you'd be out."

"It's no bother." I was out, no question. Just not in the sense she meant.

"I understand you're not feeling well today?"

"Just a flu. I'm much better now."

"Hang on."

I heard the receiver tap a desktop, footsteps, then a closing door. I pictured Jennifer crossing the office two down from mine. Identical desk, credenza, filing cabinets, and shelves, hers filled with volumes on animism, henotheism, totemism, and dozens of *ism*'s of which I was ignorant.

"Sorry." She spoke softly. "There are students in the hallway."

"I think they camp out there to avoid paying rent."

She laughed nervously. "You may be right." I heard slow inhalation, release. "OK. This is difficult."

Please, God. Not a personal problem. Not today.

"I read in the *Observer* that you're investigating the altar discovered last Monday on Greenleaf Avenue."

"Yes." That surprised me.

"Human bones were among the objects recovered."

"Yes." I had no idea where this was going.

"Last Thursday, a headless body was found at Lake Wylie—"

"Jennifer, I can't discuss—"

"Please. Bear with me."

I let her go on.

"The victim was identified as a teenaged boy named Jimmy Klapec. His body was marked with satanic symbology. Earlier, I haven't the date, another headless boy was pulled from the Catawba River. I don't know if that corpse was similarly mutilated."

Obviously she'd heard, or been told of, Boyce Lingo's tirade. I didn't confirm or deny the information.

"The police have arrested a young man named Asa Finney. He's been charged with possession of human remains and is a suspect in the Klapec homicide."

"Yes." All that had been reported in news coverage. I didn't mention that Slidell also suspected Finney of involvement in Rinaldi's murder.

"They've arrested the wrong man," Roberts said.

"The police are conducting a full investigation."

"Asa Finney is a Wiccan, not a Satanist. Can you appreciate the enormous difference?"

"I have a rudimentary understanding," I said.

"The public does not. Asa is a self-proclaimed witch, it's true. Have you seen his Web site?"

I admitted that I had not.

"Go there. Read his postings. You will find the musings of a kind and gentle soul."

"I will."

"There is a Wiccan camp at Lake Wylie. Though I don't know the exact location, I know that Jimmy Klapec's body was found at Lake Wylie. That will not put Asa Finney in a good light."

I didn't mention the books by Anton LaVey, the resemblance to Rick Nelson, or the Ford Focus seen in the area the night of Klapec's murder.

"In today's climate of religious extremism, there are those who condemn beliefs they don't understand. Responsible, intelligent Christians who would rather see people dead than following what they consider pagan practices. Their numbers are few, but these fanatics exist."

I heard a voice in the background. Jennifer asked me to hold on. There was muffled conversation, but I could make out no words.

"Sorry. Where was I? Yes. County Commissioner Lingo has twice mentioned Asa Finney by name, fingering him as a disciple of the devil, an example of all that is wrong in today's world. Given the atmosphere of anger created by Saturday's police shooting, I fear for Asa's ability to get a fair hearing."

"He has excellent counsel." I didn't mention names.

"Charles Hunt is a public defender."

"Charles Hunt is very good." In more ways than one. I didn't mention that, either.

Jennifer lowered her voice further, as though fearing her words might carry through the door.

"Asa Finney stole bones from a crypt when he was seventeen. It was a juvenile prank, stupid and thoughtless. That's a far cry from murder."

How did she know that? I didn't ask.

"The police are doing a thorough investigation," I said.

"Are they? Asa Finney is a loner. They will find no one to vouch for him. Will Asa be sacrificed on the altar of Boyce Lingo's ambition?"

I couldn't figure Jennifer's interest in Finney. Did her zeal grow from a commitment to the principles of her discipline? Or was it born of something more personal?

"I'm unclear what it is you want me to do."

"Nullify Lingo's poison. Make a public statement. You're a forensic specialist. People will listen to you."

"I'm sorry, Jennifer. I can't do that."

"Then talk to Lingo. Reason with him."

"Why are you so concerned about Asa Finney?"

"He is innocent."

"How can you know that?"

There was a moment of dead air, then, "We are members of the same coven."

"You are Wiccan?" I couldn't keep the surprise from my voice. I'd known Jennifer eight years and hadn't a clue.

"Yes."

I heard an indrawn breath then silence. I waited.

"Come to Full Moon tonight. We are having an esbat ritual. Meet us. Learn our philosophy."

My battered brain cells were screaming for sleep. I started to decline.

"You will see. Ours is a joyous religion born of kinship with nature. Wiccans celebrate life, we do not take it."

The conscience guys piped a voice through the pain in my head.

While Slidell was drowning his grief in work, you were drowning yours in booze.

"When?"

"Seven P.M."

Barring horrendous traffic, I could make it to the university and get home in time for a power nap before leaving for Full Moon.

I reached for my tablet.

"I'll need directions."

26

THE NAP DIDN'T HAPPEN. IRELAND INSISTED ON SHARING A BLOW-by-blow of her SEM prep process. Then I spent an hour creeping through a construction slowdown on I-85. I arrived at the Annex in time to feed Birdie, pop two aspirins, and set out again.

Jennifer's directions sent me along the same route I'd taken to the Klapec scene on Thursday. This time, a quarter mile before hitting the lakeshore, I turned onto a small, winding road. At an abandoned fruit stand, I made a left and continued until I spotted a hand-painted wooden plaque with an arrow and the words *Full Moon.* From then on it was gravel.

The sun was low, turning the woods into a collage of green, brown, and red. As I slipped in and out of shadow, crimson arrows shot the foliage and danced my windshield. I saw no other cars.

A quarter mile in, I spotted a wooden trellis curving eight feet above a pair of tire tracks taking off to the right. Following Jennifer's instructions, I made the turn.

Ten yards beyond the archway, the woods gave way to a clearing approximately sixty feet in diameter. At the far side, two dozen cars angled toward a crudely built log cabin. Another hand-crafted sign above the door announced *Full Moon.* This one featured what looked like a Paleolithic mother goddess—full breasts and buttocks, just a hint of head, arms, and legs.

Parking beside a battered old Volvo, I got out and looked around.

No one approached or called out. Below the goddess, the cabin door remained closed.

The air smelled of pine and moist earth and a hint of bonfire smoke. Notes drifted from the trees beyond the cabin. Panpipes? A recorder? I couldn't be sure.

Circling the building, I spotted a path and moved toward the music. The sun was down now, the woods in that murky limbo between dusk and full night. No birds called out, but now and then some panicked creature skittered away through the underbrush.

As I picked my way along, the music sorted itself into flute and guitar. A lone female voice sang lyrics I couldn't make out.

Soon I saw the flicker of flames through the trees. Ten steps and I reached a second clearing, this one much smaller than that surrounding the cabin. Pausing at the edge of the trees, I looked for Jennifer. No one noticed my presence.

The gathering was larger than I'd anticipated, perhaps thirty people. A few sat on logs placed around the perimeter of the fire pit. Others stood talking in groups.

The guitarist was a woman of forty or fifty, with long gray hair and a whole lot of jewelry. The flautist was a person of indeterminate gender with squiggly snakes painted on his/her cheeks and forehead. The singer was an Asian girl in her late teens.

Beyond the musicians, eleven women and one man followed the instructions of a woman clothed in an intricately embroidered robe.

"Raise your hands to the heavens."

Twenty-four arms went up.

"Inhale deeply. Follow your breath. Feel it enter each part of your body, moving down your throat, to your heart, your breasts, your solar plexus, your genitals, your feet. Repeat. One. Two. Three. Four times."

A lot of breathing and arm waving followed.

"With each breath receive blessings from the universe. Five. Six. Seven times."

More air intake.

"Accept a deep inner calm. Be filled with peace."

Embroidery woman drew her hands to her mouth.

"Now, thank yourself. Love yourself. Kiss each of your hands."

Embroidery woman kissed her palms. The others did likewise.

"Kiss your knuckles. Your fingers. You are love!"

Mercifully, at that moment I spotted Jennifer. She was wearing jeans and a black hoodie, adjusting logs in the fire with a long iron pole. Sparks spiraled around her, like tiny red stars carried on a cyclone.

Skirting the edge of the trees, I joined her.

"Hey," I said.

Jennifer looked up, skin amber in the glow of the flames. A smile lit her face. "You found us."

"The group is"—I was quite at a loss—"larger than I expected."

"This is actually a small gathering. Since we're between holidays, we're not celebrating anything special tonight."

I must have looked confused.

She smiled. "Let's sit down."

I followed her to one of the logs circling the fire.

"OK. Wicca one-oh-one."

"Condensed version," I said.

Jennifer nodded. "Wiccans recognize the existence of many ancient gods and goddesses—Pan, Dionysus, Diana. But we also view the God and Goddess as symbols, not as living entities." She swept one arm in an arc. "In the trees, the lake, flowers, the wind, each other. All nature's creatures. We view, and treat, all things of the Earth as aspects of the divine. You with me?"

I nodded, not sure that I was.

"The Wiccan calendar is based on the ancient Celtic days of celebration, with eight commonly recognized holidays. Four occur at the time of the solstices or equinoxes, the other four fall roughly midway between. Historical research shows that these holidays were celebrated throughout Europe and the British Isles in early pre-Christian times. Many festivals were so popular the Church couldn't stamp them out, so they appropriated and linked many to various saints.

"Brigantia, or Imbolc, the day when newborn lambs begin to nurse, became the Christian Candlemas, honoring the purification of the Virgin. Held February second, it marks the end of winter and the beginning of spring. Brigantia is the day of Brigit, the Irish goddess of smithcraft, healing, and poetry. Moving on toward spring, the vernal equinox usually falls around March twentieth."

"Twelve hours of darkness and twelve hours of light," I said.

She nodded. "Roman Catholics turned this one into the Annunciation of the Blessed Virgin Mary. Next comes Beltane, on May first."

"The day for dancing round maypoles."

"Exactly. An obvious fertility ritual. Summer solstice, the longest day of the year, falls around June twenty-first. For Wiccans, the summer solstice is when the maiden gives way to the mother aspect of the Goddess.

"Lammas, celebrated around August first, announces the coming of autumn and the beginning of the harvest. Then it's on to the fall equinox, around September twenty-third."

"The point when day becomes shorter than night and winter looms."

"Right again. The fall equinox was also the time of the second harvest, and of winemaking. For Wiccans, it is when the mother prepares to yield way to the Crone aspect of the Goddess.

"Samhain falls on the last day of October, and is celebrated today as Halloween. In ancient times, it was customary to slaughter livestock and begin smoking meat on Samhain. In the old Celtic calendar, it was the end of one year and the beginning of the next, so the separation of the living from the dead was especially dicey at this time."

"So we dress up in scary costumes to keep the spirits at bay?"

"That's one interpretation. Finally, the winter solstice falls on or about December twenty-first. Also known as Yule, this is the shortest day and longest night of the year. For Wiccans, it's the period of the year during which the Crone aspect of the Goddess reigns. Many religions have placed the birth of their gods at the solstice. Jesus, Horus, Dionysus, Helios, and Mithras all claim Yule as their birthday."

"Makes sense to me. The days begin growing longer, so it's a time of rebirth and regeneration."

"Right on, again. So, to make a long story short, tonight we're not celebrating anything special. Just coming together for companionship and to worship the God and Goddess."

I thought of Slidell's reports from neighbors concerning activity the night before Jimmy Klapec was found.

"How often do you gather?"

"Typically, the second Tuesday of each month."

Funderburke first spotted Klapec's body the previous Tuesday.

"Always?"

"Usually." Her brow furrowed. "Why do you ask?"

"What about last Monday?"

"Yes, of course. There was a planning session that night for the Samhain festival. I forgot because I wasn't here."

Maybe she was being honest, maybe not. Her expression gave no hint.

"Did Asa Finney attend that meeting?"

She looked off into space.

"No. He attends very few."

"Do you know where he was?"

She shook her head.

"Did you try contacting him?"

"I called several times to see if he would be going out to camp that night." She looked down at her hands. "I got no answer."

I watched the bonfire reshape the features of her face, elongating her nose and deepening the hollows below her eyes and cheekbones.

She looked up into my gaze.

"Asa is incapable of harming another human being."

"He's a self-proclaimed witch."

"So am I. So is every person here."

I said nothing.

"Asa is fully committed to Wicca, and, therefore, to a reverence for life. I know in my heart of hearts he could never take a life."

She shook her head in frustration.

"There are so many misconceptions about us. We're linked to Satanism, vampirism, Freemasonry. Some say we engage in group sex and human sacrifice. It's all madness, based on ignorance."

She turned to me, body tense, reflected firelight flickering in the darks of her eyes.

"Fear of women's power runs like a subtext through most of today's religions. Modern church doctrines are full of stories of sirens and witches and enchantresses under the full moon. Empowering male propaganda.

"And it's so ironic, because ancient artifacts suggest people first worshipped a female deity, a goddess or earth mother. Did you see the image over the coven house door?"

"It's modeled after the Venus of Willendorf," I said, referring to a Paleolithic figurine unearthed in Austria in 1908.

"Of course." She smiled. "You would know your prehistoric archaeology. And you would also know that the earliest written records suggest worship of both gods and goddesses. And that these early female deities eventually lost out to patriarchal storm gods like Baal, Raman, and Yahweh."

Her eyes moved over my face.

"Wiccans are modern pagans who imagine our first mother as the Goddess worshipped in prehistory, before the old boys' deity network came along. We strive to bring the subtext of female subjugation to the forefront, and to change that mind-set. We want a different world here and now, one in which women and men are equal, in which assumptions about who should hold power and what has value are different.

"But we want change brought about peacefully. Wiccans honor the feminine, but, first and foremost, we view our religion as a personal, positive celebration of life. We revere the creative forces of nature, symbolized by both a god and goddess."

She took my hands in hers.

"Let me introduce you to the others. Let us show you who we are, what we believe, what we do. You'll see. No one among us could take the life of another."

"All right," I said. "Show me Wicca."

So I met Sky Bird, Raven, India, and Dreamweaver. I witnessed dancing and drumming and chanting. I ate. I listened. I asked questions.

I learned that Wicca claims an estimated 400,000-plus practitioners, making it the tenth largest religion in the United States, behind Christianity, nonreligious/secular, Judaism, Islam, Buddhism, agnostic, atheist, Hinduism, and Unitarian Universalist.

I learned that Wicca has no official book, central governing agency, physical leader, or universally recognized prophet or messenger.

I learned that there are many Wiccan traditions, each with its own distinct teachings and practices, including Alexandrian, Faery, Gardnerian, Odyssean, Reclaiming, Uniterranism, and dozens of others.

I learned of the Law of Threefold Return, the belief that both good and bad deeds reflect back on the doer, and of the Eight Wiccan Virtues: mirth, reverence, honor, humility, strength, beauty, power, and compassion.

Despite the tarot cards, and grimoires, and crystals, and love spells, I sensed an unaffected genuineness in all I met.

I came to understand that Wiccan beliefs and practices remain largely unknown because followers hide out of fear of persecution.

Persecution of the sort sold wholesale by Boyce Lingo.

I left at midnight, still unsure about Asa Finney, but certain we needed to proceed cautiously lest our investigation be tainted by preconceived bias. Convincing Slidell would be a hard sell. But that was for the morrow.

Pulling into my driveway, the headlights swept a rectangular object sitting on the back stoop.

Charlie strikes again. I smiled, got out, and walked toward the door

The object was a cardboard box with the flaps tucked tight. Balancing it on one knee, I unlocked the door and let myself in.

"I'm home, Bird," I called.

Birdie appeared as I was removing my jacket. After figure-eighting my ankles once or twice, he hopped onto the counter.

And froze in a Halloween cat tableau, back arched, tail poofed to double its size. A primal clicking sound rose from his throat.

The skin crawled on my arms and neck.

I gathered Birdie and displaced him to the floor. He shot back onto the counter.

Blocking the cat with one arm, I disengaged the flaps one-handed and opened the box.

A dead copperhead lay upside down in the bottom, belly slit, innards billowing, glossy and red. Below the jaw, an inverted pentagram had been carved into the pale yellow skin.

M<small>Y SLEEP WAS VISITED BY THE COPPERHEAD I'D SEALED IN A</small>
trash bag and placed in the marigolds flanking my porch. In my dream
it was very much alive, pursuing me through dense trees hung with
thick Spanish moss, all the while emitting a breathy, sibilant sound. *Asa.
Asa. Asa.*

The faster I ran, the closer the snake came to my heels. I climbed a
tree. It slithered past me up the trunk and grinned down from above,
Cheshire cat–style. Its tongue flicked my face. I batted at its head.

The tongue came at me again. Above the forked tip I could see three
red sixes. Above that, a tiny glowing cross.

A tree branch morphed into a sinuous tentacle and circled toward me
holding a microphone. The metal brushed my cheek.

Again I lashed out.

And connected with something solid and furry.

I awoke to find Birdie licking my face.

"Sorry, Bird." I wiped saliva from my cheek.

The clock said 7:20.

I was making coffee in the kitchen when my cell phone rang. Slidell.
Bracing, I clicked on.

"They kicked him this morning."

It took me a moment. "Finney?"

"No. Jack the Freakin' Ripper. 'Course I'm talking Finney."

I held back a comment.

"Bleeding-heart DA agreed with the PD we got insufficient evidence to charge Finney with either Klapec or Rinaldi. And the bones rap ain't enough to keep him locked up."

Slidell's reference to Charlie Hunt caused another mental cringe. OK. No more avoidance. I'd call Charlie this morning.

"—dirty and I ain't giving up on the little prick." Slidell's voice brought me back. "Anything on your end?"

I told him about the snake.

"Sonovabitch. Who you thinking?"

I'd given the question considerable thought.

"I criticized Boyce Lingo publicly last Friday."

"Man's got a lot of fans, but they don't seem the type to be carving up reptiles."

"I'm not so sure about that."

"It made the papers you and me tossed Cuervo's operation on Greenleaf." Slidell paused, considering other possibilities. "Or maybe it was one of Finney's voodoo-ass buddies."

I told him about Jennifer Roberts and my trip to Full Moon, then waited for the tirade. Slidell surprised me.

"Gimme your take."

"A lot of ecofeminism and bad poetry."

"Meaning?"

"Though unconventional, the people I met seemed benign."

"So did John Wayne Gacy."

"Do you think the copperhead was meant as a threat?"

"That or someone's unhappy Finney was busted, decided to try a little mojo to spring him." Slidell snorted loudly. "Wouldn't that be ironical. They juju some snake, next morning their boy walks. Whatever, what ain't funny is some nutjob knows where you live. You need to watch your back."

I'd thought of that, too.

"How about I step up surveillance on your place?"

I was about to decline, thought of Rinaldi. Why take a chance?

"Sure. Thanks."

"I'll have a unit swing by every hour or so, make sure everything's kosher. Maybe we should agree on some sort of distress signal."

"A lantern in the tower of the Old North Church?"

"Huh?"

"One if by land?"

Nothing.

"If there's trouble I'll leave the porch light on."

"That works."

"You want the snake?"

"What the hell am I gonna do with a gutted copperhead?"

I told Slidell about the slides I'd left with Marion Ireland at UNCC.

"Why's it important?"

"It may not be. I'll know when I get the blowups."

I listened to a moment of nasal wheezing. Then, "Found a guy name of Vince Gunther was booked for solicitation on twenty-eight September. Spent the night in the bag until someone ponied up bail the next afternoon. I'm thinking Gunther could be Eddie's chicken hawk, Vince. I'm gonna try tracking him through the bondsman." Slidell paused. "I guess they're finding Eddie was having money problems."

"Oh?"

"Over fifty thousand in credit card debt."

"And?"

"And nothing. They're checking it out."

"He never mentioned financial difficulties to you?"

"No." Tight.

"Do they think he got involved in something that got him killed?"

"They're checking it out." There was a long pause. "I don't see it. After his wife died all Eddie wanted to do was go home, play his egghead music, and work crossword puzzles. And that other thing. That thing with numbers."

"Sudoku?" I guessed.

"Yeah. That's it. And he'd cook, just for himself. Real meals, with fresh pasta and herbs and stuff." Slidell pronounced the *h*.

Sudden stab of pain. Though I'd known Rinaldi for almost twenty years, other than the fact that he originally came from West Virginia, had been widowed and lived alone, was compulsively neat, liked classical music, good food, and expensive clothing, I'd learned very little about the man. Now I never would.

"Did Eddie have family?"

"A married son. Tony. Lives somewhere up near Boston. Has since he was a toddler."

"Did they keep in touch?"

"Yeah. But it was something Eddie never wanted to discuss."

I didn't ask why Rinaldi's son had been raised by others. "What's Tony saying?"

"Find the bastards that killed his father."

Recognizing Slidell's surliness as grieving, I let the remark go.

"Look. They got a homicide detail directing the investigation. Robbery and rape are pitching in on neighborhood canvasses, chasing witness leads, doing records checks, that kind of thing. Since the weather was crap, no one was on the street Saturday night. No one saw nothing. At least that's the story I'm getting. Members of the team don't exactly keep me on their speed dials."

I could understand that. Slidell was hard to control under normal circumstances. Given his level of emotional involvement, there was no telling what he would do if privy to even the most tenuous lead in Rinaldi's death.

"See you at the church?" I asked.

"I'll be in back."

After disconnecting, I logged onto my computer and checked my e-mail.

Katy had written to apologize for our spat. Easier than phoning, I guess.

A man in Nigeria wanted my partnership in a scheme to liberate two million pounds. All I had to do was send bank account information.

A colleague at UNCC had sent an e-invite to a Halloween party. Remembering the previous year's event, I declined.

Astall@gmail.com. Subject line blank.

Oh, no.

Oh, yes. Allison Stallings wanted to meet for a drink. She had some follow-up questions.

Bloody hell. Larke Tyrell was correct in his anger. I had talked to Stallings during my bender on Monday. But had *I* called her? No way.

If she'd contacted me, how had she gotten my home or cell number? Mrs. Flowers would never give out personal information. Nor would anyone at UNCC.

Anyone who knew. What was the name of the new secretary? Natasha? Naomi?

I looked at the clock: 8:05. I dialed.

Naomi swore she'd shared my number with no one.

Had *I*? I thought back over the past few weeks. Of course. Takeela Freeman. Stallings could have gotten the number from her.

Then why was she now e-mailing instead of dialing?

Because I went twenty-four hours without answering either line? Because those who tried my home got a message that service was disconnected?

I made a mental note to speak with Takeela.

Two messages had arrived from the entomologist to whom I'd sent the Greenleaf and Klapec bugs. Each contained an attachment. I opened and read the first.

No surprise. The insects from the subcellar suggested the chicken had died approximately eight weeks before I'd collected the specimens. That put the last known activity at Cuervo's altar sometime in mid-August.

That fit. Cuervo had his head-on with the train on August twenty-sixth.

I opened the Klapec report. In addition to species names and numbers, it provided two opinions, one concerning postmortem environment, one concerning time since death.

The first opinion was not unexpected.

The samples contain no evidence of immersion in an aquatic environment.

OK. Klapec was dumped and didn't wash ashore. Larabee and I had arrived at the same conclusion at autopsy.

The second opinion was more troubling.

The decedent was spotted in situ on October ninth, reported and recovered two days later. Temperatures reached daytime highs in the eighties for the period in question. The body was loosely wrapped in plastic. Trauma was severe. Given these factors, insect activity is unusually light, but not inconsistent with the lower end of a PMI range beginning with a minimum of forty-eight hours.

I sat back, puzzled.

Rinaldi noted that his informant, Vince, had last seen Jimmy Klapec with the violent john, Rick Nelson, on September 29. If that was true, where was Klapec from September 29 until his body turned up on October 11?

JK. 9/29. LSA with RN acc. to VG.

Were we wrong in our interpretation of Rinaldi's entry? If so, what *had* he meant?

I pictured Klapec lying on the Lake Wylie shoreline. The carved chest and belly. The truncated neck. That corpse should have been alive with maggots and eggs. Why so little oviposition and hatching? And why no interest from animals?

I pictured Susan Redmon's skull in the dark of Cuervo's cellar.

The two scenes were so different, and yet so alike, involving the macabre use of human remains. Why these two discoveries so proximate in time?

I had to agree with Slidell. In my gut, I knew the situations were linked. But how far did the web extend? And who was spinning it?

Finney? He'd denied knowing Cuervo, but tensed at the mention of the *santero*'s name. He drove a Ford Focus. And had books on Satanism.

I don't believe in coincidence. Coincidence is merely lack of full knowledge of the facts.

OK. Time for facts.

Googling the name Asa Finney got me two hits, one for an early settler of the town of Hamilton, New York, and one for the Web page of a witch called Ursa.

Asa. Ursa. Bingo. I tried the bear.

On the upper left side of Ursa's opening page a silver pentagram emitted sparks as it slowly revolved. On the right was a photo of Asa Finney in a long white robe embroidered with the constellation Ursa Major. The Big Bear. Or the Big Dipper, take your pick.

A stratified pyramid filled the center of the screen, offering links to pages within the site. Choices included: *Announcements, Book Reviews, Celebrations, Lessonbook, Magick, Moon Phases, Poetry, Rituals,* and *Samhain.*

I chose *Poetry.*

Finney favored verse about crying lilies, hearts like lighthouses, and bringing about reality through love.

I went to *Samhain.*

There was a quote from Ray Bradbury's *The Halloween Tree,* an ad for a book titled *Pagan Mysteries of Halloween,* and a lengthy explanation of the festival. Finney's account of the origin of All Hallows' Eve coincided with that provided by Jennifer Roberts. I learned, among other things, that in Scotland the practice of donning costumes involved cross-dressing, with men tarting up as women and vice versa.

I was distracted for a moment, unable to form a picture. If men wore kilts, how did that work?

The only thing of relevance was a statement that Samhain often involved two distinct celebrations, one preceding the actual feast. OK. That supported Roberts's account of an off-schedule gathering at the camp.

Returning to the main page, I clicked on *Lessonbook*.

There was Finney again, this time in closeup. The guy really did look like an acne-scarred version of Rick Nelson.

Below Finney were more tabs: *Medicine and Magick; Every Breath Is a Prayer; Rocks Are Individuals Like Us; Aphrodisiacs: Gifts from the Goddess.* I assumed each linked to a Wiccan lesson in living.

Somewhat bored at this point, I chose *Aphrodisiacs.*

The use of an aphrodisiac affects more than one person. Now there was a revelation. Aphrodisiacs exist as herbs or as food. Herbs include ginseng, garlic, and guarana. OK. I didn't know that.

Erotic foods can be anything salty, sticky, sweet, chewy, moist, warm, or cool. So what's left?

At the bottom of the page Finney had included a disclaimer, stating that his advice was for informational purposes only, and warning readers to consult health care professionals before employing aphrodisiacs as sexual aids.

Right. Hello, Doctor. I may eat a caramel. What do you think?

I was about to log out when my eye fell on a box at the lower left-hand side of the page. Finney had provided links to what I assumed were sources for his libidinous fare.

Botánica Exótica
Divine Sisters Botanicals
Earth Elements
La Botánica Buena Salud
Mystical Moods
Pagan Potions

I felt a tingle at the base of my throat. La Botánica Buena Salud. Cuervo's shop?

Barely breathing, I clicked on the listing. And got a message that the link was invalid.

Was it the same shop? An unrelated online store with an identical name?

Had I found proof tying Finney and Cuervo? If so, why had Finney lied about knowing the *santero*?

Had Finney included Cuervo's shop simply because it was in Charlotte?

Cuervo and Finney. A *santero* and a witch. What was the connection? Was Slidell's instinct about Finney correct? Was Ursa involved in more than just poetry and potted herbs? In Jimmy Klapec's murder? In Rinaldi's?

In Cuervo's? Was it possible the man's death hadn't been accidental?

Jennifer Roberts was adamant about Finney's innocence. Nevertheless, she'd been unable to contact him the night Klapec was killed.

Roberts was right about one thing. Finney's Web site seemed the handiwork of an eccentric but nonviolent personality.

Absently, I logged off.

And found myself staring at a headless body pierced by dozens of swords. Slowly, the body dissolved to black. A dot appeared and grew into an alien creature with way too many teeth.

I watched the pop-up, mesmerized, as a red circle appeared on the creature's chest. In a flash, its body exploded and flew off in fragments. Words floated across the screen. *Evil guilds. Mythic worlds. Alien universes. Prey stalking. Play. Learn cutting edge programming techniques.* The title *Dr.Games.com.* flashed orange and red, urging the viewer to click on the icon.

The pop-up had no "close" option. I moved my cursor to the X in the top right-hand corner of the screen. The thing would not go away.

Sudden thought. Finney was into gaming. Could the pop-up be his handiwork, meant to lure Ursa's visitors to another site?

OK, Dr.Games. I'm game.

Dr.Games's opening screen contained no photos or graphics. A single statement welcomed players, hobbyists, and professionals.

A bullet list offered the following choices: *How to Build the Ultimate Gaming PC. Components of a Good Game. Advice in Game Design Careers. Game Design Courses. Free Downloadable Games.*

I went straight to door five.

And discovered a chilling new world.

OF THE SIX GAMES LISTED, I SAMPLED ONLY THREE.

In *Killer Dozen* the player controlled twelve combatants who pursued and destroyed their enemies in countless gruesome ways. Bodies were torn in half, throats were slit, heads were impaled on falchions and pitchforks.

In *Reality Crime* the player was a cop looking for information on the death of his brother. Suspects were beaten and shot with a variety of weapons.

In *Gods of Combat* the player was a rebel warrior seeking revenge on the gods. Details of the injuries inflicted were appallingly realistic.

Other choices included *Island of Death, Blood Frenzy*, and *Mansion of Mayhem*. I didn't even look.

Grabbing the phone, I dialed Slidell. He answered, sounding edgy.

I told him about the link from Finney's Web page to Cuervo's shop, and about the pop-up to the gaming site. He said he'd have someone research ownership of the Dr.Games domain, and look into the existence of a second, online La Botánica Buena Salud unrelated to Cuervo's operation.

I also told him I'd received the entomology reports.

"Summarize."

"Cuervo killed the chicken sometime in mid to late August."

"I'm guessing that was before his boo-boo with the train."

I ignored that. "Klapec was never in the lake, and probably died two days before we recovered his body."

Slidell was silent a moment, thinking about that.

"Dame by the name of April Pinder sprang Vince Gunther. Wonder if she knows what line of work her boyfriend is in. Anyway, April and me are gonna become real good friends."

"I want to be there."

Slidell made a noncommittal noise and disconnected.

The clock said 9:50.

I had to hurry.

St. Ann's calls itself the little parish with the big heart. What was needed that morning was a big parish with colossal seating and parking capacities.

Driving from the Annex, I saw hundreds lining up to march. City cops and state troopers. Firemen. Military personnel. EMT's. It seemed everyone in uniform was represented.

As predicted, there was also an enormous civilian turnout. People stood three and four deep at certain stretches. Some wept. Some embraced or held hands. Many gripped or waved small American flags.

Leaving my car at the YWCA as Slidell had instructed, I worked my way to the church. From the front doors hundreds of cops in dress blues had organized into a formation that wound out the parking lot and far up Park Road.

The media were present in extraordinarily large numbers, mostly local, with CNN and FOX clocking in for the nationals. Helicopters circled overhead.

The weather was cooperating. The sun was shining and the sky was a deep autumn blue, a picture-perfect day for broadcasting from a graveyard.

After showing ID to a uniformed officer, I was checked off a list and allowed inside the church.

Slidell was seated in the last pew of a side row, hands clasped between his knees, face looking like sculpted marble. On seeing me, he shifted right, but didn't speak.

I slipped into the pew beside him.

And immediately felt the usual rush of emotions.

The somber drone of the organ. The scent of incense mingling with the sweet smell of flowers. The sunlight filtering through stained glass.

My mind flashed back to memories of funerals past.

My brother's tiny white casket. My father's gleaming bronze one. Balloons over the coffin of a little girl gunned down by bikers in Montreal. Baby's breath atop the gravestone of a friend dead of lymphoma at forty-three.

I inhaled deeply, exhaled. Focused on the music. Handel's "Dead March"? Chopin's "Funeral March"? I wasn't sure. Wasn't uplifted.

An ancient priest said Mass. Slidell's boss, Harper Dunning, offered a reading. Tony Rinaldi spoke of his father. Others talked of their colleague, their friend, their fellow parishioner. We all stood, sat, knelt. Sang "Abide with Me" and "Lead, Kindly Light."

Through it all, I kept seeing Rinaldi, all bony limbs and angles. In my office, carefully taking notes with his Mont Blanc pen. In my lab, staring at Susan Redmon's skull. On Thirty-fifth, bleeding through his perfect Armani jacket.

At the end, an honor guard of officers marched the coffin out. We exited to Mendelssohn's "On Wings of Song."

Slidell got us to the cemetery, where the scene was repeated al fresco. Cops. Mourners. Reporters. Dignitaries.

Larabee was there dressed in black. I was about to approach him when a hand touched my shoulder. I turned.

Two green eyes were gazing down into mine.

Without a word, Charlie drew me to him and hugged tightly.

Placing two palms on his chest, I pushed free and stepped back. Why? Embarrassment over his public display of affection? Over my bender? Over our roll in the hay? Rolls.

"How have you been?" Charlie asked gently.

"Good," I said, aware of Slidell ten feet away, aviator-shaded face turned to his boss, listening to us while pretending not to.

"I called," Charlie said.

"It's been crazy busy."

"I've been worried."

"I'm fine. Thanks for the food."

"I'd rather have cooked you a meal myself."

"Listen. I—"

"Don't explain. Not to me, Tempe. You did what you had to do."

"That wasn't me, Charlie." I wasn't quite sure of my meaning.

"On Thursday? Or on Sunday?"

He cut in before I could respond.

"Shall we try again? Maybe on a Friday?"

"There's been someone else, Charlie. A detective in Montreal. I'm not sure it's over."

My own words surprised me. Of course it was over. And I was over Ryan.

"He's very far away," Charlie said.

In so many ways, I thought.

"Stand by your man," Charlie sang softly.

I had to smile. The song had played incessantly on an interminable bus trip to a state tennis tournament. It became one of the team's standing jokes.

"Who owned that tape?" I asked.

"Drek Zogbauer."

"We went to school with someone named Drek Zogbauer?"

Charlie shrugged.

"I remember everyone applauded when the driver finally confiscated the boom box."

"I led the ovation. It was not the music of my people."

I cocked a brow. "Your people?"

"Yankees fans."

Again, I had to smile.

"I do understand, Tempe. Healing takes time."

You would know, I thought, recalling the photos of his murdered wife.

"I'm sorry," I said.

"I can wait." Charlie grinned. Sad, but a grin. "I'm a very patient man."

And then I hugged him.

He started to walk away.

"Charlie."

He turned back.

"Asa Finney was released this morning."

One hand went to his chest. "Really. No need for accolades."

I rolled my eyes.

"Just an acknowledgment that I'm the greatest lawyer on the planet."

"Between you and me, do you read Finney as capable of violence?"

Charlie stepped back to me and lowered his voice. "Honestly, Tempe. I don't know. Slidell's right about one thing. The guy's one weird duck."

"Thanks."

Charlie had gone barely ten paces when Slidell left Dunning and ambled back to me.

"That was touching."

"We went to high school together."

"I'm happy for you."

I said nothing.

"Dunning's pissed."

"Why?"

"Switchboard's lighting up with calls from outraged citizens wanting to know why the cops ain't rounding up witches and warlocks."

"Jesus."

"Yeah. They think He'd be all for it."

I just shook my head.

"She puts it partly on you."

"Wait. What?"

"Says you goaded Lingo."

"I *goaded* him?"

"Most callers think you're the spawn of the devil."

Thirty minutes later, the cavalcade arrived and a brief graveside service took place. Guns were fired, then the coffin was lowered into the ground. The crowd began to disperse.

The backhoe was shoving dirt onto Rinaldi when I spotted Larabee staring toward the gate opening onto Sharon Amity Road. Curious, I followed his sight line.

Like ants drawn to a gumdrop, reporters were circling a pair of men. All I could see were the tops of two heads, one silver-haired, the other buzz cut.

Boyce Lingo and his aide. Exploiting Rinaldi's funeral to spread a message of hatred and intolerance.

White-hot anger seared through me.

Elbow-jabbing Slidell, I took off in Lingo's direction, intending not to speak, but to stand front and center, a living reminder to the commissioner that he'd be held accountable for every word he uttered.

Behind me I could hear Slidell struggling to keep up. Behind him, more movement, which I assumed was Larabee.

Reaching the scrum, I pushed to the front and positioned myself opposite Lingo.

"—Finney was set free this morning. Free to live amongst us paying tribute to Satan, worshipping Lucifer and bringing evil into this world."

Silence, Brennan.

"Now, the law is the law and the man has his rights. That's as it should be. That's our system. But what happens when that system begins to crumble? When the rights of criminals outweigh those of law-abiding citizens like you and me?"

Easy.

"I'll tell you what happens. O. J. Simpson plays golf in Florida. Robert Blake and Phil Spector party in their Hollywood mansions."

"Are you saying those juries were wrong?" a reporter called out. "That these guys are guilty?"

"I'm saying our government is losing its ability to protect us against criminals and terrorists."

"Why?" another voice asked.

"I'll tell you why. Restrictive laws that tie the hands of police and prosecutors. If elected to the state senate I'll work hard for repeal of those laws."

I forgot the chief's warning. Forgot my plan of silent intimidation.

"This is hardly the place for campaigning, Commissioner."

As at our previous encounter, all eyes swung to me. Lenses and booms followed.

Lingo smiled benevolently. "We meet again, Dr. Brennan. But, yes, what you say is true."

"Asa Finney has a right to his day in court."

"Of course he does."

I couldn't let it go at that. "And to worship as he chooses."

Lingo's face went somber. "In venerating Satan, Asa Finney and his kind ignore the goodness of Jesus and show contempt for all our Savior has done for us."

Lingo raised humble hands.

"But enough. She is right. Today is for mourning a fine officer who sacrificed his life in the line of duty."

With that, Lingo turned and began walking away.

Pumped on adrenaline, I started to follow. Buzz-cut blocked my path.

"I have questions I'd like to pose to the commissioner off air," I said.

Buzz-cut spread his feet and shook his head.

"Out of my way, please," I said, voice all steely control.

Buzz-cut's face remained impassive. "Best to call for an appointment."

I started to move past him. Extending an arm, he blocked me. I stepped left. He mirrored my move.

I started to say something I would later have regretted.

"Hold on right there." Slidell was seething. "Did you just strong-arm this little lady?"

Little lady?

Folding his arms, Buzz-cut canted his head, gangsta-tough.

"What's your name?" Slidell demanded.

"Who's asking?"

Slidell flashed his shield. "I am, asshole."

"Glenn Evans."

"You his flunky?" Slidell chin-cocked Lingo's retreating figure.

"I serve as Commissioner Lingo's personal assistant." The voice was more shrill than I'd expected for a man of his size.

"Perfect. Then you can explain why my partner would be phoning your boss."

"Are you serious?"

"Deadly."

"This is harassment."

"Sue me."

"I fail to even understand your question. Nevertheless, I'll answer it. All communication goes through me, personally, and no such call ever came into Commissioner Lingo's office."

"You're pretty sure about that. Don't need to check a calendar or nothing?" Evans's belligerence was not improving Slidell's disposition. "This be easier for you down at the station?"

"You don't scare me, Detective."

Slidell glared in silence.

Evans pulled on his nose with thumb and forefinger. Cocked his hands on his hips. Drummed his fingers on his belt. "When did this alleged conversation take place?"

"Shortly before Detective Rinaldi was shot. You want, I can sub-poena your phone records. Your preference."

"This is bullshit."

"Jimmy Klapec. That name mean anything to you?"

"Who is he?"

"I'm asking the questions." Slidell's forehead vein was doing a rumba.

"The commissioner often reaches out into the community, visits homeless shelters, soup kitchens, battered women's homes, food banks, that kind of thing. He meets a lot of people."

Slidell said nothing, hoping Evans would feel compelled to continue talking. The ploy worked.

"The commissioner could have met this Klapec at any one of a dozen places."

"The kid was a runaway living on the streets. Seventeen years old. Detective Rinaldi was investigating his murder. That's why I gotta be curious Rinaldi's calling your boss."

"Wait. Are you talking about the boy found at Lake Wylie? I thought that was some kind of satanic-ritual thing."

"Why'd you think that?"

"It was all over the news."

Again, Slidell offered silence. I doubted he really viewed Lingo as a suspect, figured he was hassling Evans simply for showing attitude.

"Look, Mr. Lingo is a politician. He comes in contact with a lot of people from a lot of places. So he met some half-moon hick living on the streets, which I'm not saying he did, doesn't mean he had anything to do with the kid's murder."

As Evans talked, I studied his face. Up close I could see that his skin was pitted and scarred like Asa Finney's. But all resemblance ended there. Evans's hair was fair and shaved close to his scalp. He had close-set eyes, high, fat-padded cheekbones, and a tapering jaw ending in a prominent chin.

"Just for fun, Mr. Evans, where was your boss on October ninth?"

"The commissioner was speaking at an event in Greensboro. I was with him. If you like, I can provide a copy of the program and credit card receipts showing hotel and restaurants. Oh, and perhaps four hundred eyewitness accounts."

Again, Evans answered quickly, without giving thought to the question. I stored that observation.

Through the crowd, I could see Larabee talking on his mobile. I guessed he was putting the best spin possible on my recent outburst. Knowing Larke Tyrell, I feared the effort would fall short.

Returning my attention to Evans, I sensed interest from my lower centers.

What?

The voice? The acne? Finney? Mention of Satanism?

It was no good. Whatever cell had cocked a brow had again lost interest.

Unfortunate. A synapse at that moment might have helped save a life.

29

I LEFT MY CAR AND RODE WITH SLIDELL. SEEMED I WAS DOING A lot of that lately.

April Pinder lived at Dillehay Courts, a public housing project off North Tryon, not far from a small city park.

Pulling to the curb on Twenty-eighth Street, Slidell checked the address provided by the bondsman.

"Gotta be over there."

He pointed to one of several oblong boxes divided into two-story townhouses faced with cheap vinyl siding above, brick below.

We got out and walked in silence, each pointed at the same thought. As the crow flies, Rinaldi was gunned down just across the rail bed running to our right.

In this part of town, it was hard telling which side of the tracks was the wrong one.

Like its neighbors, Pinder's unit appeared to have enjoyed little attention since construction in the midseventies. The paint was flaking and the window AC units were rusting. Plastic lawn chairs didn't improve the ambience.

Double-checking numbers, Slidell pressed his thumb to the bell.

Dogs started barking, voices up at the glass-shattering end of the spectrum.

Slidell puffed his cheeks and shook his head. Holding comment, he rang again.

The dogs grew even more frenzied.

"I hate yappy little mutts."

How did I know that?

Slidell was about to try pounding when a voice called out, "Who's there?"

"Police."

A key turned and the door swung in. A woman peered up at us through the gap allowed by the security chain. She was squatting, holding a wriggling Pomeranian under one arm while restraining another at her feet by its collar. Both dogs were shaking and barking hysterically.

"April Pinder?"

The woman nodded.

"I called this morning." Slidell held his badge low so Pinder could see it.

The floor Pomeranian peed on the tile.

"Hold on."

Pinder rose and started to close the door.

"How about you lock up the pooches?" Slidell made no attempt to mask his disgust.

"What, you don't like dogs?"

"This pair seems a bit high-strung." Dripping with sarcasm.

Seconds later, Slidell and I were seated on an overstuffed sofa in an overfurnished living room. Pinder sat opposite in a Brentwood rocker. From the back of the unit came frenzied scratching and yipping, muted now by walls and a door.

While Slidell opened the interview, I studied Pinder. She had pale skin, bottle blond hair, and oddly lopsided cheekbones, the left jutting forward more than the right. Were it not for an overabundance of makeup, her aquamarine eyes would have been striking. I put her somewhere just south of twenty.

The apartment put her somewhere just north of eighty. Doilies. Knickknacks. Carved wooden pieces straight out of the Depression.

And photos. Lots of them. All showing people or pets. Apparently there'd been a long march leading up to the current Pomeranians.

The air was thick with odors. Fried food? Mothballs? Soiled laundry? Cigarette smoke?

I refocused on Pinder. She was describing her job at a bar on Wilkinson Boulevard. Slidell was taking notes. Or pretending to. Every now and then Pinder would pause, as though listening over the sound of the dogs. I suspected we weren't alone in the house.

"Let's talk about Vince Gunther." Slidell got to the point.

"He's my boyfriend. *Was* my boyfriend. What's he done?"

"What makes you think he's done something?"

"Why else would you be here?"

"Where is he?"

Pinder shrugged. She was wearing blue jeans and a black T-shirt that said *Cheeky Girls.*

Cheeky girls? A club? A philosophy? A rock group? Katy was right. I was growing old and losing touch. I made a note to find out. Maybe I could impress her by dropping the name.

"Wrong answer," Slidell said.

"I don't know. Maybe California."

Pinder began worrying the fringe on a rocker cushion, twisting and untwisting strands around her index finger.

"California?"

"He talked about going west to work on his tan."

"Let me explain something, Miss Pinder. You cross me, and roughly ten tons of do-do will descend on your head."

"We broke up."

"When?"

"A couple weeks ago. Maybe three."

"Why?"

"'Cause Vince's a creep."

Thumping and rattling joined the canine cacophony, suggesting the dogs were now throwing themselves at a door.

"If Vince's a creep, why go his bail?"

"He said he loved me. I'm an idiot. I believed him."

Grabbing the armrests, Pinder twisted to shout over one shoulder, "Poppy! Peony! Knock it off!"

"Explain how that worked," Slidell said, voice edged with annoyance.

Settling back, Pinder sighed theatrically.

"Vince asked me to take five hundred dollars to some office down by the courthouse. He said he'd pay me back as soon as he was out." The fringe-twisting resumed.

"He stiffed you," Slidell guessed. "Then dumped you."

Pinder's eyes came up, misty and red with anger. "Vince's a fag-fucking whore."

All righty then. A woman spurned.

"He could have made me sick." Her lips trembled and moisture welled on her lids. "Who knows? Maybe he has."

Tears broke free and rolled down her cheeks, taking a lot of mascara with them.

"My granny's got Alzheimer's. There's no one here but me. Who'll tend to her if I die?"

Granny was probably upstairs sleeping. That's why Pinder was alert to sounds in the house.

"Don't sound like Vince'll be stepping up to the plate."

I gave Slidell the Look.

He hiked both shoulders. *What?*

"You're really not sure where Vince has gone?" I asked.

Shaking her head, Pinder backhanded more tears.

I decided to try another tack. "How did you and Vince meet?"

"He came into the bar."

"How long did you date?"

"Three months." Mumbled. "Maybe a year."

"You were close?"

She snorted.

"Did the two of you talk?"

"What do you mean?"

"Did he confide in you?"

"Apparently not." Bitter.

"Did he ever mention a kid named Jimmy Klapec?"

She looked surprised. "I know Jimmy."

Slidell's brows shot to his hairline.

"Can you tell me about that?" I asked.

"Jimmy and Vince are friends, you know, both being on their own." She looked from me to Slidell and back. "Jimmy's nice. Shy, you know? And kind of sweet."

"Jimmy Klapec is dead," I said.

The heavily mascaraed eyes went wide.

"He was murdered."

Wider.

"When was the last time you saw Jimmy Klapec?" I asked.

"I don't know. Maybe last summer. I only met him once or twice when he came into the bar with Vince."

Slidell began thumbing pages over the top of his spiral. "Vince was busted on September twenty-eighth, you pried him loose on the twenty-ninth. He mention seeing Klapec around that time?"

"Sort of."

"Sort of?" Impatient.

"The night Vince got out we stayed here, caught some TV and ordered a pizza. Cheap bastard. That's pretty much all we ever did. Problem is, my granny was having her nightmares, so I ended up mostly upstairs. Vince was watching some rock-and-roll thing. Hold on."

Shooting to her feet, Pinder disappeared through a doorway. In seconds we heard banging, then, "Poppy! Peony! I'm gonna whip your butts."

Seconds later, Pinder returned and dropped into her chair.

"Go on," Slidell said.

Pinder looked blank.

"You're nursing Granny and Vince's catching some tube."

"Oh, right. One time I'm passing through the room he's pointing his beer at the TV, laughing and hooting. I ask, What's so funny? He says, Looks just like him. I say, Who? He says, Friend of Jimmy's. I say, Where is Jimmy, anyway? He says, Jimmy got into it with this dude and took off. I say, When? He says, Earlier that night. Then the asshole cracks up again. Vince is moody. I was glad he was happy. And I figured he was probably drunk."

"Who was he pointing at?"

"Some dork in a hat."

"Vince ever mention someone looked like Rick Nelson?" Slidell asked.

"Who?"

"A singer."

"Sounds like him. Jerk was always comparing people to movie stars and stuff. He once said his former girlfriend looked like Pamela Anderson." Pinder snorted. "In his dreams."

Slidell looked at me. I shook my head, meaning I had no other questions.

Slidell handed Pinder a card. "You see Vince, you give us a call, eh?"

Pinder shrugged.

Back in the Taurus, Slidell said, "Not the brightest bulb in the marquis."

I asked, "Got Rinaldi's notes?"

Slidell dug the photocopies from a grease-stained canvas bag on the backseat. As he drove, I reviewed what his partner had written.

JK. 9/29. LSA with RN acc. to VG. RN - PIT. CTK. TV. 10/9-10/11? CFT. 10. 500.

"Pinder's story supports our take on this. According to VG, presumably Vince Gunther, JK, presumably Jimmy Klapec, was last seen alive with RN, presumably Rick Nelson, on September twenty-ninth. RN's probably the violent john that Gunther quit doing."

"The guy Klapec fought with," Slidell said.

"The guy who killed him."

"And that guy's Asa Finney. Rick Nelson with pits."

I still wasn't totally convinced.

"Did you check out CTK?" I asked.

"Yeah. And PIT. No record of Finney or Klapec flying to Akron or Pittsburgh any time in the last thirty days."

I looked at Rinaldi's final entry.

RN = BLA = GYE. Greensboro. 10/9. 555-7038. CTK-TV-9/27. VG, solicitation 9/28-9/29.

GYE 9/27?

"Vince Gunther was arrested for solicitation on September twenty-eighth, spent the night in jail until Pinder arranged for his release the following day. OK. That part's clear."

"When I find the little greaseball he'll wish his ass never left the slammer."

Slidell made a hard right. I braced on the dash, then refocused on the notes.

Boyce Lingo's phone number.

"Glenn Evans says Rinaldi never called his boss. Maybe he did, maybe he didn't. What's important is Rinaldi recorded Lingo's number. Why?"

"I don't know. Yet. But I *do* know one thing. I'm gonna put a car on Miss April Pinder."

"You think she might be hiding Gunther?"

"A little surveillance never hurts."

I went back to the notes.

"Greensboro. Evans said he and Lingo were in Greensboro on October ninth. Was that what interested Rinaldi? And if so, why?"

Suddenly, a line connected two dots.

30

"R<small>N</small> <small>EQUALS</small> BLA <small>EQUALS</small> GYE." I <small>TWISTED IN MY SEAT, EXCITED.</small> "BLA. Boyce Lingo Assistant. GYE. Glenn Evans. That's got to be it."

Slidell flicked his eyes to me, back to the road.

"Check out Evans's middle name," I said. "I'll bet the farm it begins with a Y."

We rode in silence as Slidell merged onto I-277 to loop southeast around uptown.

I tried to reach out to my subconscious. Why the subliminal alert while Slidell was questioning Evans?

Nothing.

"So what's Lingo's connection? Was Eddie looking at him as a suspect? What would Lingo's motive be?"

"Sex. Drugs. Money. Jealousy. Betrayal. Envy. Take your pick. Most murders result from one on the menu."

There was another long stretch while Slidell considered that.

"What about the artwork on Klapec's chest and belly?"

I had no explanation for that.

"And one other minor detail. Evans says he and Lingo were in Greensboro when Klapec got capped."

Or that.

* * *

It was 4:40 when Slidell dropped me at my Mazda. Traffic was brutal driving to UNCC. By the time I arrived at the optoelectronics center, Ireland had gone. As promised, she'd left hard copy of her SEM scans.

Wanting to get home before celebrating another birthday, I grabbed the envelope and bolted straight back to my car.

I was on Queens Road when Slidell rang my mobile.

"Glenn Yardley Evans."

"I knew it."

"Old Glenn and I are about to have another encounter."

"I've got SEM magnifications of the bone I took from Jimmy Klapec's femur."

"Uh-huh." Slidell sounded decidedly unenthusiastic.

"Now what?" I asked.

"Now I talk to Evans and you look at your . . . whatever the hell it is you just got. We swap stories in the morning."

My thumb moved to DISCONNECT.

"And, doc."

I waited.

"Watch your back."

Knowing the larder was empty, I stopped and loaded up at the Harris Teeter supermarket on Providence Road.

It was dark when I pulled in at Sharon Hall, too late for sunset, too early for moon- or starlight. Entering the grounds was like plunging into a black hole. The ancient oaks loomed like silent black giants guarding the dark swath of drive.

Circling behind the main house, I was surprised to see a red and blue glow pulsating from the direction of the Annex.

I cracked my window.

And heard a recognizable staticky sputter.

My scalp tightened and my palms went moist on the wheel. Killing the headlights, I crept forward far enough to peek around the corner.

A CMPD cruiser was angled toward my condo, doors open, radio crackling, dual beams lighting two cops and a man.

Though my view was partly obscured by bushes and the edge of the coach house, I could see that the man stood with arms raised, palms flat to one wall of the Annex. While one cop frisked him, the other asked questions.

The man was tall and lean and wore a leather jacket and jeans. Though his back was to me, there was something familiar about him.

As I watched, the frisking cop found and examined a wallet. The man spoke. The cop pulled something from inside the man's jacket.

I couldn't stand it. Knowing I should stay back, I made the turn and rolled closer.

Porch light haloed the man's hair. Sandy. Not long, not short.

Something prickly blossomed in my chest.

Impossible.

The frisking cop passed an object to the questioning cop. Words were exchanged. Body language relaxed. It was obvious tension was easing.

Both cops stepped back.

The man dropped his arms and turned. The frisking cop handed the object to him. Tucking it inside his jacket, the man raised his chin. Light fell on his features.

The trio watched as I rolled into my driveway and climbed out of the car. The frisking cop spoke first.

"Good timing, ma'am. We were informed the porch light was a signal for trouble. Seeing it lit, we approached the premises, found this gentleman looking into one of your windows. He says the two of you know each other."

"Detective Ryan is an old friend," I said, staring into a pair of Arctic blue eyes.

"You're good then?"

"We're good." Tearing my gaze free, I turned to the officers. "Thank you for your vigilance."

The cops pulled out. Crossing to my car, I began hauling groceries from the trunk with unsteady hands. Wordlessly, Ryan joined in the effort.

In the kitchen, I offered Ryan one of the beers Katy had left in my fridge. He accepted. I opened a Diet Coke for myself.

Took a long drink. Set the can on the counter. Carefully. Spoke without turning.

"You've been well?"

"Yes. You?"

"Yes."

"Katy?"

"She's good." I didn't offer that she was out of town for a while.

"I'm glad. She's a great kid."

"This is a surprise." I didn't ask about his daughter. Mean-spirited, I know, but pain takes you past the point of civility.

"Yes." I heard movement, a chair scrape, more movement.

"You've picked a bad time, Ryan."

"I came for Rinaldi's funeral. He was a good man."

I'd forgotten. How many years now? Three? Four? Ryan met Rinaldi and Slidell while helping me with a case involving black marketeering in endangered species.

"And to see you."

Tentacles began squeezing my heart.

My eyes fell on Monday's wineglass, still upturned in the wooden dish rack beside the sink. The newly awakened beast called out.

How welcome that would be. Glowing red warmth, then confidence and conviction. Finally, oblivion.

Followed by self-loathing.

Closing my eyes, I fought to banish the craving.

"Where are you staying?"

"A Sheraton out by the airport."

"How did you get here?"

"A couple of uniforms dropped me at the corner of Queens and something. I walked over from there. I turned on the porch light and was poking around."

"And got busted for peeping."

"Something like that."

"I could have let you go to jail."

"I appreciate the character reference."

I didn't answer.

"We need to talk." Ryan's tone was gentle, yet insistent.

No, wrangler. We don't.

"I've made mistakes."

"Is that a fact?" I could barely speak.

"It is."

The refrigerator hummed. The clock ticked on the living room mantel.

I tried to think of something distracting to say, or at least light and clever. Nothing came to mind.

In the end what I said was, "Is the beer cold enough?"

"Just right."

I could barely breathe as I emptied bags and placed items on my pantry shelves. Ryan watched, silent, aware of the jolt his sudden appearance had delivered. Knowing I'd open real conversation only when ready. Or I wouldn't.

From the beginning I'd felt an almost overwhelming attraction to this man, initially resisting, finally succumbing. Right off it was more than just sex or the assurance of a Saturday-night date. Ryan and I had spent hours together, days, watching old movies, cuddling by fires, arguing and debating, holding hands, taking long walks.

Though never roommates, we'd been as close as two people can be. We'd shared secret jokes and played silly games no one else understood. I could still close my eyes and recall the way his back curved into his hips, the way his fingers shot through his hair in frustration, the way he smelled just after a shower, the way our bodies molded when dancing.

The way he could stop my breath with a wink from across the room. With a suggestive quip on a long-distance call.

Then, one day, he just walked away.

Now Ryan was drinking beer in my kitchen in Charlotte.

How did I feel?

Hostile. Cautious.

Confused as hell.

Did I still love him?

Pain also has a way of wearing love down. And Ryan had never been easy.

Nor, to be fair, had I.

Did I want that melodrama back in my life?

I felt compelled to say something. What?

The tension in the room was almost palpable.

Mercifully, my cell sounded. I checked the caller ID. Slidell.

Mumbling an apology, I walked into the dining room and clicked on.

"Yes."

"Talked to Evans."

"Yes."

"Where are you?"

"Home."

"You OK?"

"Yes."

"What? You sick again?"

"No. What did you learn from Evans?"

"Well, ain't we Miss Congeniality?"

I was definitely not up to soothing Skinny's wounded sensitivity.

"Evans?"

"He's sticking with his story. Lingo had nothing to do with Jimmy Klapec, wasn't in town on October ninth."

"Did you confirm that the commissioner was actually in Greensboro?"

"Gee. Never thought of that." Pause. "Yeah. They were both there, returned to Charlotte late the next afternoon."

"Too late to kill and dump Klapec."

"If Funderburke's remembering right about the body turning up the morning of the ninth."

"The insect evidence suggests forty-eight hours as a PMI."

"Yeah." Skeptical. "The bugs."

I was so unsettled by Ryan's sudden appearance my thoughts were all over the map.

"Couldn't you drive from Greensboro, kill someone, dump the body, and get back to Greensboro in just a few hours?"

"You'd be setting a land record."

"According to Pinder, Gunther saw Klapec fighting with someone right before Gunther went to jail. Did you ask where Lingo was at that time?"

Slidell gave me a moment of reproachful silence.

"Lingo's got his eye on the statehouse, so he's stumping hard to scare up dough. Between September twenty-eighth and October fourth he and Evans were in Asheville, Yadkinville, Raleigh, Wilmington, and Fayetteville. They've got dozens of witnesses can put 'em in each place."

"Does Lingo have a record?"

"I ran a rap sheet search. Not so much as a citation for spitting on the street." Slidell drew air through his nose. It whistled. "But I'm catching bad vibes off Evans."

"What do you mean?"

"He's hiding something."

I was about to press the point when the line beeped, indicating an incoming call.

"I'll call you tomorrow."

Lowering the phone, I glanced at the screen. Dear God. Charlie Hunt.

I hesitated. What the hell?

"You looked very down at the cemetery this afternoon."

"Rinaldi and I worked together for many years. I'll miss him."

"I'm sorry."

"I know."

Beat.

"That went badly today, didn't it?"

"It's not your fault."

"That wasn't a line, Tempe."

"I believe you." I had to smile. "You use them so sparingly."

"I really do understand how hard it is to start over. I was married eight years. I loved my wife. She died at the Trade Center on nine-eleven." Charlie sighed deeply. "Perhaps it's harder when the other person is still alive."

"Perhaps."

"I can work around that," Charlie said.

"I'm sure you can."

"Shall I try?"

"The man in question showed up from Montreal today."

There was a moment of dead air.

"I like a challenge."

"Your odds are not good, Charlie."

"I've always preferred the tough three-pointer to the easy slam dunk."

"Outside the arc."

"That's me."

After disconnecting, I stood with the phone pressed to my chest, recalling my admission to Charlie earlier at the cemetery. Until the words left my mouth I'd been in denial. Then, there it was.

Now here *he* was. Wanting to talk. To admit to mistakes.

What mistakes? Taking up with me? Leaving me? Wearing a jacket that was crazy warm for the day?

The door opened and Ryan came in.

We looked at each other as though across a great chasm.

"I've missed you," Ryan said, spreading his arms and beckoning me forward.

I stood motionless, Gran's clock ticking a metronome for my crashing emotions.

Ryan moved closer.

And that was it.

I stepped into Ryan's embrace and pressed my cheek to his chest. I smelled starched cotton, male sweat, and the familiar Hugo Boss cologne.

Ryan stroked my hair and pulled me closer.

My arms went around him.

31

I KNOW WHAT YOU'RE THINKING. ANOTHER ROMP IN THE SHEETS, slut girl.

That's not what happened.

Ryan and I talked.

Old pal talk. Mostly.

We spoke of mutual friends, old cases. Katy. Boyd. Charlie, our shared cockatiel.

Ryan relayed news of a homicide in Montreal, a man shot seven times, his chalet set ablaze. Teams were searching for the victim's hands and head. If found, the missing parts would be at my lab when I next traveled north.

I told Ryan about T-Bird Cuervo's cellar, and about the *santero*'s untimely death by train. I traced the link from Asa Finney to Cuervo via the cauldron bones and the vandalism of Susan Redmon's tomb. Finney and Donna Scott-Rosenberg to Manuel Escriva to the cauldron.

I described Finney's Web sites, and his seemingly schizoid personas, Ursa and Dr. Games. I mentioned Jennifer Roberts's conviction concerning Finney's innocence, and gave my impression of the Wiccans I'd met at Camp Full Moon.

I recounted the discovery of Jimmy Klapec, and described the 666 and inverted pentagram carved into his flesh. I summarized the entomologist's report, and shared my uneasiness about the lack of animal scavenging and the paucity of insect activity on the body.

Ryan posed exactly the question that I expected. Santería, Satanism, and Wicca? I had no explanation.

I described Boyce Lingo and his extremist brand of morality, and admitted to my unfortunate on-air tantrum. Ryan asked what Larke Tyrell thought of my performance. I shook my head. He let it go.

I explained that Slidell and Rinaldi had been lead detectives on both the Cuervo and Klapec cases. Ryan made sympathetic noises as I described the shooting in NoDa, more as I explained Slidell's continuing, though curtailed, involvement in all three investigations.

Ryan asked if those assigned to the Rinaldi murder were sharing their findings with Slidell. I passed on the information they'd given to Skinny and he'd given to me. There was no way to trace the nine-millimeter used to shoot Rinaldi. Few were on the streets that night, and those in the shops and restaurants saw little. Eyewitnesses did agree the vehicle involved was a white SUV. Otherwise, accounts were all over the map. Other than heavy credit card debt, Rinaldi had no known personal problems. No addictions. No angry ex-lovers. Except for being a cop, no associations that would put him at risk. No recently released prisoners who might hold a grudge. No unexplained financial transactions, trips, or phone calls.

Ryan asked about Finney. I said he was Slidell's prime suspect. I ticked off the incriminating evidence: Susan Redmon's jaw; the tension when asked about Cuervo; the eyewitness report of a Ford Focus, the same model of car Finney owned; the bloody Dr.Games Web site, verified by Slidell as belonging to Finney; the satanic books I'd found at the Pineville house.

I told Ryan that Finney was sticking to his story that he didn't know Cuervo, and that he was home the night Jimmy Klapec was killed, but took no calls because he was fasting and meditating. I told him that between the grave-peeing incident six years earlier and his recent arrest, Finney had had no interaction with the police. That a search, reluctantly authorized by the DA, had turned up nothing in Finney's home. That his phone, bank, and credit card records showed nothing suspicious.

I added that, save for Jennifer Roberts and those at Camp Full Moon, no one had been located who knew Asa Finney. Even his fellow Wiccans barely remembered him. He attended few gatherings, was what they called a solitary practitioner. Finney had no employer, coworkers, family, or friends.

I explained that Jimmy Klapec had no police record, but that he was engaged in a high-risk lifestyle as a chicken hawk. That questioning of other hawks had yielded little. Save for Vince Gunther, no one seemed to have noticed the kid's existence or his disappearance. That, other than the bugs and the postmortem mutilation, neither the corpse nor the scene had yielded trace or any other kind of forensic evidence. That, except for the sighting of the suspicious Ford Focus, canvassing had turned up no witness to the killing or to the dumping of Klapec's body.

I outlined what Rinaldi's informant had told Slidell concerning Klapec and the violent customer resembling Rick Nelson. Finally, I described what we'd found in Rinaldi's notes. RN, Rick Nelson. VG, the mysteriously absent Vince Gunther. GYE, perhaps Glenn Yardley Evans. Boyce Lingo's phone number.

Ryan asked my opinion of Lingo and his assistant. I told him I thought something was off there. He gave me one of his looks.

I admitted that I had no idea what the motive might be, and that Lingo and Evans were out of town both the day Klapec got into his fight and dropped from the radar, and the day Klapec was killed and dumped at Lake Wylie.

Ryan asked if I thought the Cuervo, Klapec, and Rinaldi cases were connected. I said I wasn't sure. He asked what Slidell thought. I reiterated Skinny's conviction that Cuervo and Klapec were linked, and that Asa Finney was implicated in both.

But what you have on Finney, Ryan said, is diddly.

That's what we have, I agreed, but added that Finney deserved further scrutiny.

Ryan asked about his backyard welcome from Charlotte's finest. I told him about the porch light signal and the slit-belly snake. He asked who I thought might have left the little critter. I said take your pick.

Ryan said it was good he was here to protect me. I said "my hero." Laughed.

Ryan's voice went serious. No, he said. Really.

Unsure of his meaning, I said nothing.

Then Ryan talked. About Lily. Her addiction. Her rehab. His failed attempt to reconcile with her mother.

Ryan said he and Lutetia were now living apart. Admitted he'd made a mistake. Sought forgiveness. Invited me back into his life.

How those words would have thrilled me a few months back. Now they kicked up an emotional twister.

How would my sister, Harry, put it? I'd ridden that pony and been thrown.

And that's where we left it at 2:45. Given the hour, I offered the fold-out in the study. Ryan accepted. Birdie and I retired to my bedroom.

Sleep was a very long time coming.

My clock radio said 8:14. Arrows of light were shooting the shutters and the bedroom floor. The house was quiet. Bird was nowhere to be seen.

Morning sounds drifted in through my partially open window. Bird-song. A leaf blower. On Queens Road, a garbage truck grinding from pickup to pickup.

I felt as anxious as when I'd crawled into bed.

Throwing back the covers, I dressed, did modest toilette, and headed downstairs.

Ryan was at the kitchen table, reading the *Observer*. Birdie was in his lap.

The Viking blues lit up when I pushed through the swinging door. "Bonjour, Madam."

My southern parts did that *wee!* thing they do.

"Hey." I ignored my libido.

Ryan was wearing jeans and a plaid flannel shirt, unbuttoned. Under the shirt, his T featured a fat green lizard and the words *The Dead Milkmen*.

Irrationally, the thing annoyed me.

Whatever happened to AC/DC? Lynyrd Skynyrd? The Grateful Dead? Katy was right. I really was a dinosaur.

I was also irked by Bird being in Ryan's lap. He couldn't wait for me to get up and fill his dish?

"You look good," Ryan said, taking in my quick pony and slapdash mascara.

"Don't start," I said. Joking? Maybe. "Coffee?"

"You know how to make coffee?"

"I observe while waiting in line at Starbucks."

"I'd help, but the cat might feel rejected."

The cat never raised its head.

I ground beans and measured water. Sort of. I'm more of a guesser. "Bagel?"

Ryan nodded. I popped two in the toaster, took cream cheese from the fridge. Got mugs. Napkins. Spoons. Back to the fridge for cream. Back to the drawer for knives. Back to the cabinet for plates.

Ryan's presence was making me edgy as hell.

Looking for diversion, I flicked on the tiny counter TV. It was still tuned to the local news channel I'd punched up before leaving for Rinaldi's funeral.

"So." Ryan sat back. "What's up for today?"

I was about to provide a peevish response when the newscaster's words registered.

"We could—"

"Shh." I flapped a hand.

"Did you just shush me?"

"—in the front yard of his Pineville home. Neighbors spotted the body around seven this morning. Authorities believe Finney was shot sometime between ten and midnight last night."

"Did the woman just shush me?" Ryan asked the cat.

The screen filled with footage of Finney's small yellow house. Cruisers and other vehicles lined the curb. The ME van sat with doors winged out. On the lawn, a form lay motionless beneath plastic sheeting, beside it an upended roll-out trash can.

"Jesus." One hand was pressed to my lips.

"Asa Finney was a self-proclaimed witch. One week ago, Jimmy Klapec's headless body was found on the shore of Lake Wylie, its torso carved with satanic symbols. A suspect in the Klapec murder, Finney had just been released from police custody. Authorities continue to investigate possible links between the two killings."

"That's the man you spoke of last night." All humor had gone from Ryan's voice.

I nodded.

"Sonovabitch."

Grabbing my phone, I punched Slidell's number. Four rings. Five. Six.

"Slidell." Barked.

"It's Brennan. What happened?"

"I'm kinda busy here."

"Summarize."

"Finney's dead."

"I know that."

"He was putting out the garbage when someone capped him." In the background I could hear the usual crime-scene noises. Crackling radios. Voices calling out. Others answering.

"A drive-by?"

"Larabee says the gun was fired at relatively close range. Shoeprints in the dirt by the bushes. Looks like someone was waiting for him."

I struggled to form the words.

"Same weapon as Rinaldi?"

"This was a forty-five. Eddie got it with a nine-millimeter."

"Any witnesses?"

"Neighbor two doors down saw a Volkswagen Jetta cruising the block late yesterday. Thought it looked suspicious. Got a plate number."

"What's your read?" There was no need to spell out my meaning.

"This plays different."

"How so?"

"It's sloppy. Eddie's hit was clean."

"That's it?"

"Someone really wanted this guy dead. Six slugs worth."

Dial tone.

Slamming the phone, I began pacing the kitchen. How had this happened? Had Slidell and I put an innocent man at risk? Was Finney guilty and someone felt the need to take him out?

What someone?

The someone who killed Klapec? Rinaldi? Slidell thinks not Rinaldi.

What would I tell Jennifer Roberts?

Feeling the soft pressure of hands on my shoulders, I turned. Ryan's eyes were filled with concern.

"Come." I allowed myself to be led to the table. "Sit."

I dropped into a chair.

"Deep breath."

I inhaled. Exhaled.

Ryan handed me a mug, then sat back and assumed a listening posture. OK. Cop stuff. Safe ground.

I told him what I'd learned from Slidell.

"Was Finney robbed? Was the house burglarized?"

I hadn't asked. Retrieving the handheld, I phoned Slidell again. Six rings, then I was rolled to voice mail. I didn't bother leaving a message.

I took a swig of coffee. "I can't help feeling Finney's death was my fault."

"CT." Ryan used one of our codes. Crazy talk.

Grabbing the phone, I dialed again. As before, Slidell ignored my call.

"Crap." The device hit the table with a sharp crack.

Ryan's brows floated up, but he made no comment.

I raised my hands in frustration. "Why Finney?"

Knowing the question was rhetorical, Ryan didn't answer.

"Nothing in this investigation makes sense. Cuervo, a *santero*, hit by a train. Rinaldi, a cop, shot in a drive-by. Finney, a witch, gunned down at his home."

Ryan didn't interrupt.

"Klapec, a chicken hawk, killed by Satanists and dumped by a lake. Hell, we don't even have a cause of death in that one."

I lifted, then smacked down my mug. Droplets jumped the rim and landed on the table.

"And now the asshole detective I'm working with won't take my calls."

As if on cue, the phone rang.

Without thinking, I snatched it up.

"About time." I didn't even come close to civil.

"It's Larke Tyrell, Tempe."

I closed my eyes. At that moment, my battered nerves couldn't take more strain.

"Good morning, Larke. How are things?" OK. That sounded calm.

"Not good."

My upper teeth clamped onto my lower lip.

"You spoke to the media after I gave direct orders to the contrary."

"Lingo was campaigning at Rinaldi's funeral."

"I don't care if the man was doing tai chi naked on the statehouse lawn." Tyrell was also struggling to keep his voice even. "With regret I must inform you that your services are no longer needed by this office."

My face went hot.

"Lingo is dangerous," I said.

"So is a renegade soldier under my watch." Tyrell paused. "And there's the matter of the drinking."

Shame flamed my skin with a hot effervescence.

"I'm sorry," Tyrell said.

For the second time in minutes I found myself listening to a dial tone.

"Tyrell's pissed?" Ryan guessed.

"I'm fired," I snapped.

"He'll cool down."

"Andrew Ryan, the voice of wisdom." I watched black clouds swirl on the surface of my now tepid coffee. "How can you possibly know what Tyrell will do?"

"I know you."

"Do you? Do you really?" Suddenly, I was collapsing inside. "Months go by, nothing. Then you blow in out of nowhere with your sad story. 'Poor me, things tanked with Lutetia. I'm all alone. How about a booty call?'"

I knew I was ranting, couldn't help myself. Finney was dead. Slidell was snubbing me. Tyrell had just fired me. Ryan wasn't at fault. But he was there in my face so he took the hit.

"And look at you." I flapped an agitated hand at Ryan. "You're almost fifty. Who the hell are the Dead Milkmen?"

"Beats me."

"You're wearing the T-shirt of a group you don't even know?" Disdainful.

"I figured it was a charity for the widows and orphans of deceased dairy workers." Delivered deadpan.

That did it.

I laughed.

"Sorry." I laid a hand on Ryan's arm. "You don't deserve this. Lately, I'm certifiable."

"But cute," he said.

"Don't start, big boy."

Frustrated, I got up and poured my coffee down the sink. In my condition, caffeine was probably not a good plan.

Minutes later, the phone rang again. I grabbed it.

Slidell's disposition had improved. Slightly.

"The Jetta is registered to a Mark Harvey Sharp in Onslow County.

No police record. We've got a call-in down there. Should know something soon."

Several cells opened sleepy eyes in my subconscious.

What?

No answer from my id.

It was the cemetery all over again.

Ignoring the subliminal stirring, I told Slidell I wanted to be present when he interrogated the driver.

"Why?"

"Because I do."

Dial tone.

More pacing. Pointless activity. Dishes. Cat litter.

I was sure I wouldn't hear from Detective Dickhead again. I was wrong. Slidell called back. Background noises suggested he was now in his car.

"We got us a suspect. You won't believe who was driving that Jetta."

TWENTY MINUTES LATER RYAN AND I WERE EXITING THE ELEVATOR
on the second floor at Law Enforcement. Slidell had initially denied my
request, finally relented. We could watch, but not participate in the
interrogation of the man in custody.

Slidell was at his desk. Ryan expressed sympathy to him for the loss
of his partner. Slidell thanked Ryan for traveling to Charlotte to attend
the funeral.

"There was never any question. I admired the man. And liked him."

"They don't make 'em like Eddie no more."

"No, they don't. Had it been the reverse, Rinaldi would have come
to salute at my grave."

Slidell held up tightly curled fingers. "Brothers in the uniform."

Ryan high-fived Slidell's fist with one of his own.

The two spent a few moments recalling the time the three detectives
first met.

Then we got down to business.

Slidell phoned to see if the interrogation room was up and running.
It was. We trooped down the hall, Slidell in the lead.

Same one-way-mirror window. Same battered table. Same chair once
occupied by Kenneth Roseboro, later by Asa Finney.

The chair was now holding the man suspected of killing Finney.

The suspect was around forty with flint gray eyes and short brown
hair shaved into whitewalls. Though small, he was fit and muscular.

Tattooed on his right forearm were the Marine Corps logo and the words *Semper Fi.*

I was still struggling to wrap my mind around the man's identity.

James Edward Klapec. Senior.

Jimmy Klapec's father had been stopped twenty miles south of Charlotte driving the Volkswagen Jetta spotted by Asa Finney's neighbor.

Klapec's eyes kept sweeping his surroundings then dropping to his hands. His fingers were clasped, the flesh stretched pale on each of his knuckles.

Leaving Ryan and me in the corridor, Slidell entered the room, footsteps clicking metallic through the wall-mounted speaker.

Klapec's head jerked up. Wary eyes followed his interrogator across the room.

Tossing a spiral onto the table, Slidell sat.

"This interview is being recorded. For your protection and ours."

Klapec said nothing.

"I'm sorry about your loss."

Klapec gave a tight nod of his head.

"You've been read your rights." More statement than question.

Klapec nodded again. Dropped his gaze.

"I want to repeat, you have a right to a lawyer."

No response.

Slidell cleared his throat. "So. We're good to talk here?"

"I killed him."

"You killed who, Mr. Klapec?"

"The satanic sonovabitch who murdered my son."

"Tell me about that."

Klapec sat almost a full minute without speaking, face pointed at his hands.

"I'm sure you know about Jimmy." Halting.

"I'm not judging you or your boy," Slidell said.

"Others will. The press. The lawyers. They'll paint Jimmy as a pervert." It was obvious Klapec was treading carefully, choosing his words. "I didn't agree with the choices Jimmy was making." Klapec swallowed. "But he deserved better than I gave him."

"Tell me what you did."

Klapec looked at Slidell, quickly away.

"I shot the cocksucker who killed my boy."

"I'm gonna need specifics."

Klapec inhaled, exhaled through his nose.

"Since Jimmy's murder, I start every morning with the Charlotte paper online. Cops don't bother with nobodies like me and my wife, so we have to rely on the news to know what's being done about the murder of our own son. Sad, eh?"

Slidell rotated a hand, indicating Klapec should continue.

"I read what this commissioner said about Finney."

"Boyce Lingo?"

"Yeah. That's the guy. Lingo made sense about the cops being hand-cuffed and the courts being paralyzed. About the common citizen needing to take action."

My eyes met Ryan's. I knew what was coming.

"They proved him right by setting the murdering sonovabitch free. Lingo was dead-on." Klapec's jaw muscles bunched, relaxed. "Jimmy was a homo. Even if a trial took place, they'd make him look bad. I knew justice for my son would have to come from me."

Klapec's words were sending chills up my spine.

"I owed it to Jimmy. God knows I didn't do shit for him while he was alive."

"Tell me exactly what you did." Slidell prompted.

"Borrowed my neighbor's car, drove to Charlotte, waited outside his house, and put the evil bastard out of his misery."

"How did you find Finney's address?"

Klapec gave a mirthless snort. "That took about ten minutes online."

"Describe the weapon."

"Forty-five-millimeter semi-automatic. A Firestar."

"Where is it?"

"In a Dumpster behind a Wendy's, about a quarter mile east of Finney's place."

Slidell made a note in his spiral.

"What did you do following the shooting?"

"After tossing the gun, everything's a blank. This morning I woke up in a motel and headed out of Dodge."

"Where were you going when the trooper pulled you over?"

"Home. I wanted to be sitting in my own kitchen in Half Moon when the cops finally called. *If* they called. Doubt they'd waste the time on me."

Yo!

Again, the whispered heads-up.

I closed my eyes, trying to establish a connection with my lower centers.

No go. Having signaled, my subconscious was now ignoring my call.

Slidell asked about Gunther. Klapec said he'd never heard the name.

Slidell took a moment to review his notes. Or to pantomime doing so. Then he started in from a different angle.

"Why were you driving your neighbor's car?"

"Eva needs ours to get to work."

"That would be Mrs. Klapec."

Klapec nodded.

"What can you tell me about the death of Detective Rinaldi?"

Klapec's knuckles turned an even paler shade of yellow. "That's the cop that was killed up here?"

"Where were you around ten last Saturday night?"

Klapec gave Slidell a look of blank insolence. "I'm leveling with you, here. I killed Finney because the murdering prick needed killing. Don't try putting anything else on me."

"Answer the question, Mr. Klapec."

Klapec considered. Then, "I was leaving a meeting at South Gum Branch Baptist. My wife can vouch for me."

"What kind of meeting?"

Klapec dropped his chin. I could see scalp gleaming pink through his close-cropped hair. "I attend a support group for anger management."

"Where's this church?"

"A good two hundred miles from here."

"That don't answer my question."

"On Highway Two fifty-eight, about halfway between Jacksonville and Half Moon."

Yo!

What? Highway 258? That would put the church near Camp Lejeune. I'd been on the Marine Corps base four years back, digging a dead woman from under a crawl space.

Nothing clicked.

"Hold that thought." Slidell's voice brought me back. He was leaving Klapec to rejoin us in the corridor.

Tipping his head toward the window, Slidell asked Ryan, "Thoughts?"

"He's wrapped pretty tight."

"Poor bastard just shot the man who murdered his kid."

"Maybe," I said.

Slidell's eyes slid to me, back to Ryan.

"Think he's on the level?"

"Seems sincere," Ryan said. "But he could be mental."

"Or covering for someone."

"They swabbed his hands for gunshot residue?"

"Yeah. He's fired a weapon. Dipshit's either too stupid to scrub down or smart enough to fire a cover-up shot."

"I'm sure you have a unit checking the Wendy's Dumpster."

"You bet your ass I have. And every motel along that corridor."

Slidell turned to me. "How about you? Find anything in your fandangle photos can help put this whole thing to bed?"

For a moment *I* didn't get it. Then I practically did a full-on head slap.

The SEM scans of bone from Jimmy Klapec's femur. Marion Ireland's envelope was still in my car. Ryan's appearance had blown it right off my compass.

"I'm not quite finished." I looked at Klapec to avoid direct eye contact with Slidell.

"Uh. Huh."

"I'll have at it again as soon as I leave here."

"How 'bout that's right now. This guy's life's in the toilet. Least we can do is assure him he got the right witch."

With that Slidell returned to his suspect.

RYAN AND I STOPPED AT A STARBUCKS THEN DROVE TO THE Annex. I got Ireland's envelope from my car and spread the photos across my kitchen table. Ryan sat beside me, sipping his coffee in a way that grated on my nerves.

As I viewed the SEM hard copy, I explained what I was doing.

"When Jimmy Klapec's body was still unidentified, I took samples from his femur and made thin sections for microscopic examination."

"Why?" Ryan asked.

"To allow me greater precision in estimating age at death."

"Then the kid was ID'ed by prints and that became irrelevant."

"Yes."

Ryan slurped his coffee.

"But on viewing the thin sections I noticed something wrong with some of the Haversian canals."

"Point of order." Ryan raised an index finger.

"Haversian canals are tiny tubes that run longitudinally down compact bone."

"How tiny?" Slurp.

"Really tiny. Must you make that noise with your coffee?"

"It's hot."

"Blow across the top. Or wait."

"What are these canals for?"

"Stuff goes through them."

"What kind of stuff?"

"Blood vessels, nerve cells, lymphatics. That's not important. What's important, or could be, is that some of the canals exhibit unusual patterning at their rims."

"What kind of patterning?"

"Weird dark lines."

"You're really hot when you use that scientific jargon."

I'd have rolled my eyes but they were glued to Ireland's photos.

Seconds passed.

Slurp.

"Next time, could you choose a cold beverage?"

"It's drinkable now. So what do these mysterious dark lines mean?" Ryan asked.

"With the light microscope at the ME office I could only crank the magnification to four hundred. That's not enough to really see detail."

"Enter Ireland's big gorilla."

"Mm."

"We're now viewing hard copy from her SEM analysis." Aborted slurp.

"Mm."

I'd singled out and was studying one photo. A white band at the bottom provided the following information:

Mag=1.00 KX   20μm   EHT=4.00kV   Signal A=SE2   Date: 16 Oct
$\longmapsto$ WD=6mm   Photo No=18

"What's that?" Ryan's face was right beside mine.

"Femoral section 1C magnified a thousand times."

"Looks like a moon crater circled by frozen waves." Ryan pointed at a jagged crack shooting from the crater's center. "That one of your weird dark lines?"

Without answering, I exchanged the photo for another. Femoral section 2D showed two fissures originating within the Haversian system.

One by one I studied every image.

Twelve of the twenty showed microfracturing.

"It's not an artifact," I said. "The cracks are real."

"What caused them?" Ryan asked.

"I don't know."

"What do they mean?"

"I don't know."

"Lunch?" Ryan asked.

"But I intend to find out."

"That's my girl," Ryan said.

My mind was already triaging possibilities. No evidence of a fungus. A disease process seemed unlikely. So did trauma, even repeated trauma to the femur.

I reexamined each image.

The cracks seemed to be originating deep within the canals and radiating outward. What could distribute strain so deep and so widespread within bone to cause such a phenomenon?

Pressure?

Ryan placed a sandwich in front of me. Ham? Turkey breast? I took a bite, chewed, swallowed. My mind was spinning too fast to notice.

Vascular pressure? Lymphatic?

A phone rang somewhere in the same time zone.

"Shall I get that?" Ryan asked from far off.

"Yeah. Yeah."

I heard Ryan's voice. Didn't listen to his words.

Pressure due to expansion?

Expansion of what?

Ryan said something. I looked up. He was beside me, palm pressed to the mouthpiece of the portable.

"What might expand and place stress deep within bone tissue?"

"Marrow?"

"I'm talking about inside the compact bone, not in the marrow cavity."

"I don't know. Water. Do you want to take this? The caller's pretty insistent."

"Who is it?"

"Woman named Stallings."

Anger flashed from nerve ending to nerve ending.

My first reaction was to order Ryan to disconnect.

Then I changed my mind.

"I'll take it," I said, reaching for the portable.

Patting my head, Ryan stepped from the kitchen.

"Yes." Practically hissed.

"Allison Stallings."

"I know who you are. What I don't know is how you have the audacity to phone my home?"

"I thought maybe we could talk."

"You thought wrong." My voice could have flash-frozen peas.

"I'm not trying to compromise your investigation, Dr. Brennan. Really, I'm not. I write true-crime books and I'm scouting an idea for my next project. It's nothing more sinister than that."

"Where do you get off crashing my crime scenes?"

"*Your* crime scenes?"

I was too furious to answer.

"Look, I have a police scanner. When I heard a call concerning a satanic altar, it caught my attention. Right now people are nuts for voodoo and witches. Then the body washed up at Lake Wylie and I thought the situation was worth pursuing."

"You're a paparazzo. You sell photos exploiting personal tragedy."

"My books don't make a lot of money. Occasionally I sell a picture. The income puts bread on the table."

"Mutilated children always sell. Too bad you didn't get a close-up of Klapec."

"Come on, you can't really fault me. This thing has all the elements. Satanic ritual. Male prostitution. Fundamentalist Southern politico. Now a murdered witch."

"What do you want?" Through tightly clamped molars.

"I'm neither a cop nor a scientist. To keep my work accurate I must rely on those actually involved in the investigations—"

"No."

"I know you shut me down last time we talked, but I was hoping I could persuade you to change your position."

I did?

"What did I tell you?"

"Is this a test?" Chuckling.

"No." Definitely not laughing.

She hesitated, perhaps confused, perhaps searching for the best spin.

"When I asked for your help, you said no and hung up. Then you called back and reamed me out for showing up at your crime scenes. Frankly, I found it a bit of an overreaction. When I dialed you an hour later, to see if you'd cooled off, you refused to pick up."

"Did you phone the chief medical examiner in Chapel Hill?"

"Yes." Wary. "Dr. Tyrell was less than cooperative."

"What did you tell him concerning our conversation?"

Again, she hesitated, choosing her words.

"I may have implied that you were cooperating."

The little snake had lied to Tyrell.

"How did you get this number?" I was squeezing the phone so hard it was making small popping noises.

"Takeela Freeman."

"You tricked her, too."

Stallings neither acknowledged nor denied the accusation.

"Did you *imply* to Takeela that I'd want her to help you?"

"The kid's not the sharpest tack in the drawer."

Anger made my voice sound high and stretched.

"Never call me again."

When I turned Ryan was staring at me through the partially open swinging door.

"I heard a noise."

The handheld lay on its convex back, wobbling like an upended turtle. Unconsciously, I'd slammed it to the table again.

"You're hard on equipment," Ryan said.

I didn't answer.

Ryan's mouth turned up at the corners. "But easy on the eyes."

"Jesus, Ryan. Is that all you think about?"

"Incoming." Hunching his shoulders, Ryan ducked from the room.

I sat a moment, wondering. Call Tyrell? Explain that Stallings had lied about our conversation?

Not now. Now, fired though I might be, Jimmy Klapec deserved my full attention. And his father.

And Asa Finney.

I spent another ten minutes puzzling over the SEM scans.

And came up empty.

Frustrated, I decided on a gambit that occasionally worked. When stumped, start over at the beginning.

Opening my briefcase, I pulled out the entire file on Jimmy Klapec.

First I reviewed the scene photos. The body was as I remembered it, flesh ghostly pale, shoulders to the earth, rump to the sky.

I viewed close-ups of the anus, the truncated neck, the carvings in the chest and belly. Nothing but fly eggs.

I shifted to the autopsy shots. Y incision. Organs. Empty chest cavity. Strange striated bruise on the back.

I noted the atypical decay pattern, with more aerobic decomposition than anaerobic putrefaction. As though the body was rotting from the outside in rather than the inside out.

Spreading my bone photos, I reexamined the cut mark in the fourth cervical vertebra. Concave bending. Fixed radius curvature sweeping from, not around, the breakaway point.

The fifth vertebra had one false start. I checked my notes: 0.09 inch in width.

Both neck bones exhibited polish on the cut surfaces. Neither showed entrance or exit chipping.

I slumped back in my chair. The entire exercise had triggered no epiphany with regard to cracking in Haversian canals.

Discouraged, I got up and paced the kitchen.

Why wasn't Slidell calling back? Had further questioning of Klapec, senior verified or disproved his story? Had they found the gun in the Dumpster? Had they talked to Mrs. Klapec?

I felt genuine sorrow for Jimmy's mother. First her son, now her husband. The future held no rainbows for Eva Klapec.

I paced some more. Why not? Nothing else was working.

Ryan chose that moment to test the waters.

"All clear?" he asked from the safety of the dining-room side of the door.

"Yes."

"Permission to come aboard?"

"Granted."

Ryan came into the kitchen, followed by Birdie.

"Got it all figured out?"

"No."

"Chocolate." Ryan turned to Birdie and repeated the pronouncement. "Chocolate."

The cat raised a skeptical brow. If a cat can be said to do so.

Turning back to me, Ryan tapped a finger to one temple. "Brain food."

"There may be a Dove bar in the freezer."

"What's a Dove bar?"

"Only the best ice cream treat on the planet." Then I remembered. "That's right. They're not available in Canada."

"Admittedly, we have some holes in our culture." Ryan began rummaging in the freezer.

I recalled Tuesday's morning-after mess in my sink. Maybe not, I thought.

"Yes!" Ryan slammed the door, turned, and flourished two bars. "Two frozen delights."

I took one and began peeling the wrapper.

Frost cascaded onto my hand.

I stared at it, remembering Ryan's flip answer.

Water.

Expansion.

Cracking.

Ping!

I flew to the phone.

34

THIS TIME, SLIDELL TOOK MY CALL. HOT DAMN. I WAS AVERAGING two for four.

"Klapec was frozen."

"What are you talking about?"

"I don't know how I could have been so dense. It explains everything. The distorted decomp. The lack of scavenging. The paucity of insect activity. The cracking within the Haversian systems."

"Whoa."

Ryan was listening while eating his ice cream.

"Of *course* Klapec decomposed from the outside in. The pattern makes sense if he was frozen. His outer surfaces would have warmed faster than his core."

"What's this Haversham thing?"

"Haversian. With the SEM zoomed to a magnification of one thousand, I could see cracks in the tiny tunnels in Klapec's bones. I couldn't understand what had caused them."

"Now you do."

"What happens when water cools?"

"You get out of the shower."

I ignored that.

"Most liquids shrink. So does water, until it reaches approximately four degrees Celsius. After that, it expands. When frozen it has expanded roughly nine percent."

"And this is relevant why?"

"The microfracturing in Klapec's bone is due to pressure created by ice crystal formation deep in his Haversian canals."

"You're saying Klapec was a Popsicle when he was dumped."

"The killer must have stored his body in a freezer."

Slidell made the link.

"Meaning Klapec could have died long before Funderburke spotted him at Lake Wylie."

"Maybe in September, when Gunther saw him arguing with Rick Nelson. Where was Finney around that time?"

"Home alone. And Lingo was ping-ponging all over the state."

"Did Finney have a freezer in his home?"

"You can bet your ass I'll find out."

"It doesn't confirm that either Lingo or Finney's our guy."

"It stretches our window for time of death. That's something."

I heard choked inhalation, then a sort of growl.

"I hope that was a yawn."

"I got zero shut-eye last night. I'm going ten-oh-two for a couple hours. You gonna be at your lab later today?"

"Tyrell fired me."

"No way."

I told him about the call from Allison Stallings.

"That should clear the air."

"Maybe. Tyrell's still peeved about my on-camera spat with Lingo. For now I'd better lay low."

"I knew that opportunistic bitch was trouble. Anyway, good one, doc."

I hung up and, you guessed it, began pacing. I felt frustrated with the investigation, guilty over Finney's death, and unsettled by the presence of my unexpected houseguest.

I was checking containers in the fridge for unwanted life forms when that houseguest reappeared wearing running shoes, shorts, and the green lizard T.

"Going for a run?"

Idiot. Of course he was going for a run.

"I'm glad you found your workout gear."

"I'm glad I left it here."

There was an awkward beat.

"When do you fly back to Montreal?" I asked.

"As things stand, Sunday."

"Will you be returning to the Sheraton?"

"I can." Sad face.

I hesitated. Why not? You'd do the same for any old friend.

"You're welcome to stay here."

Big Ryan smile. "I can cook."

I smiled, too. "I like that in a"—I started to say *man*—"friend."

Ryan asked if I'd like to join him on his run. I declined.

Through the kitchen window, I watched him fall into in an easy, loping stride, long, ropy legs barely straining.

I remembered those legs intertwined with mine.

My stomach did a handspring.

Oh boy.

I had to do something. But what? I didn't want to antagonize Tyrell further by going to the MCME. Slidell was power napping.

I tried grading student lab exercises from my forensics class.

Couldn't concentrate.

I tried outlining my next lecture.

No go on that either.

Phone Katy?

There was a call I'd been putting off.

I dialed. Got voice mail. Had she not taken her phone to Buncombe County? Was it not working up in the mountains? Was she still mad?

I was gathering hand washables when I spotted Ryan walking up the drive, shirt pasted to his chest, face flushed with exertion. He was speaking into his mobile. I could tell he was agitated.

Ryan rounded the corner of the Annex, out of my sight line.

Without thinking, I moved toward the back door.

"I know, sweetheart."

Ryan was speaking English, not French. Lutetia?

Cold bloomed in my chest.

"That's the way it's got to be."

Breath frozen, I leaned closer to the door.

Pause.

"No."

There was another, longer pause. Then the knob turned.

Skittering backward, I gathered the abandoned laundry into my arms.

Ryan came through the door. Met my eyes. Waggled his free hand in irritation.

"Not a chance," he said into the phone.

Lily, he mouthed to me.

"We'll talk later."

Snapping the lid, Ryan reclipped the mobile to his waistband.

"Problem?" I asked, casual as hell.

"Lily wants to go to Banff. The terms of her probation restrict her to Quebec."

"I'm sorry."

"Not your fault." He smiled at the bras and teddies pressed to my chest. "Planning a garage sale?"

"I don't do garage sales."

"Keep the leopard-skin thong. It was always my favorite."

I felt my face color.

"Mind if I use your bathroom?"

"Please. Do you want anything?"

Ryan flashed lascivious brows.

My innards went for a full double flip.

I looked at the clock. Two thirty. Dear God. What would we do all afternoon?

Remembering my quarrel with Katy, I had an idea. It would require little focus and might channel my restless energy. It would also keep me and my houseguest on neutral ground.

I flapped a hand at Ryan's shirt. "You really don't know who the Dead Milkmen are?"

Ryan shook his head.

"My daughter claims I'm abysmally ignorant of today's rock music."

"Are you?"

"*Abysmal* is a bit strong."

"Kids can be harsh."

"Tyrell canned me," I said. "Slidell's down for beauty rest."

"Don't want to interrupt that."

"Definitely not. After you shower, let's log on and look up the Milkmen."

I made popcorn to create a festive atmosphere.

Ryan and I learned that the Dead Milkmen were a satirical punk group whose first official album, *Big Lizard in My Backyard,* was released in 1985.

"Your shirt could be a classic," I said.

"Might earn my fortune on *Antiques Roadshow.*"

My mind flashed an image of April Pinder.

"Do you know the Cheeky Girls?" I asked.

"I'd like to," Ryan said, giving an exaggerated wink.

My eyes executed a hall-of-fame roll.

We learned that the Cheeky Girls were Romanian-born twins, Gabriela and Monica Irimia. Their first single, "Cheeky Song (Touch My Bum)," spent five weeks in the top five on the UK singles chart. In a Channel 4 poll, it was then voted worst pop record of all time.

"I've got to see the words to that," Ryan said, reading the title.

Finding a site that listed rock-and-roll lyrics, I scrolled down and positioned the cursor over *Cheeky Girls.*

"Cheap Trick!" Ryan exclaimed.

"What did I do?"

"*I want you to want me,*" Ryan sang. Badly.

"Did you just do air guitar?"

Ryan pointed to the group directly above *Cheeky Girls. Cheap Trick.*

"I love those guys," Ryan said.

Total blank.

"*Abysmal* may be generous," Ryan said.

I linked over to the Cheap Trick Web site.

And felt my adrenals fire into overdrive.

"Cheap Trick has been an institution since the seventies. 'Dream Police.' 'The House Is Rockin'.' You know Comedy Central's *Colbert Report*? Cheap Trick wrote and performed the theme song. Also the one for *That '70s Show.*"

Ryan's voice was barely registering. Synapses were exploding in my head like fireworks.

Rinaldi's call to Slidell, relaying information about his informant.

Rinaldi's cryptic notes. RN. CTK.

Glenn Evans flanking his boss on the courthouse steps.

"*Going to a party,*" Ryan sang.

My attention was riveted on a man holding a black-and-white-checkered guitar shaped like roadkill. A caption identified him as Rick Nielsen, lead guitarist.

Ryan misread my interest. "That's a seventy-eight Hamer Explorer checkerboard. Awesome."

Normally, I'd have wondered at Ryan's knowledge of guitars. Not then.

I stared at Nielsen, unbelieving. High, broad cheekbones. Close-set eyes. Sharply sloping jaw. Prominent chin. Baseball cap.

According to Slidell, Vince Gunther had described Klapec's violent john as Rick Nelson in a baseball cap.

Had Rinaldi actually said Rick Nielsen? Nielsen's resemblance to Glenn Evans was striking. Had Slidell gotten the name wrong? Someone Gunther's age would more likely know an active band like Cheap Trick than a dead sixties teen idol.

"Rick Nielsen," I asked, pointing at the screen. "Does he often wear a cap?"

"Always." Ryan picked up on the tension in my voice. "Why?"

I told him my thinking.

"Could be big," he said.

"Before bothering Slidell I have to be sure."

Ryan and I surfed through dozens of images. Concert shots. Album covers. Promotional pictures.

An hour later, I sat back, impressed but dubious. Unquestionably, Glenn Evans looked like Rick Nielsen. But was it merely coincidence?

Nope, I told myself. No such thing.

I dialed.

Amazingly, Slidell picked up.

"What." Barked.

I explained the resemblance between Rick Nielsen and Glenn Evans.

"Might you have misunderstood Rinaldi?" I asked.

Slidell made one of his *hrlf* noises. I pictured him sitting on a bedside in his underwear, struggling to wake up. Not pretty.

"Maybe Klapec's violent john is actually Glenn Evans." Another synapse fired. "Holy shit. Maybe CTK wasn't an airport code. Maybe that was Rinaldi's abbreviation for Cheap Trick."

Slidell started to talk. I cut him off.

"Maybe Rinaldi had Lingo's phone number because he was looking at Evans."

Slidell thought about that.

"Evans alibis out for the time Klapec's body was dumped. And for the day Klapec argued with someone and disappeared."

I had no answer for that.

"I did some checking on Evans and Lingo. Both are clean as a vicar's ass. No drugs, hookers, or little girls. Besides, where's motive?"

I started throwing things out, not really convinced.

"Maybe Evans is a closet gay. Maybe he picked Klapec up, things went south, Klapec ended up dead."

"And the Mephistopheles motif?"

I was too pumped to be surprised at Slidell's *Faust* reference.

"Maybe Evans is in some kind of cult."

"And maybe he runs bare-ass in crop circles under full moons. Think about it. Evans works for Lingo, a power-hungry Bible-thumper with an appetite for airtime. There are whole zip codes who hate the guy. If Lingo's aide swings with Satan, that fact would hardly stay hidden."

I had no answer for that, either.

"Now, since you won't let me sleep, I'm going back to goddamn headquarters."

35

"WHAT DID HE SAY?" RYAN WAS STILL AT THE COMPUTER. SOME-thing punk was blasting from the speakers. Or was it heavy metal?

"He was unconvinced. Jesus. Can you turn that down?"

"What would you like to hear?"

"The music's fine. Just lower the volume a few squillion decibels."

"Seriously. Who do you like?"

"You'll mock me."

"I won't. Well, unless you say Abba. Come on. Choose one of your CD's. You do have CD's?"

"Of course I have CD's." Two of Abba. I didn't fess up.

"Choose one."

"Oh, for heaven's sake."

Running a finger along my music shelf, I made a selection and handed it to Ryan.

"Yes! A Canadian."

"I didn't know that."

Disapproving look. "Neil Young makes up for the national flaw of not having Dove bars."

Ryan slipped the disc into the PC.

First acoustic guitar, then the familiar nasal tenor issued forth.

Synapse trip down memory lane. Pete in his marine dress whites. In jeans playing backyard croquet with Katy. In plaid flannel PJ bottoms watching TV.

This had been Pete's favorite CD.

Somewhere on a desert highway . . .

I studied the album's cover art. A scarecrow, backlit by an orange and red sunset.

Or was it a native dancer in a fringed coat?

A witch?

And there it was again. The subliminal sneeze that wouldn't break.

Witch? Pete?

She rides a Harley-Davidson . . .

I flipped the case and looked at the title. *Harvest Moon.*

The sneeze geysered into my forebrain.

"Holy hell."

Ryan's head snapped up. "What?"

"Something's been bugging me about Evans and I just got it."

As before, I grabbed the phone and dialed.

As before, Slidell answered.

I gestured at the computer. Ryan lowered the volume.

"Klapec lives in Onslow County, right? In Half Moon?"

"So?"

"I just remembered. I can't believe I missed it until now. I've been to Onslow County, know the town. I just didn't remember I remembered it."

I was so psyched I was babbling.

Ryan pantomimed inhalation.

I took a breath. Started over.

"When you questioned Evans at Rinaldi's funeral, he referred to Jimmy Klapec as a half-moon hick. I though it was just a derogatory expression, but my subconscious pricked up at the reference."

"Your what?"

"Evans meant it literally. Half Moon. It's a town on Highway Two fifty-eight, north of Camp Lejeune and Jacksonville. The Klapecs live there. If Evans never met Jimmy Klapec, how could he know the kid's hometown?"

"That lying piece of crap."

For several seconds I listened to Slidell's breathing. Then he made a clicking sound with his tongue.

"Still won't get me a warrant."

"How do you know?"

"Already tried. Got shut down. DA says it's all circumstantial.

Besides, Evans alibis out. Didn't say so, but there's also the fact that the guy works for a public figure. DA don't want to poke that hornets' nest without a smoking gun."

Slidell was right. The crack about Half Moon. The resemblance to Rick Nielsen. Lingo's number in Rinaldi's notes. It was all speculative. So far we'd found nothing to show either motive or opportunity. And Evans had witnesses putting him elsewhere on both the September and October dates in question.

I thought a moment.

"Have you checked into Evans's vehicle?"

"I've got a call in on that. By the way, Klapec's been charged. Unit found the gun. Motel manager confirms Klapec's story, and a security camera shows him checking in at twelve twenty-seven this morning. Plus the confession's clean. Looks like the pathetic bastard's telling the truth."

Ryan was still surfing the Cheap Trick Web site, the volume turned low. Seeing my face, he reached out for one of my hands.

"Feeling jammed up?"

"I keep seeing Klapec in that interrogation room. First, he lost his son. Now he's probably murdered an innocent man."

"You really think Lingo's aide is your boy?"

Raising frustrated palms, I summarized the circumstantial evidence Slidell and I had just discussed. "And Evans has an alibi."

"Let's crack it."

"According to the man who found it, Klapec's body was dumped the morning of October ninth. Evans was in Greensboro."

"Let's let that go for now. You said Klapec could have been killed earlier, then placed in a freezer."

"Yes."

"For how long?"

"I don't know." I was saying that a lot lately. "But Klapec was last seen alive on September twenty-ninth."

"By whom?"

"Vince Gunther."

"A fellow chicken hawk."

I nodded.

"Is Gunther credible?"

"Apparently Rinaldi thought so. His notes suggest he was willing to pay the kid five hundred dollars for information on Klapec's killer."

"What was Slidell's take?"

"We never questioned Gunther directly."

"That's right. Gunther's in the wind. Still no word on his whereabouts?"

I shook my head. "But we did interview April Pinder, Gunther's former girlfriend. Her story confirmed what we suspected about Klapec and this Rick Nielsen/Nelson character arguing, then Klapec disappearing. It supported an LSA for Klapec on September twenty-ninth."

"How about Pinder? She reliable?"

I waggled splayed fingers. Maybe yes, maybe no.

"Could she be covering for Gunther?"

"Doubtful. She's pissed as hell. After she paid his bail, Gunther dumped her."

I saw thought working in Ryan's eyes.

"Exactly how did Pinder's story corroborate Gunther's?"

I relayed what Pinder had said about Gunther watching TV the night he got out of jail. About Gunther telling her he saw Klapec and Rick Nelson/Nielsen arguing that day.

"And Evans was out of town at that time, too?"

"On a campaign swing across the state."

"He's sure about his dates?"

"Very."

"Is Pinder?"

"She seemed to be. But who knows? She's not all that bright."

"But, cupcake. We have a means at our disposal to check."

"We do?" Ignoring the bakery reference.

Ryan worked a few keys, checked the screen. Worked some more.

"I'll be damned." He pointed at a line of white text in a black box. "You're going to like this."

The box listed all Cheap Trick appearances, live onstage, on television, and on radio, and provided links to recent and old interviews.

I read the line Ryan was indicating.

It took a moment for the significance to register.

When it did, I took in a breath.

"Cheap Trick appeared on HBO September twenty-seventh and twenty-eighth, in a two-part special featuring seventies and eighties rockers," Ryan said.

"So Pinder had to be wrong about the date. Cheap Trick wasn't on television on the twenty-ninth." I was thinking out loud. "Gunther was in jail on the twenty-eighth. He couldn't have been watching at her house that night. It had to have been the twenty-seventh, the day *before* Gunther went in, not the day he got out."

"Does Evans have an alibi for the twenty-seventh?" Ryan asked.

"Holy mother of God."

I was so excited I had to punch Slidell's number twice. No matter. My call was rolled to voice mail.

"We've got him," I said. "Klapec was last seen alive on September twenty-seventh, not the twenty-ninth. Check Evans's whereabouts for that date. Call me."

I clicked off.

"Good one," I said, high-fiving Ryan.

He grinned a grin as wide as the Rio Grande.

Seconds dragged by. Hours. Eons.

I chewed at the cuticle on my thumb. Got up and paced. Sat down. Chewed some more.

Still the phone didn't ring.

"Where the hell is he?"

Ryan shrugged. Ate a handful of popcorn. Continued surfing.

"Don't drop kernels into my keyboard."

"Yes, ma'am."

"Or drip butter."

I looked at the clock. It had been twenty minutes since I left my message.

"Maybe I should fax that page to Slidell. Can you print it?"

Pointless. But it was something to do.

Returning to the Cheap Trick Web site, Ryan made hard copy and handed it to me. The page made me think of Rinaldi's notes. Something else to do.

I pulled the papers from my briefcase. Returned to the study.

"Look at this," I said. "Now everything makes sense."

Ryan dropped onto the couch beside me.

JK. 9/29. LSA with RN acc. to VG. RN - PIT. CTK. TV. 10/9-10/11? CFT. 10. 500.

"According to Vince Gunther, Jimmy Klapec was last seen alive with Rick Nielsen on September twenty-ninth. Rick Nielsen with pits. Gunther noted the resemblance when he saw Cheap Trick, CTK, on TV. October ninth to eleventh is the time Klapec was found. Rinaldi was meeting Gunther at CFT, Cabo Fish Taco, at ten with five hundred dollars."

Silently, Ryan and I read Rinaldi's last lines of code.

RN = BLA = GYE. Greensboro. 10/9. 555-7038. CTK-TV-9/27. VG, solicitation 9/28-9/29.
    GYE 9/27?

"Rick Nielsen equals Boyce Lingo's aide equals Glenn Yardley Evans. Rinaldi called Lingo's office, and Evans told him that he and his boss were in Greensboro on October ninth, when Klapec's body was found."

"Rinaldi must have known something was wrong with the September dates. Cheap Trick appeared on TV September twenty-seventh and twenty-eighth. Vince Gunther was in jail for solicitation on the twenty-eighth, so Rinaldi knew he couldn't have seen Nielsen, and by extension, Klapec, on that day."

"So April Pinder got the date wrong. They had their pizza party the day *before*, not the day *after* she busted Gunther loose."

"A day for which Evans may have no alibi."

"Jesus, Ryan. Somehow, Rinaldi figured all this out. Evans discovered that he knew."

My fingers were curled so tightly my nails were digging crescents in my palms.

"Evans killed him."

The phone shrilled.

I leaped for it.

Slidell sounded as wired as I felt. "Evans was in Charlotte on the twenty-seventh."

I started to speak. He cut me off.

"He drives a white Chevy Tahoe."

"Holy shit."

"Judge finally cut paper. We're going in."

"I want to be there."

"How'd I know you'd say that?"

I waited.

"Just you."

"When?"

"Now."

36

"Where's your wheels?"

Rubber squealed as we hooked a sharp right from the Sharon Hall drive.

"Ryan took my car to check out of his hotel."

I expected a wisecrack about my sex life. Slidell didn't make one.

"Tell him it ain't personal. The DA wants this handled like the world's watching."

Though Ryan's insight would have been an asset in executing the warrant on Evans's property, I couldn't fault that reasoning. Given Lingo's position, a lot of eyes *would* be watching. Perhaps courtesy of CNN and FOX.

"Is Evans at home?"

Slidell shook his head. "He rents a coach house apartment on property owned by a woman name of Gracie-Lee Widget. What the hell kinda handle is that?"

I gestured for Slidell to continue.

"*Gracie-Lee* says Evans works Thursday nights, gets home around nine. She ain't nuts for the idea, but says if I show a warrant she'll let us into his crib."

Evans lived in Plaza-Midwood, a neighborhood of winding streets, large trees, and modest turn-of-the-century bungalows. I'd been there many times. Located midway between uptown and the UNCC campus, the area is popular with underpaid university faculty.

Slidell made a right onto Shamrock, another onto a short dead-ender, and parked in front of a lowcountry house with a down-sloping roof, brown stucco walls, and green plantation shutters. The long front porch held rocking chairs and basket-hanging ferns, all looking well past their shelf life.

We got out and climbed the steps. Slidell rang the bell.

It took roughly a decade for the door to open. When it did, I understood why.

Gracie-Lee Widget's hair floated wispy white around a face shriveled by a thousand wrinkles. Scarecrow lips suggested edentulous jaws. But age wasn't the woman's most striking feature.

Gracie-Lee had one arm. That's it. No other limbs. Her left shoulder was outfitted with an elaborate apparatus ending in two opposable hooks, and she rode a motorized chair that looked like something out of *Star Wars*. A tartan plaid blanket covered her lap and what looked like two midthigh stumps.

Gracie-Lee scowled up at us, clearly not pleased.

"Detective Slidell." Slidell badged her. "We spoke on the phone."

"I don't need reminding."

Gracie-Lee snatched the badge. Drew it close to her face. Made a sound like *tcht*. Gave it back.

Slidell produced the warrant. Gracie-Lee shooed it as she might flies from a cake.

"Mr. Evans isn't here."

"That's not a problem."

"It's not right invading a man's home."

Slidell held out a hand. "We'll be real careful."

Gracie-Lee didn't move.

"Ma'am?"

"Tcht." The hook rose and dropped a key into Slidell's palm.

"Don't harm none of that nice young man's belongings."

With that Gracie-Lee pressed a button on her armrest. The chair swiveled, and the door slammed.

Slidell shook his head as we descended the steps. "Glad I don't face that every year over Thanksgiving turkey."

"She's old."

"She's mean as a snake."

The coach house was a two-story frame affair across a patch of grass at the end of a gravel drive. Double garage down, living quarters up. The second floor was accessed by an exterior wooden staircase.

Ancient myrtle grew thick at the back of the property. Though dusk was fading fast, through the foliage I could see what looked like a vast, sweeping lawn.

"Well, ain't that sweet. Evans lives at the ass end of Charlotte Country Club."

Slidell's voice dripped scorn. For golf? For being on the wrong side of the course? For those rich enough to belong to the club?

I said nothing.

We passed a koi pond that was green with algae. A brick planter overflowing with dead leaves. A birdbath lying in two pieces on the ground.

As we walked, Slidell's hand drew up to his gun butt. His eyes roved our surroundings. Neck tension suggested alert listening.

At the coach house, Slidell gestured with a downturned palm. Sensitive to his body language, I froze.

Through a dirty window I could see that the garage held only garden equipment, a wooden ladder, and a set of wrought-iron lawn furniture. A door opened from the back wall, I guessed into a small work- or storeroom.

"No Chevy Tahoe," Slidell mumbled, more to himself than to me.

"Where is CSS?"

"They're coming."

Typical Slidell. Giving himself a window alone at the scene.

Slidell moved to the stairs, but must have seen something he didn't like. Squatting, he inspected the first step. Then he rose and stepped high onto the step above.

I looked down.

A wire stretched low across the riser. I nodded that I'd seen the trap.

On the top landing, Slidell waved me behind him with another palm gesture. Then he banged on the door. "Glenn Evans?"

A train whistled somewhere very far off.

"Charlotte-Mecklenburg Police. I have a warrant to search these premises."

No answer.

Slidell drew his gun and leaned close to the door. After turning his head left then right, he stood back and banged again.

"I have a key, Mr. Evans. I'm coming in."

The door opened easily.

Every shade was down. A floorboard creaked, otherwise the interior was deathly still.

Slidell flicked a wall switch.

The kitchen was European modern. Black and white floor tile. Sleek black cabinets with lots of glass. Stainless steel appliances.

No freezer large enough to hold a body.

"Stay here." Gruff.

Glock double-fisted beside his nose, Slidell strode to an open door opposite the entrance and pressed his back to the wall. I darted to his side.

Slidell whipped my way and glared. I raised my hands in acquiescence. I would stay put.

Slidell disappeared through the doorway.

I peeked around the jamb. Darkness.

Drawing back, I waited. It was so quiet I could hear my breath rising and falling in my throat.

Finally, a second light went on.

"Clear," Slidell said.

I stepped from the kitchen into a short interior hall. Doors opened on the left, the right, and straight ahead. Slidell was banging drawers beyond the latter. I joined him.

"Real palace, eh?" Slidell's tone was once again dialed to disparaging. "Living room, bedroom, kitchen, bath. Guess Lingo don't overpay his staff."

I looked around.

The room set a new standard for understatement. Beige walls, furniture, drapes, and carpet. White ceiling and woodwork. No funny coasters or pillows. No snapshots of dogs or friends in bad party hats. No trophies, photos, mementos, or artwork.

A brass floor lamp rose from behind the couch. A flat-screen TV occupied the top shelf in a set of recessed shelving. To the left of the recess was a series of built-in drawers. That's where Slidell was searching. To its right was a cabinet.

The shelves below the TV held scores of DVD's. Pulling on latex gloves, I walked over and ran through the titles.

The Matrix. Gladiator. The Patriot. Starship Troopers. A trio of flicks having to do with Bourne.

"Evans likes action," I said.

Slidell slammed a drawer and yanked out another. Rifled with one gloved hand.

I opened the cabinet. Liquor.

"He isn't a teetotaler." I checked labels. Johnny Walker Blue Label scotch whiskey. Evan Williams twenty-three-year-old bourbon. Belvedere vodka. "The guy drops some bucks on booze."

I looked around. Slidell was on the bottom drawer. Seeing nothing else of interest, I moved on to the bathroom.

Clean enough. Old-fashioned pedestal sink and commode. Black vinyl shower curtain. Black and white towels.

On the toilet back were a boar bristle brush, a Bic razor, a can of Aveeno shave gel, and a Sonicare toothbrush in its charger.

The medicine cabinet held the usual. Dental floss. Toothpaste. Aspirin. Pepto. Nasal spray. Band-Aids. A tube of dandruff shampoo sat on the tub ledge. Rope soap dangled from the showerhead.

Slidell clomped up the hall. I joined him in the bedroom.

Here Evans had shown a bit more flair. The walls were red, and a fake zebra-skin carpet lay on top of the beige wall-to-wall. A black sateen spread covered the mattress, and a leopard-skin hanging served as a headboard. The rest of the room was taken up by a pair of bedside tables and a metal cart holding another flat-screen TV.

"Toad should have stuck with bland."

For once Skinny's comment on taste was apt.

Slidell slid back a closet door and started going through clothes. I opened a drawer in the near bedside table.

"Check this out," I said.

Slidell joined me. I pointed to a small blue package with a Texas big-hair cowgirl on the label.

"Rough Rider studded condoms," Slidell read. "So our boy's a player."

"Or wants to be. Any missing?"

Slidell counted. Nodded. Returned to the closet.

Seconds later I heard, "Hell-o."

I turned.

"Look what our rough rider's hiding with his loafers."

Slidell held a shoe box. In it were perhaps a dozen DVD's. He read several titles.

College Boys Cummin'. Gang Banging Gays. Bucking Black Stallions.
Slidell's eyes rolled up to mine. A grin crawled one corner of his mouth.

"So Evans twirls baton for the other team. Guess that takes care of motive."

Tossing the box to the bed, Slidell thumb-hooked his belt. "No room in the kitchen. So where would this douche bag stash a freezer?"

"There's an interior door in the garage."

"There surely is." Slidell checked his watch. "Let's have us a look-see."

Slidell thundered down the stairs. I followed at a slightly safer pace.

Outside it was dark, the crepe myrtles a ragged barrier between Widget's yard and the golf course beyond. No lights shone from the brooding bunker that was the main house.

The garage was unlocked. Slidell charged straight to the inside door and tried Gracie-Lee's key. It didn't fit.

Slidell twisted the knob to the right and the left. Shoulder-slammed the wood. The door held fast.

Slidell raised his foot and kicked hard. Still the latch held. He kicked again and again. The jamb buckled and splintered. A final hard thrust and the door flew in.

Slidell found a switch. The man was damn good with lights.

A fluorescent tube came to life with a loud, buzzing hum.

The room was about eight by ten. On the left was a sideboard or old bathroom vanity wrapped with padded quilting secured by rope. On the right was shelving.

Straight ahead, the wall was covered with pegboard studded with metal hooks. A tool hung from each hook. Hammers, screwdrivers, a wrench, a carpenter's saw.

My heart leaped to my throat.

No way. Klapec wasn't decapitated with a handsaw.

I scanned the shelving.

Overhead, the fluorescents hummed and sputtered.

I spotted it on the second shelf down. A cardboard box with the words *6¼ inch power saw* printed on the side.

Beside me Slidell was tugging at the rope covering the quilted object. My hand shot out and wrapped his arm. He turned.

Wordlessly, I nodded at the box. Reaching up, Slidell jerked it to the floor and tore back the flaps. Inside was an old McGraw-Edison circular saw.

Our eyes met.

"Yes" is all I said.

Unhooking a hedge clipper from the pegboard, Slidell cut the bindings on the quilt with four quick snaps. Together we grabbed the fabric and pulled.

The object wasn't furniture or cabinetry. It was a Frigidaire chest freezer, standard white, maybe eight-cubic-foot capacity.

"Sonovabitch." Slidell elbowed me aside in his eagerness to view the contents.

"Shouldn't CSS take photos before we open this?"

"Yeah," Slidell said, flipping the latch and heaving upward with both hands.

Above the whoosh of frozen air and the overhead buzzing I heard a muted pop.

"What was that?" I asked.

Slidell ignored my question. "Don't look like Evans ponied up for the auto-defrost model."

Though the comment was flip, Slidell's tone was stony. And he was right. The freezer's interior was completely crusted over with snow and ice crystals.

On the upper left was a rectangular wire basket filled with plastic bags. I scraped several to clear the labels. Frozen supermarket vegetables. Ground beef. What looked like a pork roast.

Flashback to the imprint on Klapec's back. The basket?

No. That pattern was linear. The basket was constructed of stainless steel in a woven arrangement.

I kept the observation to myself. I was mesmerized by another plastic-wrapped object tucked into a corner on the freezer's bottom.

Roughly round. A ham? Too large. A small turkey?

I reached in and lifted the frozen mass. The plastic was surprisingly frost free. What was wrong there?

The object was heavy, maybe four or five kilos. As I balanced it on the freezer's edge, my own words slammed back from the past. My lecture to Slidell on the weight of a human head. About the same as a roaster chicken, I'd said.

Hands trembling, I pressed the clear plastic against the object inside. Details emerged, cloudy and blurred, like objects at the bottom of a murky pond.

An ear, blood pooled in the delicate arcs and folds. The curve of a jaw. Purple-blue lips. A nose, flattened and pressed to a blanched white cheek. A half-open eye.

Suddenly, I had to have air.

Thrusting Klapec's head at Slidell, I rushed outside.

Gnawing at a thumbnail, I paced, waiting for Slidell to emerge. Waiting for the CSS truck to arrive.

Seconds dragged by. Or maybe they were minutes.

I heard the muffled sound of Slidell's phone.

My eye drifted to the myrtles and the hint of golf course beyond. I crossed to the hedge, wanting a peaceful vista to calm my nerves.

And tripped over something lying in the shadows.

Something with bulk and weight. Dead weight.

Heart hammering, I scrabbled to my knees and turned.

Glenn Evans lay faceup on the lawn, eyes vacant, blood oozing from a hole dead center in his forehead.

37

SLIDELL BURST FROM THE GARAGE, HEAD SWIVELING, GUN TWO-fisted by the side of his nose.

Seeing his alarm, I realized I'd cried out.

Slidell ran to me and peered down at the body.

"What the fuck?"

Heart pounding, I stumbled to my feet and drew back toward the myrtles.

Slidell stared at Evans a very long time. Then he spoke without looking up.

"Pinder owns a white Dodge Durango. Vehicle showed up at her house an hour ago. Gunther was driving it."

I struggled to put Slidell's words and Evans's death into a framework that made sense.

"Something else." Slidell's eyes rolled up and locked onto mine. They looked sunken and aged in the yellow glow oozing from the coach house windows. "Evans and Lingo were out of town the entire week Klapec disappeared. Including the twenty-seventh."

For a moment neither of us knew what to say. We just stood there.

Had we gotten it all wrong? Had Rinaldi?

In the stillness I heard a twig snap behind me. Slidell's Glock shot up and pointed in my direction.

I was turning when a gun muzzle kissed the base of my skull.

A man's voice said, "Do this right or you both die now."

Adrenaline fired to every cell in my body.

"Toss the gun." Almost a hiss.

I saw a glint as Slidell's eyes flicked sideways.

"Don't do it, Detective."

In my peripheral vision I could see the curl of a finger on the far side of a trigger guard. I could smell cleaning oil and old gunpowder.

"More police are on the way," Slidell said.

"Then we're going to move fast, aren't we?" The words came machine-gun quick.

"It won't work, Vince."

The muzzle slid forward to the soft flesh under my jaw.

"What won't work is me going to prison."

"Being in jail is better than being dead."

"Not for guys like me."

I felt the front sight dig deep into my jugular, felt my blood pulse against the nub of steel.

"The gun. Now!" Staccato.

"Let's all stay calm." Slidell extended the Glock to arm's length, then tossed it in Gunther's direction.

"Pick it up," Gunther ordered, mashing down on my back.

As I bent, he bent with me. I could smell pricey aftershave and stale body sweat.

With trembling fingers I scooped the Glock and handed it over my shoulder. Gunther took it and jerked me up by the collar of my jacket.

"The cuffs."

Slidell unclipped and tossed his handcuffs. Again, I was forced to bend and retrieve them.

"Cell."

Slidell tossed his phone. Gunther kicked it into the myrtles.

"Walk toward me, hands on your head."

Ever so slowly, Slidell raised his arms, interlaced his fingers, and dropped his hands to the top of his head. Then he began inching in our direction.

"Faster."

Slidell stopped. I could see fury working in his eyes. And something else. Fear.

"Don't play with me, fat boy." Gunther sounded dangerously amped.

"You don't have a chance," Slidell said.

"Yeah?"

I heard the swish of fabric behind me.

Slidell's eyes went wide.

Lights exploded in my brain.

Then there was nothing but blackness.

I became aware of pain first: Throbbing in my head. Burning around my wrists. Aching in my shoulders.

Then sounds: The grinding hum of a motor. The murmur of tires on pavement. Soft thumps and clanks as things jostled around me.

Smells: Gasoline. Rubber. Exhaust.

Shifting and swaying told me I was in a moving vehicle.

I tried to sit up, realized my hands were tied behind me.

I opened my eyes. Darkness.

A new sensation. Nausea.

I lowered my lids. Swallowed.

Memory crept back. Evans. Gunther. Slidell's shocked look.

Deduction. Gunther had knocked me unconscious and thrown me into a car trunk.

Dear God. Where was he taking me?

Sudden terrible thought. Was Slidell dead?

I listened for clues. My battered brain couldn't interpret what my ears sent its way.

Breathing through my mouth, I lay still and counted the left and right turns. Willed myself not to vomit.

Finally, the car stopped. Doors opened. I heard male voices. Then silence.

Again, blindly groping for a sense of control, I counted. Sixty seconds. One twenty. One eighty.

The trunk lid flew open and I was hauled upward. Trees arced past my vision. Brick. Pillars.

My stomach roiled. I tasted bile and felt tremors under my tongue.

A familiar back stoop.

Fear shot through me. We were at the Annex. Why?

Dragging me from the car, Gunther prodded me toward the porch, muzzle once again pressed to the base of my skull.

I stumbled forward, grasping for comprehension. For details to remember. To recount. To reconstruct.

Back door open. Kitchen windows casting rectangles of light on the lawn. Purse tossed, contents scattered like wind-blown leaves on the grass.

Gunther shoved me up the steps. I entered my home on trembling legs.

From somewhere in the house I heard frenzied rattling and scraping. Birdie? Too loud. Then what? I couldn't tell. Blood jackhammered in my brain.

Gunther paused, licked his lips. For the first time I had a view of his face. He looked like someone's older brother, a tennis coach, a preacher at the church. His eyes were green, but shifting wildly. His hair was chestnut and neatly side-parted. He had one thing right. Switch-hitter though he was, with his feminine good looks he'd be grade-A prime in prison.

Moving almost imperceptibly, I flattened my back and shoulders to the wall beside the jamb and raised up on my toes. Something clicked, and the light falling through the door changed subtly.

Where was Bird? I listened for the jangle of the bell on his collar. Nothing.

Pushing hard, Gunther forced me through the swinging door into the dining room, then through to the hallway.

Slidell's back was to us. He was hunched, wrenching at cuffs chaining his wrists to the newel post of the staircase.

"Easy, Detective." Agitated and tense.

Slidell whirled as best he could.

"You're going down, you dickless shit." Slidell's voice was ragged from exertion and rage.

"Then what have I got to lose with two more corpses?"

Moving me into Slidell's field of vision, Gunther jammed his gun into my trachea and forced my chin upward.

Slidell hauled on the cuffs, fury radiating from him like heat.

Gunther forced the barrel so deep I cried out in pain.

Slidell's fingers curled into fists. "You hurt her I'll fucking kill you myself."

"Don't see how you'll manage that. Turn around."

Slidell didn't budge.

"Move! Now! Or your buddies will be scraping her brains off the wall with a sponge." The calm was gone and Gunther again sounded psychotically overwrought. Was the man roller-coastering on speed or some other drug?

Eyes burning with hatred, Slidell began a slow pivot.

Lunging forward, Gunther arced the gun fast toward Slidell's temple. It connected with a sickening crack.

Slidell went down and lay still, cuffed arms crooked heavenward as if he were a supplicant in prayer.

Then, Gunther moved fast. So fast I couldn't react.

Shoving me to the staircase, he mashed me facedown, produced a key, and freed Slidell's left hand. Looping the chain through the banister uprights, he clamped the free cuff onto my right wrist. I heard movement and felt pressure on my arms. In seconds, the ropes fell from my hands.

Adrenaline surged through me as comprehension dawned. I was handcuffed to Slidell. Gunther planned to kill us both.

Stall, Brennan.

Pushing to my knees, I half turned to face my aggressor.

"You already burned a kid, a cop, and one of your ex-clients, right? Why more murders?"

"Kiss my ass." Gunther's eyes were jumping all over the room.

"He's right, you know." I swallowed back nausea. "They'll hunt you down and run you to ground. There's nowhere you can hide."

"The cops don't know I exist. Your pal here cracked under pressure. Murdered Evans, then you, then committed suicide."

"Why would he do that?"

"Despondent over the death of his partner. Over getting poor Asa Finney shot. Over killing you."

"No one will believe that. It's preposterous."

"He blamed you for making him arrest the wrong man. For goading Lingo into stirring up trouble."

Slidell groaned. I looked at him. In the murky light I could see an angry welt on his temple.

"I know what you're thinking. But I watch television."

My eyes snapped back to Gunther.

"That bruise will look wrong when they do the autopsy. I've thought of that." Gunther shot a hand through his hair. "I've thought of everything. That's where the nice bullet will blow through his head."

He's delusional. Keep him talking.

"You fed Rinaldi false information," I said. "You must have done a lousy job if you had to kill him."

"The man was a moron."

"He was smart enough to figure out you killed Klapec."

"Jimmy made a big mistake. He cut into my trade. I had to straighten up his thinking. Things got out of hand." Gunther licked his lips. "I didn't mean to waste Jimmy. It just happened."

"And Rinaldi?"

"Skank made the mistake of tying Klapec to me."

"So you eliminated the competition, then threw suspicion on your disloyal customer."

I saw Gunther's finger twitch against the trigger. "Brilliant, eh?"

"Why behead Klapec?"

Gunther snorted a laugh. "To fit him into an old crone's cheap-ass freezer."

A chill traveled my spine. The man felt absolutely no remorse.

Buy time.

"Why carve him up?"

"When that cauldron story broke, I said to myself, 'Vince my man, the devil's looking out for you. You got a frozen headless body you need to offload and ole Lucifer's offering the perfect cover.'"

Again, it was as though a switch had been thrown. Abruptly, Gunther sounded calm, confident, almost amused.

"You put Klapec's head in Evans's freezer tonight to tighten the noose."

Gunther clicked his teeth and cocked his head.

"Don't forget the saw. That was a nice touch."

"You made one mistake. You shot Evans with your own gun."

"Please. Don't be dumb. Every cop carries backup. After Slidell used his thirty-eight on Evans he came here and shot you. The bullets will match. Then, being old school, Slidell ate his own piece."

"No one will believe a scenario as absurd as that. The homicide detectives know you are in town and that you have access to a white Durango. They'll be on you within hours."

Gunther's face tensed and his eyes went hard and began to dance. "I know what you're trying to do, lady. You think you can delay me. You think you're smart. But it won't work with me."

Gunther shifted the thirty-eight to his left hand and yanked Slidell's

Glock from his waistband. The *chink-chink* of the slide sounded deafening in the closeness of the hall.

Ignoring the pain in my wrist, I hurled myself past the newel post and stretched out over Slidell as far as my manacled hand would allow.

I heard angry footsteps, then a hand grasped my hair and jerked my head up. Vertebrae crunched in my neck.

Still clutching my hair, Gunther knocked me sideways with an elbow to the face. My head ricocheted off the banister.

The room pressed in, drew back. I felt warmth trickle from my nose.

With one boot, Gunther levered me from Slidell and rolled me to the left.

"No!" I screamed, struggling to rise up on all fours.

Through a tangle of hair I saw Gunther bend over Slidell.

I stretched out a hand, tears streaming my cheeks.

Reaching down, Gunther pressed the Glock to Slidell's temple.

The moment froze into a deadly snapshot.

Unable to bear the sight of Slidell's death, I squeezed my eyes shut.

Then the world exploded.

38

AFTER PULLING THE TRIGGER, RYAN LAID HIS GUN ON THE MAN-tel, unlocked the cuffs, checked Slidell for a pulse, and dialed 911. Units came screaming from all over Charlotte. So did two ambulances, later the ME van.

Vince Gunther was pronounced dead at 10:47 P.M.

Slidell and I were transported to Carolinas Medical Center, both protesting loudly. My concussion was minor. Slidell's was severe and his scalp required stitches. We gave statements from our hospital beds.

Ryan remained at the Annex to answer questions. I learned details late the next morning.

Returning to the Annex, Ryan had seen the porch light shining. He edged up to the house and spotted my purse in the grass where Gun-ther had tossed it after removing my keys. Sensing trouble, he'd used his own key, crept into the house, come upon the scene in the hallway, and taken Gunther out with a single round to the head. Providentially, Ryan's bullet had knocked Gunther sideways, and Gunther's death throes had not resulted in a squeezing of the trigger.

At the ME office, Gunther's true identity began to emerge. Prints showed he was a twenty-seven-year-old con man with several aliases. Under his real name, Vern Ziegler, he rented an apartment off Harris Boulevard and attended UNCC. Male prostitution provided but one of many illicit income streams.

Charlie Hunt came to see me early the next morning. Held my hand. Looked genuinely concerned.

Katy called. She was still tagging documents in Buncombe County, but would return to Charlotte for the weekend. She was finding the project, big surprise, boring. The upside was she was talking about graduate studies, maybe law.

Pete also called. He was relieved to learn that I'd suffer no lasting consequences, pleased to hear of Katy's mention of law school. As we talked, Summer was out perusing china patterns.

I was discharged by 10 A.M. To his dismay, Slidell had to stay longer. Before leaving the hospital, Ryan and I stopped by his room. He'd already talked to members of the Rinaldi task force. Ryan was somber, quiet. Between us, we pieced together the story.

My wild guess had been intuitive and right on the mark. Evans was a closet gay who cruised NoDa wearing a ball cap pulled low to disguise his identity. Usually he picked up Gunther. One night he spotted Klapec and got a taste for fresh talent. Pleased with performance, he switched service providers. Gunther was furious and confronted Klapec, his sometime friend. Klapec argued free trade, things got physical, and Gunther killed him.

I remembered Gunther's words in my hallway.

"For a guy who prided himself on covering all angles, he sure hadn't worked out an exit strategy. He didn't want the body found, but he had no idea what to do with it."

Buying time, Gunther crammed Klapec into Pinder's grandmother's freezer. When he read about Cuervo's altar and cauldrons, he thought his problem was solved. Knowing nothing about Santería, Wicca, or devil worship, he decided to make the murder appear satanic. After carving symbols in Klapec's flesh, he dumped the still frozen corpse at Lake Wylie.

"Gunther knew there was a possibility Pinder or one of the chicken hawks might link him to Klapec, so he began feeding false information to Rinaldi," Slidell said.

"Do you think Gunther knew Evans was Lingo's right-hand man?" I asked.

"The guy wasn't stupid, but he definitely had some screws loose," Slidell said. "They found Tegretol in his apartment. Lots of it."

"That's a medication for bipolar disorder." Ryan.

Slidell's eyes rolled to the ceiling. "Like I said. The guy was a whack job."

I considered, decided against attempting to explain manic depression to Slidell.

"He'd stopped taking his meds?" I guessed.

"Clever move, eh? Doc said he was probably in something called an acutely manic period."

Impatient with the topic of Gunther's mental health, Slidell segued back to Evans. "Maybe Gunther learned Evans's name from Rinaldi. Or spotted him on the tube with Lingo."

"Lingo's tirades fed right into Gunther's delusion," I said.

"And set Asa Finney up as a perfect patsy to take the fall for Klapec," Ryan added.

"Here's the biggest mind-fuck," said Slidell. "Gunther didn't know Finney and didn't know he'd been shot by Klapec's father. If he'd heard that, he wouldn't have bothered with the frame on Evans, unless he just wanted to burn the guy."

Slidell shook his head.

"I was way off base on Finney. The guy was just trying to make a dime and be left alone. His income came from Dr. Games and other sites loading ads on gamers. And the Ford Focus spotted near the witch camp turned out to belong to a cousin of one of the locals."

"Did CSS find anything useful in Granny's freezer or basement?" Ryan asked.

"Enough blood for a transfusion. DNA'll show it came from Klapec."

"I suspect some of the blood may belong to Señor Snake," Ryan said.

"Gunther left the copperhead on my porch?"

Slidell nodded. "Probably meant as another satanic misdirect. Or maybe Gunther thought he could scare you off the case."

I just looked at him.

"Yeah, yeah," Slidell said. "Maybe the guy wasn't so smart after all."

"Why did Evans come home early last night?" I asked.

"Landlady dimed him. Told you that old harpy was trouble."

"Why did Evans park way up the block instead of just pulling into the driveway?"

"He was probably worried that our warrant might include his vehicle. He must have surprised Gunther sneaking in from the golf course."

"To plant the saw and Klapec's head."

Slidell nodded again.

"When Gunther learned we'd questioned Pinder he decided it was time to get the goods out of Granny's basement. After capping Evans, he saw us right there in the garage. Things were spinning out of control and he was thinking wildly. That's when he dreamed up the murder-suicide plan."

More came out over the course of that day.

At age six, April Pinder had taken a car bumper to the side of her head. The injury resulted in an inability to properly sequence certain types of information. Time was one area that caused her difficulty. Pinder had mixed up dates, confusing the day Gunther got out of jail with the day before he went in.

Turned out Gunther/Ziegler did have a record. Using a long list of aliases he'd worked a number of con games over the years, most bilking elderly or retarded women. A scam based on checking obits, then delivering COD packages requiring payment of money due. Door-to-door peddling of candy, candles, and popcorn for false charities. Sale of "winning" lottery tickets and counterfeited contest coupons. All petty stuff. Nothing violent. His boyish good looks undoubtedly served him well. It was only after going off his meds in August that he started showing bursts of violent behavior.

Overnight, the weather had turned cold and rainy. For the rest of that day and the next, Ryan and I hunkered down at the Annex. Ryan was moody, quiet. I didn't press. Shooting someone is never easy for a cop.

Katy visited on Saturday morning. She'd never heard of the Cheeky Girls. We all laughed. She talked more about law school. It was good.

Allison Stallings called shortly after noon. I didn't pick up, but listened as she recorded a message. She'd decided to write about a multiple murder in Raleigh, apologized in case her deception had caused me problems, promised to set the record straight with Tyrell.

Slidell stopped by around four. With him was a very tall woman who almost matched him in weight. Her skin was caramel, her hair black and woven into a single thick braid. From her posture and bearing I knew she was on the job.

Before Slidell could speak, the woman shot out a hand. "Theresa Madrid. This extraordinarily fortunate detective's brilliant new partner."

Madrid's grip could have cracked coconut husks.

"Chief thinks my cultural sensitivities need broadening." Slidell, out of the side of his mouth.

Madrid clapped Slidell on the back. "Poor Skinny pulled a lucky double-L."

Ryan and I must have looked blank.

"Lesbian Latina."

"She's Mexican." Slidell's lips did that poochy thing they do.

"Dominican. Skinny thinks every Spanish speaker must be Mexican."

"Astounding," Slidell said. "All those amazingly rich and diverse cultures evolving the same wife-beater shirts and plastic Jesus lawn shit."

Madrid's laugh came from somewhere deep in her belly. "Not as astounding as your girlfriend's mustache."

Slidell added another puzzle piece. It came from Rinaldi's son, Tony. His youngest child had Cohen syndrome. Rinaldi was spending all he had on his grandson's medical fees and on tuition for special schooling. And then some.

When they'd gone, Ryan and I agreed. Slidell and Madrid would get along fine.

Ryan cooked. Chicken fricassee with mushrooms and artichokes.

I worked on a lecture.

Over dinner, and later, we talked.

There had been so many deaths. Cuervo. Klapec. Rinaldi. Finney. Evans. Gunther.

Like poor little Anson Tyler, T-Bird Cuervo had met a violent but accidental end. A man alone in the dark on a railroad track. Perhaps drunk. Perhaps naive about the high-speed technology that had so recently come to his town. Cuervo was a harmless *santero.* Beyond selling a little marijuana, he'd done nothing illegal, perhaps eased the way for newcomers marginalized like himself by differences in language and culture.

Jimmy Klapec had been driven into the streets by an ignorant and intolerant father. Like Eddie Rinaldi and Glenn Evans, he died because a man went off his meds and lost touch with reality.

Vince Gunther/Vern Ziegler's life ended why? Because his own brain betrayed him? Because he was evil by nature? Neither Ryan nor I had an answer for that one.

Asa Finney's death was the most disturbing of all.

"Klapec, senior shot Finney because he was tormented by guilt," Ryan said.

"No," I said. "He was driven by fear."

"I don't understand."

"Americans have become a nation afraid."

"Of?"

"A shooter on a rampage in a school cafeteria. A hijacked plane toppling a high-rise building. A bomb in a train or rental van. A postal delivery carrying anthrax. The power to kill is out there for anyone willing to use it. All it takes is access to the Internet or a friendly gun shop."

Ryan let me go on.

"We fear terrorists, snipers, hurricanes, epidemics. And the worst part is we've lost faith in the government's ability to protect us. We feel powerless and that causes constant anxiety, makes us fear things we don't understand."

"Like Wicca."

"Wicca, Santería, voodooism, Satanism. They're exotic, unknown. We lump and stereotype them and bar the doors in trepidation."

"Finney was a witch. Lingo's rhetoric tapped into that fear."

"That plus the fact that people have lost confidence in the system on other grounds. Klapec was a sad example. There's a growing belief that, too often, the guilty go free."

"The O.J. syndrome."

I nodded. "A bonehead like Lingo stirs the public into a froth and some citizen vigilante appoints himself judge and jury."

"And an innocent man dies. At least Finney's death should put an end to Lingo's political career."

"It's ironic," I said. "The witch and the *santero* were harmless. The college boy and the commissioner's assistant led dark double lives."

"Nothing's ever what it seems."

Birdie and I slept upstairs.

Ryan slept on the couch.

39

SUNDAY, I ROSE EARLY AND DROVE RYAN TO CHARLOTTE-DOUGLAS International. Outside the terminal, we hugged. Said good-bye. Didn't speak of the future.

At eleven I dressed in a dark blue blazer and gray pants. Allen Burkhead met me at the entrance to Elmwood Cemetery. He was holding a key. I was carrying a black canvas bag.

The new coffin was already in place in the tomb. Shiny bronze, a sprightly cradle for a very long slumber.

Burkhead unlocked the casket. I took Susan Redmon's skull from my bag and nestled it carefully above her skeleton. Then I positioned the leg bones. Last, I tucked a small plastic sack under the white velvet pillow. Precipitin testing had shown that the brain was human. Maybe it was Susan's, maybe it wasn't. I doubted she'd mind sharing eternity with another displaced soul.

Weaving back through the tombstones, Burkhead told me he'd done some archival research. Susan Redmon had died giving birth. The child survived, a healthy baby boy. What happened to him? I asked. No idea, Burkhead said.

I felt sadness. Then hope.

In dying, Susan had given life to another being.

My next stop was Carolinas Medical Center. Not the ER, but the maternity center. This time my bag was pink and carried a large fuzzy bear and three tiny sleepers.

The baby was café au lait, with a wrinkled face and wild Don King hair. Takeela had named her Isabella for her maternal great-grandmother.

Takeela remained cool and aloof. But when she gazed at her daughter, I understood why she'd phoned to accept my offer of help. Seeing her baby girl, she'd resolved to reach out. To take a chance for Isabella.

Driving home, I thought about death and birth.

Things end and others begin.

Susan Redmon died, but had a son who lived.

Rinaldi was gone, but Slidell was entering into a new partnership.

Cuervo was dead, but Takeela had a new baby girl.

Pete seemed ended. Was I about to embark on a new beginning? With Charlie? With Ryan? With someone new?

Could Ryan and I go back, start over again?

Could America find a new beginning? Could we return to a time when we all felt safe? Protected? Confident in our values and our purpose? Tolerant of customs and belief systems we didn't understand?

Charlie?

Ryan?

Mr. Right?

How would my sister, Harry, put it?

No way of knowing which hound will hunt.

A CONVERSATION
WITH KATHY REICHS

Kathy Reichs talks about her cases, the inspiration for *Devil Bones*, the difference between the real Kathy Reichs and Temperance Brennan, and the television show *Bones*.

Q: Is *Devil Bones* based on a real case?

A: Strange things arrive at my lab. I've been asked to examine shrunken heads to determine their authenticity. Often they're actually the skulls of birds or dogs.

Sometimes human skulls do show up. Some are painted or decorated. Some show carbonization from candle flames. Some are covered with melted wax, blood, and/or bird feathers.

These skulls turn out to be ritual objects. They've graced altars or been used in spells or religious ceremonies. I've worked on a number of these cases and, each time, the situation got me thinking about fringe religions, belief systems that mystify or alienate the larger population.

Devil Bones is based on a mélange of cases over a long period of time, cases that sparked my imagination. Some were my own. Some were described to me by colleagues. Some were discussed in the forensic literature or in scientific sessions at professional meetings.

Q: How did you go about researching *Devil Bones*?

A: About twenty years ago, at the American Academy of Forensic Sciences, I heard a paper delivered by a pathologist who worked at the Dade County Medical Examiner's Office in Miami, Florida. His research focused on a fringe religion known as Santería.

Santería is a syncretic religion resulting from the blending of African religious practices with Catholicism. The movement emerged during the period when slaves were brought to North America and forbidden the right to follow their ancestral beliefs. As a means of survival, the traditional African deities came to be disguised as Catholic saints. I remembered the paper and tracked it down. Then I became curious about other so-called fringe religions. A McGill University colleague had told me about a graduate student who worked as a cook at a Wiccan summer camp. Initially through her I began to research Wiccan practice and philosophy.

So the research went from lab to colleagues to literature to practitioners. During that progression I met many fascinating individuals and learned a great deal about religions that hadn't been on my radar.

Q: How did you choose to write about police officers losing their lives in the line of duty?

A: Sadly, this part of the novel was inspired by events in my hometown of Charlotte, North Carolina. On April 1, 2007, Police Officer Sean Clark and Police Officer Jeff Shelton responded to a disturbance call in an East Charlotte housing complex. They had resolved the disturbance and were leaving when they engaged in conversation with a man uninvolved in the incident. As they turned to walk away, the man pulled out a gun and shot both officers in the back.

This incident had a huge impact on our community. I was in the early stages of writing *Devil Bones* when this happened and I couldn't get it out of my mind. I decided to incorporate a police shooting into the story. *Devil Bones* is dedicated to all who have lost their lives protecting the citizens of Charlotte-Mecklenburg, North Carolina.

Q: How do you manage to balance your life as a bestselling writer with the demands of your forensic work and now with your work on the Fox series *Bones*?

A: It takes a good calendar. If I didn't put everything onto my computer and BlackBerry, I think I'd probably be AWOL for half of the things I'm supposed to do.

It also takes discipline. I work a three-point triangle: Charlotte, North Carolina, where I live and do most writing; Montreal, Quebec, where I do casework for the Laboratoire de sciences judiciaires et de médicine légale (I'm also on the Canadian National Police Services Advisory Board); Los Angeles, California, where *Bones* is filmed (I am also a producer of the show).

Any time I'm not traveling—for book promotion or public speaking, for casework or testimony, for TV production—I write all day. I try to begin by eight in the morning and stay with it until five in the afternoon, or longer. If I've got free time, I write.

Q: How has it felt to see your principal character realized in the television series *Bones*? How involved are you in the production of the series?

A: The only way I can sum up working on the television series *Bones* is to say that it's been a barrel of fun. Of course, I had some concerns at the outset. What would become of my character? How old would she be? Who would be cast in the role?

I met with Barry Josephson and Hart Hanson, now two of our three executive producers, before any deal was made. Barry and Hart assured me they would keep Tempe a realistic age and keep the science honest. They convinced me that they genuinely desired my input.

I work on each episode, primarily assisting staff writers. They develop each script as an original story. They come to me with questions concerning the science and I offer suggestions. I read each script when it is finished and send my comments to the other producers and the writers.

Periodically I do go to L.A. and hang around the set with Emily Deschanel, who plays Tempe, and with the producers, the writers, the props people.

I think of *Bones* as taking place in the years prior to Tempe's arrival in Montreal, before she meets Andrew Ryan. TV Tempe works in Washington, D.C., which is where I started my career. The first skeleton I ever handled was at the Smithsonian National Museum of Natural History in D.C. The Jeffersonian in *Bones* is a thinly veiled copy of that institution.

I'm thrilled with the acting on the show. Emily Deschanel does a fantastic job as the younger version of Temperance Brennan. And David

Boreanaz is, well? What need one say? Michaela, Tamara, Eric, and TJ are terrific. In sum, I think the show has turned out splendidly. And grows better each season.

Q: Which is your favorite of all the Temperance Brennan books? Which did you most enjoy writing?

A: One of my favorites will always be *Déjà Dead*. *Déjà Dead* was the first. The adventure of being a novelist was all very new and exciting and I was totally naive about how publishing works. And of course, there was the success that *Déjà Dead* enjoyed. And continues to enjoy.

I enjoyed researching *Cross Bones* tremendously. I went to Israel with Dr. James Tabor, a colleague and biblical archaeologist with a great deal of experience in the Holy Land. He and I crawled around in tombs, visited archaeological sites, consulted antiquities dealers, and met with Israeli National Police and Hebrew University forensic scientists.

Another of my favorites is *Monday Mourning*. This plot derived from a Montreal case involving skeletal remains found in the basement of a pizza parlor. In the real case the key question was PMI, postmortem interval. How long had the three individuals been in that basement?

Though the novel spins off into completely different territory, PMI came to be the central question in *Monday Mourning* as well. I like the fact that fiction and reality started out so similarly, and that, in both the book and the real world, the cases were resolved successfully.

Q: How far do you identify personally with Tempe?

A: When I started these books I had *no* training in writing. It was a given from the outset that my main character would be based on me— a subject I might know something about.

I place Tempe in contexts with which I am familiar and comfortable. Certainly, professionally, I identify with her. In the books she's a bit younger than I am. In the TV series she's a lot younger than I am! Book Tempe is fortysomething and works in a crime lab almost identical to mine, the Laboratoire de sciences judiciaires et de médecine légale.

But Tempe's involvement in cases takes her beyond the lab, much more so than mine ever has. This is true in *Bones,* also. Tempe goes out with detectives, interviews witnesses, and pursues cases from an investigative point of view. I don't do that. My work is pretty much restricted to scene recovery, lab analysis, and court testimony. I have a little trouble with some of the impetuous things Tempe did in early books—digging up bodies and confronting victim associates and family members on her own. I would never do that.

When I created Tempe I wanted her to have flaws, to be imperfect, approachable, someone with whom the reader could identify. Tempe has problems, but problems that she's handling. Her alcoholism. Her family life. Her relationship with Andrew Ryan. Those issues belong strictly to her.

When I started writing the books it was important to me to put humor into them. We also work hard to put humor into the television series. That's an interesting balancing act. Each episode deals with death, and it's a challenge to insert humor into that context without being disrespectful.

I think Tempe's sense of humor reflects my own. Friends tell me that when reading the dialogue they hear my voice quipping the wisecracks.

Q: What is it like to work with human remains on a daily basis? Are you squeamish?

A: Working in a medico-legal lab you get habituated to what's happening around you. You get used to the sounds and the smells and the sights of death. That doesn't mean you grow immune to it.

Obviously my line of work is not for the squeamish. Archaeologists and physical anthropologists work on nice dry bone. Forensic anthropologists get involved in soft-tissue cases. Cases arriving at my lab for autopsy are homicide, suicide, and accident victims, people who have suffered violent deaths. Forensic anthropologists tend to get the most severe cases, the ones that can't be resolved by the pathologist through a normal autopsy. Our cases are the putrefied, burned, mummified, mutilated, dismembered, and skeletal.

What I always keep in mind, though, is that I work *with* the dead, but *for* the living. I work to help families when someone has gone missing. I testify in court to bring justice if there has been a violent crime.

Q: This is now your eleventh Temperance Brennan novel. How do you keep them fresh?

A: I think the thing that gives my stories freshness is what gives them authenticity: the fact that I work in a medico-legal lab. I'm around forensics all the time. Cases are constantly coming in. There's never any end to inspiration.

Each of my books is based loosely on a case that I've worked on or an experience that I've had. I never use exact details. I change the names, the dates, the places. I take the kernel of a scenario at the lab—unidentifiable body part found at a crash site, trash-bagged remains of endangered species—then spin off into a series of what-ifs.

What motivates me to stick with the same character is that she seems to have such resonance with readers. People genuinely like Temperance Brennan. The books are now printed in more than thirty languages. So the old gal has global appeal.

Q: Where/what next for Tempe Brennan?

A: The book I'm working on now starts out in Chicago. Tempe and Ryan (concerning whom she is *still* sorting out her feelings) have been asked to transport remains from the LSJML/Quebec Coroner's Office to the Cook County Medical Examiner's Office. While there, Tempe is faced with a disturbing discovery.

I was born in the Windy City and return each year to visit family. My family is large, Irish, extended. My husband's is large, Latvian, extended.

While in Chicago, Tempe also visits family so readers finally meet members of the Petersons clan. The action then moves to Montreal. Problems at the lab. Problems with LaManche. Problems with her car. Problems with Ryan. Oh, my.